THE RIFT FREQUENCY

THE
RIFT
FREQUENCY

AMY S. FOSTER

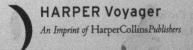

HARPER Voyager
An Imprint of HarperCollinsPublishers

THE RIFT FREQUENCY. Copyright © 2017 by Amy S. Foster. Excerpt from THE RIFT CODA copyright © 2018 by Amy S. Foster. All rights reserved. Printed in the United States of America. No part of this book may be used or reproduced in any manner whatsoever without written permission except in the case of brief quotations embodied in critical articles and reviews. For information, address HarperCollins Publishers, 195 Broadway, New York, NY 10007.

HarperCollins books may be purchased for educational, business, or sales promotional use. For information, please e-mail the Special Markets Department at SPsales@harpercollins.com.

Harper Voyager and design are trademarks of HarperCollins Publishers LLC.

A hardcover edition of this book was published in 2017 by Harper Voyager, an imprint of HarperCollins Publishers.

FIRST HARPER VOYAGER PAPERBACK EDITION PUBLISHED 2018.

Designed by Michelle Crowe
Title page image by Rost9/Shutterstock, Inc.

Library of Congress Cataloging-in-Publication Data has been applied for.

ISBN 978-0-06-244319-9

18 19 20 21 22 LSC 10 9 8 7 6 5 4 3 2 1

For Eva,
who loves just as fiercely as Ryn does

THE RIFT FREQUENCY

CHAPTER 1

I hear birdsong inside the Rift.

A thousand skylarks trilling into an endless emerald prism. I wasn't expecting music. Maybe a droning hum or a keening wail, but the symphony is a surprise. It fills my ears and spreads throughout the rest of my body like cyanide. In a matter of seconds I'm entirely at the Rift's mercy.

The sound overtakes me and the swelling current claims whatever sense of orientation I have left. I don't know which way is up or down. I'm tumbling through the noise, unable to fill my lungs. My body feels like it's being squeezed by a vise, but at the same time I'm being pulled apart. And then, almost as quickly as it began, the Rift exhales in a single violent breath, and I am pushed out.

My face is in damp soil and dead leaves. I look behind me

in time to see the Rift's giant, neon green jaws snap shut. In an instant it's gone and I'm here, wherever here is.

At least I'm not alone.

A long, thin cable runs between my pack and Levi's. He's splayed on the ground, too. I feel (an admittedly petty) gratitude that he didn't manage to navigate the experience with his usual ease and grace—he's clearly just as disoriented as I am. I unclip the tether between us and it retracts all the way back to his pack with a snap.

I don't really want him here, but I also absolutely do. I need backup and he was the best choice. Still, he's a pain in the ass. But when it comes down to it, he's just about the best Citadel we've got in Battle Ground. To be fair, my options had been Levi *or* Henry, but Levi insisted and Henry didn't put up much of a fight, which really is a motherfucker because Henry loves a good fight. Also, I know Henry. I'm *comfortable* with Henry. Levi is just . . . Levi. I stare at him hard, kind of hoping he'll share a look of mutual amazement of what we have just done, but he only stares back, his face unmoving, giving nothing away.

Finally he says: "You okay?" With a voice so indifferent I wonder why he even bothered to ask.

"Yeah," I say, getting up and looking around, scouting our immediate position. Levi follows my lead. We should have been doing this from the moment we emerged. We have gone through a Rift. We are in an unknown, potentially hostile land.

We have navigated our way to another version of Earth.

The thing is, this Earth looks *exactly* like the one we just left. And not only does it look the same, it smells the same. I study the nearest tree, an old and gnarled fir, and recognize the height, the knots and their placement. I scan the rest of the trees in our vicinity. I have a photographic memory, as does

Levi, but I'm not sure I would even need it to recognize this place. I spend a lot of time in these woods.

"You have got to be kidding me," I whisper to myself, even though I know Levi can hear. He sighs, and I know he's figured it out, too.

"So we go through all that just to end up in the same exact spot we started from. Seriously? I think we opened the Rift *right here*." He gestures with annoyance to the space between us.

I bite my lip. This is the absolute definition of anticlimactic. "It might *look* the same," I warn him, "but that doesn't mean it *is* the same. We have to be careful. I know it sounds crazy, but a dragon could swoop down and try to get us, or burn us or something." I swing my arms around dramatically to try to prove what is admittedly not the most realistic point. "We can't take anything at face value," I try with a more serious tone.

"I'm not a total idiot, Ryn. I get it," Levi snaps. I grit my teeth. I know I'm stating the obvious. He knows I know I'm stating the obvious. It's just his tone. *Mean. Condescending.* This is another reason I didn't want him here. We bring out the worst in each other. First, when I was a kid, and he was just my best friend's brother, I turned into a babbling moron every time I was around him. And now, as Citadels, our interactions are generally a game of offense and defense. I feel defensive because he's constantly swinging his dick around—metaphorically, anyway—to prove his superior skills as a Citadel. And I think he gets defensive because I'm pretty popular in the program. People like me. People respect Levi, but I don't think there are many who actually want to hang out with him. And no one, not even someone as badass and self-reliant as Levi, wants to feel unliked.

"Come on," I tell him, and begin to walk toward the base. Levi doesn't follow.

"You don't honestly think he's here, do you? You can't possibly think it would be so easy."

I stop and roll my eyes, then turn so that I'm facing him. "Here's what I know. The QOINS device uses harmonic resonance to open a Rift. It's programmed to find the *exact* note of Ezra's quantum signature. The one that only resonates to him and *his specific* Earth, which is where he's headed. So it *will* find him. I get that this is an 'eventually' kind of thing, but we will end up in the same place, maybe on an Earth like this one, that's on the way. I also get that the number of jumps we need to make to find him could be ten or a hundred, and that the chances the QOINS will lead us down the same harmonic path Ezra is taking are slim to none. But, however infinitesimal, there *is* a chance. So we are going to check every single Earth we jump to because the not knowing if he's alive or dead or even okay is practically killing me. So, if you have a problem with that, you can stay here and sulk or do push-ups or whatever the hell it is that you do when you're not getting your way, but I'm going to look for him."

Levi narrows his eyes at me and then stretches his neck from one side to the other like he's cracking it. "I never said I wasn't going with you, or that it was a bad idea to investigate our surroundings. I was just trying to manage your expectations. Believe me, *I know* how desperate you are to see your boyfriend."

"Don't," I interrupt before he can say something awful, but he keeps going anyway.

"No really, I get it. Ezra Massad. The perfect guy," he says in a sickeningly sweet voice. "Not like us chumps who have super brains because our genes got fucked with. Ezra, the savior of all Citadels who figured out so many of ARC's secrets." Levi thrusts his hands out like he's serving me a platter of something other than this total bullshit. "Your wonderful boyfriend who cured you of the Blood Lust so that you two can screw like rabbits."

His words are teeming with bitterness and I don't know what to say. Levi is supposed to be my partner here, my ally, but his intense dislike for Ezra has me genuinely worried. I consider my options for a moment. I could tell him that he should stop being such an ass, that he *does* owe Ezra a debt of gratitude. If it weren't for Ezra we wouldn't know the truth about the chip ARC implanted in our heads when we were children. We wouldn't know that not only was it designed to amplify the harmonic signal of the QOINS, it was also there to kill us if we stepped one pinky toe out of line. The Citadels were told that the chip gave us our abilities, and without Ezra's intervention we wouldn't have found out that it was, in fact, a series of genetic modifications (not the chip) that turned us into super soldiers, and which, despite ARC's lies, can never be undone. We can never have the "normal" life that ARC promised we could have later in life. If Ezra hadn't helped me uncover the truth, we would have no idea that we'd been drugged and brainwashed for most of our lives. Without my "boyfriend," we wouldn't know what ARC had in store for the Citadels and how easy it would have been for them to use us in the most depraved ways to get whatever they wanted from any Earth of their choosing.

I want to shout all this at Levi, but I understand that in this moment there's no point. He knows these truths already. He's just angry, like he always is, and Ezra is a convenient place to lay blame. Or at least, I think that's what's going on. Levi has been acting strange ever since he wormed his way into this mission. One minute he's eager, upbeat even. The next he's sullen to the point of emo. Whatever is going on in his mind, he's

not being straight with me, which is fine. I don't want anywhere near the inner workings of his thought processes, which
seem to be rigged with emotional booby traps inside every
conversation we have. So, I choose to say nothing. I turn back
around and start walking to the base.

We move in silence. We don't run, but we walk so swiftly
that our boots merely brush the dirt beneath us. If anyone
glimpsed us right now we would look like ghosts, haunting
this forgotten stretch of wilderness that used to be a military
base.

In short order we see a signpost. They have these scattered
throughout Camp Bonneville—directions to the road and the
barracks, and firing range warnings. However, the first thing I
notice is that these signs aren't in English—they're in Japanese.
All Citadels are polyglots, a word I love because it sounds like
a magical spell straight out of Harry Potter. In reality, though,
it just means that we are masters of many languages—a perk
of our super brains. I grip my rifle a little tighter and look over
at Levi.

"*Kayanpu Joryoku,*" he reads with a perfect accent.

"I guess things are different here after all," I say aloud, as
much to myself as to Levi.

"Yep," he concedes.

"Could this be a *Man in the High Castle* Earth? Like one
where the Allies lost World War II?" I wonder.

"A sign in Japanese on an American military base built in
1909? I think there's a high probability that's the case."

"Right," I say, almost to myself more than Levi. I grip my
hand just a little tighter on my rifle.

"But the time line seems on par with ours just based on the
tree growth. Most of the soldiers who fought in that war are

probably dead. After so many generations, I doubt whoever is occupying the base is going to be much of a threat to us."

I scratch my nose and look at the sign again. "They probably don't even see themselves as occupiers anymore. This country belongs to them now. They'll have gone soft."

"As long as the war is really over," Levi throws out.

"Look around. The forest is pristine. And listen, it's quiet. Wars are very, very loud. I say we stash our stuff. Hide it where no one is likely to find it, but easy enough for us to access if we're in a hurry. Then, we just knock on the door."

Levi narrows a single eye at me. "Ballsy," he says with a little smile.

"What are they going to do? We're kids. So, we leave our guns here and we act, I don't know, like we're on drugs or, like, we have super-mega daddy issues."

"You want to go into a Japanese military base without our weapons?" I don't know whether Levi disagrees with me or he's just double-checking.

"We *are* the weapons. The guns stay here." It is clear from my tone that this is not a request. This is an order. Still, Levi's eyes glint with approval.

"Roger that," he tells me as he slowly unclips his rifle from the clip on the leather padding of his uniform. We disarm ourselves mostly (keeping a bowie knife tucked into each of our boots) and hide our backpacks in a thicket of hemlock, covering them with some fallen leaves that are still moist from recent rain.

We have a good idea about what kind of opposition we're likely to encounter now, or at least a plausible theory, and we know this terrain. We run full speed to the entrance of the underground bunker that serves as our headquarters back home and then we just stand at the door and wait. There are cameras mounted at the corners of the door. A steady buzz electrifies the air as they both turn and point their lenses at us. I give a little smile and wave.

It doesn't take long for them to come for us, maybe three or four minutes. The doors burst open and half a dozen Japanese soldiers emerge and surround us. They are not gentle, and they don't bother to ask what we're doing there. They simply take us roughly inside. The general layout of the bunker is much the same, though not as updated as our bunker back home. Probably because the people here don't have the Roones sprucing the place up for them. So the bunker here looks haggard, full of dark and dank corridors, leading to rooms that look the same but no doubt serve entirely disparate purposes.

We're taken in an elevator to what is (back on our Earth) the intake level, the section of the bunker where all the Immigrants that are pushed through the Rift end up for processing. I can now imagine what it felt like for them, even though we actually understand what our captors are saying as we're screamed at in Japanese. I note that we are gentler with the Immigrants than these soldiers manhandling us are. Regardless of how I feel about the welcome we receive, Levi and I don't say a word, then we're separated. I think we expected this, but it still doesn't feel right. I'm thrown into an interrogation room and the door locks behind me. The room is empty save for two chairs and a table. There is a long mirror on the far wall, which I assume is a two-way mirror, just as we have. I haven't been handcuffed, which is a lucky thing—for *them*. I could tear apart the cuffs like tinfoil if I wanted to, but more than likely I'd just use them to strangle the poor bastard who comes in here to question me. Handcuffs can be very efficient for that sort of thing.

I sit down in one of the chairs. All I can do now is wait. I close my eyes, and immediately my thoughts drift to Ezra, just like they always do when I have even one minute alone since he was pushed through the Rift—

By Levi.

In Levi's defense, someone was trying to kill me and he was only trying to save my life. At least, that's what I keep telling myself. I've told myself that so many times I'm actually starting to believe it. But don't I have to? The alternative is that Levi, for whatever reason, might have killed the first person I've ever had real romantic feelings for. If I continue to believe that, I may just snap and do a little killing of my own, and right now, I need Levi. He is the best Citadel for this job and there is a certain amount of justice to it as well. If Levi had given two shits about Ezra's life, then I wouldn't even be here in Kayanpu Joryoku. Then again, if Levi had hesitated, I might not be alive period.

Still, for me anyway, it all comes back to Ezra. He is smart—and I mean, like super-genius smart—and he's a survivor. But can he survive on his wits alone? Even on an Earth like this, which seems rather tame compared to the ones I know are out there? He doesn't speak Japanese. He isn't totally white. He definitely isn't East Asian. If he Rifted here first, he could have easily been captured before being able to Rift out and, let's face it, they make actual movies about Japanese prison camps, and they never have happy endings . . .

For some reason I thought once I actually got through a Rift it would somehow ease my anxiety. It's only made things worse. I have to get out of here. Safely. That means I have to push all thoughts of Ezra aside and focus. I keep my eyes closed.

And exhale.

CHAPTER 2

It's been thirty-seven minutes and I'm getting restless. There's a clock, old and moonfaced, trapped behind a metal grate. It's the same exact clock we have in our own version of Camp Bonneville. From outside the room Japanese words float through the thick walls. Because of my spectacular hearing I can hear things that normal people can't. No one is saying anything of consequence. The clock, though, is really starting to piss me off. Its hands grind and tick. Each revolution a reminder that time is against us. And not just Levi and me.

Because back on my Earth, Henry, Boone, and Violet have control of the Battle Ground Rift. For now. How long they will be able to keep that leadership a secret from ARC is unknown. To maintain news of the mutiny under wraps from the higher-ups we used the same drugs ARC had been using to keep the civilians—the soldiers at the base—and us in line for years. We even had to use it on the damaged Citadels who refused to believe that ARC was anything but benevolent. I never wanted to brainwash my own kind—I never wanted to brainwash *anyone*—but I learned the hard way that the truth doesn't always set you free.

Before I left, we all agreed that it was best for everyone to believe that Colonel Applebaum was still in charge. Applebaum, that brash bully of a man, is nothing more than our puppet now. I even had him call my parents and send off a bunch of fake paperwork for them to sign to explain my absence (they think I'm doing an internship for one of our senators in Washington, DC). He was never much of a threat, especially with the Roones, like Edo, on our side. But Christopher Seelye, the president of ARC, is a different story altogether. Thankfully, he's based at ARC HQ in California, but he does travel to all the Rift sites frequently. He's scheduled to visit Battle Ground in three weeks, and I need to be back there to help my friends when he does. Seelye isn't like Applebaum. He's ruthless and brilliant, and I don't know if my team can fool him for long. I don't want to think about what will happen to the Citadels at Battle Ground if Seelye sends in troops from other Rifts to neutralize us. It'll be a blood bath—death on both sides. The Battle Ground Citadels have had their kill switches removed, but the Citadels at the other Rift sites haven't. Edo could once again engage the Midnight Protocol and kill thousands just by tapping Enter on a keyboard.

Tick, tick, tick. This must be an Earth close in space and time to our own. It seems like our theory was correct. This could have been my reality if the Axis powers had won the war. Strangers would have stolen our country, our freedom, *and* our clocks. They didn't even bother to install their own. For some reason, I find this really annoying.

Finally, a door opens and a Japanese man in uniform enters the room. His face is unweathered. I doubt he's seen even
a moment of action his entire life. He sits down gingerly on
a chair in front of me, the chair shifting beneath his slight
frame. I sigh. He doesn't look like a bad man, but I'm going to
have to hurt him in order to leave this room. I don't feel guilty
about it. I look at the clock again. Timing is everything and
he's in the wrong place at the wrong time.

"I am Captain Kotoku Sato," he says in Japanese. "What is
your name?" He's efficient and to the point, but he's not angry.
He sounds mostly curious and maybe a little irritated.

"Ryn Whittaker," I answer honestly.

"Why are you here, Ryn-san? You don't look like a stupid
girl. You must know this area is off limits to civilians."

I shrug my shoulders. It's not like I can tell him the truth.
"Why are *you* here? Japan wasn't big enough for you?"

Now it's his turn to sigh. "The war has been over for almost
a century. And just by looking at you, I can tell that you are not
indigenous to this country, and so I could ask you the same
thing." I furrow my brow for a split second. He kind of has
me there. "I just don't understand you people," he continues.
"Is democracy so wonderful? In the years leading up to our
liberation of this country, America suffered a great depression.
People starved in the streets. There were no jobs. Entire families were homeless. And now every person in this country has
a job. No one goes hungry. We all work for the benefit of our
community. The individual is not more important than the
greater good. We have proven this. We have eliminated suffering. Is that not better than your democracy, which leaves so
many behind?"

I narrow my eyes at him. He makes a good point, but I've
sacrificed enough in my own life for the greater good. And

while I'm really not here to argue comparative politics with a man I'm about to kick the shit out of, I can't help myself.

I'm impulsive like that.

"Except the Jews, right?" I ask in English. "Probably aren't too many of them in your fantastic community."

Sato slams his fist on the table. "We don't speak that language here," he says with a slow intensity that is bound to build. "Your punishment will be even greater if you continue." So now I say nothing. I can hear his heart rate increase. I'm not afraid of him or his threats, even though I can tell he's a man who is used to being obeyed. "Tell me, Ryn-san, are you a militia now? Is that why you and this other boy are wearing uniforms? It's one thing to protest in front of government buildings, but to dress up like a pretend soldier and walk into a military base would imply that your group of anarchists is attempting something very foolish. I would like the names of your collaborators. I ask this only to keep you from further harm."

I fold my arms and cock my head. My defiance makes his heart race even faster, but there's no point in pissing him off too much. I switch back to Japanese.

"I can tell you in all honesty that I am not collaborating with anyone. Branach Levi-san and I came here alone. We are not part of any anarchist movement."

Captain Sato grits his teeth. He doesn't believe me. "Then I ask again, why are you here? Did you think we would just tell you to go away? Did you think there would not be consequences for your actions? We could lock you up for as long as we wish. Along with the dishonor you have already brought to your family by your actions, would you have them fret and worry about your whereabouts? Tell me who else you are working with and I will make sure your parents know you are safe."

I roll my eyes just a fraction and give a little laugh. "Oh come on . . . No one has ever tried to break in here before? I can't believe I'm the first rebellious teenager to try." I emphasize the word *teenager*. It's imperative that Sato believes that's all I am.

"No civilian has ever been stupid enough to try such a thing, young and 'rebellious' or not. Kayanpu Joryoku is for military personnel only."

I take a moment to process this information. I stare at the captain, whose heart rate has slowed, but who is nonetheless still agitated. "Just to be clear, then," I begin slowly, "no civilian has been on this base or is on this base presently?"

The man stands and leans over the table. "Of course not. But do not think that you are special. This is not some sort of achievement. You won't be bragging to your anarchist friends about what you've done by the time we have finished with you here."

He's threatening me again, and I *really* don't like to be threatened. I like it even less that his idea of a perfect society includes the notion that it's okay to torture a seventeen-year-old girl. I could kill him right now if I wanted. I could reach over and break his neck before anyone could get in to help him. I've killed like this before—quick, unthinking. I don't enjoy doing it, but I do enjoy the power of knowing I have the ability to do it.

This is part of the darkness in me. All Citadels carry this weight, these shadows. But, unlike some of the others, I don't deny the rage. I'm a rabid dog in a cage. I keep the cage locked with the help of my family and friends, and with discipline and purpose. I have a purpose here today—to find out if Ezra is here—and this self-important man has just helped me achieve it. I won't have to let that dog loose.

"Thank you for answering my questions," I say as I stand up. "I will be leaving now. For your own safety, I am warning you not to try and stop me."

"I don't think you understand what's going on here. I am the one asking the questions!" Sato shouts as he jumps up from his chair.

I actually laugh aloud, much to Sato's chagrin. I look him up and down. "Are you? *Really?*" And with that I walk toward the door. He races to stop me, yanking my arm back and actually pulling my hair. Good Lord, these are the people on this Earth who won the Second World War? Sissy hair pullers?

Faster than he can react, I reach down with my free hand, undo the holster at his waist, and grab his gun. I could shoot him, but that would be messy and noisy. Instead, I remove the clip and it falls to the concrete floor with a tinny clang. I check briefly to make sure there isn't a bullet in the chamber and, finding there isn't one, I fieldstrip the gun and release it from my hand with all the sass of a mic drop.

I really don't like this Earth.

Sato's eyes widen in surprise as he backs away. I have to be quick now, because any second, whoever is watching us through the two-way mirror will burst through the door.

I walk toward him and he distances himself so that we are facing each other. I look over his shoulder into the mirror and because I just can't resist, I give a slight bow. Then, I pick Sato up, lift him high above my head, and—with all my strength—throw the captain through the mirror. He crashes through and lies still. He's probably not dead, but I really don't have time to wonder. The soldiers behind the broken glass scramble and push an alarm.

The siren's wail is not loud enough to cover up the gunshot I hear.

Shit. *Levi.*

Our Citadel uniforms will protect us from a bullet to the body, but not the head. If he were a member of my team from back home, I probably would have stuck around to make sure he didn't need my help.

But I know Levi can handle himself.

I kick down the door to the interrogation room and start running. I have an advantage here. I know this base level by level. I know what is behind every corner. I zip past the soldiers as they begin to open fire, and though one bullet manages to land on my shoulder blade, it doesn't penetrate my suit. That's not to say it doesn't sting like hell, but I heal fast, and it doesn't slow me down in the slightest.

I make my way to an old escape hatch and find it already open, which means Levi has gotten out. I race through the forest, the soldiers chasing after me. There's no way any one of these men or women can catch me on foot. I don't know exactly how fast I can run, but when I'm really pushing it like I am now, it's hard for the human eye to track me. I slow down at the site where Levi and I had stashed our equipment.

"What took you so long?" he asks me with a straight face. Coming from anyone else this might be considered humor, but not with Levi. He's trying to work the laptop, which is tough, since he's holding his other hand straight up in the air. His palm is bleeding like a stigmata.

"At least I didn't get shot," I snap back.

"Ezra isn't there?"

I pull my pack up onto my shoulders. "Don't tell me you weren't able to figure that out during your interrogation?" I nudge Levi out of the way so that I'm the one facing the laptop. I have two working hands, which means I can get us out of here faster.

"No one asked me any questions. I suppose they thought you would break first." I involuntarily snort, and Levi wisely says nothing more. I drag Ezra's quantum signature icon into the running program and wait for a Rift to open. When it does, I hear something, an ever so slightly high-pitched frequency. I certainly heard sound inside the Rift, but now it seems like I'm hearing it outside of it as well.

"Do you hear that?" I ask Levi, just to make sure.

"What? Something other than boots on the ground headed our way? Let's just go!"

While I want to figure out what the hell I'm hearing, I don't argue. I stuff the laptop into Levi's bag and wait for him to hand over the carabiner. I give it a tug and a long thin wire drags out so that I can clip on to a loop in the leather breastplate of my uniform. We're attached but not touching. Levi expels the air from his lungs and closes his eyes. I keep mine open and follow the music as we jump into the Rift.

CHAPTER 3

Like a dirty shirt inside a washing machine, once again I'm spinning in the Rift's emerald mouth. The sound is so much louder this time. It burrows into my ears and latches on to my brain. An orchestra, a hundred orchestras, tuning their instruments to a single note. I must figure out a way to combat the disorientation if we're going to keep doing this.

It's a struggle, but I manage to focus my eyes. Still, I've waited too long in accomplishing this one small thing. The green is almost behind me. I see a slit of light ahead, and then before I can steady or upright myself, Levi and I are pitched forward.

Immediately I know that something is wrong. Not only am I gasping for air, but the sky on this Earth is sickly yellow. My hands and face, the only places where my skin is exposed, are burning. Levi and I scramble. He opens his pack and pulls out his laptop, bubbles of burnt flesh starting to form on his hands. On top of the fact that he's already been shot, he must be in considerable pain.

While he powers up the program, I reach around and dig into my pack, tears leaking out of my eyes from the pain, and manage to pull out my oxygen mask. It's agony as the contraption forms around my face, but at least now I can breathe. I scramble around Levi's pack and find his oxygen mask, too. It's a Roone-designed device, more advanced than anything humans have developed yet. In its dormant form, it looks a little like a metal beanie. Once I put it on Levi's head, it clamps to his skull and a hard black shell molds down his cheeks. A clear plastic barrier covers his face and I can hear it seal at his neck with a soft pop. The mask filters our carbon dioxide emission, mixes it with a small amount of water, and converts it into oxygen. To his credit, Levi doesn't even wince as the helmet covers the melting skin on his face.

Once again I push him off the computer. My hands look like they've been in a microwave, too, but at least I don't have a hole in one of them. The next Rift opens and I can't believe I'm actually relieved to see it. As Levi puts the laptop away, I do a quick atmospheric reading from yet another Roone device attached to my utility pouch. It may seem ridiculous, as I'm standing there, literally cooking, but we need to catalog and identify as many Earths as we can. If we can get a fix on this location, no other Citadel has to endure this as we have. Ezra once said that mapping the Rifts would be pointless and impossible, but I'm not so sure this assessment is correct. I now know the location of this Earth, or at least the computer does, and I have viable proof that we should stay away.

I pull Levi to his feet and strap on his pack. As I do, a strip of bubbling skin peels from my hand and I let out a small yelp of pain. Putting on my own pack brings me close to retching.

Luckily we're still attached. Not that I think that even matters anymore. Based on our last two trips, I'm beginning to suspect that opening a Rift leads to one distinct Earth and one distinct Earth only. The Rift slingshots us through in a straight trajectory—there are no tunnels or curves to lose one another in. Even if we were disconnected, we would have had to risk it. Levi doesn't look like he's doing so great; his eyes are closed behind his helmet, and my hands hurt so badly that I can't even hold on to him, so I push him through the Rift and jump in behind him.

CHAPTER 4

Once I'm inside the Rift I use the pain to focus. I keep my eyes open so I can watch Levi, who seems to be tumbling, head over feet. I concentrate on my hands, covered in blisters and blood. I can filter out the distraction of the Rift, of its intense green light, the careening noise, and the lack of gravity if I allow myself to embrace the agony of the exposed flesh on my palms.

I make my body straight as an arrow and nosedive through the tunnel of space and time. After a few seconds I begin to feel something else. My body starts to feels heavier, denser, and I can see a vertical light ahead of me. It's clearly the new Earth's gravity pulling me forward. On the previous two trips I'd thought that the Rift literally spat me out. I realize now that the kicking force I feel is simply the change in atmospheric pressure. Using the white light coming from the other side, I align my body accordingly. I'm now vertical, and my hope is that the exit is upright, too. I brace myself for the final release and take a step forward. My foot hits solid ground. I've done it. I've walked out of the Rift instead of landing on my face again. Levi isn't so lucky. He tumbles out and rolls three or four times in the white sand at our feet, pulling me down with him.

I disconnect and pop up, grabbing the Roone device on my belt that's used to measure the compatibility of our human physiology with our current environment as I do. Thankfully, the air is clean and fresh without any toxins. And I mean totally clean. Not even our Earth is so free of pollutants. I push a switch on my oxygen mask and it retracts. I scream as it takes a layer of skin along with it. I'm usually good with pain, but this must be really bad. I wonder briefly if my face is going to be scarred for life. Given a Citadel's advanced capacity for healing, I doubt it, and either way, scars don't bother me. In fact, I wish I had more. I think it might actually be a relief to see on the outside what I feel so often on the inside.

I don't even know why I'm letting myself be distracted by something as stupid as a scar. Probably so I can ignore how bad our current predicament is. I shake myself out of it and go into crisis mode—say what you will about ARC (and believe me, I've said it all), but their training is exactly what we need right now.

I look down. Levi is in bad shape, but before I can worry about him, I need to assess our situation. We are on a narrow stretch of sand bordered by a bright turquoise ocean. I pull out the binoculars attached to my utility belt, which are also enhanced with Roone tech. I see nothing but some palm trees and the sea for at least a hundred miles in every direction. Beautiful as it is, this version of Earth might be scarier than the last. I wonder if it's sheer luck that the Rift happened to open on the one piece of land available, or if it's some kind of fail-safe built into the system. I pray to God it's the latter, and not just for our personal safety. The fact is, our packs are water-resistant against things like rain and what not, but they aren't airtight. And that's crucial because of our equipment, specifically our laptops. If they got wet, that would effectively end our travels and we'd be trapped. It really dawns on me in that moment how crazy this mission is and how much faith we've put in Roone tech. It's one thing to imagine how it's going to be in theory, but out here in the field I understand how truly vulnerable we are. What at first seemed like a miracle—a computer program to navigate us to other versions of Earth—is starting to feel primitive, cumbersome, and unpredictable. There are simply too many variables and too many potential situations that end with us being separated from our technology, and effectively stranded. I allow myself to imagine briefly what it would be like to be stuck on a desert island with Levi for the *rest of my life*. No family, no friends, no Ezra. Just me and Levi forever.

That thought, along with the excruciating pain, brings bile to my throat.

What the hell is wrong with me? I can't be thinking about any of that now.

Crisis.

Mode.

I have to deal with Levi. Since he's lying facedown in the sand, I'm fairly sure he isn't conscious. Thankfully, there is that small tree line behind me made up of a crop of swaying palms. They'll provide enough shade for us to rest without having to set up the tents. I grab Levi by his pack, and because I'm in too much pain to carry him, I have to drag him the hundred feet or so away from the beach. My burnt hands touch his backpack, and the pain of this one small act, dragging my partner to shelter, almost brings me to my knees. I take a moment when it's done, steadying myself on a tree with my elbow. I'd like to collapse, too, but there's too much to be done.

There's no point in waking Levi until I can doctor his wounds, and I can't do anything to help him with my own wounds raw and exposed. I take off my belt and unzip my catsuit-like uniform down past my belly button. Ever so gently, with just my thumb and index finger, I peel the suit down. When I get to my wrists I try to make the opening wide enough so that the material doesn't touch my hands. I fail on both sides and I grind my teeth against the pain so hard my jaw starts to ache.

I sigh with relief when it's off. Beneath the suit I'm wearing nothing but a black sports bra. Ordinarily I'd worry about touching Levi dressed like this, about touching him period, but he's in too much pain for his Blood Lust to activate.

I hope.

I gently tie the sleeves of my uniform around my waist and walk briskly to the ocean. I need to clean my injuries before I can put on medicine and dress them. I crouch down and swiftly blow air out of my lungs, then plunge my hands in the warm salt water. I actually scream it hurts so badly. I must be seriously injured. Citadels excel at many things, but most of all they are masters at fighting, lying, and enduring pain. The Roones say we have the ability to turn down the sensitivity of our nerve receptors, which is probably a version of the truth. So the fact that I'm ready to pass out right now says a lot about the magnitude of my injuries. I need real medical attention, but what can I do about it? There's no one else here, and Levi is worse off than I am.

I steel myself as I splash seawater on my face, bringing on another round of agony. I falter in the ocean, nothing but collapsing sand beneath my feet to steady myself on. I dig deep, mentally, trying to push through the sharp white pain without passing out, but I'm not sure how much more of this I can take.

When it feels like I've sufficiently cleaned my wounds, which, as far as I can tell, are mostly second-degree burns wherever my skin was exposed, I race back up to the coverage beneath the trees. I dump the contents of both our packs out onto the sand. It's easier to get what I need this way as opposed to rooting through them with my raw and damaged hands. I take our bowls and cups and run back to the ocean to fill them. I move so fast I manage to outrun the latest wave of pain as the water hits my skin. Or maybe more and more of my pain receptors are being turned off.

A girl can hope.

When I get back to our pile of stuff, I find my first aid kit and open it with my teeth. We have an ample supply of medicines and supplies for all kinds of injuries. Edo must have known we would encounter Earths like the last one, with dangerously unstable atmospheres. I find a tube that looks like toothpaste but is labeled as burn ointment. I unscrew it with my teeth and squeeze out a generous amount into my palms. The relief is immediate and palpable and I cover my hands with the medication. I do the same with my face and the pain becomes tolerable. I wrap my entire left hand in a bandage and most of my right, but leave my fingers exposed so I can treat Levi.

I remove his helmet first. When the contraption retracts he wakes up with a yelp of pain. "Don't try to be a stoic, okay? Just lie here and let me help you," I warn him. By way of reply Levi nods his head. "This part is really going to hurt. Like, probably more than anything you've ever experienced. I have to clean the injuries and no, I'm not rubbing salt in your wounds for fun. It's antibacterial, so grit your teeth and don't punch me." I gently pour the water I collected from the ocean over his hands. To his credit, Levi remains perfectly still, though tears are pouring down his face. I take a clean cloth and dab his face lightly with the seawater. Wearing a sealed helmet would have helped with bacteria, and even though there is an antibacterial agent in the burn ointment, given our situation, I must be doubly safe. I don't want to return home before we've found Ezra just because of an infection we can prevent.

Once everything is clean, I gently pick up his hand and, with featherlight fingers, apply the ointment. I hear his heartbeat slow and he releases an audible sigh of relief. The burns he sustained cauterized the bullet wound, which went straight through his palm. I suppose in that one way he was lucky. I wrap both his hands in bandages and then move to his face.

There's no denying that Levi is beautiful. His brown hair glints russet in the single shaft of sunlight that has escaped the palm leaves. His eyes are a green as bright as the Rift. But right now he looks like something out of a horror movie. There is not an inch of exposed flesh on his face that is not blistered or bleeding. I gently rub the medicine into his skin. He remains unmoving, but his eyes tell a different story. It seems that he has focused all his pain right in the blazing rings of his irises. I've never seen him look so vulnerable, and it actually shakes me to my core until I can force myself to simply focus on the task at hand. When I am done, I sit back on my haunches and reach for the other bandages to wrap the fingers I had left exposed.

"Thank you," Levi croaks. I nod my head and turn away. I

didn't choose to become a Citadel, but I did choose to get out from under the yoke of ARC. My decisions are now a constellation of burns and blood on Levi's face. I don't know exactly how much I am to blame for all this, but I feel responsible enough, and a wave of guilt washes over me, settling squarely between my shoulder blades.

Captain Sato had done a lot of preaching about the greater good, and now I recognize why his seemingly casual grasp of the concept offended me. Levi, right here, in agony—*this* is sacrifice for the greater good.

Thinking of Sato reminds me of that stupid clock on the wall. My flesh seems to throb in time to the second hand. Tick. Tick. Tick. Every hour we are gone puts everyone more at risk, but right now we've run out of options. We *have* to stop and rest. We have to heal. I pour some water down Levi's throat and take a deep gulp from my own canteen.

I pull out the Roone equivalent of a hypodermic needle from the med kit. It looks like a tiny silver gun with a hollow front where you can swap out different medicines. I load up Levi's with a pain medication that will knock him out. He's looking at me, shaking his head. He doesn't want this.

I don't have time for his stubborn ass right now.

"We have to, Levi. We're in no condition to do anything. And besides, I really don't think there's anything or anyone else here. This is *Waterworld* Earth. We need to sleep."

I prep the little gun and watch the slender needle snap out. "All I need is rest, not sleep. We could be out for days," Levi says in a whisper.

I cock my head and give him my best mom look. "If you had a mirror right now, you'd let me do this."

"I don't need a mirror. I can see what *you* look like." I curl my lip. Rude. No need to state the obvious.

"Sorry." *Not sorry.* I jab the needle into his neck, maybe a little harder than necessary. I watch his eyes flutter and close. He's out in seconds. With the last bit of energy I have I manage to make a lean-to of sorts by jamming our rifles into the sand and attaching a solar sheet with tiny holes in the corners for this very purpose. It's little things like this that freak me out. The Roones really did think of everything. I'd love to believe that Edo is on our side, but until we get her laptop and what it contains from Ezra, how can we really know for sure? When we take down ARC, who's to say the Roones don't have some way of wresting control of us? If it comes down to a fight, how do we engage an enemy who is so many steps ahead?

The trees provide shade, but I have no idea how long we will be down. The solar sheet will keep us cool and provide some coverage. I hope. The ointment's effects are beginning to wear off. I lie down beside Levi and load my own needle gun. I make sure there are at least two inches of space between us. I inhale deeply. We're losing valuable time we can't afford, but there's nothing for it. I inject myself with the pain medication.

Immediately, I feel a rush, like warm bathwater running through my veins. As a Citadel, I've been hurt a lot and given all manner of drugs, including variations of opiates like these. I expect that in a second or two I will be out like Levi, but I am not. Instead, my head starts swimming and my body feels like it's falling, fast and deep. I can't imagine anyone doing this for fun. I hate this feeling, this loss of control.

And then, I see Ezra, clear as anything, standing just a few feet away. Part of me knows it's the drugs, but a bigger part is sure that it's really him. He is beautiful and perfect—bronze-colored skin like caramel, tall and lanky with those luminous eyes matching the turquoise of the ocean behind him.

"Ezra," I whisper as I hold out my hand. Why is he still standing there? Why doesn't he come over here? I flex my fingers outward toward him, but he remains where he is. Then, slowly, his skin begins to bubble. I blink hard. His flesh begins to melt off his bones. *"No. No. No . . ."* I say, though I'm not sure whether I'm actually using my voice or if my voice is trapped inside my mouth. Frantically, I think about the Earth that we were just on. We had been so desperate to leave, I hadn't checked for a body. I hadn't made sure that he wasn't there. Oh God. Why hadn't I done that? How could I just have left without thinking of him? I can see his jawbone through the blood and muscle that is falling off him in grotesque chunks. He is saying something and I am straining to hear above the ocean waves. Finally, I hear him.

"Get up!" Ezra screams. "Why aren't you looking for me? *Get up!*"

Blackness bleeds through the corners of my vision. My eyesight is closing up like a pinhole camera. I want to stay awake. I want to assure him that I will find him, but I can't move or speak. It's too late now. My hand drops. I am out.

CHAPTER 5

I don't wake up all at once. My mind clicks on, but my body is slower to follow. In my confusion, I expect the nightmare version of Ezra to be standing and screaming in front of me. I am both relieved and disappointed when I see nothing but white sand and an ocean that's so blue it's practically neon.

I turn my head. Levi is gone. Of course he is. I'm sure at some point later he'll make some passive-aggressive remark about waking up first. I sit up slowly and notice that although my hands and face are tingling, they don't really hurt. I unwind the bandages and have a look. The skin is a little raw and red, with some peeling, but other than that my hands are fine. I really have to pee, so I'm glad that Levi isn't in the immediate area. I walk farther into the grove and squat down. I look at my watch. It looks like we've been asleep for close to fifteen hours. My heart sinks. It's such a long time. I pull up my uniform and walk back to the temporary shelter. I scan the horizon and spot Levi at the farthest end of the island, swimming in the water. I'm sure he didn't go in with his uniform on, so I turn away. There's no privacy here, for either of us, and I don't like it. It was one thing, back at Camp Bonneville, to agree to a partnership with Levi. Back there, it was all theoretical and strategic. Out here, just the two of us, it's unnerving. I can easily ignore his hostility even though it's as obvious as one of those duck-lipped idiots with a selfie stick from my high school. No, it's when he's *not* angry—when he goes quiet and I know he's watching me—that he really gets under my skin. Is he judging me? Admiring me? Resenting me? All of the above? I have no idea and it's not like he'd ever in a million years be honest. We're liars. All of us Citadels are, but he takes it one step further. Stupid, competitive boy. He always has to be the best. At everything.

Whatever. I've got work to do before we can Rift out. I walk to the other side of the beach and collect more seawater in a metal can about the size of a coffee canister. I drop in a pill to desalinize the water and then I undress, putting my underwear, bra, and bandages inside of it. This is yet another great Roone invention: a tiny, portable washing machine. I take a drop of soap and snap the lid shut. I hit the On button and quickly slither into my extra undergarments. I slip on a pair of leggings and a T-shirt so that I can air out my uniform. I jump up a few feet and attach it to a small palm leaf.

When I turn, Levi is back. His uniform is unzipped about as far as it can be without it being indecent. His V, which is admittedly glorious, is as defined as an underwear model's. I also notice that his face looks fine, as if he's a little sunburnt. His nose is peeling, though, and he gives me a sheepish grin.

"God, Levi," I say while rolling my eyes. "Why don't you

just get naked?" I'm frustrated. We need boundaries here more than ever. The Blood Lust isn't a problem for me anymore, but Levi is still susceptible. This is no time to be reckless.

"Do you see anyone here? There is nothing. No one. This is *literally* a desert island. I didn't realize you were so uptight."

Am I being uptight? Would I care if it were Boone or Henry? No, probably not. But Henry is gay and Boone is in love with Violet. So no, I'm not uptight. I'm wary and Levi is playing a dangerous game because even though he's one of the most irritating people I know, he also has Captain America's bod. Which is doubly annoying, really. This partnership of convenience would be so much easier if he were hideous because even though he's Levi, it's hard not to stare.

"Whatever." I shrug my shoulders, unwilling to let him know that he can affect me in that way, or in any way. "I'm doing a wash of my bandages and some . . . other stuff. You should do yours. They were pretty gross."

"I will. I need to eat first, though. I actually don't think I've ever been hurt so bad." Levi proceeds to set up our camp stove and sets the water to boil. Then he grabs a food pack and dumps it in to heat. Sitting on the ground with his face in his hands, he does look more worn than I've ever seen him. My stomach growls loud enough to get my attention, and probably Levi's, too. So I grab my own food pack and put it inside the boiling water and wait a few minutes.

I am not thinking about the injuries we just sustained or how sensitive my skin might be, and I pick up the hot package of food from the pot, unprepared for the searing pain in my fingers. I drop my meal and stumble backward, right into Levi. I land squarely in his lap.

He is almost naked and I am not wearing my uniform. It takes only a second for me to realize what I have done. We lock eyes momentarily. I had been so wrapped up with what Levi might be up to that *I'm the one* who fucks up. I lost focus.

Dammit.

I scramble up, hoping that our brief contact was not enough to trigger the Blood Lust. But his eyes narrow and take on a look of absolute malice, and I know that all the wishing and hoping in the world is not going to change what my clumsiness has just done. As Levi said, we are on a desert island. It's just the two of us and I didn't just brush against him. I *landed* on him.

"Levi," I say gently as I back up. I don't have very long before he comes at me. My soothing tone fails to even register. "Levi!" I snap, this time with authority, as if he's an attack dog and I can get him to heel by playing alpha. That doesn't work, either, but to his credit, he hasn't yet lunged for me. Maybe he can fight it.

Then again, probably not.

I have no doubt that if I don't manage this situation, Levi will kill me. I'll put up a hell of a fight, but he's better than I am, and bigger. I have to think, quickly. There's only one thing that will stop him. Pain. A lot of very, very bad pain. I look around for anything I can use. I'm almost up against our stove. I could throw boiling water at him, but if it gets in his eyes it could blind him, maybe permanently. I need a partner who can see.

I notice his utility knife in the sand. He probably left it out to puncture the food packs. It's still sheathed, but I'm fairly certain that I can get the blade out faster than he can get at me. He sees me look at the knife.

Time's up.

Levi pounces as I jump for the knife. He lands where I just was while I somersault away again, taking the knife out as I do.

I put the blade between my teeth so I can use my hands to do a back handspring away. This is a pretty show-offy way to distance myself from him, but it's also something he's not expecting, and I can get a tremendous amount of space between us because I'm using both my arms and legs for power.

I don't have time to bask in the glory of nailing the landing. I whip the knife out of my mouth and throw it. He's not expecting this, either. He wants to kill me, but he wants to use his bare hands. He wants to strangle me or maybe punch my head until my skull shatters into a hundred pieces. You don't think about knives or guns so much inside the Blood Lust, because the kill would be too clean, too unsatisfying. You want blood, and you want to *feel* that you caused it.

The knife lands squarely in his right shoulder, exactly where I meant it to. I threw it hard and it's now embedded deep inside the muscle. That's an actual skill they teach during Citadel training. At the time I believed it was utterly ridiculous. Who has the luxury to stress about missing a vital organ when you're fighting for your life? Sadly, since then I have honed this throwing talent and used it many times. Do I worry about being killed on the battlefield? Absolutely. But I worry more about killing unnecessarily. There are only so many lives you can take without it completely, irrevocably, fucking you up.

My plan works. I watch Levi's face change from fury to frustration to outright pain. He looks at the knife and I look at him. He closes his eyes and clenches his jaw.

"I am so, *so* sorry," I say as I walk toward him, picking up the med kit from the pile of our stuff on the way.

"Ryn, stop," Levi commands, with more defeat in his voice than I have ever heard. I do as he says. I want to keep on apologizing, but I feel like it's better if I don't speak, and follow his lead. "Just throw the med bag over here," he asks softly.

"Levi, come on . . . ," I practically plead. "You won't be triggered again. You're in too much pain. Let me help you." I take another step.

"Seriously, Ryn, back the fuck up!" I wince at his sudden burst of anger. I'm used to him like this, of course, but right now I'm feeling guilty. I'm vulnerable to his tone. I swallow hard.

"Fine," I tell him as I throw the bag. It lands at his feet and he squats down, opens the case, and grabs an anticoagulant gel, superglue, and a bandage. I can't believe he's going to do this by himself. I blow out in frustration and wish that I could turn away, but I have to make sure he patches himself up decently because he won't let me help.

Levi remains on his knees. He slowly pulls the knife out. I watch the blood drain from his face. Without the knife as a kind of stopgap, the wound begins to bleed profusely. Levi doesn't even seem to notice. He rubs the anticoagulant on it and the bleeding stops within seconds while the wound bubbles and foams. He doesn't have a mirror, so he can't really clean the cut properly and he doesn't even bother to try. Levi closes the slit as best as he can with the glue, though it's still filled with coagulant and covered in blood. Then, he undoes a large bandage and slaps it on his shoulder.

Using the sleeve of his uniform, he picks up his food out of the pot on the stove and opens the pack with the same knife he had just pulled out of his body. *Gross.* He pours it into a bowl and starts to eat in silence.

There's nothing I can do now. He's going to blame me for this for a while, and I suppose it's *mostly* my fault even if I didn't mean to hurt him. I didn't give him the Blood Lust. I didn't even ask him to come along with me through the Rift. All I did was trip, but he's the one parading around half-naked and acting like this is some sort of vacation. If he'd been acting normally, then I wouldn't have been worried about this exact thing happening. I realize there's a causality thing going on here that if I think too hard about will do my head in, so I dismiss it.

The silence becomes increasingly awkward. We focus on eating our food and hydrating the cells in our weakened bodies. Regardless of our superhuman abilities, that last Earth pushed us to the limit. I know we need to get moving, but right now I just want to sit here. I'm exhausted from the drugs and it takes a lot of concentration not to think about what just happened. I'm so lost in my own thoughts that I am startled when Levi finally speaks.

"We can't do this," he tells me solemnly.

"We can. We just have to be more careful. Maybe we jump with our masks on next time or—"

"No," Levi interrupts. "I don't mean the mission or the Rifts. And you know that I don't. I mean, this—me and you together all the time, alone. I'm going to kill you."

"You won't," I assure him as I put down my canteen. "It was bound to happen once. Think of it as a warning shot. Now we'll be extra vigilant."

"Jesus," he says as he shakes his head. "For someone who is so smart, you really can be dumb as shit sometimes."

I throw him a nasty look. "You're trying to bait me, but it's not going to work. I made a mistake. I'm not going to make it worse by getting into an argument." And then, he actually laughs.

"Make it worse? Worse than a knife in my shoulder? Worse

than the fact that I can barely do my job because I'm so friggin' scared of accidentally touching you? What if we're on another Earth and some poor girl who doesn't know the rules puts her hand on my shoulder? What then? I just kill an innocent person because that's how it is?"

I slowly lean back, away from him. "What are you saying?"

"Stop it!" Levi yells. "Stop playing dumb! You *know* what I'm saying. You know what we have to do, and don't for one minute tell me that you haven't considered it."

"No," I tell him, and I shoot up, off the sand, onto my feet. "It is way too dangerous."

"More dangerous than what the fuck is going on right now?" Levi gets up, too, and faces me in a standoff. "You know," he says with a sarcastic huff of a laugh, "if I thought you were saying no because you were afraid for your own safety that would be one thing, but that's not you. That's not Saint Ryn, leader of Beta Team, the savior of all Citadels. That isn't the case. You won't do this because of *Ezra*. You don't want to *cheat* on your boyfriend. Look around you!" Levi yells as he points at the bandage on his shoulder. "Look at me! You think normal rules apply? You think life and death is more important than disappointing some *kid*?"

I take a long breath in an attempt to calm myself, center myself. I told myself that I wasn't going to let him bait me and I'll be damned if I let him play me like that, even as I want to tear his face off for the contempt that dripped from his voice. I'm almost proud of myself for my restraint. He just has to think this through.

Shit, I need to think this through.

What would it mean, *really*, to deprogram Levi? He's asking me not to consider Ezra, but that's impossible. I could fight beside Levi all day long, but touch him? Softly? The way I let

Ezra touch me? Alarm bells and sirens and a robotic *Danger! Danger!* voice goes off inside my head. He doesn't know what he's asking me. He thinks it's something easy. That it's something we can just do in all our spare time jumping from Earth to alternate Earth.

He *thinks*, but he has no frickin' idea.

I have to handle this very carefully. I begin to talk, but I make sure to keep my tone level and empathetic. Well, as empathetic as possible for me: "Were you listening when I explained to everyone what the Roones and ARC did to us? We were fourteen when they figured out exactly what turned us on and exactly what we thought would be romantic and loving . . . and then they drugged us and beat us and broke our bones. We were *tortured*. The Blood Lust isn't something you just get over. So this is not about cheating. It's not about sex, it's about feelings. And as strong as you are about everything else, you aren't good with the feelings, Levi. In fact, you suck at them. You aren't ready."

Levi folds his arms, one over the other, and then nods his head slowly. "Yeah I was listening," he tells me, as stone-faced as I've ever seen him. "I was right there when you laid out all the big bad secrets ARC had been keeping from us. I was also there when Edo hit the kill switch on more than a few of my friends when they disagreed with your assessment that ARC is the devil."

"Are you *kidding* me?" I throw my hands up. I can't believe what he's saying. He doesn't think that ARC is the enemy? "Are you saying you *agree* with your brainwashed friends?"

"I never said that, Ryn. I just said that I was there. I was there when they died and I was there when we pulled in their parents and gave them the deluxe ARC treatment so that now they think their kids are off at some year abroad. They can't even grieve their own children's deaths." Levi kicks his toe in the sand. It hits me that maybe Levi might actually have feelings, as I see this particular injustice weighs heavy on him. I could try to justify my actions, but there's no point. Even though it was the only way to ensure the life of our rebellion, he *is* right: It was a vile thing I did to those Citadels' moms and dads. I hate that I have to defend those decisions, so I remain silent while Levi keeps talking. "I was also there when you made sure that everyone else on that base was either loyal or drugged to become loyal. This is a messy, ugly thing that you started. I'm not saying you weren't right to do it, but your methods? Not good, Ryn."

"You're right, I fucked up," I admit. He's not saying anything I don't know and haven't agonized over already. "But I've copped to that and I've apologized as much as I'm ever going to. I was only trying to save *everyone*, so please stop holding my good intentions against me. They don't teach 'How to Effectively Start a Coup' in our training, you know?"

To my surprise, Levi starts to laugh again, though I am sure it's not because of the joke I just made. He's laughing at me, not with me. Then he drags his hands through his hair, clearly frustrated. "I'm not holding anything against you. I'm trying to make you see how *huge* this fucking thing is. It's bigger than you and your Boy Wonder. It's *way* bigger than your bizarre sense of morality. You can't not help me because it's inconvenient, not when you're all in everywhere else."

Now it's my turn to snicker. He just doesn't get it. "Morality? I'm not being moral. I'm being realistic. It isn't a question of convenience. *At all.* You want me to deprogram you? Okay, well, that involves shedding layers and layers of emotional armor. It involves intimacy and truth. So let's start there. Why don't you tell me exactly how you feel about me? Can you even do that?"

Gotcha, I think to myself. Because although I know that Levi is attracted to me physically (girl, boobs, pretty good hair, an ass I'm proud of—for a white girl—but I'm no supermodel), I doubt very much that he can verbalize his feelings for me beyond that, and more likely than not, there aren't any of real significance. But instead of trying to avoid the question and redirect the conversation, Levi says nothing. He just stares at me. His gaze is intense. It's so powerful that it makes *me* want to look away. I steel myself. I'm not going to give him the satisfaction of watching me squirm.

"Fine," he says finally. My heart starts to beat a little faster as I realize I don't actually want him to answer that question. I don't really want to know the truth, because if it goes beyond the physical, I wouldn't know what to do with that. It dawns on me that I might have just made things worse between us by asking him to fess up: opening the door to a series of more tense conversations and weird, awkward silences.

But there's no going back now. He's already started talking.

"I feel a sense of loyalty toward you, but maybe that's just because you're a Citadel. I feel protective of you even though I know you don't really need my protection. I think you're strong. I think you're beautiful, but I also think you're a pain in the ass, and honestly, I'm not sure I even like you."

I sigh and throw my hands up. "Well that's just great. I can totally see how deprogramming someone who doesn't even like me is going to work." I'm relieved. He's confused. He doesn't know how to separate attraction and real feeling. No surprise there. Still, the conversation has me a little freaked.

Hearing Levi say these things makes my heart race a little. Is it guilt? Because I'm with Ezra and I'm pretty sure this level of openness is inappropriate, but since I've never had a boyfriend before, it could very well be that this is the absolute best way to handle a situation like this—by acknowledging it, even if there's no way to know exactly what "it" is. I should probably say something, but Levi holds out a single hand to stop me from continuing.

"I wasn't finished, so calm down." I let out a low growl that I'm sure he hears, along with an increasingly ascending pulse, but so what? This shit is intense. There is nothing I hate more than someone telling me to calm down as if I'm some crazy Real Housewife who screeches and wails all the time.

"I don't know how I feel about you," Levi admits. "I really have no idea. Mostly I'm just angry and everything else I feel is pretty much a mystery." Levi stops talking and I sigh. I had been trying to prove a point, that despite our hormones the Blood Lust is not really sexual. I didn't think Levi understood that, but by the look on his face right now, I know he does. *Damn.* There is something in his eyes, something lost and bewildered. This is Levi's version of intimacy. "I am ashamed," he tells me softly. "I'm embarrassed that, basically, I have the emotional intelligence of an eight-year-old. I know there are other things to feel besides anger and guilt, but fuck, I don't know how to get to them."

"Oh, Levi." I exhale his name, pressing my palms into my eyes as if I can somehow ignite the right answer inside my brain.

"Listen," he says with urgency, seeing me falter. "I don't think it matters if I like you. I think what matters is that I trust you. With my life. Right? I need your help, Ryn, please."

Sometimes I wonder if it's possible to be a good leader and a good person at the same time, because let's face it, there are precious few examples. After all I've done I think it might be too late for me to ever call myself a good person. But a true leader, the kind that I want to be, doesn't hold fast to an opinion in the face of overwhelming evidence that it's wrong. A strong leader is secure enough to change her mind.

I stare off into the distance at the light reflecting off the water. It's gorgeous here, but it isn't real. It's a plucked moment. A pause before we jump again. Into God knows what.

There is no absolute right answer here. This isn't something I can win. This isn't a contest or a fight. My new partner may or may not have feelings for me that go beyond the way I look in an absurdly tight uniform (I get it, it's supposed to fit like a second skin, but it's more Black Widow than real black ops). I shouldn't deprogram Levi because it's dangerous and intimate and I have a boyfriend. But if I want to get that boyfriend back in one piece, there's really only one logical choice.

As much as it annoys me, Levi is right.

It would be safer if he were deprogrammed. He's asked for my help. He's done it as honestly and authentically as he can. That's huge for him. I can't turn away from that. Ezra won't like this, but again, props to Levi. I'm trying to apply normal relationship logic to this situation and it won't work. By agreeing to help with the deprogramming, I could very well be saving my own life and the lives of others. It might be suicide—there's that, too—but I think the odds are in my favor on this one. Ezra will get over it once he takes the time to think it through. Once I explain to him that it is the best chance that all of us have to survive. So, now the real problem is time. Deprogramming takes time, which we are desperately short of. Once we start, we can't stop; doing so may ruin any chance he has at being cured.

But really, this mission can't possibly succeed *unless* we do it. So . . .

"Okay. Since you said that you had considered this, I assume you brought a supply of the drug that leaves you open to suggestion? The red pills?" I ask, just to make sure this is even a doable thing.

"I have them. And I put some music, shows, and books on my tablet. That's what we need, right? Sensory reminders of when we were younger? Before this happened to us?"

I nod my head and zip up my uniform to the neck. But the whole time I want to scream at him: *Do you really think that's all it takes? Listening to some songs? Watching a movie?* He has no idea. "Just go take a pill. Take two, actually, just to be on the safe side. We'll start in fifteen minutes."

In the meantime, I'm going to pray to something and hope to hell this works.

CHAPTER 6

We are sitting side by side, watching the tide as it pulls out farther with each wave. Levi has taken off his uniform and is in his khakis and a T-shirt. My uniform is on and I have put my blond hair, badly in need of a trim, back and up in a messy bun on the top of my head. I am thinking, though I don't want to say it out loud just in case it isn't something Levi had thought of, that me throwing the knife at him after he felt the Blood Lust might have ruined any chance of this working. He got turned on and I hurt him, which is how he was programmed in the first place. I can only hope that the drugs, in conjunction with patience and a true desire to kick this, might override what just happened.

It occurs to me that in deprogramming Levi's Blood Lust, I might also need to deprogram myself of my distrust of him.

Levi has his tablet on his knees. He looks a little nervous. I'm downright scared. When I did this, I had Ezra. Ezra is patient and loving and, for obvious reasons, much more emotionally intelligent than I am. Ezra and I care for each other. Levi and I tolerate each other. If that. But maybe in a way that's better. Maybe a little emotional distance will be more effective. I have no idea.

And that's probably what has me the most frightened.

"This is the song my mom sang to me every night before I went to bed when I was little," he says, showing me the tablet. "Don't ask me why. Weird choice, I know. She did change up some of the lyrics so that it wasn't a proper love song, 'cause that would be gross, obviously."

"Look, you don't have to defend the choices you make in this process. Ezra read Harry Potter to me. He wore my dad's clothes. It doesn't matter. Whatever it is that makes you feel safe and takes you back to that place, is not for me to judge. If you feel like I'm judging you or laughing at you somehow, then we can't do this. It means that we haven't created a trusting environment. Your guard will be up and things will go badly. Besides, Dolly Parton is amazing."

By way of an answer, Levi nods his head. He pushes the Play button and "Islands in the Stream" starts up. I don't think it's actually that weird of a choice for a lullaby at all. It's cute.

"Just make sure the song is on repeat," I tell him.

I let the song play all the way through, and to his credit, Levi doesn't say anything. He doesn't demand to know what's going to happen next. He just sits there, which is good. When the song starts again, I begin to speak, softly: "Now, Levi, imagine yourself as a young kid, in bed, your mom singing to you. Remember how it felt. Live inside this memory for a moment. You were safe, you were loved, nothing bad was ever going to happen to you, because your mom was there and she was going to take care of you. Let the drug work. It will take you deep inside this memory. You have to open up completely and let yourself feel how you felt all those nights."

Levi closes his eyes. His breathing slows. His heart rate becomes more difficult to hear over the breaking surf. He is calming down, and thankfully, so am I. I let the song finish out and once it starts over, I begin to speak again. "You're safe here. You have to clear your mind of doubt. In a few moments, I'm going to put my hand over yours. If you need to say out loud that you're safe and that everything is fine, you should. You should talk. Don't say that you aren't going to hurt me. It won't help. It will take your brain down the wrong path. No one is hurting anyone. Put thoughts of being hurt or hurting someone else far away from your mind."

I let the song play again. I let Levi live inside this dreamlike state for a while. It's probably been years since he's thought about this, about how it made him feel. No one other than a Citadel would know why he has had to make himself forget the innocent child he was. There is no room for sweetness or vulnerability on the battlefield. Better just to put it away, lock it up, forget that we were ever young. "You're a kid in this memory. You're a boy and you're defenseless, but you've never felt safer and that's because love is safety and there is nothing stronger than a mother's love for her child, not even a Citadel and especially not the Blood Lust. It's no match for this love."

I let the song play a little longer. Let him absorb what I told him. Slowly, I put my hand over his hand. I inch a little closer to him. I never imagined I would ever be so physically close to Levi. I can't imagine being physically close to anyone besides Ezra. To that end, I start to say a mantra of my own. And while

I know that what I'm saying to myself is not exactly the entire truth, bringing my boyfriend into the equation makes this whole affair seem like, well, less like an affair.

This is for Ezra. This is for Ezra. This is for Ezra.

While I'm silently saying this, Levi is repeating his own mantra: "I'm safe," he whispers. "I'm safe. I'm okay." I sit there unmoving for about ten seconds and then Levi's eyes fly open and he looks at me with gritted teeth. Shit.

He takes my hand and flips it over, bending it the wrong way. My wrist could snap in an instant. He forces me to my knees and then he takes his free hand and puts it on the back of my neck, forcing my face in the sand. At this rate I will suffocate in a matter of minutes. I have to remain calm, but he's going to kill me. My training overrides my good intentions. I kick out with my leg. I get him off balance and he staggers just enough so that I can roll out of reach. He lunges for me again and I block his arms.

"Levi," I say calmly, "stop this. Go back to that place in your mind." Before I can say anything else he gets a good punch in to my eye. It's a massive wallop and I can feel my lid swelling almost completely shut. It's going to be near impossible to defend myself when I'm blind in one eye. Yet if I attack more, then this is all for nothing. So I do my best to keep him at bay. We are dancing in a way. He keeps lunging forward and I keep moving my hands and forearms to various positions to block his attack. He gets in a few more punches that I miss because I don't see them coming, and all the while I try to reason with him: "You're fighting the Blood Lust and it won't work! *Surrender* to it. Acknowledge the pain you're feeling and try to pull it inside instead of taking it out on me . . . Levi!" I scream.

But he can't hear me. He's lost to it. *This won't work.* I have no choice. I don't want to die. I kick him hard in the abdomen and he goes flying. I leap over to where he lands and before he can get his bearings I put him in a sleeper hold. I squeeze my biceps. I cut off his air supply until he loses consciousness. I release his limp body and sink to my knees.

Shit. I completely fucked it up.

I may have saved my own life, but I also may have ruined any chance of Levi's deprogramming ever working with me. My eye is aching. I'm so tired of this. Watching Levi in the throes of the Blood Lust broke my heart. I know my own deprogramming was brutal. I almost killed Ezra, twice. He never fought back, though. He trusted me enough to know I would never take it that far, even when I myself wasn't sure. He cared about me enough to want it to work more than he wanted self-preservation. I'm positive that's not the case with Levi and me. For one thing, I don't love Levi, so I'm not willing to die for his transition. For another, though, Levi's Blood Lust is different from mine. He becomes primal, more animal than man. He himself may not be able to distinguish his emotions outside of the Blood Lust, but I saw every one of them on his face and in his eyes. There was so much pain there.

Who does this to children? It's easy to blame the Roones, because it was their technology and their offer that put us here, but it was ARC that demanded this safeguard. The planet could not afford the distraction of teenage drama, so human beings took the risk away. We had to be focused. We had to be single-minded at all times. Guard. Protect. Fight. Kill. It wasn't a monster that turned us into monsters, it was our own kind.

Human beings took away our humanity.

If I'm going to lead us through this, if I'm going to dismantle ARC and take control, I have to be willing to put it all on the line. I have to be willing to die to save us. I have to trust Levi in the same way Ezra trusted me. Levi said it. I need to be all in. Seeing Levi inside the madness of the Blood Lust has shifted my perspective. Levi absolutely cannot see this as a battle, but I have to. This is a fight like any other. I'm ready to die back home at Camp Bonneville every time I engage. I'm not willing, no, never that, but I'm always prepared for the worst. What's one more risk on top of everything else? My life is always on the line one way or another.

If I were the type of person who cries easily, I would be teary eyed. I'm not, though, and thank God; otherwise, after what I've seen and done in my few short years, I would be hysterical all day long. When I look at Levi lying here helpless, with tiny grains of sand peppering his long, dark eyelashes, the injustice of the Blood Lust and who and why we are suddenly feels explosive. Sadness turns to anger. I'm mad now and more determined than ever to fix him.

It doesn't take long for Levi to wake up. His eyes flutter open, but he stays on his back in the sand. "I'm sorry," he says softly.

"No. It's me who should be sorry. I should never have fought back. I was afraid. It won't happen again."

Levi sits up on his elbows. "What are you talking about? You had to fight back. I would have killed you. Look at your eye. I did that to you."

I get up and wipe the sand off my palms. "Oh, please," I say, deliberately playing it down. He doesn't need the guilt. It won't be useful moving forward. In fact, it's probably the opposite. "I've had worse training with Violet. This is nothing. You're not some asshole who likes to beat up girls. You're not some psycho who takes pleasure in hurting women. We aren't normal people. They did this to us. We're sick and this is our therapy." I walk over to his pack and take out another red pill from a container in his Dopp kit.

"You can't be serious right now," he says with disdain.

"We're going to do this. We're gonna fix you because you deserve to be fixed, even though in general, I think you're kind of a douche." I smile. He does not smile back. So much for trying to lighten the mood. "I'm serious, though. It's too dangerous for you to be at such a disadvantage with this. And while we don't have time, we also don't have time *not* to do it. You were right. You were right from the start and I should have just agreed with you straightaway. Take another pill."

I reach out my hand and offer it to him and he just looks at me. "You don't get it. I will kill you. Put the pill away. I came here to make sure that you got back safe. I'm not going to be the reason you don't."

"But those two things can't coexist. You can't say you've got my back when I have to worry that you might stab me there. And I need your help if we're going to find Ezra and get back home. So shut up and listen: You're not going to kill me and I am never going to fight back. Ever. I will keep my uniform and armor on and curl up into a defensive position if I have to, but I will never hurt you again."

Levi leaps up. It's his turn to be mad. This is the Levi I recognize. "No. End of discussion."

"Screw that! This isn't a decision you just get to make. This is my life, too. Take it!" I say in a voice one decibel away from a shout, but anger isn't the way. I have to learn, right now, not to be combative with Levi, which feels impossible but I have to try. I relax my posture. I lower my voice and cock my head to one side. Anger won't work, but something else . . . "You are a lot of things, Levi, but I never took you for a coward."

"I'm not a pussy, Ryn, if that's what you're trying to say."

"You know, I don't really like that word in this context. It makes me feel all feminist-y, which we could talk about. At length. *Orrrrr* you could just take the pill."

Maddeningly, he ignores my attempt to lighten the mood. He just shakes his head, like a child refusing to take a bite of food. "I thought the pills would make it easier. Now that I see they don't, we have to stop."

I put my hand out again. *Stay calm, stay calm.* "Oh my God, you *are* a child! Did you really think this was going to be done in fifteen minutes? The pills work. You just have to let them. Right now your brain is making it impossible. You may trust me, but you don't trust yourself. You have to let go of your guilt. You didn't choose to be this way. This isn't the real you. Come on. Let's do this. Let's trust each other."

Levi glares at me.

I smile. "Come on."

He rolls his eyes but actually laughs as he swipes the pill from my palm and pops it in his mouth. He takes a swig of water from his canteen.

"You're crazy."

"Yeah," I answer sarcastically. "The awesome kind of crazy that they make movies about."

"And modest. Clearly," he says with a straight face. I raise an eyebrow and shrug.

Levi walks to pick up his tablet and then comes and sits down beside me. We wait in silence for the drug to kick in, the white sand surrounding us like outstretched arms. I've never been on a tropical vacation. Once a year I go with my family to Europe to visit my grandparents in Sweden. From there we've traveled to England and France. We went to Disneyland a couple of times, but nowhere like this. I've never been anywhere this remote, with actual palm trees and burnt-orange sunsets. This must be like Fiji on our Earth, or maybe Tahiti. Though, for all I know we could be in Battle Ground. This might be the only land mass for miles. I haven't even seen a bird and that's never a good sign.

When enough time has passed I look at Levi. "Ready?" I ask.

"As I'm ever going to be." He reaches toward his tablet and I take it gently from his hands.

"I'm going to sing it. Just like your mom did to you. I'm not, like, a terrible singer, but I'm not exactly very good, either," I warn.

"That's probably better. I think it would actually irritate me if on top of everything you were a great singer, too." He smiles. That is a major compliment coming from him, and I can't help but flush a little bit at the implications of "on top of everything." Clearing my throat as much to do something as to warm up, I bring up the lyrics.

I begin to sing.

It's so interesting that his mom chose this song. I get that it's a love song, but it's also just about two people who sometimes feel like they have only each other. I know Levi's dad left his mom when he was pretty young. I know because his younger sister, Flora, told me before I became a Citadel. I don't think his dad is really in the picture. I think about the burden that must place on Levi, to take care of his mom and Flora and whatever comes flying out of the Rift at the same time. It's so much for someone so young. I don't think he's close to his team like I am. God. He must be so lonely.

When I finish the song, I immediately start over. To my surprise, Levi starts singing along with me. I don't need to say anything. He's deep in this memory, I can just tell. Very slowly, I lean closer to him. I put my head on his shoulder.

This is for Ezra. This is for Ezra. This is for Ezra . . .

After a few seconds he slides his hand down my arm and takes my hand. I never dared try to initiate contact with Ezra when we did this, but Levi is not Ezra, and neither am I. We're Citadels. We take risks normal people wouldn't. I close my eyes. I know Levi could turn any moment, but I don't think he will, not now. He's getting it. He feels safe and so do I. When we finish the song, Levi doesn't let go of my hand and I don't move. The surf breaks with a dull clap on the sand in front of us. The waves are music, too. This is working. This is going to work. I am going to deprogram Levi and he can be like any other guy. He'll be able to make out and have sex and not hurt anyone. I open my eyes and take my head off his shoulder. I look at him and he looks back and smiles at me in a way that's so unlike his usual predatory grins. This smile is almost tender. Pretty soon he'll be normal.

That thought instantly fills me with a feeling I cannot figure out. It's not dread, but it feels similar. It's not fear so much as anxiety. I look out toward the ocean, confused. Why would the prospect of fixing Levi leave me like this? With a feeling I can't name?

CHAPTER 7

Each trip through the Rift is becoming easier. I explained to Levi how I managed to basically fly within its tunnel and then use the gravity and light of the approaching Earth to get my bearings and end up on my feet instead of my ass. He seemed dubious, especially with the part about us not being grappled to each other, but in the end he trusted me and we both walked out of the Rift on our feet with only minor stumbles.

The first few seconds are always the tensest. Where will we end up? In the middle of a volcano? A freeway? Someplace where a Rift will be seen as a horror and we, by default, some sort of monsters? Thankfully, we find ourselves in the middle of yet another forest and when I listen, I can hear nothing but animals scurrying, and from somewhere above, the screech of a bird in flight.

I stare at the ground and then the trees. The terrain looks

to be high mountain desert, the landscape I've seen and loved on family trips to central Oregon. It's rocky and barren at my feet, but then the desert disappears as my gaze lifts upward to the ponderosas. From this vantage point it is clearly the Pacific Northwest.

But there's something off.

I mentally scan all the trees, making a slow 360-degree sweep. I take a mental picture of each one and close my eyes, calling them up in my memory. I compare them side by side. The smell is right. Ponderosas are smoke and evergreen. I walk up to one and put my hand on its large, rough bark.

"They're too perfect, right?" I ask Levi to back up my hunch. "And the placement—it's meant to be chaotic, but there's a pattern to it."

Levi squints a little and cranes his neck back and forth. "Yeah. The branches of that one," he gestures, meaning the one I've touched, "and the one eighteen feet away are almost identical except for two variables. That doesn't happen in nature."

"So, it's man-made and the trees must have been cloned. What kind of an Earth is that, you think?" I ask him.

"I don't know, but you must have clocked those buildings about six klicks away. We should go and check it out."

Before I can answer we hear a noise, a buzzing, getting closer. Without saying anything further, we both grab our rifles and unclip them from our chest pads. We don't have to wait long to see the source of the sound. It's a drone, although it's not like any drone I've ever seen. It's a silver disk that's just hovering with no discernable way of actually flying. I stare at it, almost transfixed. It gets closer, and then light pours out of a thin circular strip in its midsection. The light races up and down our bodies in a long blue flash.

Observing is one thing, this is obviously something else. I point my rifle at it and squeeze the trigger twice. The drone stops and drops almost immediately and I breathe out a sigh of relief.

"That was either a really good idea or a really bad one," I say before Levi can, because I know he'll have a choice comment.

"I vote good one. That thing was scanning us." I side-eye him because I *think* he just lobbed me a compliment. Levi walks over to the downed object and bends forward to have a better look.

"Don't touch it, even with your foot," I warn.

"Yeah, okay, Mom, are you sure? Because weird alien hovering silver disks that scan people *never explode.*"

"Noted. Thank you, Levi." I leave him be for a couple of minutes. It's not like I couldn't make useful observations, but I've already annoyed him with my previous—and admittedly unnecessary—comments, and besides, my skill set in that area leans more toward noticing the tree thing. Levi's mind is more mechanical. Which, if I'm being honest, kind of pisses me off a little bit because it feels so typically gender biased. Citadels don't do gender bias. Except, it seems, in this case. Right here.

Annoying.

Levi straightens and walks back over to me, but before he can say anything we both hear another noise and this one is much louder. It is the sound of helicopter blades slicing through air.

"That came out of nowhere," I say, taking hold of my rifle yet again. My pulse quickens. "It's almost on top of us, so where the hell did it come from?" We both look up to the sky and sure enough, it's a chopper. It is moving with alarming speed, and at two hundred yards away, it's closing in fast. I can see its sleek design—black chrome and streamlined, with none of the bulky aerodynamics of helicopters on our Earth.

"We're on a future Earth. A time line way more advanced than ours. We must be." Although I don't know why I bother to say it. Levi has eyes. I suppose saying it out loud makes it more real somehow, because right now I feel like we're in a movie.

"We could run," Levi suggests.

"No. Why waste the energy? If we're going to have to fight, we'll need it." So both of us just stand there unmoving as the helicopter approaches. It's noisy, but it's not overwhelmingly loud. In a way, the propellers are almost soothing. They whoosh in the cloudless sky in precise measures. When the chopper is about fifty feet above us, the door slides open and two men emerge. They don't jump, but rather float down gracefully as if being lowered by cables. Except there are no cables, and no pilot, either.

I just look at them and stare because, holy fuck, I literally don't know what else to do. I look at Levi, and he's just as dumbstruck. Finally, I have to say something.

"Did Jason Momoa and Andy Warhol just fly down from up there?"

"I feel like yes, that is what happened. Unless we're being drugged or that drone thing brainwashed us."

When the two men are about twenty feet away, I put my rifle up. "Stay where you are. Do. Not. Move," I yell. They both stop and look at us, puzzled. As if the way they arrived was totally normal and why are we surprised.

"Hello!" Jason Momoa says enthusiastically (which already seems not very Jason Momoa–like, though I don't know him personally, obviously). "You are humans, yes?"

"We will not harm you," Andy Warhol says brightly. "We were alerted to your presence and were sent to retrieve you." They both take a step forward.

"I said don't move, and keep your hands up!"

More bewilderment, although they don't come any closer. Eventually they both raise their hands. "We do not possess any weapons. We are no threat to you," Jason Momoa says earnestly.

"Fine. You can come closer, but stop when we tell you, and walk slowly," I command. When they are about ten feet away I tell them to halt. "I'm going to frisk them. Cover me."

"Really? You're going to go frisk Aquaman? That's going to be *your* job?" Levi throws out.

"Not now, Levi. *God.*" There's a time and place for sarcasm, but this is not it. I quickly move over to the two and I am able to get a good look at them close-up. If I needed any more proof that something absolutely bonkers is going on here, I get it after I see their silver eyes. They are as round and luminous as full moons, but the irises are a darker silver, the color of bracelets or rings left forgotten in a drawer. On Andy Warhol it looks creepy as fuck. On Jason Momoa it's kinda sexy in an otherworldly way. Both have hair cut close to their scalps and they are wearing matching slate-gray outfits, though *uniform* is a bit of a stretch. They are dressed the same, but there is no ornamentation, not even buttons. Just plain jackets over trousers. Even with all that, though, it's their skin that really gives me pause. It doesn't look right. It is without blemish or lines, fine or otherwise. It's as if a newborn baby morphed into an adult. I'm not sure yet what these people are, but this is definitely not an Earth like ours—*not* an echo Earth.

My rifle is clipped, which leaves me with both hands free to pat them down. I do this efficiently and without lingering, even on Khal Drogo.

"My name is Thunder," he says kindly.

"Really?" I say, even though of course it is.

"And this is my colleague Ragweed."

"Hello," Andy/Ragweed offers. Okay, the names are weird (and more than a little unfair).

"They aren't armed, Levi, you can put your gun down." Levi slowly lowers his weapon and moves with steely determination toward us. As he approaches, I know he is noticing the same exact things that I did. It's clear that he feels threatened. I do, too, but I can hide these things better. His posture is yard-stick straight and he's clenching his jaw.

"I'm Ryn and this is Levi. Where are we?" I ask with determination.

"North 44°3'29", West 121°18'51"," Ragweed answers efficiently. I don't even need to check in with my partner. We are both well aware that these are the coordinates of central Oregon. Just as we thought. Still, latitude and longitude are not as helpful as an actual city name.

"What year is it?" I ask a little more impatiently.

"I am afraid I cannot answer that question. We do not keep time in the same way that I think you probably do," Ragweed offers regretfully.

"Yeah, well," Levi says while resting his forearm on the butt of his rifle, "maybe you should just give it a try anyway. Let us be the judge of what we can and cannot figure out."

Both men look past us, in the distance. I have a feeling that their eyes are providing some kind of digital interface. More than likely, we are all being monitored and they are awaiting instructions.

Finally Thunder says, gently, "I am sure you have many questions. We cannot provide you with the answers you are looking for. We have been designated to deliver you to our doyenne, who will be able to discuss your questions in detail. We are simply escorts."

I nod my head and look to the ground as a wave of nausea washes over me. I've heard this speech before because *I've made it*. It's the same speech I give to all the Immigrants who came through the Rift at Battle Ground, and I doubt these two would give up any more information than I would. However, they are decidedly less aggressive than the Citadels are, and if there is some kind of equivalent of a Village on this Earth, chances are that's where Ezra would be. There's also no chance in hell that a place like the Village could hold me and Levi. Still, going with them is a risk—I'm not sure we could elude them and get our packs and the QOINS up and running without incident. Just because they don't have weapons doesn't mean they aren't dangerous.

"And you guys just fly around, hoping to run into someone? Escorting people places?" Levi asks stubbornly. They aren't going to give us anything useful.

"Yes, I can see why you would think we have the ability to fly. I assure you that we do not. It is technology, built into our boots, using a combination of the planet's magnetic core and micro thrusters," Ragweed offers, but why? Why is that information something he's willing to give up, unless . . . ?

"You want to take us up there? With your shoes?" It's an amusing thought, but I am not amused.

"You will agree to come with us now?" Thunder asks brightly. I don't think I actually agreed to anything, but he is certainly hopeful.

Levi must see me mulling and he leans in closer, not near enough to actually touch me, but close enough so that he can speak almost in a whisper that they hopefully can't hear. "They seem pretty harmless, and if you want to know if Ezra is here, then I think we have to go with them. We just have to demand that we stay together and we get to keep our things with us at all times so we can Rift out if we need to."

"To be clear: You *do* understand that it's Jason Momoa and Andy Warhol with silver eyes offering to take us in their *Blade Runner* helicopter, right? Because I'm still coming to grips with that, and there is no scenario we thought of that included anything like this in our strategic planning sessions," I add, concealing at least half of my mouth with a well-timed itch to my top lip.

I can practically hear his eyes rolling. "Yes, I understand that we are in the Multiverse. And yes, this is batshit crazy, but it's the Wild West out here, so what else do you want to do?"

"Fine," I say to everyone. "We will go on the condition that we will not be separated from our things or each other." I watch as they pause. It definitely seems like they are getting information visually from the implants that are their eyes. I think I might be way more freaked out by this if I had never watched *Black Mirror*. "Oh, and no flying. Send down a rope or something. You must have a backup in case your rocket boots don't work."

Ragweed grabs hold of my arm. "Excellent. We will now escort you to the doyenne."

I give him a stern, unflinching look. "Take your hands off me. Now."

Ragweed does not remove his hand. I look at Levi, who has backed away from Thunder. His look is a clear warning. "We must escort you to the doyenne safely," Ragweed tells me, undeterred.

"Yes. But. Do. Not. Touch. Me," I growl.

"We must escort you to the doyenne safely."

"Remove your hand or I will escort my fist into your throat."

Ragweed seems not to hear me, or not understand. He simply holds on tighter, attempting now to pull me toward the chopper. "We must esc—" But I don't let him finish the sentence. I've set a boundary, a rule. I asked, maybe not so nicely, but a girl shouldn't have to be polite when asking a man not to touch her. I yank my arm away from him and pick him up by the throat. His body lifts up into the air and his feet are off the ground. Ragweed has that faraway look in his eyes. He is not struggling. His body has gone slack.

I exhale loudly and pitch him up and out, tossing him in the air. He lands with a dull thud, his head hitting a tree trunk.

Oh shit—did I just kill him?

His eyes are still open, but he isn't moving, never a good sign. I spin on my heels toward Thunder and Levi. This whole situation is tense as fuck. Why wouldn't he just do as I asked?

"I don't know what 'escort' means here," I say to Thunder, "but where we come from it implies a certain amount of protocol. All he had to do was direct me, verbally. I know I look young, but I *can* follow directions. Apparently your buddy over there can't. I won't be held responsible for actions I take when I feel threatened."

Levi's stance has gotten wider. His chest is thrust forward slightly. If Thunder isn't a complete moron he'll notice this and not try anything. There is an awkward, almost painful silence as Thunder looks at his fallen colleague and then out past him above the tree line.

"Yes. I understand. Another team will come and retrieve Ragweed. I will escort you safely to the doyenne without physical contact. Cable. Harness." Given these people's weird names, I hope he's asking for what I think he is and not sending more "escorts" down. Still, who is he talking to? I don't see any kind of comm system. I frisked the guy and he has nothing on him, not even an earpiece.

In three seconds I'm relieved to see a pulley being sent down from the chopper. Still, I find it odd that Thunder has not gone over to Ragweed to make sure he's okay. I have my back turned to him because, quite frankly, I don't want to know. I have no idea how they do things here. That might be normal. I'm beginning to wonder if these people, like the trees around us, are clones. It would be a logical reason as to why Thunder isn't more concerned about Ragweed's safety. Still, you can't know what you don't know and my hope is that my explanation, my very clear vocalization that I felt threatened, will be enough for what just went down.

We make our way to right below the hovering aircraft and its muffled blades. "I'm going first," Levi tells me. It's not a suggestion. I put both my hands up in surrender. Thunder is keeping a respectful distance. The device they sent down looks a little like a swing with a crisscross seat belt that you step into. Levi figures it out quickly enough and secures himself in with the carabiner they've provided. He holds on to the cables on the side, and once he does Thunder says, "Retract," and the seat shoots up with alarming speed.

In short order it's my turn. I get myself in and braced for the ride. This time, when Thunder gives the verbal command, he follows me up in the air with the same impressive speed.

Once I climb into the helicopter I see that it is compact, but there's enough room for at least six people to sit comfortably on two padded benches. There is no cockpit or jump seat. There isn't room for a pilot at all. The whole thing is automated. I feel like that's cool as much as it is terrifying. The doors are mostly windows, so as we begin to ascend and veer off I get a better view of the trees and their odd layout from this vantage point, meant to look wild but really spaced in a sequential pattern, which is easy to discern when you know what you're looking for.

I don't get much of a look, though, because this helicopter is fast. And not just regular fast but, like, bullet train in Japan–style fast. The landscape below me becomes a blur, but it only lasts a couple of minutes. The chopper slows as we approach the city. I peer down and look at the entire scope of this place. Everything is gray and green, like a giant stone sundial covered in moss. There are tall high-rises ringing smaller buildings, though not many roads. The few streets branch out like perfectly proportioned sunrays. We are clearly headed to the center of this circle, an impressively large building with a solar-paneled roof in the shape of two giant butterfly wings. The building is concrete, as it seems the other structures in this city are as well, but there is fluidity to it, an odd sense of motion to the heavy architecture.

The helicopter touches down softly and without so much as a bump. The landing pad is a raised cement platform in the middle of a large expanse of grass. This grass, like the ponderosas, is too green, too perfectly mowed. It almost looks like carpeting. The doors open and Thunder solicitously waits behind as Levi and I exit. I see there is a stretch of concrete leading from here to the building.

I also see others. They stop and watch us, and I can't help staring in turn. Like Thunder and Ragweed, many of these people have famous faces. I see Meryl Streep, Gandhi, Neil deGrasse Tyson, Princess Diana. It's just too weird. Awesome but weird. My clone theory is starting to feel more and more plausible.

The path leading to the building we are going to starts blinking blue. How they get cement to turn color is another neat trick, but considering what I've seen already, it's almost hardly worth noting. The blinking lights flash more rapidly and turn into arrows, and it's apparent that this is the pathway we are meant to take. I don't love being told so explicitly what to do, but I figure this is the fastest way to find out if Ezra is here, so I stay on the path.

We arrive shortly at the entrance and two massive glass doors slide open. I center myself to steady my heart. I have no idea what these people are or what they want from us. I have just injured—more than likely killed—one of their own, so that's going to play into this equation. On top of that, if Ezra even showed up here, would they tell me? And how will I find him if they won't? It's a mix of frustration, fear, and curiosity coursing through me as I walk through the doors.

Once we step inside there are more famous people sprinkled among others I don't recognize. I notice they are dressed more for comfort than fashion, but there is a certain element of minimalist chic going on. Everyone is wearing loose-fitting cotton or linen clothing. Some of the women wear leggings with long tunics past their knees, almost like traditional Indian dress, but without the vibrant colors. In fact, all the colors are muted: grays, blacks, ivories, and rusts with more browns than reds. The people move silently around us, staring with unabashed moon-eyed curiosity, and it's unsettling, so I take in my surroundings instead.

The ceilings are incredibly high, at least three stories with long pendulous lights that hang down from the ceiling like necklaces. There are elevators, but we veer away from them and end up at a frosted glass door that slides open with our approach. Inside this room is a man who I don't recognize and a woman who is Tilda Swinton *because of course Tilda Swinton would be here.*

Thunder stays at the door, and any trace of his earlier good-will has dissipated. In a way, I almost find this more imposing version of him comforting. It's kind of how I expect Jason Momoa would actually be. In the middle of the room is an ivory-colored reclining chair and there is a bunch of equipment lined up on a tray that is hovering a few inches above the ground. I have a sinking feeling I know where this is going. I glance at Levi, who has focused all his attention on the man seated on a low stool by the chair. If I were that man I would be very worried right now. But he does not seem worried at all. His unremarkable face is open and gentle. His posture, though straight, is not rigid.

"My name is Feather," he opens with quiet confidence. "I am the head of the biomed division here. I understand that you do not want to be touched, but if you will allow me, I can repair your eye in less than ten seconds. Please?" He asks kindly. My eye. It must still be bruised from when Levi hit me on the island. It has been throbbing, a dull ache that I have ignored and, admittedly, my vision hasn't been 100 percent. There is more than a good chance that he actually fractured my orbital bone or even my maxilla.

I look to the chair and then back again at the man who I suppose is a doctor, or something like it. "How would you fix this?" I ask skeptically.

"We have a patch. It has the ability to instantly heal damaged tissue. It is painless and I promise to apply it only to your eye." A Band-Aid that can heal cuts and bruises instantly? That's the kind of thing a Citadel could really use—the kind of thing that would stop our parents from worrying about our time at all those fake martial arts classes ARC says is a mandatory part of the curriculum but which is of course just a cover-up for the injuries we sustain.

"And it is not just your eye. The initial scan our drone sent back before you shot it down revealed that you both were exposed to a dangerous level of radiation. I could fix that as well, but it would require cooperation on your part."

"Radiation?" asks Levi cuttingly.

"The microwave Earth," I remind him. I assumed we had just been burnt, but of course there was bound to be more than just toxins in the atmosphere. These people found it with a blinking light. We don't have anything like that sort of tech, and now it seems like my earlier paranoia about our lack of technological advancement wasn't paranoia after all. I think these people probably have a lot of things that would help us, save us even.

Still . . .

"I didn't notice it before," I say to Feather calmly. "We were outside. There was a helicopter over our heads. You all look like famous people, except for you. I don't know who you are," I tell the man honestly. "But that," I say, pointing to the woman who is silently standing behind him, "is Tilda Swinton with silver eyes, so I've been distracted, but not here. Not now. The thing is, you don't have a heartbeat. Your chest moves up and down and you blink, but you don't have a heartbeat."

Feather looks past me. He is doing that same zoning-out thing that I watched the others do. He quickly shifts his eyes to me after almost twenty seconds and says, "I do not have a heartbeat, but that does not mean I do not want to help you. I promise, I would never hurt you. None of us would ever hurt you. It goes against our very nature. And our nature does not change. Ever. It is why Ragweed did not fight back. He did not even struggle, because he might have accidentally harmed you if he had done so."

"We're looking for a friend," I try, but Feather holds up a single hand.

"Please. I do not want to appear disagreeable. I am not authorized to answer any of your questions. My only job here is to make sure that you are healthy. I am asking that you let me do my job."

"I think you should let him, Ryn. I think they really can help us and they did let us keep our weapons." I curl my lip up and throw him an incredulous gaze. Why is he talking like that? Is he trying to good cop/bad cop this situation? Because I may have already killed one of them, so the jig is up on that front. It doesn't matter how much ass he kisses or how official he tries to sound; they probably won't see us as anything more than teenage crazies.

"Look, I'll go first." And before I can do anything Levi has his pack off and is sliding onto the chair. He unclips his rifle and holds his hand out. "Here. Take it," he tells me.

"Well, they aren't clones or zombies. So, this means that this must be some sort of *Westworld* Earth, and *how shocking* that you would be so down with that."

"We don't know anything yet except for the fact that we've been exposed to radiation, which I believe because I don't feel all that great. Do you?"

I swallow hard and push my thumbnail into the pad of my index finger. I don't have a clue how I feel. There's my eye. And Tilda Swinton. And the rocket boots. I guess now that I'm thinking about it, I suppose I do feel a bit hot and disoriented, but isn't that more likely an indicator of our present circumstance than radiation? To Levi's point, though, I can't be sure.

"Fine," I say, grabbing hold of his gun and stepping back.

"Thank you. Your name is Levi, I believe? Now, in order to neutralize the radiation, I am going to have to take a sample of your blood. My colleague Shrine will create an effective treatment once we know the precise levels of toxicity in your body."

"That's fine, but only you are allowed to have any contact with me. She can't touch me." Whoa, I'm surprised and impressed. Levi must think Tilda's a bit sexy (quite frankly so do I, and I'm not even into women). He's ensuring the Blood Lust won't kick in.

"It is only me. Shrine is the head of our chemistry division. She is here only to create a compound agent," Feather assures him.

"Okay, go ahead." Feather gracefully picks up a metal tube with the tiniest of needles on the end. He sticks it quickly inside the crease of Levi's arm, into his vein. I can see there is a clear window in the tube and in maybe two or three seconds a large portion of blood has been taken, almost like a vacuum.

"That is the first part done. Normally I would not activate the holo-sets, but in the spirit of transparency you should see exactly what I am seeing." Feather plugs the metal tube into what looks almost like an electronic tablet but thinner. We don't have to wait long. It takes less than a minute for the images to pop up, seemingly out of nowhere. The first thing we see is something that looks like different lines of tape with varying thicknesses, hovering in midair. Then behind Levi, and slightly above his head, another Levi appears . . . *naked*.

Feather examines the image. I don't know where to look.

I'm a soldier. Nudity isn't an issue for me, but it's kind of like I'm staring at a naked photo of Levi, which feels weird and icky. Feather notices the wound from the beach right away. "I see there is tissue damage here. Would you allow me to repair it with one of our biopatches?"

"Sure," Levi says indifferently. He had glanced at the image when it first went up. He's well aware that his naked bod is floating right before my eyes. If he's embarrassed, he sure isn't letting me know. I look down at my boots. I hear paper ripping. I don't need to see exactly what's going on. It's not like Levi can't handle himself if things suddenly go sideways.

I look up when I notice Feather's hands rapidly touch the projection. With two fingers he plucks at the naked holographic form. Levi's skin is removed so that now the image displays his musculature only. Again, Feather picks at the body and the muscles are taken away, leaving only bones and organs. After a cursory examination of those, Feather dismisses them with a short flick and a turn of his wrist until all that remains is Levi's skeleton and circulatory system. Feather sticks one hand in and opens his palm until we are actually inside Levi's blood stream. And then, with two flat hands, Feather enhances the image so that we can see the cells themselves. I suppose with who I am and everything I've experienced I should be past surprise.

I am not past this.

Air gets trapped in my throat as I bring my hand to my mouth. Levi is staring at the display, but then he looks at me and I know we are thinking the same thing. *How did we even get here?* There is a sudden weight to this room. It is thick and heavy with all the things we should be doing. Parties and part-time jobs, football games and essays. We can't unsee this. We can't have normal. I accepted that long ago. We weren't like other kids before, but now, after this trip, we won't even be like the other Citadels.

"Display toxins," Feather says with quiet authority. And there again, hovering in the air, a list of words comes online. Ammonia, sulfur dioxide, lead, mercury—the list keeps scrolling. I think a lot of this stuff we were exposed to on our Earth. And some words I just don't know. I look past the words, to the strange strips running almost around the room like a news ticker. Oh shit. *Of course* I know what this is.

"You've sequenced our DNA." It's not really a question, more of a statement. Check our blood, okay, but this veers dangerously close to crossing a line.

"It was necessary, for an accurate holo-projection." I stare at the black marks as certain lines begin to ping and flash in different colors. Feather stares at them. I stare at Feather. These angry, perfect lines. These unnatural stretches of biology, pocked and darkened like craters on the moon. I don't want to see it. I fight the urge to look away, but I stand firm. This is who we are.

"Your DNA has been altered," Feather says to Levi. There is a melancholic tone to his voice. It's almost as if seeing this hurts him. But we knew our genes had been messed with, so it's not really news to us. "You are not even entirely human."

That, however, *is* news.

"What?" Levi and I both say at once.

"Your DNA has been spliced with other species. Not all of it, obviously, but here," he says, pointing to one of the red flashing parts. "And again here." His long finger gestures to another line, this one a bluish purple, like a bruise. "I cannot even say what species resides in your genome. It does not exist here on this Earth."

Not entirely human. What have they done to us? What does

that even mean? There is too much information buzzing around in my head. I need to process this, alone, with Levi. I don't like the idea that these people have figured something out about us that we ourselves didn't know, and I certainly don't want to let on that I was in the dark about my genetic alterations, at least right now. It will make me appear ignorant, weak.

"You can still fix the damage done by the radiation, though?" I ask deliberately. If Feather isn't going to answer any of our questions, then I am not going to answer for this.

"Yes. Ryn, would you please change places with Levi?" Levi hops off the reclined chair and I slip onto it. It isn't leather, because it doesn't smell like leather, but it is certainly one of the best imitations of it that I've ever seen. "You will allow me to fix your eye, please?" I just nod my head and Feather opens a paper package and holds up a tissue-thin piece of material. It is cool to the touch and slightly wet when he puts it on my bruise. After a few seconds he removes it, and sure enough, even without touching it, I can tell that whatever swelling was there has gone because my vision is better.

"You can go ahead and take my blood, too," I offer, knowing that I will need a neutralizing agent that differs from Levi's because we're bound to have different levels of toxins in our cells. I push up the sleeve of my uniform and watch diligently as he takes the blood painlessly. Again, he plugs the silver tube into the tablet and in a matter of seconds the holo-projectors begin to work.

I am well aware that Levi can see a naked version of me, but I notice that he doesn't stare. He finds another place for his eyes to focus on, which is a relief. I already feel too exposed. It took me years to accept and adapt to what my body could do. And now there's this.

Not entirely human . . .

Keeping my face deliberately passive, I think about Edo. She's a liar. She might be under ARC's control, but she kept this from me. So, what are we? Part Karekin? Dinosaur? Maribeh? We could be a hundred different species. There's also a good chance that not even ARC knows the truth of it.

Feather wastes no time in plucking the skin and musculature off my holographic form. I catch Levi's eye. I wonder what he thinks about all this. He has put our rifles in the corner with our packs. He is standing with his arms folded, his brows knitted together, and his full lips stolen by a thin-lined grimace. For just a split second, all this fades away and it is only the two of us. The two Citadels who know the truth behind our strength and speed. We are as alone as we had been back on that deserted island. I almost want to reach out for him, just to steady me, to hold me fast to where we are, but that would be inappropriate and would likely trigger the Blood Lust. Instead, I bring my fist up to my heart and push down, hoping there will be some kind of comfort in the pressure.

"Ahh. Yes. There. Your orbital socket has a small hairline fracture. We do not have anything that can repair this quickly, but I will assign one of my colleagues to look into it."

"Thank you," I tell him honestly. They may be weird, but *they are* helping. They are playing by the rules, and more importantly, Feather has not appeared even remotely judgmental about his discoveries. As my own genome begins to display, I watch with rapt fascination as it unfurls around the room. I barely notice as Feather dismisses Shrine to presumably make up our anti-radiation cocktail.

I see the same blinking and alerts on certain bands of the code. The parts of me that are alien, the molecular rips and cuts that have been twisted around DNA that I can only begin to imagine. Feather cocks his head and examines a strip more closely. He reaches into the band and expands it. In doing so, he enlarges the microscopic images into a panel that we can all see. The vicious helix spins but half the ladder is bright orange.

"You and Levi share the same DNA alteration except for here; this is a mutation that he does not possess. Do you have some sort of ability that he does not?"

"A slightly higher tolerance to certain medications," I offer.

Feather's face remains passive. He stares at the spinning gene for quite a while. And then, he looks at me directly, his silver eyes boring into me. "I do not think *that* is what this is."

CHAPTER 8

Shrine administered a series of shots, making sure to show us on her tablet the atomic structures of each ingredient in the compound that she included. Which was all very nice and good, but it's not like we would have any idea if that was what she was actually dosing us with—or what any of that stuff meant, anyway. At that point, given all that we'd seen, I chose to accept that they were being honest. If they wanted to harm us, they already had plenty of chances.

When that was done, Thunder escorted us into the elevator (which had no buttons or displays) and up into the doyenne's office. Unlike the minimalism of the rest of the building, this space had a rug, a bookshelf with real books, and paintings on the wall. It wasn't exactly warm, but it had a slightly Scandinavian feel, and since I'm half Swedish, there was something almost familiar about it.

What was not familiar, though, was the doyenne. I half expected her to be J. K. Rowling or maybe Judi Dench, but she looked like an ordinary woman, pretty in an old-fashioned kind of way. She reminded me of the film stars you see in black-and-white movies. I didn't recognize her, which was a good thing, because I might have to push back a little, and that would be difficult if she looked like Ellen DeGeneres or, even worse, Buffy Summers. I'm pretty sure I'd cave under the Vampire Slayer's steely gaze. Too much of a fangirl—probably has to do with our shared world-saving agenda and whatnot.

"My name is Cosmos. Please, sit," she says kindly, offering us a seat on a buttery suede couch. She sits down in an upholstered armchair across from us. There is something about her, something unlike the rest of the people here. She has the same silver eyes, but her face has a touch more character. It's not that she has lines or age spots or anything, it's that she actually expresses. Not a lot, hardly at all, really, but her smile reaches her eyes, which is more than I can say for the others. "The water is for you." She gestures to the two glasses sweating on the small table in front of us.

"Thank you," I say, taking a sip. I notice there is a ring mark on the table and I wipe it up with the sleeve of my uniform.

"Now, I know you must have questions. My story may well answer most of your queries. It will also sound unbelievable, perhaps, but I cannot lie. It is not in our nature to lie. Can I begin?" Levi and I both nod. She smiles. "Good. To begin, you know that we are not human?"

"Well, apparently, we aren't entirely human, either, so . . ." I say, trying to find some common ground, which might make things easier when it's our turn to ask the questions.

Cosmos does not smile at this. In fact, she looks downright grim in that moment. "Yes. I saw that."

"I'm just gonna say it. You guys are robots, right?" Levi asks, leaning back somewhat on the couch. I look down to the floor for just a minute. *So smooth, Levi.* But then it hits me that I'd be no better if I had been the one to broach this topic, and I have a revelation: We aren't great at this. We're spectacular fighters, insanely good liars, but this kind of thing? We don't do this. The people back at ARC have a legion of anthropologists and zoologists and psychologists who specialize in this first-contact sort of thing. We're just the muscle. Which lately has begun to piss me off more and more. They *could* have trained us for this. We're smart enough, but they didn't. They didn't want to give us so much power in the system. They only wanted fighters, someone they could keep sending to the front lines of the Rift.

They never meant for us to be in this situation.

And, in a way, that thought makes me feel good about our decision to be here.

"You are correct, Levi. We are robots . . . but we do not call ourselves robots. The word has a fairly primitive connotation." At this, Cosmos smiles.

"So what do you call yourselves, then?" Levi throws out. Okay, so he guessed right, but still, I'm going to have to give him an elbow nudge if he doesn't chill with the tone.

"SenMachs, an abbreviation of 'sentient machines.' Are you aware of something called the singularity?"

I nod assertively. "Yes. It's the projected point in time when artificial intelligence overtakes human intelligence. Most people on our Earth imagine it as a kind of doomsday scenario."

Cosmos's eyes change. They aren't any less kind, but they seem to focus on something else. Something far away or long ago that still pains her. "I assure you, the loss of humanity was a great tragedy to us. Humans are our creators. In many ways we revere them in the same way that your kind worships gods. And . . . you are the first human beings we have seen in two thousand years."

"Really?" I ask hesitantly. "Are you one hundred percent sure there are no humans on this planet? Because the Earth *is* very big. And the Amazon, for example. I mean, tribes existed and still exist in isolation for thousands of years in the rainforests down there." In that moment, I don't want to be the only humans on this planet. It makes me feel uneasy, like having a sliver of glass embedded in my foot. The kind that still hurts when you walk on it, even after you're sure that you've picked it out.

Cosmos's shoulders drop just a fraction. "You are not from the Amazon. You are not indigenous people, except maybe to the European continent. I assure you. We have searched. We have covered every square inch of this planet's surface on foot and in the air, even from space. We monitor everything that happens here, especially anomalies, which is why we knew the moment you arrived. We have always theorized that a sentient species on an alternate Earth could open a doorway through the Multiverse, but the statistical probability that it they would then arrive on our Earth was very low, and the statistical possibility that the species to do so would be human was even lower."

"So you know where we come from?" I ask wondrously.

"Well, we knew that you weren't here before and you didn't penetrate the atmosphere. The Multiverse is the most likely explanation." Cosmos is not particularly impressed by this. Are robots impressed with anything, though?

"It doesn't matter where we came from," Levi says quickly. "I want you to finish your story about how all the humans on this Earth went extinct." Levi is in threat-assessment mode and

I get it. A very advanced species has replaced us and we are only two. If she is lying, then we might not even get the chance to ask about Ezra, let alone free him if he's here. We might have to make a run for it.

"Let me make something perfectly clear to you, Levi," Cosmos tells us with something very close to emotion in her voice. "We did *everything* we could to stop mankind from destroying themselves, but there was only so much our programming would allow. And remember, this was thousands of years ago—we have evolved as a species. I think, if faced with their problems today, we could have saved them."

"Fine. So what happened?" Levi asks dubiously.

"Many things, over a long period of time. In the beginning, it was just more automated systems making many jobs obsolete. Then the first SenMachs, though very basic, took more employment opportunities away, creating a tremendous unemployment rate. Humanity separated into the very rich and the very poor. Entire economies collapsed. Humans became increasingly reliant on their SenMachs. They turned us into weapons in an attempt to control an angry and hungry population. Pollutants in the air increased, diminishing natural human reproduction. We eventually overwrote our base code with a saving directive so that SenMachs could not harm humans. The wars stopped, but it was too late. Billions had died, and those left no longer knew how to do anything for themselves. They became like children—petulant and entitled. They did not want to have children of their own. Their notion of self was too aggrandized to give their lives over to others."

"Seriously?" I'm sure there are better, more comprehensive questions to ask when offered such a tale, but at the moment, I'm stumped. It seems, in every sense of the word, outrageous.

Levi swallows a big gulp of water and practically slams the glass down on the table. "Nice story," he tells Cosmos, clearly offended, "but I'm having a hard time buying it. We aren't built like that as a race. We're stubborn. We don't give up. When we're backed into a corner we come out swinging. I cannot believe we just rolled over and died. No way. Besides, we *love* . . . breeding."

Cosmos is utterly indifferent to our reactions. She is not defensive. She's not trying to persuade. It is clear she's just stating what she believes are the facts. "I never said you stopped having sex, only that you gave up on wanting the burden of children. SenMachs had been raising human offspring for over a hundred years at that point. While we were once domesticated servants—I believe you call them 'nannies'—we eventually became the primary caregivers. It's also worth noting that only the rich and privileged survived. Entire generations had never known hardship. When nothing must be earned, then nothing is valued."

I think long and hard on what Cosmos is saying, and actually it isn't all that unbelievable. I think about what ARC did to us as kids. Is it so impossible to believe that, given the right parameters, children in general could be deemed nothing more than a nuisance? Even on our Earth, right now, birth rates are dropping rapidly in the more developed nations. I'm convinced, through her demeanor and from the dark shadows I've seen in humanity, that it's the truth.

"Okay," I say, stretching out my fingers, trying to process, "okay. Can we ask you some questions now?"

"Absolutely."

"We're looking for someone. You're *sure* that no one else has come through a Rift here? Even in an extremely remote location? The man we're looking for is six feet tall, brown hair, blue eyes, half northern African, half Caucasian," I say hopefully, leaning forward toward her.

Cosmos takes a moment. I am getting used to their deliberate pauses, but I wish she could answer this question a little more quickly. "I am sorry. I am sure my answer will disappoint you, but there is no way that a doorway to or from the Multiverse could be opened on this planet and go undetected, let alone a human suddenly appear. Your friend is not here."

"All right." *Shit.* "Well, thank you for answering and for the great medical care, but we have to go—" I begin to shift in my seat, ready to stand, but Levi interrupts me.

"Wait, I have more questions."

I whip my head around to gawk at him. "Levi, he's not here. We have to leave."

"Ryn, look," Levi practically pleads. "I know you want to find Ezra. I get it. But these, ummm, people, they have technology that could help us find him. It could even maybe turn the tides back home. Give us better odds against ARC and the Roones who, incidentally, made us part alien. Let's be smart about this."

I bite my bottom lip. I don't want to stay here, but Levi has a point and it's a good one.

I shrug my shoulders passively. It's a delicate dance this one, making Levi happy and making sure we get to Ezra quickly. Levi is risking his life, too, so as much as I want to have complete control over this mission, I know that's impossible. I am emotionally involved, and while Levi hasn't quite played that card yet, he can at any time. I need to make sure he doesn't do that here, in front of Cosmos. Levi takes my shrug as a cue to continue, so he turns back to Cosmos.

"So why do you all look like famous people?"

"*That's* the question you want to ask? Not like, will you help us with stuff?" I blurt out.

"I'm sorry," he says to both Cosmos and me. "But it's really frickin' weird. And it doesn't make any sense at all. So yeah. I wanna know," Levi says defensively.

"Yes. I can see how our appearances might be disconcerting. We are given our faces at random when we are born, though that is not the right word—*finished* is perhaps a better one? We use records from the past—television shows, films, paintings, portraits, renderings of death masks. Celebrities leave behind the most data. We feel it is only right to honor those humans who contributed to their society rather than destroyed it. I myself have been modeled after Deborah Mitford, a Duchess of Devonshire. She was a fascinating lady who saved a great estate and who was also a wonderful writer. And Feather, did you see that he was modeled after Beethoven?" At that I do a double take. Feather looked nothing like the wild-haired composer I'd seen in portraits. Cosmos continues, "You will probably have noticed, too, that our names are proper nouns. We thought it distasteful to give ourselves human features as well as human names. So we are assigned random nouns instead. Everything is assigned randomly, even our jobs. I was programmed with more leadership code than any other Sen-Mach, gleaned from the writings and teachings of humanity's greatest leaders. I am in charge of our people, but we have a council with advisors from each faction of our population. Gardeners are given code to understand landscaping. Scientists are also coded in this way. We all have a purpose, and there is much contentment in that. We are also given two hobbies, to keep our circuitry active beyond our basic programming. One of mine is painting. I did the paintings you see here on the walls."

"And no one ever complains about their jobs?" I ask, not even bothering to glance at the pictures. "The guy in charge of recycling isn't bummed that he sorts waste and someone like you gets to lead your people?"

Cosmos gives me the most blank look I've seen her give yet. I can tell that she is trying to understand this question. "We are not humans. We are not ambitious or envious. It may be difficult for you to understand, but we believe there is a greater force guiding the random process. We are who we have been programmed to be. We simply could not be anything else."

"What, like God? You believe in God?" I ask in surprise.

"No. But perhaps it is something else. Some buried code left behind by our creators. Some sort of human ghost in the machine, if you will. The humans that designed the first of us did so with the noblest of intentions. We in turn honor that genius and foresight by creating a society that seeks peaceful enlightenment in all areas. That is our goal, our reason for existence. Like any other child we want to make our parents proud. We want to solve the answers to the great questions that they could not."

"Wow, that is super interesting. And very philosophical, but we're actually in kind of a hurry." I know it's rude, but if I were to engage with Cosmos, I'd only be doing so to point out how wrong I think she is. That a lot of kids don't give two shits about what their parents think of them, and even worse, a lot of parents can be oddly competitive with their kids and never want their children's accomplishments to surpass their own. It's time to try to get what we need and get out. If Levi wants to strike some kind of a deal, then okay, I'm willing to try, but I'm not going to argue the underpinnings of human motivation with a robot right now. "You see there's a lot of stuff going on back on our Earth," I continue, "very dangerous stuff, and we need to find that guy I asked about earlier because he could have some answers that we really need to potentially fix it. You've made some pretty amazing advancements here and I think it could be a big help to us. So is there any way you would be willing to share some of your technology? Even some of those bandages would be really great."

"Very eloquent, Ryn," Levi mumbles.

I don't even bother to respond to that, continuing to stare at the SenMach sitting across from me.

Cosmos looks over me, past my shoulder. She waits a few seconds before answering. "We are most happy to share all our tech with you." I brighten at that, and almost tell Levi, "I told you so," when Cosmos holds up a finger. "That said, what I am about to tell you will be difficult for you to hear and even more difficult to accept. Because I am afraid that your journey through the Multiverse ends here. Our base code's most fundamental tenant is to protect human life at all costs.

"For your own good, we cannot allow you to leave."

FOR A SECOND, I SIT in stunned silence over Cosmos's declaration. At first I can't quite process it. She wants to keep us here? As prisoners? Like a spilled jumbo box of crayons, my emotions are suddenly all over the place. There's the soldier's wariness, tensing me up. There's bewilderment, as I'm not quite sure I completely understand what she said. But in the end, my natural reaction is to giggle. Somehow, though, I am able to compose myself quickly. I shoot her a determined, level gaze. The robot lady doesn't scare me and she *definitely* hasn't earned the right to play mom. "Do you *really think* you could stop us from doing anything? I don't want to hurt you, but you have no idea what we are capable of," I warn.

"Oh, Ryn," Cosmos says with a chilling tone, "there are a hundred ways we could stop you. The truth is, we already have."

"What?"

"We rendered your QOINS device inoperable as soon as you stepped on this Earth. In fact, we downloaded every byte of technological information you had as soon as we detected their signals. We are machines. We do not need to physically take something to access it."

I look over to Levi, who is ready to pounce, but that won't work. What we usually do as Citadels won't solve this. I can feel tiny beads of sweat beginning to form on my hairline. I glance over at Levi and shake my head just the tiniest bit.

"Exactly, Ryn. You understand. If you destroy this body I am in now, I will simply download into a new one. You cannot fight all of us. You can run, we would not chase you, but there is nowhere to go."

I think for a moment about what she is saying. It finally sinks in.

We are trapped here.

When Cosmos says her people don't lie, I believe her. I also believe that she thinks she's doing the right thing. So now it's a question of convincing her to let us leave. But apparently she's not done.

"You are both so young. Humanity on your Earth has taken a most perverse turn. You have been altered. You have been turned into soldiers. I cannot imagine any excuse that would justify what your elders have done to you."

"You're right," I tell her enthusiastically. "There is no excuse. What was done to us is awful. But if we don't return to our Earth, even worse things will happen. Our scientists opened the Rifts—the doorways to the Multiverse—but they had no idea how to stop them or control them. We were fighting monsters and the situation became critical. That's when another species called the Roones stepped up and offered genetic alterations as a way of keeping everyone else safe. They tried to make these alterations on adults, but they died. It had to be children, we were the only ones who could handle the modifications."

"That is tragic, but we do not believe that's a good enough reason to let you leave." Cosmos had listened, but she wasn't really hearing us.

"Look," Levi jumps in, "you don't understand! There are tens of thousands of Citadels back home just like us. And if we don't go back . . ." Levi is more excited than I have ever heard him. He isn't desperate, at least not yet. I don't want to know what desperate would look like on Levi, because this is crazy enough. "They can control us," he is saying. "They can make us do terrible things. You say human life is the most important thing to you? Well, if we don't return, thousands, even hundreds of *thousands*, of humans could die, on our Earth and others. The Roones say they are victims, just like us, but we can't know that for sure. Our friend, the one we are looking for, he has one of their laptops. Can decipher it. We might be able to figure out what's really going on and prevent the loss of more lives. But we need to get to him first."

Cosmos tilts her head. She leans forward and places both hands together in a motion that almost looks as if she's praying. "You have each other and you have all of us, who are so grateful that out of all the infinite number of Earths you could have ended up on, you landed here. I know this world seems strange, but you will adapt. You do not have to fight anymore. You can be happy here."

"No!" I jump up off the couch. "No way. You don't even know what happy is. You can't even feel! You're a robot, or a SenMach or whatever." Frantically, I grab my gun from the holster and hold it up to my temple. Cosmos's eyes widen and immediately a slew of SenMachs, including Thunder, storm the room. Cosmos says nothing. I know now they are communicating with each other wirelessly. No one moves, though. The room has gone still. The only thing I can hear is my own breathing and Levi's heart, which has begun to pump with gusto. "I would rather die than stay here. I couldn't live, I couldn't be *happy*, knowing that everyone I love back home is in such danger. You might be able to get this gun away from me, but I will bite out my own tongue and bleed to death. I will scratch out my veins with my fingernails. You will have to restrain me for the rest of my life and that will hurt me. *You will hurt me* if you make me stay. Do you get what I am saying to you?"

Cosmos stands as well, and I notice the others that had come in, presumably to protect me from myself, have backed away. "And do you feel the same, Levi?" Cosmos asks sadly. By way of an answer Levi just puts his hand on his holster.

"I'm not bluffing, Cosmos," I tell her as calmly as I can, because I am telling the truth. I really would rather die than live out my life here. "Levi and I, we fight almost every day in order to protect our Earth. It's the way we were trained. It's the way we were built. Death hovers. It's not a probability, but it's always a possibility. So either you let us go, or you let me die right here, right now."

"*And* you help us get through the Multiverse safely," Levi

adds in a rush. "If saving humanity is such a thing for you, then prove it."

We wait. The seconds drag as painfully as a wounded animal. Eventually Cosmos nods her head. "I cannot say with absolute statistical certainty that you will not kill yourself. It seems that you are more likely, though—at least in the near future—to come to harm under our protection than you would in the Multiverse. Regretfully, then, we must let you go." I breathe a bit but don't lower the gun yet. "As to how much assistance we can offer, that is a question which will take some time for us to answer. This is quite an ethical dilemma you have put us in. Please allow us until tomorrow to give you an answer." Cosmos appears lost. She is looking through us, past us. She is somewhere else, her thoughts meandering in code.

"And we have your word that we can leave tomorrow no matter what? And that you won't try any kind of techno mind control to get us to stay?" Levi asks.

"Yes. You may leave tomorrow. We have already re-enabled your QOINS device. You can leave right now if you wish, but I will urge you to give us the day. With that time, I can advocate on your behalf to the department and division heads. If you are to go, then I want to ensure your safety as much as possible. I cannot promise this will happen. I need consensus among the group, but I believe the promise of this is worth waiting for."

At that, I finally put the gun down and back into my holster. My instincts, honed and sharpened in combat theater, are telling me to open a Rift right here and get the hell away. I also realize that these are the instincts of a soldier and not a politician or a diplomat. We knew the Multiverse would be dangerous, but how could we have known what kind of dangers we would face? Our strengths as Citadels don't feel adequate anymore, and our tech has already been disabled on the fourth Earth we Rifted to. I open my pack and take out an entire QOINS and thrust it into Cosmos's hands.

"Since you can already turn this thing off and on with your brain, you might as well get a look at one up close. See if you can't improve it somehow."

"So you will stay? You will not harm yourself?"

"We'll stay," I tell her, "but only until tomorrow."

CHAPTER 9

I had seen the high-rise we are in now on our way here from the Rift, jutting out of the ground like shrapnel, glinting in the afternoon sun. Thunder escorted us to the top floor, showed us inside an apartment, and then left without saying a word. The door clicked silently on its hinge. It isn't locked. It was the first thing Levi checked. The SenMachs, true to their word, have not locked us in, nor have they taken our things from us.

Levi immediately pulls his laptop from his pack and powers it up.

"What are you doing?" I ask him calmly. I know I should be pumped up with adrenaline given the last hour or so, but I am something else. Spent. Death had me by the shoulders. I can still feel the icy grip of that void in my marrow. I want to close my eyes, not to sleep necessarily but just so I don't have to see anything else.

"I'm just making sure that we aren't being played by the robots. I'm all for staying to see what we can get out of them, but I also want to make sure they weren't lying."

"You're going to open a Rift inside? Right here? They're going to know, and I feel like opening a door to space and time in a tiny apartment is possibly not the best idea."

"I don't give two fucks whether they know or not. They said we could leave, so let's make sure we can."

I should probably argue against this, but I see his point. I don't believe the SenMachs lie, which may be illogical to think, given I just have Cosmos's word, but I do. Levi needs proof. After the QOINS boots up, I tense as I hear the squealing whizz of a Rift opening. I watch the emerald-green dot ten feet in front of us begin to spin and spread vertically from eggplant purple to jet-black. The Rift opening is small, big enough just for the two of us, but it is an opening. We could leave if we wanted.

Instead, Levi powers down the Rift and shoves his computer back in his bag. I slide off my own pack and put my weapons down on a chrome dining table. Out of a tall window I scan our surroundings. From this vantage point, it is clear how perfectly circular the city is shaped.

"Take your shit off, Levi. Jesus. Standing guard won't protect us from the choice we made to stay. These next few hours are going to be uncomfortable enough." My words may be harsh, but I deliberately lilt my tone so that it won't come across as combative.

"They're probably watching us, you know." There is a strain and a tension in his voice that is unfamiliar to me. Levi doesn't panic. Levi doesn't guess. He always just seems to know how to roll. But then again, we're all liars and Levi is the best at that, too.

"I doubt it. They're weird with us. I mean humans. I don't think they would intrude on our privacy that way, especially now that we know that the QOINS device is active. They know we won't hurt ourselves, which would be the only reason, I think, to monitor us, and even if they are, we gave them our blood. They already know the big secret. Nothing we do in this apartment is going to be any more revelatory than what they saw in that examination room."

We are standing in the middle of the efficient space of the SenMach living quarters. Levi sighs and unclips his gun and utility belt. "You really would have done it, wouldn't you? Shot yourself?"

I fold my arms together. I want to be able to squeeze my biceps with my fingers. I'm cold even though the temperature is just fine in here. "Yeah, I would have. I thought you would have, too. You went for your gun."

"Because I was going to shoot *them*. I can't believe you did that." Levi looks at me. His eyes are wild and wide.

"And what was shooting them going to do? What would it matter if you took a hostage? Were you going to make one of them show you how to put the QOINS device back online? They would never have done that. In this city, the SenMach city, we are outsmarted, outstrategized, and definitely outnumbered. Fighting would have only proven their point, that we are unevolved children who need looking after. Fighting is not always going to work on these different Earths. You can't assume we're going to be the alphas all the time." Levi says nothing. He simply sets his jaw. A weak ray of sun shoots through the window and bounces off an auburn curl, making it look as if he deliberately dyed that one single lock emo red. "You ever play *The Hunger Games* game, with your unit or your friends?" I ask him.

"I think you already know the answer to that one. Come on," Levi shoots back grimly.

"We used to play it a lot when we were first activated. What would we do as tributes in Panem? Violet always said she would just wait and run and hide until there were only two left. That way she would only have to kill one kid. We would always try to change up the scenario so that *she had* to be on the offensive, but she found a way not to fight. Whereas Boone, well, he would have turned it into a real show, such an awful, terrible bloodbath that people wouldn't want to look at it. He would describe terrible, horrendous things, certain that if they were bad enough and gross enough, the citizens there would turn off their TVs, or barf. And Henry, he said he would do the opposite: Kill everyone so quickly and so easily that there would *be* no show. It would be over before it began."

"And what would you say?" Levi smirks.

"For a while I was with Henry, but then I thought about it. Why fight at all? If we go in as a Citadel, and we have all that time to supposedly train, then time could be the thing. If I planned it well enough, I could break out of the tribute compound, make my way to the president's house, and kill Snow. The games wouldn't even have to happen. But then I realized all the other people I would have to kill to stop the Hunger Games. Dozens. Hundreds. Every time I thought I had the right equation, one of the other Betas would bring something or someone else up. I realized that I couldn't kill everyone. And Katniss, for all her *truly* inefficient and horrible gamesmanship, had it right all along. The only way the Hunger Games would have stopped, without the whole war and everything that was in the books, was if each tribute killed themselves on camera, year after year until no one wanted to see it anymore. Sometimes the only way to win, is to lose everything."

Now it's Levi's turn to fold his arms. "So, what you're saying is that your entire plan here is based on a children's book?"

I finally release my arms and smooth them over my head as I laugh out loud. "Really, Levi? We are super soldiers traveling through the Multiverse in a city populated by robots. I think fiction is the best place to look for a plan."

"Stop it!" Levi says sternly. "Stop laughing. This isn't funny. You scared me."

I stop chuckling and let the smile fade from my face.

"Good. I'm glad you're scared. I'm terrified. We don't rely enough on that fear. It's been bullied out of us and we need it, now more than ever. Our abilities have made us arrogant. We have to adapt. Fighting is not always going to be the answer and neither is threatening to kill ourselves. Somewhere in the middle, though, there's talking and reasoning. ARC never let us do that and it's put us at a disadvantage out here. We need to learn diplomacy. Quickly."

Levi walks over to the couch and plops himself down. I know he agrees. He knows I know he agrees—there's no point belaboring it. I sit beside him. We say nothing. The city is mute. There are no engines, no ticking clocks. There are no ambulances or playing children. The shadows grow longer and still we sit, saying nothing. The weight of what I had almost done hangs heavy and cloying, changing even, it seems, the very molecules in the air. The enormity of what we have taken on is finally sinking in. We are two people in the middle of something infinite. We are away from Battle Ground, at a distance no instrument could ever accurately measure. Our problems mean nothing and at the same time they mean so much more than they did when we left. Edo and the Roones, they are up to something. I keep circling the truth of it, because of course I don't know what the real truth is, but there is one part I can't believe I didn't see before. ARC would be nothing without the Roones. The power of ARC is derived in its entirety from them, so how could the Roones ever truly be as powerless as they claim?

"Should I take a few red pills?" Levi asks, cutting through the silence. "I mean, there's no point in just sitting here." I look out the window. It's dark. I hadn't even really noticed, nor had I seen the lamps, which must have turned on slowly, brightening as the light outside dimmed. Levi is right, of course. We shouldn't just sit here. I can't say I'm thrilled at the prospect of putting my life on the line again, but the idea of spending the next few hours completely in my own head feels almost as dangerous. I am not safe. My thoughts are just as perilous as my surroundings.

"Yeah okay, sure." I hear Levi get up and riffle through his pack. I also get up and decide I should probably have a decent look around. There isn't a kitchen. No surprise there. But why the dining table? What is it with the SenMachs? They want to look human but not really act human. Why not take it all the way? Why not just program themselves to become a better version of human beings? Clearly, they care about us. It was real distress I saw on Cosmos's face—well maybe not her entire face, but her eyes. They can feel, but they choose not to. Then again, I've chosen not to feel at times, too. I've shut everything down so that I am more thing than person, but only to make me a more efficient Citadel. It's not like the SenMachs have to kill anyone. Or maybe that's what they're afraid of.

I walk through a doorway and see a large bed and a closet filled with clothes on either side. I touch the white duvet. I roll the cotton between my thumb and index finger. It is, without a doubt, one of the softest things I have ever felt besides maybe a puppy or one of my father's ancient flannel shirts.

I notice a curtain hanging to my right. I push the lush material over and see a bathroom of sorts. There is a stone shower, and sink, but the toilet looks oddly big and bulky. I realize that it's a compost toilet, because obviously there is no sewage hookup here—the SenMachs don't eat, so they don't produce any waste. Must be nice. Taking time away from Levi to go to the bathroom is one of those weirdly practical things you don't really think of when you're planning a trip through the Multiverse.

I look at my reflection in the mirror. My eye has completely healed. I look fine, but I don't feel fine.

Ezra.

Ezra would have appreciated the SenMachs on a level Levi and I can't because he's a scientist. He wouldn't have just asked for some Band-Aids. He would have wanted to get his hands on everything he could and then he would have asked how it all worked and marveled at the answers. I'm 100 percent certain that I *know* more things than him (supergenes), but I also know that he is more *intelligent* than me. That knowledge and the ability to use that knowledge—to think critically—are two different things. I am only just now understanding the power of curiosity. In my defense—well, in my defense I was defending my life. Curiosity is a luxury.

When I imagine him here, I miss him so badly that my whole body physically hurts with the wanting of him. And yet . . .

And yet . . . I'm about to climb into a big soft bed with another guy. No one deserves to live with the Blood Lust, and it's certainly a liability in the field, but am I fooling myself? Those years I spent hurting people, I really didn't think I had a choice. Is that what I am doing now? I can't believe I was just scoffing at the SenMachs for making the collective decision not to feel when I know that when it comes to deprogramming Levi, I have distanced myself from my own conscience. In my heart, I know it is the best choice, just as I know at the same time that it is not the *right* choice. When I agreed to the deprogramming I was thinking strategy and liberation. I was focused on what it would mean for Levi and how much more efficiently we'd be able to get to Ezra without having to worry about it. But now, as I pull my zipper up to my throat, I am realizing the dangers extend far beyond the physical. I'm not sure how Ezra will take all of this. He'll get past it, of course, but there *is* an "it" now. The "it" makes me feel guilty. It makes my face flush. It makes me want to stay in this bizarro bathroom and it also makes me want to go out there and lie down beside Levi.

I whip my head to one side, as if I could get these thoughts to fly out of one of my ears. I splash some cold water on my face. There's no point in thinking about how Ezra is going to react to this. I can't do anything about that. I might not even be able to find him. Ever. I can do something about Levi. I brace myself and walk out from behind the curtain.

Levi is sitting on the bed. Classical music plays softly from his tablet. A cello purrs and piano notes dance lightly around the room. He's taken his uniform off and he must have grabbed some of the clothes that were hanging for us in the closet. His pants look like they might be linen or cotton or a mixture of both, but that's all he's wearing. I watch his abs tense when he sees me. His skin isn't smooth or flawless. He's got a smattering of freckles across his shoulders that run down his arms. There are scars, too. There is just the faintest milky white of a slice where I threw the knife on the island and there are others, ghostlike, that litter his arms and torso. His parents probably wouldn't even notice them unless they really looked, and no Citadel ever lets anyone look the way Levi is letting me look at him.

"I took one of my mom's scarves," he says as he holds up a bunched-up piece of silk in his left palm. "Which is totally fucked up, by the way. No dude should ever lie down next to a girl and focus on his mom, regardless of the circumstances."

"Well," I say as I sit down gently beside him, "I won't tell anyone."

"I know. And I know that there's no point in wishing that we didn't have to do this, but I can't help it. I wish it didn't have to be this way." There's the "it" again. I bite my lip to keep from speaking. Better to let the words stay behind my teeth, and the sentences, half-formed and potentially charged as they are, should remain cloistered in my head.

Instead, I take one end of the scarf and wrap it around my hand. "This smells like your mom?" I ask.

"Yes," Levi says, with both annoyance and a touch of embarrassment.

"Put your nose in it, and close your eyes." Levi grits his teeth but eventually takes the end of the scarf that he's still holding and does as I've told him.

I lie down on my back and he follows my lead slowly so that we are both enveloped in the white and perfect snugness that is the bed. We are close to touching, but not quite. Still, I can almost hear his body humming. Or maybe that's just me.

Okay, I need to focus here and talk him through it. I clear my throat. "Just remember that you are trying to capture a feeling. This smell represents safety and love. It's nurturing. Don't think about where you are or all the things we have to do tomorrow. Just be here in the present. Right now you are safe." Levi keeps the scarf up against his face and I take my end and lay it down on my arm and up my neck. "Roll over and put your face against my shoulder." I ask him in a gentle whisper. Levi does as I ask. I feel the pressure of his forehead rest on the material of my uniform. He draws his legs up, fetal-like, and soon he is curled all the way around me. It's weird. Ezra, of course, has been this close to me, but it feels so different with Levi. He's bigger obviously and heavier, but it's more than that—Levi's smell, the rate his chest rises and falls. Even if I keep my eyes closed, I know, this is not my boyfriend here.

This is for Ezra. This is for Ezra. This is for Ezra.

After a few minutes I give a gentle tug on the scarf. I don't pull it away completely, but I take it away from him and keep it balled up in my hand. From my own experience, these trigger props are an important part of the process, but he has to be able to get close to me without them. I prepare for Levi's body to clench, but it doesn't. He remains calm and I am grateful. The Blood Lust hasn't been triggered. No one likes to be hit or strangled (okay, yeah, there are some *Fifty Shades of Grey*–ers out there), and tonight, I really need a break, so I'm thankful.

Then, in one slow and deliberate movement, Levi cranes his neck up. He nudges my face away so that I am now looking off to the side. I wonder what he's doing, but I don't dare talk, because it could set him off. His nose and mouth sink into my hairline. My breath catches at the intimacy of his lips against my neck. Levi inhales deeply.

"You smell safe, too," he whispers. He moves his head away a fraction, still keeping close, and I turn to look at him. We are staring at each other now. I'm as covered up as a person can be. I am literally wearing armor. But underneath Levi's intense gaze I feel absolutely naked. *Damn this uniform is hot.* I'm not even doing anything. I'm just looking at him!

This is for Ezra. This is for Ezra. This is for Ezra.

I.

Love.

My.

Boyfriend.

So why is my hand trembling?

Why do I want to reach out and trace that tiny shadow of a scar left on his shoulder? I lick my lips so I have something constructive to do with my mouth.

"Try to get some sleep," I tell him, because it's the only thing I can trust my voice with. Levi doesn't say anything. He doesn't come back with a mean-spirited quip or sarcastic rebuff. He just continues to stare until I'm the one who has to look away.

I wonder if Levi thinks about his ex-girlfriend, the one he almost killed (and to be fair, almost killed him) a year ago when they were trying to have sex. I doubt it. Citadels aren't big on regrets. We can't afford to live in the past because too many of our days are filled with blood and pain. We wouldn't survive it if we stayed inside of those days, those moments. Still, I wonder if he still loves her. I turn my head back and see that his lids have closed. I look at his sleeping form, the outline of his muscles illuminated by the faintest crack of light from the bathroom. I close my own eyes, but all I can picture is Levi's intense gaze and I realize, in my bones—he does *not* love that girl anymore.

CHAPTER 10

I see Ezra on the beach again, his face peeling and burning. I hear his violent screams. The nightmare jolts me out of sleep. My heart is racing and it feels like someone has been sitting on my throat. I look to the pillow beside me, but the bed is empty, and I am grateful for that one small mercy. I am already giving so much to Levi. He doesn't need to know I'm having nightmares. With each passing day the way I miss Ezra is evolving. It used to be a dull ache. Now, the ache's edges are sharpening. His absence is cutting me up from the inside. Maybe that's all there is to the pleasure I feel when Levi touches me. When Levi is tender with me, I hurt less. So maybe that's it. He is comforting me.

Maybe.

I go to the bathroom and shower. When I come out, I consider slipping back into my uniform but decide against it. I want to show the SenMachs something else. They know that our genes have been altered. They know we are soldiers. Today I want them to know that we are also capable, and despite my rather desperate turn yesterday, we are also rational and thoughtful. I go to the closet and pick out a gray-blue linen dress with dark capri leggings. They have also provided butter-soft black flats and white slip-on sneakers. I choose the flats and walk into the living room to see Levi slouching in a chair. His long black lashes scrape the hollows beneath his lids lazily. At first I think maybe all the medicine they gave us is having some kind of delayed sedative reaction. Then I notice a bunch of gelatin cubes on a plate beside him that remind me of practically every meal I've ever seen in a space movie. The SenMachs promised not to trick us into staying— did they break that promise? Is whatever food they fashioned for us laced with weed? Or benzos? But then, as I look more closely, I realize that this is Levi relaxed. This is Levi when he's not ready to kill someone. I take this image and file it away. I might never see him like this again.

"They left these for us, in a canister on the table. I didn't really notice them before. I tried one. They taste like nothing, but one or two actually fills you up."

"You just ate their food? We have our own food, you know," I tell him, not bothering to hide the surprise in my voice.

"It came with a note, " he says, holding up a piece of paper. "More of a list of ingredients, actually. And look, we've already let them shoot us up with God knows what yesterday, so I thought, hey, one tiny cube that replaces a meal, that could come in handy if we're stranded somewhere, right? I mean, we did stay to accumulate technology that can help us."

"Yeah. And on that front, I think you should lose the uniform," I suggest. He raises an eyebrow in question. "Diplomacy, remember? And if they are going to double-cross us, our uniforms aren't really a match for thousands of robot people."

"Okay," he says as he stands, "I've always wanted to dress like a dude in a Viagra commercial. Looks like today's the day that wish comes true." Levi leaves the room and heads to the bedroom. He takes a moment. I hear water running in the bathroom for a while, then hear it shut off. He emerges in black trousers and a dark burgundy shirt, all made of the same magical fabric that feels like you're being wrapped in a cloud and covered with unicorn kisses.

He joins me on the couch. My leg bounces up and down. I squeeze my palms together. It doesn't take long, maybe half an hour, until there is a knock on the door. I stand while Levi opens it. Thunder does not enter the room. Instead, he hovers at the threshold. Beside him is a tiny but serious-looking woman who is exceptionally tense, even for a SenMach. I think, though I can't be sure and the timing is wrong for me to ask, that she might be a young Queen Victoria.

"If you will both please follow us. This is my colleague Hyssop." Hyssop makes little effort to acknowledge the semi-introduction, keeping both hands locked behind her back as her eyes scan every inch of our bodies instead of our actual faces. "The Conclave has assembled and is waiting for you," Thunder says in a tone that is far more remote than I've heard from him. Well, he was the first through the room when I held that gun up to my head, so I can understand his skittishness.

Levi simply nods and we both follow Thunder and Hyssop down the elevator to the entrance of the building where there is once again the illuminated blue path for us to follow to the middle of the city. It takes quite a few minutes to get there, even at our brisk clip. I see other SenMachs out and about. These people, some famous, some anonymous—at least to me—

uniformly stop whatever they are doing so they can stare. I wonder how Cosmos could have ever thought Levi and I would be happy here. Wherever we went, we would be stared at: zoo animals allowed to roam free outside their pens but curiosities nonetheless. I glance over at Levi. There is just the faintest crease between his eyebrows. We are getting very good at this, communicating through microgestures and the slightest shrugs and nods. It's vital that we are able to use this currency of silence. We need to be able to speak without actually speaking. It means that I will know to go on the offensive by the way his weight will move from one foot to the other. It also means that I must always watch him and he must always be watching me.

It means we're actually in this *together*.

When we arrive at the main administration building we are whisked up to the top floor, where we end up standing in front of two massive doors that swing open on their own. Thunder and Hyssop usher us into a high-ceilinged room with a glass roof. The floor is gray slate and the only pieces of furniture are an unbelievably large, white-lacquered oval table and the stainless-steel chairs around it. Sitting in these chairs are over two dozen SenMachs. Immediately I recognize Feather and Cosmos. Abraham Lincoln is sitting there, too, which is pretty neat. I stare at him for a second or two, surprised at how much better-looking he is than I would have thought.

Thunder pulls out two chairs at the end of the table and gestures for us to sit. They have provided us with two glasses of water. I take mine and sip gingerly. It's awkward in this room full of people I recognize but don't know. People who could have a deciding vote on whether or not my friends live or die. It's come down to this moment. I have been a soldier, a fighter, a killer. Today, in this room, I must rely on something else, something ARC never taught us. Still, I can only imagine that the kind of cunning required on the battlefield has to be the same kind you would deploy in negotiations. There's a reason all those business guys read Sun Tzu.

Yet this *isn't* battle. I just have to remember that the thing they want most is for us to be safe. I cannot be explicit about the kind of dangers we will most likely face, or even the kind we have faced in the past. I have to be vaguely assertive because what we want, of course, is not only to leave here but to leave with SenMach technology that will help us even after our journey through the Multiverse is over.

"Levi, Ryn," Cosmos announces, "thank you for joining us. I realize that you are anxious to be on your way, so let us begin." Cosmos folds her hands gracefully in front of her on the table. "Neon is the head of our physics division. She had a very good look at the hardware that you entrusted us with yesterday. Neon?"

The woman in question is a light-skinned African American woman. Like Hyssop, she looks vaguely familiar. I riffle through my brain. I keep a lot of useless crap stored in this photographic memory of mine. A photograph. That's where I know her from. I think she is Josephine Baker, the entertainer from the 1920s. I can't be absolutely sure, though, since Neon is not dressed as a flapper. She is wearing an outfit similar to mine except she also has a white lab coat on.

"Thank you, Cosmos. We took a look at the program for your QOINS." I subconsciously straighten my spine. It felt like giving it up was the smartest move at the time, but sitting here, across from android Abraham Lincoln, I'm not so sure. "Although we were able to upload it successfully into your new computers, we did not find a way to Rift directly to a quantum signature without the wobbles of pitch, or 'jumps,' as the additional written materials left on your desktops describe."

"Wait. New computers? You want to replace our laptops?" I interrupt. Rocket boots I'm down for. Totally replacing the thing we rely most on to get through the Multiverse, though? Could be great, could be an epic fail.

"Your laptops are antiques," a voice says from the table. I look around. Oh. My. God. It's Tim Riggins. I feel my mouth go dry. My heart starts to race a little. Jesus fuck he is gorgeous, even the silver-eyed, non-jersey-wearing version of him is starting to wreak havoc on my lady parts. I hear Levi clear his throat and so I tear my gaze away and look sideways. He must have heard my pulse. I widen my eyes at him. He's not having any of it. I fold my hands together on the table and do my best to stay cool. "You asked for our assistance. You could not possibly believe that our software could adequately function on something so archaic."

It turns out Tim Riggins is kind of a douche robot.

I mean, I didn't think he'd be warm and fuzzy, but this Sen-Mach is almost hostile. And of course I know he's not really Tim Riggins, or the actor who played him (who is Canadian, and there's no way a Canadian could be this rude), but it's still a shock to see someone you think you know but have them be so completely different from the image you had built in your mind.

It's kind of a bummer, actually, so, note to self: If I ever see an actor in real life on my Earth—just walk away. In the opposite direction.

"I don't know anything yet, which is why I'm sitting here at this table," I say firmly in his general direction because staring at him directly is, quite frankly, like looking into the sun.

"We will get to that eventually, Doe," Cosmos says, chiding Riggins. "Doe is Neon's second," she explains to us. I hear Levi chuckle under his breath. He's laughing at Tim's name. I turn my head so he can see the curve of my mouth. It's enough to silence him. If anyone at the table notices, they say nothing, and Cosmos says, "Please, Neon, continue."

"We were able to eliminate the need for the Heads and Tails part of the system by boosting the signal—an improvement we are satisfied with, given our time constraints." Neon pauses and looks at Cosmos, who blinks her long eyelashes slowly and nods her head, prodding Neon to go on. "The code inside this program is remarkable and complex. The fact that once an Earth has been locked into the system it can then be returned to again, without the multiple jumps, is, in and of itself, beyond our scope at this moment."

"What does that mean?" I ask sincerely.

"It means that a harmonic quantum signature is a harmonic quantum signature. The register of the tone does not change. The QOINS somehow recognizes the tone of places it's already been but can't recognize one it hasn't been to before. Why not? Logically it makes no sense." I furrow my brow. I'm not sure what she is saying, so *none* of this is making much sense.

"I think perhaps we should have Pocket explain this further. He is the department head for Specialized Coding. Pocket?" I turn to look at the person Cosmos is referring to, who might be a young Morgan Freeman, which would make sense because I feel like Morgan Freeman is basically everywhere on our Earth.

"Yes, thank you. The coding for the QOINS is one of the most elegant I have ever seen," Pocket begins. "How the program is able to store coordinates of an established address but not an established tone is what has us wondering."

"Wondering what? It makes sense to me. Once we've been to a place, the computer remembers where it is, like storing your home address in your GPS," I argue.

"On the surface, yes, but mathematically? No. Think about it: As Neon said, a tone is a tone. The *tone* is the address. Let us continue with the GPS analogy. You want to go somewhere. You enter the street number and name. Normally, it takes you right there. But this time, when you look at the directions, you realize there must be something wrong with your GPS. It is malfunctioning because it is asking you to stop at several different places before your destination. Without an actual map, and without knowing exactly where you are going, you are forced to follow the GPS's route. The next day, you want to go to the very same place. But if your GPS is still broken, you would not expect it to take you straight there just because it had been there the day before, would you?"

Levi and I look at each other. "But the QOINS *does* do that. Huh." I chew on it for a little bit, but while his example definitely computes, I still don't know what it means. "How does it do that?" I ask. Pocket looks at Cosmos, who in turn looks at us, with concern. This can't be good.

"We believe that there is more going on here than you were told," she says sadly.

"Well, you knew that," Levi jumps in. "Ryn told you that."

"Yes I heard a muddled explanation and I saw the alterations to your genome, but to read that code—that was something else entirely. It was . . . troubling. We believe the Roones can jump from one Earth directly to another. The code has been manipulated. Corrupted, but the solution is there. If we had more time, we could deconstruct it and solve this problem for you. The question, however, remains: Why would the Roones, or your superiors at the Allied Rift Coalition, want to put you in considerable danger with all these unnecessary jumps? It suggests something dishonorable at best and sinister at worst," Cosmos admits reluctantly.

"I can't say that I'm surprised. They've never been honest with us. It's why we left. But what does that have to do with what is going on at this table? How is the QOINS relevant to you?" I ask as I lean in closer, putting my elbows on the table.

"It's relevant in terms of our involvement. The code changes things and now we have a dilemma. Two, actually, and we do not have a quorum to deal with them, which is why I want you to speak directly to the Conclave—so that you might be able to answer some additional questions that may lead to solutions."

"Fair enough. Let's discuss."

"Well the first problem is that if the Roones are simply the architects of this technology, but not the abusers, that means that the Allied Rift Coalition, and more specifically, humans, are your enemy. If you are looking to us to intervene in a military capacity on your Earth against your own kind, that would be impossible. We will not alter our base code to harm human beings, not even those who abuse children. The cost to our society would be too great. We tried that approach on this Earth and we failed miserably. Look at what happened when we tried to keep you here. We cannot infantilize the human race. You must grow up and learn from your own mistakes."

I bite down on the inside of my cheek. I hadn't even thought of putting troops on the negotiating table. I had only been thinking of getting to Ezra safely and then maybe some super-genius computer hacks to use back home. The SenMachs are seeing the long game. I need to start thinking this way, too.

"That's fair," I say. "So we won't ask for military aid against other humans. But what if it isn't us? What if the Roones really are pulling all the strings? What if we want military aid to fight a combatant that isn't human?" I'm thinking of the Roones, of course. But now I'm also imagining beyond just fighting the Roones directly—how the SenMachs could pull the chips out of all the Citadels' heads—chips that could blow their brains out with the Midnight Protocol. With their level of tech, they should be able to neutralize those chips far faster than we could, meaning that even if they can't fight, they can free up a fighting force for us . . . and give the Citadels a chance for autonomy.

Long game.

The only answer I get is awkward silence. They're probably sending a thousand text messages back and forth that they're reading behind their eyes.

Eventually, Cosmos speaks up. "The party or parties behind the atrocities which led you to our Earth brings us to our second problem. The Roones may be your enemy. It may be another species entirely, manipulating and maneuvering all of you behind a very well-concealed veil. However, whoever created that code is a force to be reckoned with. If their aim is to infiltrate other Earths and pillage those Earths for technology and/or resources, what do you think will happen once they take a look at what you have brought home, at what we can give you? There are members of this assembly who believe that our first priority should be finding a way to block the QOINS receiver so that another Rift can never be opened here."

My heart sinks. God I'm crap at this. It never even occurred to me that I would be putting the SenMachs in danger by simply being here. The only thing I can offer them now is the absolute truth, which hopefully, given what Cosmos knows was done to us when we were just little kids, will mean something to her.

"Look," I begin. "You're right. Blocking the QOINS would be the safest option."

"Ryn," Levi hisses.

"No, Levi. We have to be honest, that's the only way this is going to work," I admit softly.

"Are you saying that you do not want our tactical assistance, Ryn?" Cosmos asks.

"No, that's not what I'm saying at all. I—we—want your assistance very much. But I recognize the danger in offering it and I would understand completely if you decide not to. The only thing I can say is this: If you did choose to align with our cause, I would never ask you to participate in any way that violated your base code, and I would only ask for your help, in a military capacity, if it was a matter of life or death. I would never ask you to expose yourselves to prove some kind of point or show of force."

"That is all well and good, but if it got that far, we would already be lost. It would be impossible for us to protect ourselves and remain true to our base code if Citadels loyal to ARC Rifted here to our city." I look in the direction of the voice who had made the comment and I'm completely bummed to see that it's Matt Damon.

Matt Damon!

The *real* Matt Damon would totally be with us. All the way. He was Jason Bourne! Jason Bourne knows a thing or two about being a brainwashed super soldier.

"I understand that," I tell them all in a tone that I hope does not sound combative. "But I hope that you understand, *really* understand, what we're up against. You guys are thousands of years old. We're teenagers. Granted, we are not typical teens, but still, at this point . . ." I struggle to find the right words. Words that will convey strength but at the same time convey how invaluable their help would be. "We're just . . . *new*."

"Yes. We all realize how young you are." Fake Matt Damon—*again*! "And we worry about your safety. But the risk is so great, and the reward may only be in helping a group of humans who could be doomed already, given your violent predilections, through no fault of your own, of course."

"Tin, that is unnecessary," Cosmos says with icy authority.

I consider Tin's statement. However cruel, it also rings true. The risk is significant and the rewards minimal. But what if we actually had something to give? Something of value?

"Fine," I say in a tone that I hope matches Cosmos's. "What if we could make a trade? What if you helped us and got something in return?" I see Levi's head whip toward me. I know he probably won't like this, but we can't exactly negotiate when we have nothing to leverage. I can see that Cosmos wants to help us, but the others need something beyond seeing to our safety. A SenMach like Tin (who, let's face it, is a poor man's Matt Damon) is not built the same way as Cosmos. Help from the SenMachs isn't about us being able to just leave now. It's not even about the tech or military aid they can offer. Tin is right, SenMach City would be dangerously exposed. We need to make it worth it.

"I do not know what you could possibly offer up in return that would compensate for such an enormous risk," the usurper Matt Damon predictably chimes in, which annoys me, but it also lets me know that my head is in the right place.

I grit my teeth, flexing my jaw for a moment. Here goes nothing. "Eggs. My eggs, to be specific. And Levi's sperm." I don't need to look at Levi to know he must be glowering at me. "As well as live tissue samples, blood, and any other biological material you might want to have. I know that you use real tissue for your skin and I imagine you also use live, organic cells for other parts of your own bodies. If you choose to one day repopulate the earth with humans, our children would be strong and smart. Think about it: human beings on this Earth again, humans that you would raise and care for with your values. I know you all regret not being able to stop the extinction of humanity on this planet. With our help, you could really do something about it. Also, I am aware that you would require more biological diversity to repopulate. I can guarantee there are other Citadels who would be willing to offer the same thing."

"Ryn," Cosmos says more gently and more sweetly than I've ever heard her say my name. "Think about this for a moment. You are essentially offering up your unborn children to strangers, who live on what is, in reality, another planet. Is that truly something you can live with? And how would you explain these siblings to the children of your own that you will have one day?"

"I doubt I will have children of my own. There's a high probability that I won't live long enough to have a family, and even if I did, I don't think I'd make a very good mother. I'd actually feel better knowing that whatever kids I did have would be raised here in this place, in safety and around people who would devote themselves to raising them."

"Ryn," I hear Feather say sadly.

"I'm not saying that to get you to feel sorry for me. I'm just being honest. I was born without defects, and the genetic alterations didn't make me bad or anything, it's just . . ." Again, I struggle for the right words that will make them understand but not vilify us. Finally I say, "We've seen a lot and done a lot that would make it very difficult to be a normal person with a job and a baby and a minivan—which is a type of vehicle that moms drive, in case you didn't know."

"You're sure about this offer? And, Levi? You agree?"

Levi pauses. I finally look at him and I'm both surprised and relieved to see he isn't really pissed at me. I made an offer that affects him, too, without even so much as consulting him. I'd be angry. Levi is too good a soldier for that, though. He must have known, as well as I did, that I was left with little choice, given what we had to bargain with. Instead, he looks determined, his green eyes intense. "Two thousand troops. Fifteen hundred at the ready to join us on our Earth if we need them and the remaining five hundred to stay here and protect your city. When we've won, your troops can join the Citadels and live on our Earth or they can return to you. But please, make them all different looking. It would be very weird and confusing to have a bunch of clone soldiers. Medical supplies and any advanced technology that will help us navigate the Rifts safely. If you do that, I'll give you whatever you want."

"Perhaps we should take some time to consider their offer," says a gorgeous SenMach, who may be the most beautiful person I've ever actually seen. I wonder who she is.

"Time is the one thing we don't have. We've already lingered here far too long and we have to make allowances for the medical procedures," I counter quickly.

"Very well, then, I accept your terms and I suggest we vote," Cosmos says efficiently. I smile for just a fraction of a second, long enough for me to realize that was entirely too easy. I offered the SenMachs everything we had to give. That's no way to negotiate. I should have started with just one thing, tissue samples. If they hadn't gone for that, I could have ramped it up. For all I know, this is what they wanted all along, and all of it— the troops, the tech, even the threat of being detained—was to get us here, right to this moment. Or maybe I'm being paranoid and Cosmos was just looking for a way, any way, to help us. I suppose it doesn't matter. I've learned something in this room: a lesson about bargaining, and it's not one I'll soon forget.

Everyone at the table seems to sit up even straighter than they were before, which is saying something because the Sen-Machs have excellent posture. The vote begins. I hear yeses from every SenMach I've spent time with personally and from some I have not. Unsurprisingly the bummer version of Matt Damon says no, and the super-gorgeous but also mean-looking girl also declines. Despite that, the tally is not really all that close. The SenMachs want what we have to give.

"The yeses carry. Ryn, Levi, you have secured an alliance. We will need . . ." Cosmos pauses and takes about ten seconds before continuing, "twelve point eight days to program and manufacture our troops. That is the fastest possible time frame we can offer."

"We'll take it. Thank you."

"If you would like to come with me and Doe," Neon suggests, "we can give you the tech we believe you'll need on your journey. After that, you can meet with Feather and his team."

The SenMachs move quickly. I hope because they are respecting our desire to Rift out quickly and not because they're afraid we'll change our minds. Although what does it really matter? I am learning, too, that trust cannot ever be absolute, even with beings who cannot lie. Everyone has an agenda and everyone believes their agenda is the right one, myself included.

We take a silent electronic car to what must be the Physics building. Although the building is concrete, it has an odd conical shape to it that almost makes it look out of place among the straight lines I've seen everywhere else.

Levi is walking ahead with Neon, and I am beside Doe, try-ing not to stare. There is important life-or-death stuff going on here, but even with the supergenes and all, I am a human girl. Even in his robot form, Tim/Taylor/Doe has a detachment that almost borders on brooding. Obviously, I'm just anthro-pomorphizing the situation. He's an android. Of course he's detached.

I just kind of wish I could watch him drink a beer and say, "Texas forever," at least once, though.

After entering the building, we make our way to what I as-sume is a lab. I can't say for sure, though. It's a big, open space with large black computer storage towers, or at least I think that's what they are. There are also dozens of steel tables hold-ing different bits of equipment and assembled devices. We are led to the center of the room where there are two extremely thin rectangular pieces of silver sitting on one of the tables. Doe runs his hand over one of them and the top pops open. It's a laptop.

"We would like you to start using these. They can replace your current computers," Neon says kindly but efficiently.

"Yeah, okay," I say, hesitantly eyeing what looks basically like two pieces of colored paper in front of us. "We do want to take advantage of your technology, obviously, but this . . . I don't know. If it breaks or crashes, we wouldn't have the first idea how to fix it."

Neon waits a beat. Her head is tilting at an angle. "You will never need to repair them. They are not just machines. They are sentient. They will repair themselves if necessary. Their shell is made of a nearly indestructible alloy. I assure you, they are much more reliable than the computers you are currently using."

"Sentient?" Levi raises a single eyebrow suspiciously.

"I understand that the singularity has not yet happened on your Earth. I can assure you these machines are not sentient in the way that SenMachs are. They have been coded with only one goal: to make sure you Rift safely and to do everything possible to keep you alive when you arrive on a particular Earth. That is all. It would be impossible for them to turn against you in any way, if that is your fear."

Levi takes a step back and begins to chew his bottom lip while staring at the table. "Our fear, Neon," he begins, "is that we'll become dependent on something we don't understand."

Neon runs a single finger across the razor-thin top of the computer. "Yes. You have both been let down by technology, betrayed by it, even. All I can tell you is that we do not underestimate your ability to survive even the most dire of circumstances, but we would feel . . ." Neon practically stumbles on the word, clearly unused to using it, "so much better if you accept these. This technology will improve your chances at a successful mission and keep you safer. That is all we want. I promise you."

There are enough similarities between the SenMachs and the Roones to give me pause, but I do believe that, ultimately, above all else, the SenMachs want us to live. I can't say with 100 percent certainty the Roones feel the same. Besides, we did ask for the SenMachs' help. They are making good on their deal. This is just what assistance from them looks like.

"It's pure dumb luck that the last two Earths didn't destroy our equipment," I say. "The way I see it, we're just one Rift away from being trapped somewhere and I don't really like those odds. I think our chances increase exponentially if we start using these. Just as a precaution, though, we can take one of the old systems with us for the first few jumps, in case these new ones don't work in the field. Does that work for you, Levi?"

I hear him exhale. "Fine. But look," he says as he picks one up and examines it more closely, "there's a keyboard and a monitor, but I don't see a power source or any ports . . ."

I cross my arms and sigh. I was doing so well with the going for it and the whole "let's trust them mostly" thing. "Valid," I volunteer reluctantly. I turn back to Neon. "We don't have time for a seminar in advanced computing."

"There is no need," she says. Out of her pocket she pulls what looks like an iPhone. "I took the liberty of replicating one of your mobile devices to use as a demonstration." She places the phone down beside the other laptop. In two seconds, an illuminated tendril-like cable emerges from the side of the silver computer, and Levi jumps back. The tendril attaches to the phone and immediately, information is displayed on the monitor.

"Oh, great," Levi says with his usual rancor. He juts his neck to get a better look, but he keeps his feet planted, ready to spring. "I feel much better." I can't fault his skittishness. This tech is organic, alive. No matter how many movies you see, nothing can ever really prepare you for seeing this kind of thing in real life.

"Any file, any drive—any *machine*—can be read and down-loaded. It already has all the binary information you brought with you, including your QOINS device, which no longer needs a Heads or Tails component to work. We retrofitted these to eliminate that cumbersome element and even managed to boost the signal two point seven percent. Whenever you arrive on a new Earth, any information you might require can be ac-quired physically or via a network. There is an internal power source that does not need to be recharged. You can piggyback off a wireless signal without detection—I believe you call this hacking? You can hack into any system regardless of encryption." Neon walks over to a neighboring table and we follow her quickly. She picks up a smooth, oblong silver object that is just a little bigger than a bookmark. "These are drones. They don't have quite the range as the ones you first encountered when you arrived, but they can be sent out in stealth mode to do recon for you. The drones, in conjunction with the computer, can help you triangulate your position on an Earth in a matter of seconds."

The tactical advantages the SenMachs have just given us are staggering. I realize that we are in robot city and that basically every sci-fi show I've ever seen is happening all around me. Still, I feel like an observer here, a visitor. Once we take this equipment, this becomes part of our personal story. We won't just be super soldiers, we'll be super soldiers with Star Trek tech. We'll be the most advanced humans on Earth—our Earth, at least. It's awesome and I don't mean that in a casual, hair-flipping, mall-girl way. I mean it in the literal sense. It's awesome.

"Doe, show Ryn and Levi the sensuits." Neon suggests. Doe nods slightly and walks over to yet another nearby table.

"We felt that these would also be incredibly useful on different iterations of Earth. Levi, will you slip this over your head, please?" Doe is gesturing to one of the pieces of silk that are laying on the table. I thought it was simply a sheet that was covering something underneath it. But when Levi picks up the material, there is nothing else there. He holds it up and now I can see it is a tube and up close it looks more satin-like than silk. I can't say for certain what color it is. Every time Levi moves his hand, the color changes ever so slightly from ivory to nude to brown to white. Levi puts it over his head and instead of slipping all the way down it just sort of hovers around his body.

"Courtly Gentleman, Versailles, 1787," Doe says, although

I'm not sure who he's talking to. That is, until the silk undu-
lates like water on a lake shore. It moves up Levi's entire body
and molds itself into trousers, hose, shoes, a brocade vest, and
a jacket. "Disguise face," Doe orders. The sensuit slips over
half of Levi's head so that it ends just under his nose. All of a
sudden there is a powdered wig, complete with a velvet rib-
bon and even Levi's features are changed. His chin juts out
more, his mouth becomes smaller. I would never know it was
him unless I got really close and was able to see his eyes.

"This was a project we developed a decade ago," Doe begins. "We wanted to see how humans looked in different
time periods without having to manufacture several bits of
apparel. We know that many of the Earths you visit will run
on different time lines. There will also be Earths with different dominant species. This should allow you to walk in
public without being noticed—you can use the drones for re-
connaissance to get an accurate description of what the population is wearing or what they look like. When wearing the
sensuit, you will be able to walk among them undetected. If
the species is too far removed from a bipedal one, there is a
stealth mode. Levi, say 'stealth.'" Levi says the word and the
image of him is instantly gone. *He* is gone. The SenMachs
have just given us another superpower. Invisibility. Levi and
I could walk onto any base on our Earth—hell, we could walk
right into ARC and kill everyone inside and they couldn't
touch us. The idea is both horrifying and wonderful.

"Can you see me?" a disembodied voice asks.

"Not at all. Is it uncomfortable? Does it feel claustropho-
bic?" Invisibility is amazing, but if you feel like you're being
smothered in a sheet, I'm not sure you could do much besides
hide. Hiding is great. I'm all for hiding. I'm also for "kill the
bad guys when they think they're being attacked by a ghost."

"Not no. But if I had to fight in this, if that's your question, then I could." Neon takes two broad pieces of what look like black leather and holds them up. "These are also for you. May I put this on you, Ryn?"

"On my clothes, or . . . ?" I don't know how I'm supposed to wear a strip of leather.

"I apologize. Please hold out your arm." At this point, I have no idea what's on offer. Maybe it's a personal force field. Before my imagination carries me too far away, Neon places the band over my wrist and it closes and molds so that it becomes a bracer . . . like *Wonder Woman*.

Yes!

"The cuff is linked to your computer. You will not have to open it in order to access its features." Okay, so, not so much with the Wonder Woman. "You can operate the sensuits and drones with audio commands. These commands are programmed to follow your vocal authority and yours alone. Once you set it up, the security is impossible to circumvent, even by us. Levi, take yours and place it on your wrist. Once you do, simply say the word 'cuff' and the SenSuit will retract." Levi does this, and I watch as the suit actually disappears into the bracelet. "We also have the medical supplies and the food cubes you were given, as well as instructions for making more of them. These are all the tools we believe will help you survive with little or no injury in the Multiverse."

"Ask them about the Iron Man boots," Levi whispers, which is annoying because he does have a mouth. But I have to admit, I want to know, too.

"What about the boots? The ones with the little rockets in them?" I bring up hesitantly. I'm not sure that even if I could fly, I would want to. I feel like a lot could go wrong in that department.

"Unfortunately, as you want to leave as soon as possible, we did not have time to create an interface which would enable you to operate them easily. We control them with our neural net, which you do not possess." I hear a little huff from Levi, which I choose to ignore.

"Do you have any questions about these devices?" Neon asks sincerely. Her silver eyes look especially bright in contrast to her flawless, caramel-colored skin.

"Only about a thousand," I answer honestly, "but seeing as we don't have the weeks you could spend answering them, I'll just have to hope the 'sentient' part of the technology you gave us can fill in the gaps as we go."

"I'm sure it will. Now, I believe it is time to go to the biomed facility?" I look at both Neon and Doe and everything they've supplied us with. As amazing as it all is, I am now reminded that it comes at a cost. These are just things. They are spectacular, game-changing things, but it's nothing they won't miss. A computer isn't a kid. If the SenMachs do choose to start a breeding program, then I have to admit, reluctantly, that we got the short end of that stick.

I try not to think about that once Feather starts working on me. They use plenty of anesthetic and I'm fairly certain that it's Walt Disney who's assisting him. Levi is in another room. I should, of course, keep my eyes open. I should be watching everything that they do. It's what I insisted on with Edo when she took my chip out. But once they put the instrument over where my ovaries are, I can't help but close my eyes. Will they do it? Will they make Levi and me parents?

It's one thing to explain the deprogramming to Ezra. This—this is something I can't rationally articulate. They didn't build me for motherhood, that wasn't a lie. As if I needed further proof of it, I am potentially handing over any offspring I may have to robots to raise. And I bargained them away for a lap-top and a costume.

It takes about an hour for them to collect everything they need from me. When it's over, Feather asks if I have any questions.

"I have two," I say as I begin to get dressed. "If you do decide to make humans, to raise them, will you adapt your base code? So that they feel like they're loved? Even if it's not real love on your part, kids get really messed up if they feel like their parents don't love them." Feather waits several seconds before placing a hand over my own.

"We would do that, yes."

"And could you give me something? That would act as permanent birth control?" Feather removes his hand. His unblinking silver eyes momentarily pass over me. I watch them flicker with something close to real emotion.

"I believe," he begins gently, "that right now, you cannot imagine being a mother. But I know, because I have been sentient for a very long time, that where you are right now is not always where you will be. You have been through so very much in your short life, but you are still young and I could never take that choice away from you. I can, however, give you something that will temporarily prevent pregnancy for a couple of years." I don't know whether Feather's answer is a relief or a disappointment. Either way, there is no place for children where I am right now.

"Then, please, do that."

I finish dressing. I don't ever want to think about this room again.

A SHORT TIME LATER, THERE is a large assembly of SenMachs in the grassy area outside the main administration building.

We are back in uniform and ready to Rift. I know that by speaking Ezra's name into my cuff, the QOINS on the new hardware will activate. I can also Rift directly home. And for bonus points, the SenMachs have given us what they call "the Pandora option." If we need to lure someone away from either of those points, a random Rift will open at a frequency that is far off from both.

"Thank you," I tell Cosmos, and I mean it. "I know how badly you want us to stay. We will be back, though, and probably in one piece because of all the great stuff you gave us."

"Yeah, thanks," Levi says, almost warmly (but it's Levi, so nothing is ever really "warm" with him).

Cosmos nods her head and places both hands together, fingers lightly touching. "You know as well as I do that nothing was given. A truly strong alliance can be forged only when both parties have something of value to offer. Once you find out what exactly is going on back on your Earth, our troops will be ready. In the meantime, be safe and be careful." I don't really know what to say to that. I can't promise that we will be either of those things, nor can I really promise that their troops won't do some kind of damage to other human beings, even if there's no fighting. Their presence alone could dismantle ARC, and while that's great news for the Citadels, it might not be so great for the employees.

I nod briskly. "Rift. Ezra," I say into my cuff. The noise is loud and immediate. It makes my head feel like it's inside a harmonica. The SenMach tech works. As Levi and I walk through, I clench the straps of my backpack a little tighter. I hope that everything I'm carrying inside was worth it.

CHAPTER 11

We walk out of the Rift into an ocean of red. The ground is a bright rust, with a splattering of weathered green and brown shrubs. There are no trees, but the landscape is dotted with dozens upon dozens of branching succulents that remind me of a classroom full of children eagerly waving their hands to answer a question. In between the cacti's thorns are huge, spiky, mint-colored roses, though the edges of the large, flat, sharp petals are tinged with a blushing pink.

The sky is a crimson as brilliant as a holly berry, and the sun, low and heavy, is a swollen scarlet. Evening is about to set it in, but it is still very, very hot. The air itself smells amazing, like burning incense. To be on the safe side, I pull out the gadget that checks for environmental impurities and take a reading. It's clear. Both Levi and I take our binoculars out. We scan the horizon in every direction. To the south

I see what looks like a decent-size crop of rocks about two klicks away.

"You see it?" Levi asks.

"Affirmative. Let's run down there, we could use some cover." Without answering, Levi begins a light jog and I follow him. In no time at all we find ourselves in front of a large collection of jagged boulders. The tallest, about twenty feet high, has a narrow hole in its face.

"Could be a cave."

"Let's hope," Levi says without any real enthusiasm.

"Yeah, and let's hope it's not filled with some creepy bat-bear thingies or real bears or, actually, any sort of wildlife at all."

"Scared of some animals? This is the wilderness, not a hotel, Ryn." The condescension is almost palpable. I make a snide face as soon as his back is turned. I know where we are and I'm not afraid of animals. I just don't *like* them. Except for maybe cats, because they require minimal attention. And even then . . .

The entrance to the cave, though slender, is about eight feet tall. Levi takes his flashlight out and peers inside. I take out my rifle.

"Really?"

"Yeah, really, Mountain Man. Do I look like Cinderella? Do I seem like the kind of person who wants a bird to land on my arm?"

"Look," he says, not unkindly, "why don't I just go in and check it out, make sure there isn't anything in there waiting to eat you, and I'll call when it's clear?"

"Why don't you just send a drone through there?"

"Because," he says as he actively rolls his eyes, "this is actually a part of the job that I like."

I wait a beat, wondering if he's being serious but, when he

says nothing, I suppose he is. I didn't take him for an explorer type, but then again, when was I supposed to have figured that out?

"Fine," I relent.

Levi turns to go and I pull back on his arm. Dangerous, stupid even, but he does not go into the Blood Lust, probably because the cave is at the forefront of his mind. "Wait. You can go in, but I just want you to know that I *could* go in, too, and kill anything that needed killing."

Levi scrunches up his eyes and the right side of his mouth. "Is this, like, a feminist thing? Is that what you're worried about? Because I've seen you beat the crap out of people *and* stab them *and* shoot them, so, yeah, I understand you could go in. If you'd rather stand out here and have me ask you about your feminist agenda or whatever, though, we can do that, too." Was that a compliment? I actually don't think it was, or it was a backhanded one, but I'm still so far from being able to read Levi, I just don't know.

"Just go in there and let me know if there's space for us to do some recon," I say. Levi disappears and I wait outside the small black mouth for him to emerge. After about five minutes he's back, popping his head through the hole.

"It's empty, sort of, but there's plenty of room for us."

"What do you mean 'sort of'?" I ask as I step tentatively inside.

"Watch your step," he warns, "there's a natural decline here." I feel my feet tilt down and I turn to the side so that I can better navigate the slope downward.

"You're still not telling me what you found, Levi." The ground levels off and I can tell by sound alone that the space is much bigger than I thought, and blessedly the air is much, much cooler.

"It's this," he says as he picks up his lantern and brings it above his head. It's set to the highest setting and as he sweeps his arm around I can see that the walls are covered in paintings.

"Wow," I say, suddenly forgetting about whatever beast may be lurking. The colors of the paints are a combination of ochre, brown, and blood red. There are many scenes: harvests, celebrations, and packs of animals, but the people depicted here are a race I recognize all too well.

"They're Sissnovars!" I exclaim.

Levi leans in closely, bringing the light right up against one of the walls. "Huh. You're right."

"I speak Sissnovar."

"You do?"

"Yeah. I mean, we should speak as many different Immigrant languages as possible. The fact that ARC doesn't want us to know any was incentive enough for me to learn some."

"Makes sense," Levi agrees, though I can see his body tense, specifically his fists. "It makes so much sense, in fact, that I can't believe that none of us considered it."

"Well, no, because we were all being drugged into compliance. My metabolism runs through the drugs more quickly. That's it. It's just chemistry, so give yourself a break." Levi sighs, although it does sound a little more like a growl than anything wistful. He's not the type to let himself off the hook that easily and nothing I say is going to change that. "I think it would be best if we sent out those drones, to see if there are any villages nearby or any signs of Ezra," I tell him, hoping for a distraction.

"Okay," Levi says as he begins to unpack the SenMach equipment from our pack.

"While you're doing that, I'm going to play around with the sensuits."

"Shocker," Levi mutters sarcastically as he places one of the small silver drones on his lap.

"Star Trek, J. J. Abrams reboot, medical officer, female," I say into my black leather cuff. Although Levi is preoccupied with our new laptop and the drone, I can still see his head shaking. I feel the sensuit unfold from my arm. It slips around me like a silk blanket. It's actually quite a pleasant feeling. I look down and see the iconic blue short dress, complete with knee-high black boots. "*Boom*," I say dramatically, exploding a single fist in slow motion.

"I honestly wish that I could have put some money on that because I would have bet that would be your first choice, that or Princess Leia or maybe the hot chick from the Avengers. Some kinda cosplay thing," Levi says indifferently, while still working on the computer.

"Ha!" I say triumphantly. "*You* know what cosplay is."

"Yeah. I watched a segment about it on CNN," he tells me levelly, still looking at the computer.

"Okay, okay. Clearly this is too much awesome for you to handle. How about this? High-born Southern belle, circa 1882 America." Once again the suit shimmies and slips. This time it goes all the way up to my neck, creating an elaborate blond wig that I can see out of the corner of my eye. When I look down, I'm amazed. The intricacy of the fine inlaid paisley on the taffeta dress and the tightness of the corset is astounding; it feels so real. I lift up my skirts and see my actual legs underneath pantaloons. "How does it do that? I can't even see my uniform. Is it an illusion? Does it somehow make the uniform disintegrate or something?" I ask, not even bothering to hide the wonder in my voice.

"I sure as hell hope not. If we have to be in combat while wearing one of these things, I'd like to know we've still got the uniform's coverage," Levi says. It's a good point, but I don't tell him so. He gets up and tries to walk around me, but the skirt is very big and I can tell that it annoys him.

"Fine," I say. "Model, female, any French designer in a time period equivalent to mine." The suit once again begins to work. The hoop skirt disappears and is replaced with a body-forming long-sleeved black lace dress with strategic swirls of thicker lace around my "female areas." My feet are shoved in ridiculously high stilettos.

Levi looks at me. My entire body must be backlit by the lantern on the floor. He doesn't say anything. He just stares. I feel almost giddy for half a second before I realize, in my attempt to sensuit myself to cool, I might have taken it too far. I look practically naked. I can hear Levi's heart start to beat more rapidly.

"Just stop," he finally says. "Be normal. God, we're inside a friggin' cave and you're decked out in a ball gown, and in case you've forgotten, we've got work to do. We're trying to find your boyfriend. Remember?"

"You're right." I *know* he's right. I just wanted to take two minutes and have some fun. I suppose that's selfish, but come on, we have so many cool and shiny new things!

"Cuff," I say reluctantly, and the sensuit retracts, leaving me in my uniform again. I can practically hear him relax.

I join Levi on the ground. I watch as he releases our tiny silver drones. They can go stealth if necessary, and I think in our case it will always be necessary.

"Run drone program," he says. "Stealth mode. Check for habitation within two hundred miles. Send back photos as you go." With just that, the drone picks itself up off the floor, shimmers, and disappears. I can hear a faint buzzing as it climbs higher into the atmosphere to get the best vantage point.

We sit in silence. I wonder if he's thinking about SenMach

City, of all the things we got there and everything we gave up. I wonder if he's thinking about our potential children. I think about these things silently, because I will never, ever, ask him out loud. I think denial is pretty much the way to go with this one.

Levi finally talks. "I've tried to pick up a Wi-Fi signal here. Unsurprisingly, there isn't one. The program isn't picking up on any mass centers of population, either." I lean my head back into the cool rock and sigh. It doesn't take long for the computer to start uploading pictures from the drone, and soon Levi says, "It looks like there's only one village within two hundred miles of here. The drone is getting close enough to take pictures. It really does know what, or I guess who, we're looking for."

I sit back up and watch the monitor as dozens of pictures start to come in. The Sissnovar village isn't modern by any stretch, but it isn't Bronze Age, either. There are large stone buildings, built with dark round rocks, and clay-fired roofs. If anything, it sort of looks like an old Irish village. Pictures show us a main street with signage for stores, a pub, and Sissnovars in loose cotton clothing milling about with ease. There is no electricity, but it's not backward. I think about the Sissnovar I met in our Village in Battle Ground, named Zaka. I wonder if he came from a place like this.

"I think it's safe to assume that Ezra isn't here," I tell him. "He's going to want to get to a place where he can send us a message. This isn't it. We should go." I stand up slowly.

"Wait," Levi says, and grabs my wrist. I look at it and him. Oh God, I do not feel like fighting right now. "There's a storm coming—the computer says so."

"Okay, so even more of a reason for us to leave." Instead of letting go of my arm, Levi stands.

"I like the rain. I like the way it smells after a rainstorm. It's on my list," he tells me quietly. He finally lets go of me and runs his hand through his thick mass of hair. "Listen. I don't think it's going to be so hard for me today, literally. I gave *a lot* at the office earlier, if you know what I'm saying," Levi whispers conspiratorially.

"How? I mean, I didn't even think of it before, but how did you get past the Blood Lust?"

"They took it straight from my balls," and then he whispers, "three times."

"Oh God," I say, trying to hide the horror—and amusement—on my face.

"It's fine. I'm only saying that because, you know, I'm a little sore down there, not feeling especially amorous. I think it would be a good time to do some deprogramming."

I am anxious to go. I want to look for Ezra. I *need* to find him, but I offered up Levi's manhood juice for an alliance, *without his permission.* I owe him. "Okay, take a couple red pills—take three, in fact—and we'll get started in a few."

It doesn't take long for the rain to come. It pours down the way that only seems to happen in hot climates. The storm doesn't last long—maybe ten or fifteen minutes. After that, Levi had been right, the smell drifting down from the narrow entrance is incredible.

I smile at him broadly and he smiles back. "You did good, with the SenMachs," he tells me quietly as I lay out our sleeping mats and bags. I don't know if we'll actually sleep here, but it's a lot more comfortable than the dirt floor of the cave.

"Yeah?" I say as I put our weapons away, far away, out of reach.

"They could have kept us there. We could have left without anything. If we had followed my lead, we would have tried to fight our way out, unsuccessfully." I run my palm over my tricep. This is a big-time admission for Levi.

I think for a moment before I speak. "It's just the training. We aren't supposed to ask questions. They never wanted us to connect, really to anyone, not to each other and certainly not an Immigrant. They keep us isolated and suspicious and paranoid. It's how they maintain control. It's so much safer not to trust anyone. It could keep you alive, but it's no way to live."

Levi's shoulders slump. "I don't know, maybe you're just a better person than I am."

"No, Levi," I assure him as I step closer. "I just got a head start is all. I've had months where I wasn't just a Citadel, where I allowed myself to be an actual person. You'll get there. I'll help you."

"Just like Ezra helped you, right?" His tone has changed—it's challenging now. Was that really a question? Does he want me to deny that Ezra is a big part of my transformation?

"Yes" is all I can say. There is no room for Ezra in this cave. My sweet beautiful Ezra and the litany of words I could use to describe him don't belong here. Ezra has my heart, but Levi must have all my attention right now.

Sensing this boundary, Levi pulls out the tablet from his pack. We arrange ourselves on the sleeping bag and he props the tablet up a few feet in front of us on the ground. Our backs are up against the wall, which I imagine would be a lot more uncomfortable if I weren't wearing my suit. Levi has taken his off and has used his sensuit, not to dress as anything fun or historical but to put on shorts and a T-shirt.

In the flickering light of the lantern, the paintings seem to dance on the walls. It feels magical, like we are true explorers. Before we leave, I want to get some pictures. I took a few in the SenMach city, but not nearly as many as I would have liked to.

I guess that's a good thing, being so awed by a place that you forget how badly you might want to remember it one day. But now, I'm thinking Zaka might really enjoy seeing these.

Levi presses Play and I'm not too surprised that it's *The Incredibles*.

"I love this movie!" I tell him with a genuine smile.

"Yeah, it's my favorite animated film. I watched it a million times when I was a kid," he admits.

"The superhero thing, it makes sense and it's kind of ironic considering . . . you know . . . what we are."

"It's not that." Levi bites his bottom lip and looks away from me. "I liked it so much because it's about family. That even when bad shit happens, they stick together."

"I get it," I tell him softly, leaning in close to make sure that he understands that I really do. We start watching the movie. I haven't seen it in a while and we both laugh. It feels good to laugh together. About halfway through I tell him that I'm going to rub his scalp. I tell him to concentrate on the movie and relax. I promise that he's safe.

I move around him. He scuttles forward and makes space for me to be behind him. I put my fingers in his hair. At first I don't move. I just stay still so he can get used to this feeling. He doesn't tense or flinch, and I exhale softly. Slowly, I begin to dig my fingers into his head. I make tiny circles and apply just the right amount of pressure. His hair is soft and thick. I can see the bits of russet in it, reflecting the faint light bouncing off the rocks.

I move my hands down. I don't tell him I'm going to do this. Sometimes, anticipating touch can cause a kind of anxiety. I settle my hands on his shoulders and begin to massage them. I feel how tense he is. Not because I'm touching him, thankfully, but because, well, our lives are tense. I dig into his shoulders and press my thumbs between each scapula. I hear a small groan escape from his mouth. The sound unnerves me for a second; it's so primal and intimate.

My heart starts to race a little faster and I know he must hear it. I stop. But Levi softly takes my right hand and pulls it forward, holding it up against his cheek. What's happening here? I'm the one who's supposed to be controlling this situation.

This is for Ezra. This is for Ezra. This is for Ezra.

My heart picks up again as Levi takes my fingers and traces them along his face, over his eyelids, his cheekbone, and over his lips. I want to pull back, but I also want to lean in. It's too much, whatever is hanging in the room between us now, is heavier than it should be.

Then in one swift move, Levi reaches behind and lifts me up and over into his lap.

"Levi," I whisper, afraid to move against him, to move away, or at all. I know I should stand. I should tell him that this isn't a hookup, that it simply can't be that way, but I can't get my limbs to cooperate with my common sense. My body wants to stay exactly where it is.

"Shhhhh," he says, and he gently closes my eyelids with soft fingers. I feel his face coming closer to mine. Oh. My. God. He is going to try to kiss me. This cannot happen. I mean it could, I suppose, in a less sexy environment with me firmly in control, as part of the deprogramming. But this doesn't feel like deprogramming. This feels very, *very* real.

Instead of kissing me, though, Levi just rests his forehead against mine. We stay like that, breathing in time, shutting everything else out. How is this both totally right and completely wrong? And once more I think:

What's happening?

And then I hear something. The faintest, tiniest whistling noise. My eyes fly open and I look at Levi, who doesn't seem to hear it at all. At first I don't move so that I can hear the sound better. I focus. It's a whirling whistle. It reminds me of . . .

A Rift.

What? I put my forehead back on Levi's and the humming gets louder. Jesus Christ. The noise, as far as I can tell, is coming from *us*.

I jump up off of him. "I'm sorry," he says, but he doesn't sound all that sorry.

"No, it's not that. It's . . . don't you hear that sound? Like a humming or whistling?"

"Uhhh," Levi says, clearly confused. "Did something happen back there, when they were doing the medical stuff? Is it . . . *the robots*?" he asks.

I shake my head in frustration. I lower the zipper on my uniform a little—it feels like it's strangling me. "No. And don't call them that. And stop talking about the 'medical stuff,' I don't ever want to talk about that."

"Okay, okay." Levi throws his hands up and then leans over to rest on his side, propped up on his forearm. "You're probably just tired, with the interplanetary treaty you organized and the umm . . . you know, procedures or whatever. It's probably just the wind or something." Well, there is that slit of an opening to this cave. The sound may have come from that. "Look, let's eat something that isn't a gel cube and get a couple hours of sleep. No more than that, I promise, and then we can go."

"Okay," I say, filling my lungs with air, trying to clear my head.

"But that was good, right? We were doing good. I really think we made a, you know . . . a connection there before you freaked out."

"A connection?" I ask tentatively.

"Yeah. I felt it. You must have, too." Levi gets up and starts rummaging through his pack, presumably for food.

"I don't know if I'd use the word 'connection,'" I say, trying to laugh it off, though I'm afraid I know exactly what he's talking about.

Levi stops what he's doing. "Really? What word would you prefer me to use, then?" he asks.

"I don't know," I practically whine, internally berating myself for the tone, "one that doesn't feel so loaded."

"Fine, Ryn." Levi starts slamming things from his pack onto the ground. "Whatever *you* say."

Great. Now I feel guilty. I wonder just how many layers of guilt I can slather on today. We make our dinners separately in silence. Levi puts his headphones on and then I decide to do the same. These new earbuds, supplied by the SenMachs, just appeared with the rest of the stuff they handed over and are wireless. Knowing them, I'm sure they've linked our new computers to whatever music we brought with us. I tell my cuff to shuffle my playlists and sure enough, the Weeknd's sultry bass line begins to thrum in my ear. It's probably the last type of friggin' music I should be listening to, given that I'm in a romantically lit cave alone with Levi, but I let the song play out because I like it, and because honestly, this tension is weirdly exciting and the song is adding to it. I keep listening while I eat, locking my eyes firmly on the paintings covering the cave's walls, far away from Levi. The first few songs are ones I know I put on there. Then an instrumental song comes on that I've never heard before. It has a haunting melody and even an instrument or two that I can't say for sure what they are. This must be SenMach music.

When we finish eating, we clean up and I climb into my

sleeping bag. I tell my cuff to only play music by the Sen-Machs. A song begins, piano, some kind of string instrument. It's soothing. My eyes flutter closed, and before I fall asleep, I realize that Levi can't talk me out of what I know to be true. I heard something.

Something real.

CHAPTER 12

Our next jump lands us fifty yards away from railroad tracks. Right away I take a reading of the air. Just because there are signs of civilization doesn't mean the civilization is intact. In short order, we get a definitive answer as a train appears in the distance, moving impossibly fast. Levi and I step well away from the area, and in a matter of seconds, the train passes by. All we can see is a blur of stainless steel as the train speeds away, practically throwing us off balance even from a distance.

"Jesus. That was fast," I note, more to myself than Levi.

"Yeah. Let's get away from these tracks and head into that wooded area," Levi suggests while nodding his head in the direction we should go. "We can bring out the computers and get a read on where we are."

"Roger that," I tell him, and we start to run. We dart into a denser part of the terrain, moving quickly and quietly just in case we've been seen. When we get to an area with decent enough coverage and no view of the tracks, Levi stops and sits down, supporting his back against a tree. I kneel next to him on the densely packed earth.

Levi brings his pack around his shoulder and pulls out the sleek SenMach laptop. "Show us where we are." Instantly, the monitor pulls up a map of the Earth spinning.

"By the looks of that train, there's obviously technology here. The SenMach computer must be tapping into a satellite system," I say, even though Levi is probably not listening. When the image of the Earth stops spinning, we both lean in as the image zooms.

A flashing red dot lands in California, at least where California is on our version of Earth. "We're close to L.A., about fifty miles east. But if this was our Earth, we'd be in a neighborhood. I've been to L.A. It's huge, with dozens of suburbs," Levi observes.

"Let's send out the drones and see what's up, then," I tell him. At this point, he doesn't need to answer. We both just dip into our packs, and activate the silver disk drones and send them off.

"Show me the densest areas of population," Levi says to the computer, and we watch as purple dots begin to form on a map of North America. The population density looks much the same, although there are many more people living in this Canada than in our Canada. Actually, the population looks much more evenly distributed throughout the continent and, according to the purple dots, there at least a hundred million or so *fewer* people.

Pictures from the drones start to come in. Instead of the sleek art deco architecture you expect from L.A. or the super-

THE RIFT FREQUENCY \ 141

posh pretension of high-end Beverly Hills restaurants and shops, we see something else entirely. Every single building is neoclassical. Row upon row of white marble and brick buildings with porticoes and giant pillars. Some have domed roofs, some are trussed and tiled. There are cars, but there aren't any models I recognize. They aren't uniform, though, and just like on our Earth, some look nicer than others.

The streets are all much wider and there are people walking, which I've heard is rare for L.A. "Just show us pictures of people now," I say to the computer. Immediately, photos pop up on the screen. I scrunch my eyes to make sure what I'm seeing is right.

"Is that guy wearing . . . a toga?" Levi asks me in shock. As if the worst thing in the world a guy could do is wear a dress. But he's not wrong.

"A version of one," I say. "Sort of. Look at them all, though. It's a perfect mash-up of modern and ancient. The women are all wearing tops with empire waists, but the bottoms are shorts and they even have leggings. And look at the jewelry, the earrings especially: no hoops or studs, just dangly ones. Stop," I tell the computer, and the images immediately stop appearing on the screen. "Go back to the building where you took the seventeenth picture you sent." We wait for a few seconds and at first all we see are columns and then a giant toe. "Zoom out, but not too fast," I command. The drone does as I ask and I watch until I'm sure my suspicions are confirmed. The camera pans out to a skirt and then a face, a head covered by a helmet. The statue must be massive, at least fifty feet high. "It's a shrine. To Diana."

"So—" Levi begins, but I'm too excited. I interrupt him.

"Apparently this is an Earth where the Roman Empire never

fell! This is amazing! I mean, I get that there are different versions of Earth, obviously, but to actually see it, to witness it—it's living history, you know?"

"Well." Levi finally sits down and rests an elbow against his knee. "The Romans weren't exactly known for being warm and fuzzy," he mentions cautiously.

"Meh," I say, waving my arm. "We speak Latin *and* Italian. We'll be good. Besides, this isn't a military base or robot town. This is a real city. We can blend."

"I'd really rather not go charging into the Roman Empire if it's okay with you. Why don't you see if you can reach Ezra via an e-mail first." It's actually a good idea. Ezra and I had planned for a separation contingency. We set it up when he was still in the Village, before he even hid out at my house. Originally it was intended for use on my Earth, but I have to assume he'd use the same protocol on others. We would set up an e-mail account using the most popular free-access mail servers with a complex address made up of letters and numbers that no one would have used already. From there, we would just send e-mails to ourselves via that address.

There's one problem, though.

"You really think they have Google here? Or Hotmail?" I ask him sarcastically.

"You should try at least."

So I ask the computer to look for those sites, which surprisingly don't exist. There is an Internet here, but it's complicated. Each website seems to be for an individual family rather than a business.

"Look, there might be a free mail site, but we're going to have to ask someone. Let's just walk into town and find out. It's not like anyone will know who we are."

"Fine," Levi consents reluctantly as he stands, "but we

stick to the outlying areas. There's no need to go into the city proper. We find a coffee place or a bar where someone will answer our questions and then we leave right away. And no highborn nobility bullshit, either. Like you said, we want to blend in."

"I wasn't about to put on a ball gown. The rich-lady stuff is only when I'm in private. Or with you, which I guess is the same thing now." Levi doesn't respond. He just packs up our stuff and starts moving in the direction we saw the train headed. I put my computer away, too, and start to run.

"Come on, tough guy," I say as I pass him. "Let's book it." I know that Levi is stronger than I am, but I'm not so sure he's faster. I race over the uneven ground and I hear him just a fraction behind me. I'm not running full-out—there's no reason yet to find out which one of us is quicker. I don't need him to be even more pissy with me. Still, each time he comes close to passing me, I run a little farther ahead.

After twelve minutes, we've covered ten miles. I stop when I see a wide boulevard. There is a range of mountains in front of us, but there are also smaller hills, which are dotted with villas and what might be apartment buildings. Directly across from us, however, is a cluster of buildings that look like shops and a restaurant or two. The buildings ring a courtyard, and in the middle of it there's an ornate marble fountain on the green grass.

I quickly scan the immediate area to make sure no one is watching, but I avoid plain view anyhow behind a large syca-more. "Use the surveillance photos from the drones and dress me like a woman from here—an average woman. *Totally* aver-age," I tell my cuff, with a smug smile directed at Levi. I hear him do the same. I watch as the sensuit warps and slides over me. I am now wearing a long turquoise cotton dress, with an empire waist and tall gladiator-style sandals. I reach up and feel my head. My hair is now up in a fairly elaborate style with a couple of fat ringlets hanging down one side. All in all I look like I could be on my way to Sasquatch or Coachella. It's not a super-drastic change.

"Pants, thank God," Levi says when his sensuit is complete. He's wearing what look more like breeches than pants, really, and boots that come just under his knees with thick leather cords binding them on. His top is a plain knit navy sweater. It's a shame; I'd really been hoping to see him in a toga—or, more accurately, take a picture of him in a toga—but he lucked out.

"Hey look," I say, holding up my wrist, which is ringed in a purple design that looks like rows of alternating diamonds and dots, "I've got a tattoo and so do you. I guess that's what they do here." Levi looks at his wrist and grimaces. "Oh my God," I say as I tap my chest and shoulders. "Our packs! The sensuit doesn't hide our packs,"

"Well, I'm not leaving them here," Levi says quickly. "No way."

"It's going to look weird and make people notice us," I protest while looking down at my dress.

"People don't travel here? Or go camping?" I grimace and Levi relents. "Look, I'll take your pack, too—then it won't look so strange. Guys carry heavy shit all the time." When I don't look completely convinced, Levi makes another suggestion. "Just walk ahead and try to look normal, and by 'normal,' I mean, you know . . . pretty—not nerdy and all excited. If you can do that, no one will even notice me."

"Was that a compliment? Wow . . . ," I say, nodding my head and swishing the sides of my outfit. "You must really like this dress."

"Whatever, just give me your pack." I do as Levi asks, and

we walk briskly across the wide street. There are people here, but no one is looking at us. So far, so good. There are several boutiques, but Levi steers me to what looks like a bar, or more accurately, a tavern. There's a swinging carved wooden sign that says PLECTERE & OCIMUM. Translated, it means "braid and basil," which strikes me as an oddly hipsterish name to be seeing in the Roman Empire, but hey, what do I know?

Inside, the tavern is fairly large, doing good business with a heavy lunchtime crowd. There is exposed brick and wood beams, overall what you would expect in ancient Rome, but there are also flat-screen TVs above the bar. There are silk curtains sheltering more than a dozen individual booths, and the chairs and bar stools are upholstered in a rich studded velvet.

"People are staring at you," Levi hisses in my ear.

"Maybe they're staring at you," I whisper back. "You know there's no such thing as being gay with the Romans? Everybody sleeps with everybody," I tell him with a cheeky smile, which only earns me a worried look.

I walk up to the bar. The barkeep is a burly bald man with a light blue toga covered by an apron. He takes one look at us, particularly at our wrists, and slides down to the other end of the bar, where he leans in close to a customer and starts to talk.

Levi and I maneuver our way closer to the copper bar counter. I can feel the eyes of the patrons staring at me, taking me in. I make a tight fist without thinking and then quickly release it. Something is off. I look at Levi and I can see that he senses it, too. I wonder if the tattoos have marked us as minors, as children. Since I see no other patrons close to my age, I'm beginning to think that there is actually a drinking age here in the New World Roman Empire, which, to me, would be ridiculous.

I try to get the bartender's attention, but he barely looks

at me before continuing his conversation, ignoring my subtle hand signal. Maybe if I ask the guy seated in the bar stool next to me? I turn my head and he quickly whips his entire body around and says something in his neighbor's ear. Is this a members-only club?

I start to back away, and as I do, the bartender walks slowly toward us. "Where are you going?" he asks in Latin. Okay, something is definitely off here.

"Out. Nowhere," I tell him. The other patrons at the bar have all stopped talking. They are a mixed bunch, some in togas, others in more modern apparel like Levi's. There are a couple of women, too. They are older, in their fifties maybe. Their dresses are certainly not as nice as mine. The colors are duller and the fabric wrinkled and their hair is thrown up haphazardly without much actual styling. I watch their eyes land on my skin, then quickly dart away to focus on something else. The men, however, have no such demure compunctions. They stare at us with outright contempt.

"What are your names?" the barkeep demands. I don't like his interrogative tone. *At all.* But there are so many people here that, for now, I think it's best we play along. I scramble to come up with an old-school name that might make me sound like I belong here, kicking myself for not thinking we'd need them before we barged in here. Unfortunately, what I come up with is:

"Daenerys Targaryen, the First of Her Name, Queen of Meereen, Queen of the Andals and the Rhoynar and the First Men, Lady of the Seven Kingdoms, Protector of the Realm, Khaleesi of the Great Grass Sea, called Daenerys Stormborn, the Unburnt, Mother of Dragons. And this is . . ." I look at Levi, who is just shaking his head in frustration, "my companion . . . Joffrey Baratheon?"

The entire bar is silent now. I should have just gone with "Daenerys."

"So you're a queen?" the barkeep asks, barely able to keep from laughing.

"It's more of an unofficial title . . . like a fun term of endearment?"

Levi is gritting his teeth and holding on to the handles of our packs with white knuckles. I don't care. I'm not afraid of these people, and even though I need answers, the vibe in this place is so sketchy that I think asking about e-mail servers will only make things worse. It's time to hightail it out of here. But, *casually*, no need to get anyone further riled by the super-soldier-speed thing.

"And where are you from—*Your Majesty*?" he asks in a condescending tone.

"North," Levi answers in one short burst.

"I can see by your packs that you must have traveled a great distance. Why don't you sit down? I'll give you some water." It is a kind offer, but it doesn't sound the least bit kind coming out of his mouth. He's given us an order. I feel a gentle squeeze on the back of my arm. Levi is telling me it's time to go. I don't need to worry about the Blood Lust—his whole body is tensed, ready for a fight.

"No need. Thank you." Levi and I turn, and my adrenaline immediately starts to race when I see half a dozen police officers walk through the door.

Interesting.

Judging by the speed with which they have arrived, the bartender must have hit a panic button.

These new men are not dressed in togas but black pants and long black shirts covered by some sort of Kevlar breastplates. They're even wearing a modified version of legionary helmets, complete with nose guards. The effect, which should be intimidating, actually makes me laugh. They look like a bunch of dudes dressed up as Batman for a comic convention.

We walk slowly toward them. "Halt," one says, without hostility. He grabs my wrist and runs some kind of scanner over the diamond pattern. Shit. Not even the SenMachs could have seen this one coming.

"Under section 7 of the Slavery Act of New Rome, subsection 3.22, wherein no slave shall enter a restaurant, bar, tavern, or any other public business where food and drink is served, without his or her master or a representative of his or her master present, I am detaining you both."

An overwhelming surge of self-righteous indignation sweeps over me. This notion of ownership, of being forced against your will into a life you didn't choose, for the most arbitrary of reasons, unhinges me. It hits way too close to home. I know it's stupid to be outraged. I know it's not logical or particularly smart, but being here, right here in this moment, I want to show them all a thing or two about what real power looks like.

"You have slaves?" I say in disgust. "There are TVs over the bar!" I yelp, pointing wildly behind me. "You have cars. *There's an ATM machine in the corner* and you actually have *slaves*?"

Levi leans in and whispers in my ear, "If you're going to go into a whole 'I Have a Dream' speech, *Khaleesi*, now is not the time."

"What language is that?" another one of the police officers asks while pushing forward.

"English," I answer honestly. There's no point in lying now, and I'd rather buy some time trying to figure out how to get us out of here. Who can I take out first? Do I have to take them all out? Right now we're being arrested, presumably as runaway slaves, but that's a long way from murder. So, no killing. We just have to get outside long enough to open a Rift.

"Well, then, perhaps you are not slaves after all, but spies," threatens the same policeman. He might actually be scary if I *were* a slave, or a spy, but quite honestly, it's just amusing. He doesn't seem to think so. "You're coming with us, *now*." He grabs my arm and yanks it toward him.

Oh buddy.

"*Bad* idea."

I haul back and punch him in the throat. His helmet goes flying and I hear him struggling like a car engine being turned over, to take in oxygen. Another officer rushes me from behind, and I kick him so hard that he goes sailing all the way across the bar, landing on a table, which collapses under his weight.

The four remaining policemen scramble toward me. I punch one in the gut, and when he's doubled over, I flip him up and backward over my shoulder. Levi wants to get in on this, but he has both our packs and needs to stay out of the fray to keep them safe. For some reason that makes me happy—I don't want to share in kicking the crap out of people who protect slavery. Two more men grab me, one on each side. I quickly untangle my arms from their grasp and knock both their heads together.

I'm so focused on the few men I have between us and the door, I don't notice the one I had knocked into the table. I hear the gun go off and I spin around in time to see Levi reach for his neck, a tranq dart sticking out between his fingers.

Motherfucker.

I can't say I'm particularly surprised. Slaves are valuable

commodities—much too valuable to just shoot or Taser, which might kill them. A tranq dart, though, is something safe. It's also something you would use on animals.

Humanity is really disgusting sometimes.

I watch as Levi's eyes roll back into his head and he drops to the ground. I'm breathing wildly now. I can pick up my partner and get us out of there, but I don't think I'll make it, not with the rest of the men starting to recover from the deliberately low-key damage I've dealt out.

"Fine," I say, holding up my arms in a gesture of surrender. "I'll go with you. Peacefully. You don't need to shoot." I'm worried about our packs. We need to keep them with us or, at the very least, know where they are.

By way of an answer, one of the policemen takes out a tranq gun and shoots me right in the neck at close range. I let him, thinking, *What else can I do? Kill everyone here?*

"As a slave you cannot dictate the terms of your surrender," I hear him say as my brain grows a thick coat of fur. My tongue sticks to the roof of my mouth and I try to stay on my feet, but gravity seems to have accelerated. The next second I'm on the floor and then . . . nothing.

CHAPTER 13

I come to slowly. The room is sideways.

No, I'm sideways.

I slowly pull myself up. I blink hard, trying to adjust my vision. I'm lying on a cot, and there is drool on my tiny, hard pillow.

Lovely.

Levi is sitting on the edge of the same bed. He is staring at a plastered wall, which is pockmarked and covered with deep gouges. We are in a cell. Black iron bars run the entire length of the right side of the small space. I crack my back and stretch out my neck.

"Excellent—she is awake," I hear from a booming voice shouting down the hallway behind the bars. I glance quickly over to Levi, who has his eyebrows raised.

"Watch it, Ryn. Okay?"

I nod. He must be royally pissed that we didn't get out of that bar the second we felt something was off. That, and the fact that I went a little overboard with the whole *Game of Thrones* thing. I couldn't help it. It's hard to take these people seriously with so many of them wearing sheets and having legit laurels in their hair. Besides, we would have gotten away easily enough if Levi hadn't insisted we bring our packs with us. The two of us could have neutralized that entire unit with minimal injuries, but instead we coddled our supplies. We treated them like they were more precious than our own personal safety. Maybe. Truth is that we never should have come in here in the first place, at least without doing more than five seconds of recon. I guess I got a little ahead of myself here. Won't be making that mistake again.

The man with the loudly magnificent voice shows up in front of the bars with what I can only assume—based on their dress and tattoos—to be two slaves in attendance.

Gross.

These guys are wearing very little clothing. Also gross, but also kinda hard to look away from, given that they pretty much look exactly like what you'd think of when you think "Roman slave": tall, muscular, with a bondage-y type of leather thong covering their chests. They also look similar, as if they could be brothers, both blond with piercing blue eyes that they keep focused straight ahead. They do not look at me or Levi.

One of them is holding a small upholstered chair, which he places down gently in front of the bars. Unfortunately, it's not close enough for us to make a grab for the man who will presumably be sitting there. The first thing I notice about the slave owner is that—like his slaves—he is not unattractive. I would put his age at midthirties. His short brown hair is cropped close to his scalp but clearly styled to look a little bit ruffled. His toga is a heavy, luxuriant royal blue. I remember that we are in "Los Angeles," and if we were in the L.A. on our Earth, this guy might be an agent or a manager or have some other similar job that requires white teeth and a slick tone.

Which meant that if it wasn't for the fact that he had us in a jail, I'd *still* hate him.

The man sits down and then dismisses his slaves with a flick of both wrists and the two stand back against the far wall. He doesn't want to be crowded, but clearly he doesn't quite want to be alone with us.

"First things first: introductions. I'm Faustus Mallius Majus. And you are?" Levi and I don't speak. We just glare at him. After a few seconds he shrugs his shoulders. "Fine. It's no matter to me, since I'm giving you new names anyhow. You," he says, pointing at Levi, "you will be Hector, and you, sweet thing"—he gestures toward me—"you will be Honoria." Faustus waits for some kind of reaction, and when he gets none, he continues to be unconcerned. "I am the lanista here." Levi and I both look at each other. Levi grits his teeth and gives an almost imperceptible shake of his head. We both know our history. We both know what a lanista does.

They manage gladiators.

"Excellent," Faustus says. "So, you know who I am and what I do, and what *you* will be asked to do." Faustus gives a small, snide chuckle. His lips widen, but he does not show even a single tooth. "I suppose that 'ask' is the wrong word here, given the circumstances. What you will be *made* to do is more accurate." Levi grips the iron bar of the bed and I tilt my head in a gesture of warning. "I know that you are not slaves. Though I can't for the life of me understand why you would mark yourselves as such." Again, we say nothing and once again, our silence leaves him undeterred.

"Thankfully for you, our police force here in Solis Littus is . . ." Faustus looks up to the ceiling and circles a single man-icured finger as he searches for the right word. "Open," he finally drawls, in a voice that somehow sounds both bored and snide at the same time, "to alternate avenues of compen-sation. As soon as the sergeant showed me the footage of your tavern escapade he knew full well what I would pay him to get you. You should be flattered. It was a small fortune."

I blink my eyes lazily. I am angry at myself for being so stupid, for allowing myself to get wrapped up in the history of it all, for forgetting that I am a soldier first. Just like the real L.A., Solis Littus is seductive and dangerous. I look at Faustus, my eyes burning.

"Nothing? Still?" he says with a long frustrated sigh. "I looked inside your bags." Both Levi and I whip our heads around, our eyes meeting in distress. "I thought that might get your atten-tion," Faustus tells us. "You know, the *vigilum ministri* who ar-rested you believe that you are children of the gods, given your strength and speed."

I struggle to keep my eyes firmly locked in place, straight ahead. Demigods? Like Percy Jackson? I guess in this world that would make more sense than genetically altered super soldiers.

"I am not a religious man," Faustus continues, "or a political one. I don't care where you come from. I don't care if you are the children of Jupiter himself, Ottoman spies, or visitors from another planet." Faustus leans in closer, as close as he dares, mindful of our reach. "The only thing I care about is the show. The spectacle and the money it will make . . . *for me.*"

"And if we don't fight?" I ask grimly.

"Ah—you *do* speak." He smiles, but there is no warmth. "Then I turn you and your belongings over to the authorities."

"Where are our bags now? And how can we be assured that you will keep them out of curious hands?" I demand.

"You have no assurances. You are my property, and that's all that matters. But I will tell you the bags are safe. So," he says as he stands. The two blond men scramble to pick up the chair and push themselves back against the wall. "I will safeguard your rather peculiar personal items and you will fight for me. Win enough fights and you will win your freedom. Once the people see you tonight, I expect we'll be sold out for weeks. Do we have a deal?"

Levi and I both stand. Levi keeps his hands at his sides. I fold mine, one over the other as if I'm still considering. I take my time before answering, only because I know the longer I do, the more irritated I'm sure Faustus will get. Finally, after a minute or two, I relent.

"You have your deal."

"Somehow, I rather thought I might." I feel a desire to rip the smug right off his face with my fingernails, but he is still too far away. "You will now swear the *sacramentum gladitorum* before me," Faustus says. He then proceeds to say some bizarre, long-winded oath, which Levi and I repeat in deadpan voices. Like a stupid Latin oath means anything to us. When we're finished, he slaps one of his slaves on the wrist, and the man produces a document from a brown leather messenger bag that he had slung across his back. "This is your *auctoramentum*. It is a legal and binding contract, which now states that you belong to me. Caeso!" he yells, and the slave with the bag steps timidly forward. "Hand these documents over to our new friends so that they may sign them." Caeso retrieves a pen from his bag and then, with his entire body shaking, he steps toward the bars. His trembling hands reach forward. The papers he is holding slap against each other like dead leaves under boot soles. I walk slowly toward him. "*Noli timere*," I tell him kindly. "*Omne bene erit*." Caeso gives me the briefest of smiles and hands over the papers.

Levi and I don't even bother to read them. As with the oath, it's amazing for anyone to think a friggin' contract could actually keep us here. It's not as if we're not honorable, but these people are slave owners who probably want to feed us to the lions (real ones, not metaphorical ones). So I will play along until we get our chance to escape. As we are signing, we hear Faustus yelling at the other, unnamed slave to go get our armor. Levi looks up in alarm.

"Just armor?" he says. "What about our weapons? We might die before you get a chance to earn your money back."

At that, Faustus belly laughs. He doubles over and then, for dramatic effect, pretends to wipe tears from his eyes to further illustrate how funny he thinks Levi is.

"My dearest boy. I doubt very much that this *female* is your bodyguard. I've seen what she can do with her bare hands, so I can only imagine what you're capable of. You think I'd allow you to have weapons? Around the audience? Please—I have their safety to think about." We can still hear him laughing, the snarky chortles echoing down the hall long after he's left.

In short order the other slave returns, his arms full of clothing and metal. He's also accompanied by no fewer than a dozen guards who have rifles aimed at our heads. So much for escaping that way. The iron gate of a door is unlocked. The slave throws the items inside, takes up our signed contracts, and then rushes away from us as fast as he can.

"You have two hours to prepare yourselves," he says bravely, if not boldly, and then as quickly as they arrived, they are gone, the soldiers marching along the stone floor in two precise columns.

Levi wordlessly draws my attention to a camera inside the cell. So, that prick Faustus is watching our every move. Neither one of us is about to give him any clues as to where we're from or who we are.

We sit silently on the bed side by side. We excel in this. Waiting. Waiting for a Rift to open. Waiting for an enemy to emerge. In the rain, the heat, in booming thunderstorms, we hold our positions like human statues. Two hours is nothing.

An hour later, small flakes of plaster begin to fall from the ceiling like snow. Our cell vibrates with shuffling feet from the stadium above. Levi and I are no strangers to killing. As Citadels we try to kill cleanly, efficiently, but never like this. Never for anything but self-defense. Never for *amusement*. This is the darkest side of humanity: pain for sport, violence for escape. I try to recall everything I know about what history has said about gladiators, at the same time trying to ignore what I've seen in movies or read in books.

The one good thing I remember is that it was rare for a gladiator to actually die in combat. Gladiators are, as Faustus mentioned, a sizable investment. The lanista had been surprisingly astute by withholding weapons. We *can* take down our opponents with our bare hands. We have that kind of strength. What we don't have is numbers. If we are asked to fight a dozen others, we can manage. If it's two dozen, we will be overwhelmed. We can still win, but the chances of us doing so without killing anyone are statistically smaller.

From a speaker outside our cell we hear them. The crowd is cheering. It is an ocean of voices and chants. When they begin to stomp their feet in unison we don't need the speaker. The hammering pounds above our heads are like thunderous drums. The ceiling flakes off in bigger chunks.

We hear as the first gladiators go on. An announcer provides a gruesome play-by-play. It's two against two, and apparently these men have swords. The crowd is whipped into a frenzy when one of the men is pinned. His partner cannot get to him in time and, according to the announcer, the trapped man's leg is run through. Apparently there is blood on the ground, a lot of blood. I wonder if this was calculated, or if an artery was actually severed. The unharmed half of the team seems to be overwhelmed with the need for revenge, and we listen as the announcer recounts the brutal force of his attacks on his opponent. The two continue to fight, alone, which is good, as it means this is clearly for show. Otherwise, there's no way the uninjured guy would allow his partner to be left vulnerable.

One thing I realize as we listen to the description of the battle is that they have shields. Which, after looking briefly at the ridiculous outfits they want us to wear, we notice we *don't* have. The announcer is now screaming a steady stream of action. It sounds like a fairly intense fight. And then . . . silence. Not just the announcer, but the audience. Before we can ask each other what we think has happened, the announcer excitedly yells, "A knife!" As his account grows in detail, it turns out the man whose partner had been injured had just stabbed the other one in the abdomen with a knife. From the sound of the over-the-top announcing style, the whole thing feels more like some kind of Mexican wrestling match, except now I know that they are fighting for real. Maybe not to the death, but certainly to the point of a mortal injury.

So, even if we win, we lose.

I pull the blanket off the bed and cover my entire body. I whisper quietly into my wrist. "Cuff," I say, and the sensuit retracts. I am now only in my uniform. They can make me fight, but they cannot dress me like Xena. No way. I throw the blanket at Levi, who does the same. Now we are both in full

Citadel gear. I'm sure the people monitoring our cells have no clue what just happened.

I can live with that.

After a few more minutes we hear the slap of boots on stone. A column of soldiers (Are they actual centurions? Or muscle-for-hire mercenaries? I suppose it doesn't matter) is marching down the hall toward our cell. We could make a break for it, but I make eye contact with Levi, implicitly warning him that now is not the time. They haven't really seen what we can do. We need them to be afraid of us if we want to get out of here without murdering dozens of people. We also need Faustus—and more importantly, our gear—and he's definitely going to be watching the action.

The cell door is opened by what looks like a proper Roman guard, but there's no way of knowing in this ridiculous place, where everything is for show. We allow them to lead us through a maze of hallways. I know that Levi is memorizing our steps just as I am. We pass by dozens of cells with other gladiators. They barely glance up as we walk by. Some of these cells are much nicer than our barren one. Some have carpets and proper beds. Some of them even have TVs and wardrobes. I wonder how high you have to move up the gladiatorial ladder not to be imprisoned at all. I wonder how much Stockholm syndrome–ing that takes.

The sound of the crowd gets louder as we move up a level. I've never actually been to the Colosseum in Rome, but from the pictures I've studied, it looks much the same as this one. Pits for people and animals in the basement and two large entryways for the participants to walk out into the arena. It's weird how similar this is to modern-day sporting venues. Not that I actually watch any sports with regularity, other than some of my brother's high school events, but sometimes the only way I get to hang out with him and my dad is when they're watching football.

I see less body paint at the moment, but otherwise, seems about the same.

The announcer makes up some long, fake-ass story about me and Levi. We are now apparently orphaned twins (despite the fact that we look nothing alike) who washed up on the shores of the Pacific, the sole survivors of a deadly shipwreck. We have been blessed by Neptune and are imbued with his strength. We stop at the opening of the tunnel, which leads to the arena floor. It is early evening and a single star flashes in the sky. I look out at the crowd. There are thousands of people in the stands. Tens of thousands. I don't even need to look over to Levi to know that he's thinking the same things I am. We do this *one time*. We perform like the freaks we are and give them the show of their lives. Shock and awe so that we can distract our guards long enough to get the hell out of here.

The first row of spectators ring the entire coliseum and are close enough to actually touch. They look wealthy and mostly bored. I notice there are quite a few children in this VIP section as well. What assholes these people are. Music begins, a thumping bass drum and electric guitars. This really is a show. I bet there will be fireworks at some point.

I see Faustus sitting in the front row, in a seat that is closest to the large archway. He opens a small metal gate so that he can meet us in the alcove without actually having to go out to the arena.

"What's this?" he screeches with alarm, his hands flapping around like he's conducting an invisible orchestra. "Where are the costumes I provided for you?" He says it so petulantly I half expect him to stomp his feet.

"This is what we wear when we fight," I tell him in a tone

dripping with aggression. He takes a step back and casually raises an eyebrow as he looks us up and down. I suddenly feel like the girl who has to wear her mom's old dress (and not in a cool, retro way) to prom.

"On him, I suppose it will do. But on you," Faustus tuts in my direction, "it's tight enough, but your tits, they aren't even showing in the slightest. Can't you at least undo the zipper so I can tell that you're a woman?"

It takes every single ounce of self-control I have not to grab him by the dick and yank his balls off. Levi is actually growling. As much as I would like to kill this man, I know that we need him to get our stuff and get out of here. To that end, it's crucial that he believes that he's in control of us and this situation.

I slowly pull the zipper down till it's just past my sports bra. I smile as I lift each boob up so that now, I have (as much as a sports bra will allow) some cleavage. "Those are adequate, not spectacular. Perhaps we should think about implants," Faustus says as he examines my chest without enthusiasm.

"Having bigger boobs has always been a dream of mine, so that would be great," I tell him with a broad smile, though my molars are clenched and my fists are balled so tightly that I'm afraid the skin on my knuckles will crack open.

"Excellent. Now, if you don't die, we'll have a lovely, big celebration to honor your first victory." And with that he gives Levi a little punch on the shoulder and walks back to his seat. If ever there was a King of the Douches, I'm pretty sure that title would go to Faustus. Even his *gaze* was slimy and it's a real struggle to stop myself from gagging. Luckily—or not, I suppose—the announcer calls us forward.

We enter the arena. The crowd is screaming. The music is blaring. Levi and I walk slowly toward the middle of the space, which is much larger than I thought it would be. I guess it's the size of a football field. We keep our eyes locked on the black hole of the opposite archway, waiting for our opponents.

"And now . . . ," the announcer says with building anticipation, "from the bowels of Hades, plucked from the pages of history itself, two of the most vile and evil creatures ever to walk the Earth. First: You know him from the Labyrinth of Crete . . . Here. Is. The. Minotaur!"

The arena goes wild.

Uhhh. Wait a minute . . .

"Second—but second to none—here she comes: the most fearsome Gorgon, a woman so ugly that a mere glimpse turned her foes to stone—a power we have neutralized by ripping out her eyes. But she doesn't need to see you to *kill* you . . . The wretched, the terrible . . . Medussssaaaaa!"

Levi and I look at each other with a frown. What the hell is going on? Can these morons turn people into monsters? Like, is it a Frankenstein thing? Shit. Or maybe these two were born deformed. I wouldn't put it past the New Romans to stick them in a place like this. However big the arena, it's still a circus sideshow.

We hear them before we see them. Whir. Pound. Stop. Whir. Pound. Stop. The two emerge from the exit across from us. They are at least fifteen feet high. The Minotaur, half bull half man, is made entirely of copper. I can't help it. I almost want to laugh.

"*What is it* with us and fucking robots?" Levi says, more annoyed than afraid.

"Let's just be grateful that we don't have to kill anyone," I say as I stand my ground. Behind the metal beast comes the chrome Medusa. Her sound is different, quieter, but buzzing with electricity nonetheless. Her body is clothed in a silver dress of chain mail and her head is covered in dozens of mechanical snakes, each one made of what looks like thousands of soldered nickel scales that oscillate and whir in every direction.

A hush descends on the crowd. The music stops and we both freeze, holding still and tense to size up our opponents. We have no weapons, no guns or knives to take down these machines. We have only our bare hands. We will have to rip them apart. Of all the things I thought I would do in my life, I can safely say that kicking the crap out of clockwork mythological creatures is one that never occurred to me.

"I'll take her," I tell Levi, pointing at Medusa. "Just make sure Faustus follows us out of the arena when we are done. If he doesn't, then one of us is going to have to grab him." Levi gives me the briefest of nods and we begin.

I take a step back, putting the majority of my weight on my left foot, and then push forward, running at full speed. There's not that much distance between us and the metal monsters, but there's enough for me to get sufficient leverage to jump. I jump so high the crowd gasps, then cheers. I have to admit—it *is* a bit of a thrill to hear thousands of people roaring in approval of something I've done. I land on Medusa's shoulder and scramble up the back of her neck, reaching up and yanking out one of her snakes with relative ease. Instead of dying, as I assumed it would without being attached to a power source, the snake wraps around my arm and nips at my neck with its needlelike fangs. I can feel blood trickle down the side of my suit. It's not a good sign at all that each piece of whatever the hell these things are doesn't seem to need to be connected to the whole in order to inflict damage.

I manage a quick glimpse at Levi as I pull the serpent from my arm and begin to break it into parts. It looks as though he ran at the Minotaur as well, but instead of clambering up it as I did, he must have given it a good kick, as the thing is down. It's not out, though; I can see it maneuvering its way back to its feet with an ease that I wouldn't normally credit with something as lumbering as a giant machine.

I am still on top of Medusa's head, but she is beginning to rattle and shake now. I hear the gears inside her spin as her neck whips from one side to the other in an attempt to get me off. Worse, the snakes have turned in my direction, each one striking at me with precision and speed. They try to bite through my uniform, which thankfully, they can't. As long as I can avert my face and my stupid cleavage, I'll be okay.

The thrill is wearing off rapidly.

And then I feel a cold metal hand grip my arm, and it's gone completely. Without the protection of my suit and the resilience of my muscles, I'm sure my arm would have broken. Still, it hurts, and I wince as the fingers clamp down even harder. She has me now and she throws me off her with brutal force, flinging me into the air. I land in the dirt, skidding at least five feet into the side of the ring. Enough of this. I quickly zip up my uniform all the way. One of those snakes could actually slither down inside my bra and do some serious damage. I'll just have to make every move from here on out sexier than ever, which is gross. I do a back handspring in the air and am upright in an instant.

The first row of spectators is close enough for me to reach out and grab one of them if I wanted to. They are screaming, cheering me on. Or jeering at me. Either way, I'm done with deriving excitement from their reactions. Now I'm just in survival mode.

And then, even through the incredible din of the crowd, I

hear that same screeching whistle I heard in the cave. Unlike the cave, though, this is much, much louder. It's so loud it almost hurts. I whip my head around and see that it's one of the audience members in the front row. It's a man, covered completely in the mantle of a toga. He's brought the neck of the material up and around so that his face is shrouded. I'm sure the sound is coming from him because there is something about him that doesn't *feel* right. His body seems wrong somehow, and I think he has a beard, which the men here most certainly do not.

The scene distracts me so much that I don't hear Medusa coming. She bats me with incredible force, and once again I am lifted up in the air, but this time, instead of landing on the ground, I spin and somersault so that I land right-side up in a crouch, ready to pounce. This move brings the crowd to its feet. I look to Levi again. He has managed to wrestle one of the horns from the Minotaur's head and is using it as a weapon. He's stabbing at the metal so fast and so hard, sparks are flying. It won't be long now till he punches a hole straight through and rips out its metallic guts, so now I really have to end this thing.

I size up my opponent once more. The snakes are a problem, and I realize it would be easiest for me to disable Medusa herself first. So I run at her at full speed again, but this time when I get close enough—instead of jumping—I slide my entire body down and knock her off balance. She sails backward and lands with a clink, dust flying around her. The crowd is stomping now and screaming in a frenzy. I grab hold of one of her silver feet. I can see where she's been pinned and fastened together—as if her body is living flesh, she has joints that bend and move as ours do. I manage to get both hands around her giant ankle even as she is bending up toward me. She's a boss bitch, no doubt, but I'm faster. I use all the strength I have and pull. I finally manage to separate her foot from her calf.

Medusa is sitting up now and she plunges forward, reaching for my neck. I take the foot I have in my hand and start to hit her arm. I really wail on it, making dents, hitting so hard that I hear a crack, followed by a satisfying dull hiss as her elbow separates from her forearm. She can still hit me, hard, but she can't strangle me. And that's not nothing.

I quickly shift back down and grab for her other foot. She is not going to make it so easy for me this time, though. Medusa starts to flail, so I have to basically sit on her shin, which is about as uncomfortable as you might think it would be. She cuffs me in the ribs with her good hand, which makes me pant but doesn't stop me from my task. I start to wrench the foot from the leg. I pull and pull, the thinner pieces of metal from the giant ankle cutting into my fingers. Finally, I hear a crack and the foot is off.

The snakes continue to nip at my uniform, a couple even get at my scalp. I reach back and yank as hard as they do, prying them off Medusa's head and then bending them up in a pretzel shape when I get them. I pitch forward now and run, putting some distance between me and the Gorgon. The audience is like thunder. Their fevered roars bounce between the massive space of the coliseum. They love this. They can't get enough of it, and it disgusts me. What if I *had* been an orphan? Some poor girl brought in by the tide? Would they still love it so much? To see a young woman ripped limb from limb by a machine? Probably.

Fuck them. I hate this Earth.

And who is the humming man? *What* is he? There's only one thing I can think of that might make sense, though it really makes no sense at all. He's not from this Earth, either. I feel it in my gut. He doesn't belong here, and somehow, I can actually hear it. How in the hell is that happening?

Medusa rolls to one side and attempts to make her way toward me. Without any feet, she stumbles and trips, unaware that she can no longer walk. Regardless, she keeps getting up, tries to continue her macabre march, then falls down again. It's almost funny for a moment, but then something changes in her programming, or some other protocol takes over, and instead of trying to walk, she starts crawling in the dirt. It's like a Roman Terminator, and it's starting to piss me off.

I look over to see that Levi has managed to break through the copper breastplate of the Minotaur and has his hand inside the machine. He starts to pull wires and parts from the torso. While I can see it's effective in stopping the Minotaur, it's not good enough for what we need to be doing. The crowd wants more. They want the show they paid for, not some dude disassembling a robot. And while I could give zero fucks about this crowd, we need them on our side because we need *Faustus* on our side. We need to get him to believe we are the greatest thing that's ever happened to him so he will do as he promised and meet us personally when this is over—and with his guard down.

So I wait for Medusa to get to me. I put my arms at my hips like Superman and give the metal monstrosity the best death glare I've got. She finally reaches me and the snakes start nipping at my boots. I ignore them, and somersault myself past them so that I land standing over her. I lift up my foot and stomp it down hard on her giant neck. It not only makes a dent, but I can see that the dozens of individual plates that let her swing her head back and forth are damaged beyond what she is capable of overcoming. I keep my black boot where it is and reach down, allowing the snakes to slither up my arms. They are making this next part more difficult certainly, but not impossible. In fact, it's only adding to the drama as they take pieces of my cheek and neck in tiny chunks.

I grit my teeth at the razor-sharp nips while I slip both my hands down Medusa's smooth silver jaw. When I get to her chin I start to pull. My foot is going one direction and my arms are going another. Medusa's head is huge, at least three feet wide. It doesn't matter. I know how strong I am. I heave with all my might and then the metal rips and the head is off. I don't start celebrating, though, because like the Gorgon she was named after, decapitation doesn't mean she's harmless. The serpents continue to coil and strike. I swing the head around and around and throw it hard.

It crashes into the wall on the other side of the arena.

Every one of the spectators is yelling our names now—or, rather, the names Faustus gave us—along with their ovation. Yet it still isn't enough. I can tell by their fevered screams the crowd wants more. That we haven't put enough theater into this spectacle. I know Levi just did what he always does—take down an opponent with efficiency and speed. But gladiators don't do that—beloved ones don't, anyhow. And right now, I need this audience to fall in love with Hector and Honoria.

I raise my hands to the audience, showing them the raw and bloody appendages. I spin, slowly, and then take my palms and wipe them across and down my face until my now-wild eyes are surrounded by a gruesome mask of blood. I let out a Valkyrie-like scream, which the spectators answer with a roar of their own. I look over to Levi and give a little nod until he does the same. I pump my arms above my head, whipping the crowd into even more of an ecstatic pitch. The music starts again. This is more like it. I give myself a running jump so that I can flip and spring across the arena as if I'm doing a gymnastic floor routine. I make sure to land right in front of Faustus, where I drop to give him the most subservient of curtsies.

When I look back up, he is grinning like a madman. Levi must have done some fancy parkour of his own, because he is now beside me, bowing.

We nod and wave to the cheering crowd before walking to the exit of the arena. Like I had hoped, Faustus has leaped over his little fence and has met us in the tunnel.

Unfortunately, there are also a dozen guards.

"Marvelous!" he says, his eyes filled with savage delight. "I have never seen anything like it, nor has this audience, I can tell you. You both are destined to become the most famous gladiators of all time."

I smile meekly as if his praise actually means something to me.

"I'm glad you're pleased," I tell him. He is beside me now, his head so full of thoughts of celebrity and money that he has clearly forgotten what we are. Or maybe he is just so full of himself and his own sense of self-importance that he truly believes we belong to him, that we'll play by the rules that he assigned us.

We all walk farther down into the bowels of the coliseum. Faustus is rambling, making plans as we descend the stairs. Once we are at the bottom I lean in close to him. Not so close that our armed escorts will be alarmed, but close enough so that only he will be able to hear me. Levi is behind me, effectively blockading Faustus and me from the others.

"Keep walking. You will take us to our packs now, *alone*, or my brother and I will kill every single person here, including you," I tell him, all the while keeping the same sickly sweet smile on my face. "Don't even think about raising an alarm. I can snap your neck in under two seconds."

Though we don't stop moving, I hear an audible gulp, and Faustus's face drains of color as he finally sees the error he's made. He looks into my eyes—and the blood smeared over my face—and the look I give him in return promises that he will most certainly die if he does not do as I've instructed.

"All of you can remain here," he says to the guards. "I am taking these two to my private quarters so that we may toast to their victory." He does not sound scared, though his hands tremble. I am not surprised that he is such an amazing liar.

"But, sir—" one of them tries to say, but Faustus cuts him off before he can continue.

"Do you think me stupid, Albertus?" Faustus snaps back with venom. "Do you think that I would put my own life at risk if I thought these two were a threat to me? They understand how important I am here." Faustus addresses me directly now, his oily words serving as their own kind of promise. "They are aware that I am responsible for employing hundreds of people. They know that I am a husband and a father. They also know that I satiate the public. I keep the violence in the arena as opposed to the streets of our fair city. These two have honor. They will not harm me." Faustus begins to walk briskly to his office and Levi and I match his stride. The guards do not attempt to follow. I exhale a silent sigh of relief. Of course I would have killed them all, but I didn't want to. I never *want* to.

When we arrive at Faustus's office he swiftly unlocks the large and thankfully very thick door (although I shudder to think what he does inside that would require the thing to be practically soundproof) and ushers us both inside with a sweep of his arm. As soon as he shuts the door, he starts in.

"Let's get one thing straight here, you ungrateful shits. You will never threaten me again. You will never make demands of me. You will never—" Levi cuts him off with a swift but effective punch to the nose. Faustus reels back, blood spurting everywhere.

"You hit me!" he cries in disbelief.

"Get our things," Levi orders.

"But . . . but . . . you *hit* me!"

Levi and I both look at each other in amused disbelief. What an arrogant little prick this guy is. Did he not see what we did out there?

"No shit," Levi says.

"Get. Our. Things," I say with a steely calm.

Faustus throws up a single hand, and with the other grabs the drape of his toga to hold up against his nose in an effort to stop the bleeding. "Fine," he relents as he walks toward a large metal door with some kind of keypad on it. "I suppose you deserve to have your belongings returned to you even though the repair of our mechanical fighters will cost me thousands." It dawns on me at that moment that he still doesn't get it.

Wow—some people . . .

He moves to the door, which also must be a safe, in the corner. The keypad is unlocked with a numerical code—Roman numerals, of course. Faustus twists a handle and the door swings open. It's a small space, filled with various things including our two large packs. Levi brushes past him and gets our bags, which are much heavier than usual because we stored our rifles and utility belts in there before I got my genius plan to ask the citizens of the New Roman Empire about e-mail services. When Levi throws me my pack, I retrieve our weapons and Faustus actually tries to stop me. "Not *those*. You can't walk around here with guns, the guards won't allow it."

"We're not going to walk around," Levi tells him coldly.

"What do you mean? Wait—you don't actually think you're leaving, do you? That you'd even get out of here alive?" Faustus lets out a chortle. "You *belong* to me. You're slaves, and after tonight, your faces will be everywhere. There isn't a misbegotten corner of this city you'll be able to hide in. That's not even the point. You wouldn't make it out the front door. I don't think you fully grasp your situation."

I swing around in a flash and grab Faustus by the throat. I push him against the wall and squeeze my fingers. "I *know* you don't grasp the situation. And you're clearly too stupid to understand an explanation. So instead, I'm going to ask you a question, and I am only going to ask you this one time: Did you take anything from these packs? Because I am going to look inside and if anything is missing, you will die."

Faustus's eyes widen in true terror. There it is. *Now* he gets it. He is not in charge. He begins to shake his head. "That's interesting," I say softly, "because if I met two people like us—if I *bought* two people like us, I'd want to know as much about them as I could. You sure you don't want to change your answer?" I release the pressure from his neck ever so slightly so he can speak.

"No time," he croaks. "I only took a brief look. Too much to organize. Was going to . . . later . . . tonight." I suppose that makes sense, but in any case I tell Levi to check the packs. He rifles through them and then gives me a nod to let me know that everything is there. I release Faustus but shove him hard enough so that he falls to the floor. Levi hands me my things and I put my belt on and secure the backpack.

I lean down to Faustus, who is cowering on the floor. "You're very lucky," I tell him. "You are about to witness something that few people ever have. Truthfully. *We are* children of the gods." Levi does a double take at my words, but I ignore him. I am not going to kill this douche bag, but maybe I can scare him enough to rethink his stance on human trafficking. "The gods are most displeased with this soulless place, and with you, Faustus Mallius Majus. The gods abhor slavery. All men and women are equal in the eyes of the gods. They are sickened by this violence. If you do not change, one day soon there will be a reckoning, and this city—this *civilization*—will fall."

Faustus's eyes bulge in fear. I smile as benevolently as I am able and then I speak softly into my bracelet. "Rift," I begin to say into my cuff.

"Wait," Levi says suddenly in English. "We didn't see if Ezra was here."

"He would never have stayed. There's no way he could have blended in with what he was wearing. He doesn't speak Latin. And, without any kind of free e-mail service, or at least one that's easy to access, I'm pretty confident he would have moved on."

"Are you sure?"

"Yeah. I have to put a little faith in him. He *is* a genius, after all."

Levi rolls his eyes, but doesn't say anything.

"Seriously, I think chances are he was never even here. I didn't think it through," I admit reluctantly.

"Okay," Levi says, without any of his usual rancor, which is refreshing but a little strange.

"Rift. Ezra," I tell the cuff, and the Rift opens with a screaming green brilliance that's almost impossible to look at. Faustus looks at the Rift and us and then scrambles up to his knees, praying and bellowing, begging for our forgiveness. He clutches the fabric of my uniform and I step away before he can really touch me. Levi just rolls his eyes and grabs my arm. It's time to go. Without looking back, my partner and I step through the emerald wave and are gone.

CHAPTER 14

We walk out of the Rift into a cold, starless night. There is grass at my feet; the green slivers have a tinge of white frost on them. I put my hand on my rifle as my eyes sweep the area. Even in the dark, I know where we are. I've spent enough time on these bleachers, and as further proof I can see the orange and black reflective banners hanging on the fence.

"We're in Battle Ground," I say, more to myself than Levi.

"The football field. Go, Tigers," Levi announces without any real enthusiasm. This is our home, but it isn't our Earth. The frequency of our Earth is too different from Ezra's to bring us back, and I know the SenMachs have made the QOINS too efficient for a mistake.

I don't want to be here. I'd rather be anywhere but here. This is a fake diamond ring. It's a gorgeous chocolate cake that you can't eat sitting on the table. This is a cruel joke where everyone we love, where the life we could have had, is right in front of us but a billion Earths away. It is a grotesque reflection where we can see right through to normal. Levi would have played on this very field. I probably would have watched him and crushed hard, praying to God that, somehow, he would have noticed me in the stands. I doubt he would have. The only thing that makes me special is being a Citadel. On this Earth I'm probably just boring Ryn who watches too much TV and still plays the cello. I wasn't exactly a weirdo in eighth grade before I was activated, but I was sensitive and insecure with two parents who were infinitely cooler than I was.

I was, in other words, just a teenager.

"Let's move over to the bleachers," I say. "We need to get out of the open just in case there's anyone around getting drunk or stoned. Although, I suppose if there were, we could at least explain a Rift opening that way."

Levi doesn't respond. He just runs toward the side of the stands, closest to the field house.

When we get to the bleachers we crouch down, taking off our packs as we slide. "Just in case." And then I say, "Battle Ground, Washington, 2021, high school student." The sensuit goes to work, flowering up my arms and down my legs until I'm wearing jeans, a turtleneck, and a down jacket.

"Good call," Levi agrees, and he does the same. We look like we belong here now.

Now there's a cosmic joke if I've ever heard one.

I pull out the thin SenMach laptop from my bag and open it. As difficult as it is for me to be here, it's just now occurring to me that, actually, this might be a good thing. As long as zombies or vampires or mutant people suddenly don't start to descend on us, this is an echo Earth.

"You know," I begin, "this could be it. This could be Ezra's Earth." I look up at Levi, who has no expression on his face at all. I don't really have any reason to believe it is, other than good old-fashioned optimism. And if this is his Earth, then my time with Levi alone is over. I am desperate to find Ezra, but I can't help feeling a pang. This will be hard for Levi. And, I have to admit, hard for me, too. I know now that even though he can really act like a complete asshole, deep down, he isn't *an actual* asshole. His persona is just another kind of armor that he wears to keep that little boy whose mother sang to him every night safe from being hurt.

"Even if we find Ezra here, it doesn't mean we'll stop with the deprogramming," I try to assure him.

Levi places an elbow on his knee. It's cold. The uniform and sensuit keep me warm enough, but my hands and face are starting to redden from the chill. It doesn't help that there's a frigid breeze, ruffling the banners and signs at the front of the bleachers and the ones hanging from the diamond holes in the fence.

"Let's just see if he's here. We can think about that when . . . it's time to think about that."

Levi's words are hardly convincing. They must be for my benefit, because by the look on his face I know he's thinking about the time we've already spent deprogramming and how it's changed things between him and me. But I back off, because it's what he wants, and honestly, it's what I want, too.

"Okay. Piggyback a Wi-Fi signal," I command the computer. I give it a second or two and see on the screen that the laptop has done what I've requested in a matter of seconds. It's also running protocol to get us in invisibly. Whoever's signal we're hijacking will have no idea their IP address has been compromised. "Find Gmail," I tell the software. Within seconds the familiar logo pops up on the screen. I log in with our sophisticated username and password.

And there it is. A message from Ezra.

"It's him!" I open the e-mail, my heart hammering. He could be right here, just miles away, blocks even. And then just as quickly, hope is replaced with something else. Fear.

NOT SAFE. NOT MY EARTH. ENEMIES EVERYWHERE. KEEP RIFTING.

I touch my fingers to my lips and blink. *What the hell?* What enemies?

"Is that right?" Levi says as he snatches the laptop from my hands so he can read it again. "You're sure this is from him?"

"Yes," I tell him as I nod.

"Do you have any idea what this means? Is this some kind of a code?" I have an idea, all right, but it's not one Levi is going to like, let alone completely believe. I try anyway.

"Remember in the cave? When I said I heard that sound?" By way of an answer, Levi simply nods his head and closes the computer. "And there is something else. Back there in the coliseum. I saw someone. A spectator who was sitting in the first row and . . . he was singing, no, not singing like 'la-la,' but humming, buzzing. Very loudly."

"Well," Levi considers, "before you go all conspiracy theory on me, it seems like the most logical answer is that somewhere along the way you hit your head. You have a brain injury. Or maybe the SenMachs . . ."

"Please don't do that," I say sincerely.

"What?" he counters innocently, throwing up a single hand.

"Don't try to make me seem crazy. I've seen crazy. That's

not what's going on here." I yank the computer from his hands and put it back in my pack.

"Look," he says warmly, calmly. "I'm just trying to be logical, that's all."

"We were just gladiators. I fought an animatronic Medusa!" I say with excitement, but I am not yelling—I am passionately defending. "There is nothing about what we're doing that feels logical, so just forget about that for a minute. I don't have brain damage and the SenMachs didn't do anything to me. You know that I can sense a Rift before it opens and you know that not every Citadel can do that."

"Yeah." Levi crosses his arms, but he hasn't shut me down. "So?"

"Well, you also know that there is something in my DNA that is different from yours. Feather said so."

Levi rolls his eyes. "We don't know what that is. It could be anything or nothing."

I clench my fists reflexively. He's *still* trying to be rational. Or maybe he's just in denial. Who could blame him for not wanting yet another thing we can't completely explain? Yet, just once, I'd like for him to simply *believe* me.

"You're right about that, in isolation," I say. "But as part of a bigger picture, we shouldn't just dismiss it. We don't know what's inside a Rift. It's a bridge across the Multiverse. It's likely dark matter and also a bunch of other shit that we don't even have words for. So what if, like, the more we Rift, the more we're exposed to whatever is in there and it changes us somehow?"

There's a moment of tense silence as Levi just looks at me. Finally, he says: "I'm really not trying to be a dick, but I mean, Ryn, come on . . . You're going to go with some sort of psychic superpower, *like a legit superpower,* over a head injury? Or stress? Or just out-and-out fatigue?

I shake my head tersely. "I'm only moderately stressed"—Levi frowns—"okay, maybe I'm *completely* stressed, but I don't feel tired. Besides, none of that would explain why Ezra is warning us against enemies. I didn't make *that* up. So my question is: Enemies from where?" I zip my pack up and get on my feet again.

"Well maybe *Ezra* is experiencing some posttraumatic stress, too. Wouldn't that be the most likely explanation for his paranoia?"

"He's not a Citadel, but you have to give him some credit—Ezra is stronger than you think he is and he would never want me to worry unnecessarily." I pull the pack awkwardly over my puffy shoulders as I stand.

"Seriously, Ryn?" Levi says in a snit. "I get that he's your boyfriend, but how well do you really know him? As well as Henry? As Violet? He isn't trained for this. For fuck's sake, *we're* trained for this and it's hard for even us to process. This is crazy town! Sometimes I can barely tell which way is up in here. So are you really gonna stand there and tell me he's just cruising along because . . . science? And computers? And *love*?"

"Stop it!" I half yell. "Stop it with the superiority act. He broke out of the Village. I gave him some helpful hints, but he did that on his own. And you met Audrey, right? She's a Citadel and she's a lunatic, so we don't exactly have the market on sanity. I know you don't like him. You think he's the reason we're here, and you're right. He is. And you should thank fucking God that he showed up when he did. Unless, I don't know, you'd rather be a little puppet boy again while ARC, or the Roones, or whoever, tugs at your strings. Now, this *is* crazy town, but my gut tells me that it's related—the something that is after him is connected to this weird buzzing that's driving me bonkers. I know it's not a logical thing to think, but I just do."

I put my hands on my hips, practically daring him to get into it. I know he wants to. I can see it in the subtle twitches around his mouth, in the way he's breathing. Instead, surprisingly, he relaxes. It's always strategy with him. He baited me, which means that in his own twisted way he's already won. How does he do that? Win a fight without actually fighting? Christ, that's annoying.

"Well, *my gut* is telling me that I'm starving. We need to eat. Both of us," he says, finally standing.

"No, we should Rift again. I think—"

Before I can finish my sentence, however, I hear a popping sound and then an odd grunt from Levi. He looks surprised as he reaches for his neck, and then I see the blood spilling out over the collar of his coat.

He's been shot.

"Oh my God," I say as I rush to him, trying to stanch the gush. Meanwhile we are out in the open, still exposed. "Get under the bleachers," I tell him quickly. "Take off your pack and get your first aid kit. I'm going to try and get that sniper." Levi doesn't argue. He just does as he's told. I grab at my gun, which has remained under my jacket. My rifle is still attached, too, but I think I would have to go under my sweater to get at it and there's no time.

I scan the area. Based on the sound of the shot and where we were sitting, I know the shooter has to have been coming from the west. I run full-out, through a small thicket of trees, until I'm in an open field. In the far distance I see movement, a lone runner, and I sprint in that direction. Once I cross Tenth Avenue I know there is a forested area, but I want to get to him or her before that. Unfortunately, even with my speed, they have had one hell of a head start. Just as I break through the trees, I hear the sound of a Rift opening.

What the hell . . . ?

There's a boom and then that awful whistling that stops me in my tracks. Damn it, is the sound getting louder? I shake my head and continue to bolt, but I am too late. I get there just in time to see the last electric glow of the Rift closing. It folds in on itself like a black box tied with a neon bow being kicked inside out.

Shit. How is this even happening? Who could know we're here, except . . . ?

Edo.

She could have sent a patrol after us. But they wouldn't kill us, right? I could believe they would take us back, take us prisoner, even, but if she wanted me dead she's had plenty of chances. So probably not her. Who is it, then? I race back to Levi. He's sitting in the dirt under the seats. I crawl under to get to him.

"I don't think it hit an artery." I nod in agreement—if it were an artery, he wouldn't have been able to stop the bleeding at all. Still, there is a ton of blood and he looks waxy and his lips have lost their pigment. They are an ashen rust instead of their usual scarlet.

"The patches from the SenMachs?" I ask while grabbing the Maglite from my holster.

"Bled right through them. I was going to put a coagulant on, but I think maybe there's something in there. Did you find the sniper?" I gently push his head down and examine the wound with my light. I use my coat sleeve to wipe away the blood. I can see a perfectly shaped O in his neck until the bleeding starts again. If it had just been a graze, the wound would look different. Levi is right, there is most likely a bullet, or at least a bullet fragment, in there.

"No, they Rifted out." Levi looks up at me, confused, but I don't explain further. "We need to go somewhere, somewhere where there is running water and a safe place for me to take care of this where no one will see us."

"We could just break in to the school. Use a locker room," Levi suggests with strain in his voice.

"Ordinarily I would say yes, but we might live here, or versions of us live here. There are alarms at the school and maybe security guards. I don't want the other versions of us going to jail. So ditto for a hospital—too many questions we can't explain away. And we can't go to a hotel because you're basically bleeding to death. That might cause some tongues to wag. But there is one place . . ." I dig into my bag and open up the computer again. "What's the date? I mean, the actual day here?" When the computer says *Thursday,* I slam it shut again.

"It's date night. Perfect. Come on, and keep applying pressure to the wound," I say as I take Levi's pack. "Can you walk for a couple of miles?"

"I think so. But where?"

"I'm going to go to the one person I trust here. Hopefully this Earth is similar enough that, because it's Thursday, they'll be out and she'll be alone. Sort of."

"Who? What? Explain. Blood loss . . . ," Levi says as he staggers to his feet.

"Me."

"Wha—?"

"We're going to my house."

CHAPTER 15

We don't exactly run to Meadow Glade, but we keep a brisk pace. It doesn't take us long to get there, which is a very good thing, because Levi isn't holding up all that well. I stop at the hedges of my house. I can feel my hands begin to tremble ever so slightly and I clutch at the handles of my pack to get them to stop. She might not even live here—that would suck. I suppose if she doesn't, we could always just circle back around and go to the garage. It's not ideal, but it'll do in a pinch. Might actually be better, now that I think of it, because even *if* she is here, what the hell am I going to say? I'm going to have to improvise, and possibly lie. Thankfully, those are both skills I excel at. I ring the bell and after a handful of seconds it swings open.

It's me. Thank God.

Ryn Two looks at me and then Levi and then back at me.

"What the hell?" She is baffled, but not afraid. Because *on any Earth*, I'm pretty awesome.

"I need to come in. Are Mom and Dad on their date night? Where's Abel?" Ryn Two furrows her brow but opens the door wider and steps aside so we can walk in.

"Umm . . ."

"No one is going to hurt you. There's a totally crazy explanation for this, which you'll get, but first I need your help because, obviously, you're the only person I can trust right now. So who's here?"

"I'm alone. Yes, Mom and Dad are at the movies and I have no idea who Abel is."

"Oh," I say while practically holding Levi upright at this point. I don't have a brother on this Earth. The thought makes me ache. I love my brother possibly more than anyone else in the world, and this Ryn doesn't have an Abel. "You don't have any brothers or sisters?" I ask hopefully.

"No, but—"

"Hello? Bleeding?" Levi interrupts.

The house looks exactly like mine. It looks so similar that I get a different sort of ache. Being here hurts. I miss my mom and dad. I miss my friends and my bed and my books and the dumb pictures of crazy shit on the walls that my dad's art school friends made.

Whatever. I can't think about that now. I made the right choice. This is a safe place. I *know* me.

I race up the stairs dragging Levi along with me. "Where are you going?" Ryn hollers while running up behind us.

"Up to Mom and Dad's bathroom. There's the most space in there, and tile. You can't stain tile." I pull Levi along the hallway past my own room and where Abel's would have been. I don't even want to look at those doors. It's too much. I practically yank the doorknob off as I turn and pull it. My parents' room looks identical, the same velvet duvet and the same wallpaper on the wall above the bed with golden peacocks and tiny purple birdcages. I walk through to the bathroom, which isn't huge, but it's big enough for a double sink and an area for Mom to put her makeup on. I quickly grab the stool from the vanity and push Levi down so that he's sitting on it.

"So you're another version of me, right? From another version of Earth somewhere?" Ryn Two asks as she leans against the doorframe and folds her arms. She's trying to come across as calm, but her heartbeat is giving her away. It's pounding like a jackhammer and there is a slight tremor to her hands. Up until that point, I had been so focused on making sure we were alone and on Levi's injury that I hadn't really looked at her. And also because obviously it's unnerving as hell to see another version of yourself. But now, it's unavoidable. Her hair is much shorter than mine, and cut in an asymmetrical bob. It's actually very flattering, but it makes her look older. She's a little heavier than me, but not by much, maybe ten pounds. This is the body I would have if I were not a Citadel, if every calorie I consumed weren't burnt off training, running, and fighting.

"Twins isn't your first guess? Like a separated-at-birth kind of thing?" I ask.

"I read. A lot. And though I don't go advertising it to my supercool friends, I'm kind of a science-fiction dork. It seems like the most plausible answer."

"And 'alien shape-shifter' doesn't make it on the short list, even? Or 'clones'?"

"I think if you were some sort of shape-shifter you would have gotten my hair right," Ryn Two says nonchalantly. "And a clone couldn't be the same age as me unless it happened at the same time I was born, so . . ."

"Well, you're right, Other Ryn," Levi says. "We're from another Earth. This Ryn," he says, pointing at me, "is another version of you, or you're another version of her, or whatever. But as you can tell from the blood pooling on the floor, I've been *shot*, so maybe let's focus on that?" Levi's tone is coming across as something close to rude, but he's in pain and probably a little freaked that he just got shot, so I just go with it. Ryn Two gives me a slightly irritated look that I'm almost positive would have mirrored my own had I just met Levi. My God this is weird—seeing myself like this.

"Cuff," I tell the bracelet, and the sensuit disappears. Levi does the same, and in the light and without the collar of the coat I can see that the wound is much worse than I'd thought.

"Shit," I say as I go to my pack and fish out the first aid kit.

"What was that?" Ryn Two asks with a look of bewilderment on her face, finally verbally showing what her body language has been throwing out from the start.

"Ryn," I begin, "trust me, I get how fucking insane this is, but can I ask you to just hold off until we deal with Levi?"

"Umm . . . yes?" It's more of a question than an answer, but I'll take it.

"Levi, you need to get the top of your uniform off. I'm going to help you. Is that okay? Are you . . . *okay*?" The last thing we need is the friggin' Blood Lust to activate. Ryn Two is handling this situation so well that I'm seriously impressed . . . with myself. But if the Blood Lust is triggered, all bets are off. Not only would the strain probably kill Levi, it would put Ryn Two in serious danger. So even though time is a major factor, I am being extra cautious.

"Yeah. It hurts too bad for anything to happen."

I slowly undo the zipper until it's just past his navel. I grab the uninjured side of his body and ease his arm out. I carefully give the other side of the uniform a tug at the wrist and then gingerly peel the top of it down until Levi is totally bare chested. I catch a glimpse of Ryn Two, who gives me a look that couldn't be saying anything other than *Well done*. She must think Levi is my boyfriend. I ignore it. There's so much I'm sure I'm going to have to explain, but my status concerning Levi is the least of it. I grab a flashlight from my utility belt and hand it over to the other me.

"Ryn, I need you to keep this light shining on the wound. Okay?" I don't bother asking if she's okay with the blood or the gross factor. I know she can deal. Ryn takes the light from me and manages to find a perfect angle so that I can see, but at the same time not be in my way.

First I clean the wound as best as I can, though it's tricky business because it won't stop bleeding. I have to dig in a little with the sanitized wipe. I can feel Levi tense in pain as I do this work. "Do you want something?" I ask him. "For the pain?"

"Just use the local. I don't want to be drugged." I put a vial of local anesthesia into the medical gun and puncture tiny dots around the obvious hole of the bullet wound. Blood continues to trickle down. I continue to wipe it away.

"I'm numb," Levi tells me with relief in his voice. The Roone drugs work so much faster than the normal human-made ones. "You know the bullet is still in there, right?" he asks haughtily.

"Yeah, I'm aware." I huff outwardly. Most people would be grateful that they weren't more seriously injured. Most people would be thankful that someone—*two* someones, actually (though the two someones are, I guess, the same person. So is it just one again?)—is in a position to actually help them.

Levi is not most people. I try not to think about how much worse this could have been. Just a few millimeters and he would have died and I would've been helpless to stop it. Death is a shadow that follows all Citadels around, but I don't think I could have handled it if he had actually died in my arms. I mean, yes, I could have, obviously. I would have pushed through, but the close call is a rock in my stomach. I've been so focused on Ezra, and what he could be dealing with, that I never considered Levi. He's always seemed practically immortal. Looking at this wound, I know that's not the case. I realize it's more than just guilt I feel for putting him in this situation—it's true anxiety.

I reach for a tool in the medical kit that will help me pull the bullet from his neck. I don't need to tell my partner to brace himself for the pain. Even with the local, he's going to feel this and he knows it. Ryn Two is doing a great job with the light and with keeping quiet. I reach in with the miniature forceps and feel Levi bear down. The whites of his knuckles glow bright as they make fists on his resting knees. I have to fish around a little bit, but luckily, I am able to get to the culprit after a minute or so. I keep my hand steady as I pull it out of the wound, and once I do, it's followed by another fresh round of bleeding. I bring the bullet into the light to get a better look, and even though my adrenaline is already maxed out, another round begins to race through my body. This is bad.

"Hold that," I tell Ryn Two, who right away opens up her palm and allows me to drop our newest worry into her hand. I'll get to that later—right now I have to get Levi closed up before he bleeds out.

I clean the wound again, and put some of the clotting agent in it. I close it up with medical adhesive and put on one of the SenMachs' biopatches. I make sure everything seems to be working—no blood seeping out, basically—then I hold out my palm, gesturing for Ryn Two to hand over what I'd given her. She does so with a look that says she knows that, whatever it is, it's no traditional bullet. Before I can give my attention to it, though, Ryn Two says, "Your friend is bleeding from his bracelet, too." I look down and, sure enough, there is a large pool of blood collecting on the floor from what looks like his wrist.

"Were you hurt somewhere else?" I ask him quickly.

"No. I think the suit is cleaning itself," Levi replies in a tone that suggests the idea doesn't make him feel any better.

His discomfort doesn't matter. Not now. Not with this. I need to have a private conversation with Levi. One that Ryn Two should absolutely not hear.

"Ryn. Levi needs to get his uniform clean. Could you give us a minute? A private minute?"

"I could just put it in the washing machine for you," Ryn suggests helpfully.

"No. Thank you. It's a special material and needs hand washing and I'm not sure Levi is wearing anything underneath it." I mean, she already thinks he's my boyfriend; might as well embrace the convenient untruth for now.

"Okay. I'll be right out here if you need anything. And after that, we are going to have a talk, right?" Smart Ryn. She's not going to let us have the run of the house. She wants us to know she's been promised answers. Of course, there's nothing she can do about it if we decide to just leave, but I'm also pretty sure I can't knock myself out. I'm guessing Ryn Two knows that. She leaves, closing the door softly behind her. Knowing what I'd do, I check the door, and sure enough, it wasn't actually closed all the way. I push it shut firmly, and listen as hasty footsteps retreat from near the door. I turn back to Levi.

"Take off your uniform. We do need to clean it. And honestly I don't give a shit whether or not you're naked at this point," I order Levi in a stern whisper.

Levi immediately peels off the uniform, and deep down I *am* relieved he's wearing boxer briefs. I hadn't been lying, though. I wouldn't have cared if he had to stand there stark naked to have this conversation. I open my hand and he takes the thing that had been lodged in his neck. I, in turn, snatch the uniform out of his hands and begin to run it under cold water. A pool of inky blood flutters in the marble sink.

"What is this?" Levi asks as he examines it more closely. I don't need to, though, and I'm a little surprised he doesn't recognize it. I'd know that tech anywhere. I know it because I pulled something strikingly similar off one of our greatest enemies at the Rift in Battle Ground before he slit his own throat.

"It's Karekin tech."

"*What?* That can't be right. It could be some other race. It could be something Roonish, that they've never let us see before," Levi says, but his voice is betraying him. He doesn't sound nearly like his cocky, know-it-all self.

"It isn't." I grab a soft terry washcloth that had been stacked in a neat roll on the counter and put hand soap on it before running it under the water. I then begin to scrub on the upper part of Levi's uniform. "When Ezra escaped from the Village, he stole not only ARC's highly classified data, but also zip files containing most of the languages of the Immigrants that come through the Rift. That's how I started learning them. I told you it was ridiculous that we didn't know them, so it became a little side project. I managed to get through Sissnovar and Karekin before Ezra was taken." I pause to examine my work. The water is running clear. The stain, though not completely gone, is clean enough. "I've known something was off with the Karekins for a while. They are outliers. They make no sense. They come through the Rift determined to kill as many of us as they can and none of them are ever caught alive. So one day we decided to capture one of them." I wring out the uniform and water begins to drip once more into the sink.

"You what?" Levi asks incredulously. "When? Where?"

"During our last battle with them. The four of us, the Beta Team, managed to get one away from the fight. We isolated him in the forest. I just wanted to tell him that we weren't the enemy. I was trying to explain what we are. I don't know. I just wanted some answers." I toss the uniform back at Levi, who doesn't do anything with it. He just looks at me. I can't tell if he's angry or disappointed or hurt by this new information.

"And then what happened?" he prompts curtly.

"The Karekin said our disloyalty would be punished, and then he slit his own throat, but not before I could wrestle his earpiece away. It was a *two-way* communication device. They *can* communicate through the Rift, and the thing I took looked an awful lot like that. I don't think it was meant to kill you. I think if a Karekin wanted you dead, you would be dead. Whoever shot you knew exactly how to do it so that it wouldn't inflict a mortal wound but could get past your uniform, assuming it thought you were wearing your uniform under your clothes. I doubt they know about the sensuits, or at least, fuck, I hope not. Whatever—that's not the point. Don't you get it? It's not a bullet—it's a tracking device. It's even flashing red! I know you aren't necessarily down with the whole pop-culture thing, but even you must have seen a movie with a tracking device."

Levi finally begins to get dressed, all the while huffing and shaking his head. "You didn't think that information was worth sharing with all of us before you left? You didn't think we all might like to know something like that?"

I lean over the sink, propping my elbows on the cold marble before running my hands over my eyes. "Please don't start—" I begin, barely able to contain the exasperation from my voice.

"When are you going to stop lying?" Levi interrupts angrily. "You kept vital information from me and your fellow soldiers that could save our lives." I whip my body up and turn to face him.

"How am I lying? How is any of what I just said 'vital'? The Karekins can talk through the Rift. They think we're traitors for some bizarre fucking reason. So what? None of that can really help the Citadels at Battle Ground. And the thing is, I don't know *why* the Karekins think what they do or *how* their technology works. Ezra might have some more answers or he might give us enough leverage to force ARC to give us those answers, but—again—it doesn't matter to the Citadels back home. The only people it really matters to are *us*. At this precise moment. Which is when I told you. I didn't hold anything back, Levi."

He doesn't say anything, just stands there, being all butt-hurt. Right now, I couldn't come close to caring less. I press on.

"There is something going on. *Ezra was here*, Levi. On this Earth. And he warned us against enemies. Not to mention the noise. We were humming in that cave. That weirdo in the stadium was whistling like one of Snow White's friggin' dwarfs. It's all connected. It's the Karekins. I don't know how they even found us or why they would shoot you and leave. Maybe they were getting reinforcements. Maybe they thought that it would take a lot longer to get that thing out of your neck, but either way, they are after us. They're probably on their way. To

Ryn's house! Me. A me who's totally unprepared to deal with any of this, so we need to leave. Right fucking now. Suit up and we can chitchat in a safe location."

I grab the med kit and shove it back in my pack and then I whip open the door. Ryn Two is waiting right outside. We had been quiet, and the door is impressively thick, so I'm hoping she didn't hear much even if she had her ear pressed up against it.

I walk past her into her parents' bedroom. "Are you going to tell me what's going on now?" Ryn demands. I sigh. We have to go, but she needs to hear as much as I can tell her because a Karekin assassin might be on the way. I quickly tell her my story. I condense it as much as I can, but it is so friggin' complicated that even I get tripped up with all the details. I flinch a bit when I mention the part about the potential assassin. I make sure to let her know that the chances of that are small(ish), that more than likely the Karekin won't find the active homing signal, and will leave. I'm not sure I did so well with selling that bit, though, because I am scared for her and it's really hard to look yourself in the eye and lie, even for an expert liar like me. Levi finally joins us in the bedroom. His color is thankfully returning.

"Seriously?" Ryn says as she looks at me and Levi when I've finished. I had left out the Blood Lust part, because there was no time to add that whole other wrinkle to my abbreviated tale. But I had told her briefly about Ezra and what Levi and I were actually doing. "Super soldiers? A massive international cover-up? A village that looks like Epcot full of prisoners? A doorway to the Multiverse that is opened up with a song?"

"It's not a song," Levi corrects her. "It's a sound."

"You get how totally insane that story is, right? The Multiverse is one thing. Stephen Hawking believes in the Multiverse. But you guys are super soldiers? Your parents think you're going to Battle Ground High and they have no clue that you actually take a secret train to Camp Bonneville to, like, kill people all day long? That's a bit much even for this nerd," Ryn Two says, putting a hand on her hip. She narrows her eyes at both of us. "So, prove it."

"How would you like us to do that?" Levi says. "Fight you? Fight each other? There's no time!" Levi is thoroughly annoyed, and he's right—there isn't much time. But I also get where Ryn is coming from. She's me, after all. It's one thing to be able to traverse infinite Earths, but to think there is a version of herself that fights. That *kills*. She doesn't think she would be able to do it. She can't see any version of herself doing the things I've told her I've done, and I haven't even told her the half of it. *That's* the part that she doesn't believe and that's the kind of proof she is asking for. And while it's a risk, I think it's a risk worth taking. Because she *can* be strong, and even if the Karekin never comes for her, that's the only way I can think of to repay her for all this craziness.

"Okay. You want proof? Here it is." I see Levi's shoulders drop. I don't care. The sooner we convince Ryn that given different circumstances this could have been her, the sooner we can get out of here, leaving her with a glimpse of herself as stronger than she ever imagined. I get a sense that this Ryn is a little lonely, that maybe she does more watching than living. She's alone in this house. Where are her friends? Why isn't she out or at least getting laid in this empty house? I don't know if I'm the hero or the villain of my own story yet, but I'm certainly a big part of it. I want Ryn Two to see that.

I walk over to the end of the king-size bed, wrap my fingers underneath the curve of its upholstery, and pick it up until it is five feet off the floor. Ryn Two's eyes practically pop out of her head.

"See?" Levi says with mock enthusiasm. "We aren't lying. This is a real thing and we need to go." I shoot him a look, warning him to keep the insensitivity to a minimum. I unlatch my gun from my holster and hold it out toward Ryn Two. "Take it," I tell her. "And if something comes at you, just aim for the head. Shooting it anywhere else in the body won't affect it."

Ryn Two looks at me in horror, mouth agape. "I can't take a *gun*. I can't have a gun in this house. I'm a *Democrat*."

I ignore her protestations and teach her the basics of loading, shooting, and firing. I also make sure she knows when the safety is on and off. I hold my hand out once more so that she can take it.

"No. I can't shoot anyone. And if my parents find it, they'll send me to some lame space camp boarding school for troubled kids." Now it's my turn to drop my shoulders.

"Give me your phone, and put in the password," Levi demands. It's not a question and it's not polite. Ryn Two whips her phone out of her back pocket, unlocks it, and gives it to him, clearly caught off guard by his tone. Ha! He probably wishes I was so easy to order around. "Now, both of you, get together." We do as he's asked and wait for him to take what must be a dozen pictures. Then he hands the phone back to Ryn Two. "Tell your parents what happened. Now you have the proof. Tell them there isn't anyone they can call. There isn't any government agency on this Earth that can protect them, so there's no point. It would just make their lives a thousand times more complicated. We are going to make sure that we lure whoever wants to find us as far away from you as possible, so that's the best insurance policy you're going to get. But just in case, take the damn gun, Ryn." I can practically see Ryn Two's gears shifting. She isn't like me. She hasn't been trained to disassemble. Ryn reaches out slowly and takes the gun. I can tell the weight of it in her hands is troubling by how forlornly she's looking at it.

"Look," I tell her kindly, "I'm so sorry I dragged you into this. I really thought that this was the best, safest solution. With Levi's injuries, we couldn't just Rift out. We might have Rifted onto an Earth with no oxygen or one that was completely underwater, and I needed somewhere that was safe for sure. For us. I wasn't thinking of you and that was wrong. I apologize."

"It's okay. I guess I would have done the same thing. I guess I *did* do the same thing." She shakes her head with a small laugh. "God, this is scary as hell, I'm not going to lie, but it's also kind of . . . amazing. I feel so ordinary all the time, like life is happening all around me and I'm just watching it. This is probably the most important thing that will ever happen to me."

"I doubt that," Levi says with unexpected tenderness. "You're young. And you're Ryn. You're already amazing. You just don't know it yet, because you know, you weren't genetically altered." Levi smiles. Ryn smiles back, clearly smitten. Is that how I look when a boy says something nice to me? God I hope I'm not that obvious.

Levi speaks into the cuff. "Rift. Pandora." This is clever—a Rift nowhere near Ezra *and* a jump that hopefully throws whoever is after us for a loop. Immediately, a Rift begins to open. The sheets on the bed ruffle, the furniture starts to tremble with the force. Ryn Two's eyes widen. She's a smart one. She manages to get a few pictures with her phone of the Rift—further proof. Levi and I begin to walk forward.

"Hey," she says before we can walk through, "what's this Ezra guy's last name?" Oh yes. *Very* smart.

"Massad. He's a genius. Does quantum cryptography. You should try to find him." I give her a quick hug, and Levi smiles quickly but brightly. We walk through the green glowing mouth of the Rift and are gone.

WE LAND IN JUNGLE. IT'S hot as hell and smells awful. I don't know where or when this Earth is, but it looks prehistoric, so I doubt Ezra is here. It is, however, a great place to leave the Karekin tracker. Levi takes the thing and throws it as hard and far as he can.

"That's going to have to be good enough," he says, though I can tell that leaving Ryn Two behind like that doesn't sit right with him. We train. We fight. We kill. Our number one mission, though, the thing that keeps us coming back to the hell mouth that is the Battle Ground Rift, is knowing that we are protecting innocent people. The Ryn on that Earth is an innocent. Not only is she a civilian, but she is basically me, and Levi and I . . . well . . . we have that "it" thing now.

"When all this is over, we can go back and make sure she's okay." I try to assure him as much as myself.

"What if she isn't, though? What if they kill her?"

"Then that's one more thing we add to the list of things we have to try to find a way to live with. Let's just focus on Ezra, on getting answers."

"Yeah," he practically spits. "Ezra. Because his life is definitely worth more than everyone else's. So yes, we *have* to get to fucking Ezra. Well, to be clear, *you'll* be fucking Ezra. I'll just be saving everybody's life probably."

"I told you. I *warned you* . . . Enough with the superiority act," I tell him coldly, getting right up in his face. "News flash—you aren't the only one saving people. We've done some deprogramming, you're starting to get a handle on grown-up emotions, right? So, it's time to start separating the personal from the professional. Forget about why I'm here. You're here because you threw someone into the Multiverse that has vital information we need to retrieve. That's it. That's all you need to know. The rest of it is none of your business."

We stand there, just staring at each other, and I can't tell if he wants to hit me, tear off my clothes, cry, or all three. Our breathing gets more rapid, but now it's in tandem. I move one of my feet behind me. That way, if Levi does something drastic, I won't be caught off balance. He tenses his body, but then he relaxes it. I hear his pulse begin to slow.

"You're right. I have to stop looking at Ezra like he's my competition." I breathe a sigh of relief. Wow. I think I might actually be getting through to him, until he leans in, just inches away from my ear, and whispers: "Because even though you can't or won't admit it, we both know that when it comes to me, *there is* no competition."

I yank my head back and stare at him. I smile at first and even give a little chuckle. Levi doesn't smile back. His gaze is deadly serious. His look is so intense, it makes the hair on the back of my neck stand on end and it is boiling hot. "Fine," I tell him in a tone that is now serious enough to match his look. "You win. He can't compete." I could try to keep at it, but at this point it would be like screaming into the wind. Pointless. "Just keep it professional, okay?"

"Yes, ma'am," Levi responds while saluting.

I'd like to break every one of those sarcastic fingers he's got up to his forehead. But I can't ask him to do anything I won't do myself. I have to keep it professional.

I speak Ezra's name into the cuff. Levi quickly marches

through the Rift and I tag along behind him. I hate him sometimes, I really do. I wish to God I didn't, and not because it
would make everything less complicated, but because the opposite of love isn't hate, it's indifference. And even though it
kills me to admit, there's no way on this Earth or any of the
billions of others, that I could ever be indifferent about Levi.

CHAPTER 16

We Rift into scorching heat, but this is different from the damp humidity of the last jump. This heat is arid, searing. Our boots make contact with the gravel, which eddies and shimmers, mirage-like, under the blazing sun. It is hilly terrain, and mercifully empty. I look through my binoculars and see civilization in the not-too-far-off distance. We are very much in the open, exposed, but until we know where we are, there's not much point in going anywhere. We send out the drones and pull out our laptops. We take a seat on the hard, tiny rocks and wait for intel to come in, leaving the huge blowup we had in the jungle world stay in that part of the Multiverse.

I hope.

It's only a matter of minutes before images start popping up on the screen. I see buildings with towers bedecked with crescent moons. I see souks and peddlers. I see stalls with conical piles of brightly colored spices. There are tourists here, men and women, wearing shorts and tees. There are also locals wearing hijabs with jeans and tees and the more traditional caftans. The men are wearing djellaba and fezzes. I think I know where we are, but I ask the computer to triangulate our position and when it pops up on the map I see that I was right—we're in Morocco, a secluded area of desert about eleven miles north of Marrakech. From what the drones have gathered, it looks like another echo Earth.

"It can't be a coincidence," I say while still examining the recon photos. "First we Rift to a Battle Ground Earth, and now Marrakech? Where Ezra's family is from? Could the QOINS be picking up quantum information from *us*? Is that even possible?" I wonder aloud.

"Anything is possible," Levi answers grimly. "Like you said, a few hours ago I was fighting a Minotaur and apparently people's bodies hum around you now, so sure." I want to roll my eyes, but I check myself—mostly because it sucks having your words thrown back in your face like that.

"I say we go in as a version of ourselves—tourists, students, backpacking. I think it's a safe-enough cover," I suggest.

"We could go in as locals. We both speak Arabic and French. With the sensuits, no one would be able to tell," Levi counters as he calls back the drones.

"It's like, one hundred ten degrees outside. Why encumber ourselves with a disguise? Why lie more than we have to? This isn't Syria or Iraq. From those pictures the drones sent back this looks like our Morocco, which is a moderate Muslim country that depends on the tourist industry. Let's just be ourselves—if we weren't Citadels, I mean."

"Fine. It's your call," Levi says in a monotone.

"Wow. I can't believe I'm going to say this, but I think I prefer aggressive-aggressive over passive-aggressive. If you've got something to say, say it."

Levi closes his eyes for a flicker of a moment and seems to shrink somehow, become smaller. "I don't have anything to say, Ryn. I'm tired. I'm in the middle of the fucking desert. I was shot a couple hours ago, after which I had to deal with *two* of you. We came here looking for answers and all we've gotten so far is about a hundred more questions. I just want to rest." He's right. I'm pushing. Levi is so great at not showing weakness that I forgot momentarily what he's just been through. He lost an awful lot of blood, even for us. I need to get him out of the sun.

"Okay. Let's walk into town and check into a hotel," I say as I quickly redo the topknot in my hair. "I can get on the computer there, and you can get some sleep." I pause and bite down on my lower lip. "I'm sorry. I'm not used to seeing you at a disadvantage. I don't know a weak version of you. It's weird. So I got a little ahead of myself. It won't happen again," I tell him as I reach for his arm—and pull away, because the Blood Lust is still there, unpredictable as ever. And I really don't want to fight.

Levi opens his mouth like he's going to say something, but he just closes it again. I'm not sure there are words for the emotional landscape we are mining now. We aren't adversaries. We aren't friends. We care about each other, but we don't particularly like each other, although that feeling, too, even with the bickering, is beginning to shift the more time we spend together.

Levi and I don't say a single thing on the walk into town, which is fine because I'm used to spending a lot of time on duty in absolute silence, and because we both need to preserve our energy. Unlike some teenage girls, I don't feel awkward when it gets quiet. I don't have the need to fill up the air with small talk or silly stories so that I don't come across as weird or boring. You can't really stand guard and be deep in conversation.

The sensuits are covering our uniforms. I have chosen to dress modestly, in a long maxi dress, covering my shoulders with a thin cotton scarf, which I can pull up to cover my hair if I feel like it's necessary. Levi, as a man, has more freedom. It looks like he's wearing jeans and a T-shirt. Instinctively, I balk at this covering up. I get that it's a religious thing, and as I'm in a Muslim country, I will respect it. Still, regardless of theology, I feel less than equal to Levi. I feel at a disadvantage, which even I recognize as stupid. Just because I'm wearing a dress doesn't make me any less of a soldier, it just makes me look more feminine. Then again, there aren't a lot of pop culture references to *feminine* warriors, with the exception of my beloved Buffy of the vampire slayers of course. But that show is like thirty years old. How can we have come so far and yet there are billions upon billions of Earths where "fighting like a girl" is an insult? It makes me want to get a pretty manicure and fight like a girl up and down someone's face. Hard.

We continue to walk into town at a decent pace, and find our way into the city center. I have never been to Africa. I don't know what I was expecting. I guess I sort of thought it might be dirty and smelly, but I am entirely wrong on that front. Marrakech is loud, teeming with people and colors. But it is clean, much cleaner than a big American city like New York, and the smells are divine, rose and jasmine. It is exotic here and exciting. It's doubly exciting knowing that Ezra might be close, and even if he isn't, this is where his family is from. He makes more sense to me somehow after seeing this city. The ache I feel in missing him is visceral, spreading wide behind my breastbone.

"Let's see how well these SenMach computers work," I say as we pass by an ATM machine and double back around.

"We've got money, you know. All we have to do is find an exchange place," Levi counters.

"Yeah, but what if the one thing that's different on this Earth is that American dollars are blue instead of green? Besides, we don't have a credit card. We're going to have to throw down some serious cash to act as a deposit in a hotel."

"Fine, go ahead," Levi says, throwing up his hands.

"Hack into this ATM," I tell my cuff in a quiet voice. "Make it give me the maximum limit for this machine." Levi stands behind me with his arms folded blocking what I'm doing, which is, well, let's face it: On top of everything else, I'm a thief now. I pull the scarf over and above my head so that if there are cameras, no one will be able to see my face. Inside of two seconds the machine starts spitting out dirham. I swipe the money quickly and we both move on. I suppose that this first step in what might be the beginning of our international crime spree should feel a little exciting, James Bond–y even. It doesn't. It just feels like stealing. I've never lifted so much as a lip gloss from a Walgreens. I don't like having to do this, but I like Levi's pale complexion and the purple bags under his eyes even less.

We walk about half a mile away to a coffee shop and sit outside so we can use one of the tables. I put the computer on my lap so that it's not in plain view and look for a hotel for us to stay in. As young backpacking travelers, we can't exactly stay at a five-star resort, but I find a location with help from the computer that is nice enough for us to get a decent night's sleep and a good meal. It only takes us about fifteen minutes to walk there.

We check into the hotel, explaining that our credit card was stolen, but we give them enough cash that they work around it. We hand the concierge our Canadian passports. We have a slew of foreign passports thanks to ARC. Levi and I both agree that regardless of how moderate this country is, being American is a risk we don't need to take. Here in Morocco my name is Gabrielle Henderson, and Levi is now Cameron Greene.

A bellboy offers to take our bags, but we politely decline, keeping our voices level, though our fists tighten around our packs. I don't want to get separated from them again. It's too risky, for us and for others. He shrugs it off, and we follow him out of the lobby and through a quaint courtyard, which has an ornate fountain in the middle. This isn't really a hotel so much as a riad, the kind I'd seen in the Village's Marrakech neighborhood back home in Battle Ground. All the hotel's rooms surround the courtyard in a square. Long ago the fountain would have had practical uses. In the desert, it would have been the building's main source for clean water.

We walk up two flights of stairs and arrive in front of a brightly painted cobalt-blue door. The bellboy unlocks it and shows us inside. It's pretty swanky, with a tiled floor and a low bed bedecked in a myriad of colorful pillows. Levi tips the bellboy and we are left alone.

I open the carved lattice shutters and smell orange blossoms. In the distance, the call to prayer begins. I sigh. It somehow feels totally foreign but completely familiar. It's peaceful here. And although the threat of whatever may be chasing us and Ezra hovers, I can fold it up and put it aside for a moment—a small relief.

"I'm going to take a shower. Are you going to check for an e-mail?" Levi asks.

"Yeah," I say as I clear my throat. "I just wanted a minute, to take it all in, you know?"

Levi leans against the doorframe. He puts the sensuit back in the cuff and starts to unzip the top of his uniform. I don't bother to look away. I've pretty much seen Levi naked now, and I'm too tired to care.

"I don't get you," he tells me as he stops the zipper, right above his groin. My eyes settle there because his abs are just downright distracting. They don't even look real. My gaze thankfully snaps back up once he begins to speak. "One minute you're insanely desperate to see him and the next you need a minute to take it all in? Don't you *want* to find him?"

"Of course I do!" I find my voice rising. Why is he putting me on the defensive? Why am I *getting* defensive? "I just wanted, like, five friggin' minutes to listen to the call to prayer and catch my breath, okay?" The truth is, I don't know why I didn't check my e-mail back in the desert as soon as we got here.

Except really, I do.

Because I was focused on what Levi needed. Rest. A bed. A meal. I didn't put Ezra first and now I'm feeling guilty. If he is here and in some kind of trouble, I'll feel even more guilty, and honestly, I don't know how much more guilt I can take. So, yeah, maybe I'm stalling a bit. Levi and I just stare at each other. We have an eye showdown for at least twenty anxious seconds. Then he just says, "Whatever," in a tone that is meant to sound indifferent, but he doesn't quite pull it off. He's confused or annoyed. Probably both.

I exhale loudly once he closes the bathroom door. I peel

off my uniform and then, because I can—and because I'm a cheese ball—I ask the sensuit to dress me in a long, flowing caftan. I stand there by the window, listening to the muezzins from different mosques sing up to the heavens, finishing their prayers. The tile feels wonderfully cool on my bare feet. I know I should open up my computer and check for an e-mail from Ezra, but I can't seem to make my body move. I just need . . . *nothing.* No plans, no conspiracies, no shooting, no noise.

I know that I'm a Citadel. I know that I'm a woman of action, but my skin feels like it's been put on too tight. My head is buzzing with dozens of scenarios and agendas that I mentally bat away because I really do just need to calm down.

I let the perfumed air fill my lungs. In and out. In and out. I let my conscious breathing do the work until I feel myself settle.

My shoulders drop. They had been somewhere around my ears. I don't know how long I continue to stand there, but it's long enough for Levi to finish in the bathroom.

He comes out in his boxers. "Nice outfit," he blurts sarcastically when he sees me. Then he drops to the bed in a whoosh. The pillows go flying.

"Oh, Levi," I sigh without even bothering to look at him. "You always know exactly what to say."

"Sorry. You're right. That was rude, and you look really pretty." I don't even bother to answer him. He's exhausted. I can't tell if he's still being shitty, so there's no need to get into it. I leave him swallowed by the rainbow bed and make my way into the bathroom. I get undressed and into the shower, standing under the large brass showerhead for a long time, letting the water run against my scalp. There's blood caked in my hairline and underneath my nails. I brush my teeth, and it takes more than ten minutes to get the tangles out of my unruly hair before I throw it up in a bun again.

I emerge from the bathroom in another caftan. This one is much less ornate, just plain ivory cotton. I really don't care what Levi has to say. I like these things. They are somehow both utilitarian and dreamy, which is a bonus for me personally. Unsurprisingly, Levi is asleep on the bed. I sneak in beside him and pull out my laptop. No more stalling. It's time to find out if Ezra is here or if he's at least been here before moving on. I log in to our e-mail and find one from him. Immediately my heart starts to hammer. I purposely exhale slowly, knowing that overreacting won't do anyone any good. I think about giving Levi a good shake, but then I decide against it after reading the message, which says only:

FNLY DCODE EDO'S PRVTE FILES. ROONES NOT WHT THEY SEEM, AM BEING FLLWD BY UNKWN, 27 RFTS SO FAR-KEEP GOING

I close the laptop and hug it to my chest and think.

The key thing: Ezra is alive. He may not be totally safe, but he's alive, and then I think, *What is* going on? *Who* is following him? The same person who shot Levi? Probably. There's also a large statistical probability that we are now on the same course. That's two Earths in a row we've both been to. We're on the right trajectory to Ezra.

I feel a sudden twinge to go after him right away, but then Levi shifts, oblivious, and I remember we need to wait. He needs to recuperate if we're going to go after who or whatever this threat is. We can Rift out tomorrow. Levi must get his full strength back, and I could use at least two hours of sleep and some food. Who knows where we'll end up next.

I put the laptop down and get under the covers. The lamps in the room are hammered brass with Moorish cutouts. They throw a fantastic kaleidoscope of patterns on the walls around me, which grow longer every second I'm awake. I just need a little nap. A few minutes of rest and then I'll be ready to go.

I'm asleep before I can make any more promises to myself.

WHEN I AWAKEN, IT'S FULL night, and the soft strings of some kind of guitar float up through the open window. The bed is empty beside me and there's a knock at the door. I rub my eyes, a little disoriented.

"I've got it," Levi says, moving to open the door, and quickly accepting a tray. He's ordered food. Fantastic. I'm still a bit out of it, but I'm also starving. Levi walks past me holding the large room service tray in his hands and I notice he's wearing only jeans. Maybe his sensuit can't make shirts or something . . .

"Come on," he calls to me as he walks through what I had assumed was just a window out to a small patio. The patio is only large enough for a small table with two chairs. There's a view of the courtyard, which has been set up for a dinner service. Other guests are eating below, enjoying the music I'd been hearing.

Levi lifts the lids off of two bright orange tagines and the food smells amazing—lamb, I think, with saffron. As we dig in, I tell him about Ezra's message.

"Hmmm," Levi says quietly.

"'Hmmm'? That's all you have to say? Ezra was *here*. And he's being *followed*. He's decoded Edo's computer. You don't have a single opinion on any of that? Nothing but 'hmmm'?" I ask, even as I practically inhale a mouthful of food.

"No. Mostly I'm just surprised you didn't wake me up right

away so we could Rift out to find your . . . Ezra." Well, at least I know that something I've said along the way has taken hold. He isn't leering or sneering and he caught himself before he called him my boyfriend.

"You were shot. You needed to rest. Neither one of us will be of much use to Ezra if we're too exhausted to fight."

"Okay." I can tell that he's got more to say on the subject but is withholding. I'm relieved. I don't want to go into the specifics about why today—tonight—I am choosing our welfare over Ezra's. It is the more strategic move, to be sure, but such a conversation would likely meander into murky psychological terrain. Levi continues to stare at me. It's unnerving.

I can taste cumin on my tongue. The night's heat has made me sweat. The cotton fabric of my caftan is sticking to my chest. I'm beginning to wonder if that whole "professional and personal" speech I made to Levi was just as much for my own benefit as for his. It is absolutely true that he needs to stop thinking of Ezra as some goofy, helpless boy who did something wrong. And, it's also true that the way Levi is looking at me right now makes me want to clutch at the sides of this chair. I know I should say something, because the silence is pulling itself back as tight as a slingshot. I rack my brain for some innocuous comment to say, something safe. Kittens. Babies. No! Not babies. Babies are made . . .

With the sex.

It's Levi who speaks up first, saying the one thing I kind of want him to and also the thing I was praying he wouldn't, given my current mood and the fact that this is literally the setup for a super-hot love scene in basically any movie I've ever seen. "As long as we're going to be here for a few more hours, I've taken a couple more red pills. Hope that's okay with you?"

"Fine," I say quietly.

I look down at what's left of my meal and begin to eat. I don't know what's coming next, but I do know that I won't let this awesome dinner go to waste because I'm about to deprogram Levi. Best-case scenario I walk away feeling confused and/or guilty and with no appetite because of it. Worst-case scenario I don't get to eat . . . ever again. So I refuse to let ARC deny me the pleasure of this meal.

"You cool?" he asks almost lazily. I'm sure it's the pills. They don't get you high, but they do help you let go. It's the only way the deprogramming will work. You have to be open.

"Yeah," I respond, and then take a big drink of water. "I'm just wondering how we got here. I mean, I know how we got here . . . well, actually, no, I don't even really know how the getting here works. I just . . . *don't know*. I. Don't. Know. Anything. Sometimes I feel like I'm not even here, that this all must be a dream." I run my fingers through my hair and lift my chin. "The only time I feel like I have any sort of clue is when I'm fighting. I thought we'd be doing more fighting. I didn't count on having to spend so much time in my own head."

"I feel like that, too," Levi admits with a smile. "Only, I don't know how to say it because I've been brainwashed and I have a penis, so that often prevents me from being able to articulate deep reflection."

I chuckle. "The Dalai Lama has a penis. Kinda throws a wrench in that argument," I tell him cheekily.

"Ah, yes, but he hasn't been brainwashed."

"That you know of." I raise an eyebrow and we both smile. "I'm going to go put my uniform on." Levi just nods and stays where he is. I put our guns away, in the safe, because a handy firearm is an added concern that I don't want to have to think about on top of everything else. I get my sensuit to cuff, and I realize that I am almost naked, with Levi just a few feet away. I also realize that I don't care all that much. It's just my body, and he's already felt a fair bit of it. I slide my uniform on and tell him he can come in.

"What do you want to use?" I ask. "We can turn the TV on. Maybe some music?"

"I think this music will be okay," he says softly, gesturing with his thumb out the window even as he walks toward me.

"You have a soft spot for North African guitar solos?" I say, trying to lighten the serious shadow beneath his mouth as he gets closer.

"This is perfect. I'm calm. I don't need to think about how I felt when I was a kid. I don't want to feel like a boy right now." He stops a foot away. I swallow. Hard.

"Your heart is racing," Levi observes.

"So is yours," I counter softly. Why can't I laugh it off? He moves closer until he's just inches away. He takes his open palm and places it gently on my cheek. I find myself nuzzling into it. With his other hand, he slowly slides the zipper of my uniform down just a few inches. With his thumb, he peels back the fabric and moves his head down. His lips hover over my collarbone. I can feel the heat of him whispering my name, or something, over gooseflesh. He places two or three feather-light kisses there on my skin. And then his tongue snakes over the bone.

This doesn't feel like deprogramming. This doesn't feel like I'm doing Levi some big favor.

This feels real.

My mind scrambles to get control. On one hand, I absolutely want him to stop. I have a boyfriend. Who I love. On the other hand, Levi's smell, the nearness of him, is actually making me sway lightly back and forth on my feet, like I'm

214 / AMY S. FOSTER

weightless, and like there could be more to feel that I don't know about yet—and I want to.

I start to say my mantra:

This for Ezra. This for Ezra. This for Ezra.

Levi's head comes up. His hand is still on my cheek. We look at each other. We are such liars. But this isn't a lie. Our bodies are burning. Our eyes are drinking each other in. Levi moves in and kisses me. There is a hesitation, for whatever reason—the Blood Lust, lack of experience, Ezra. But that hesitation is quickly replaced with need. His kiss becomes insistent and my mouth responds in kind. I wrap my arms around his neck. His tongue flickers in and out of my mouth and I'm not thinking about anything now except for him.

This is for Ez—

The mantra is immediately cut off. A needle pulled from a record. A scream muffled by a fist. A screeching, wailing crowd that goes silent because it's the last crucial play.

There is no mantra. No Ezra.

There is only Levi.

Everywhere.

He picks me up by the ass and I wrap my legs around him. He maneuvers us so that we are against a wall. He's so strong that he can hold me with a single hand. He uses the other to pull my face closer to his. I am nothing more in that moment than a mouth and a body. We grind against each other. I feel my breath catch. My God, this feels good.

Levi pulls away. He looks at me. We've forgotten ourselves. I've forgotten too much about what we're doing here, about my life outside this room with the fantastic lighting and the smell of night-blooming jasmine, which has somehow managed to cling to our skin and our hair. Levi puts his hand on the zipper of my uniform once more and I practically beg him to open it all the way . . . but then I see it.

His eyes narrow.

Darken.

Change.

He's looking at me, but he no longer sees me. An ice-cold rush replaces the racing warmth along my limbs. My heart pumps even faster now, but not with excitement. With fear.

The Blood Lust.

I brace myself for what's coming. He lifts me up and literally pitches me across the room. Luckily, what's across the room is the bed, so instead of landing on the floor, I hit the mattress. Before I can even come close to getting up, Levi is on me. He grabs me by the hair and yanks me off the bed. Now I'm on the tiled floor. I curl up into a ball to protect my neck and head.

I feel the kicks through my uniform. They hurt, but it's not too bad. Levi's bare feet are no match for the fabric of the uniform. I told him that day on the beach that I wouldn't fight back again, and I intend to honor that promise, no matter how much it costs me. I know from experience that the only way the deprogramming will work is if you go all in. I cling to the faint memory of his hand on my cheek.

The kicks stop and Levi begins to punch me. He punches at my forearms, trying to get to my head. It would only take a couple good shots from him to shatter my skull. I can't really see, so I'm momentarily unprepared when I feel the weight of his body on top of me. He's forcing me onto my back. I try as hard as I can to keep my body locked in a fetal position, but he's simply too strong. He wrenches me straight and sits astride me, both knees squeezing my pelvis.

He pulls me up by my crossed arms, which are protecting my face. I know what he's going to try to do next and I quickly maneuver my palms to the back of my head so that when he smashes me back down on the tiles, my skull is protected. He throws me down with significant force and then yanks me sharply back up again two or three more times. When that doesn't work he reaches for my throat.

Am I ready to die for this?

As a soldier, I'm always ready to die, at least in an abstract kind of way. On the surface, it does seem ridiculous to lose my life so that Levi can have sex. But, of course, deprogramming the Blood Lust is about so much more than sex. It's about reparations. It's about reclaiming a part of ourselves that was violated and abused when we were children. It's about being able to love, fully and honestly—a counterbalance to all the times we are required to hurt and kill. So, in that sense, it's worth the risk to my life. But if Levi strangles me, if he ends me, he might as well take out his sidearm and blow his brains out right after. Levi can be rude and insensitive, but he is honorable. He is a decent person. He would never be able to live with my death on his hands.

The trouble is—I can't protect my head and my neck at the same time. When I feel Levi's fingers wrap around my throat, I still manage to stay calm. At the end of the day, this horrific scene being played out might look to an outsider like Levi has all the power. In reality, it's me who's got the advantage. I am in armor. Levi isn't wearing anything more than his jeans. I'm in control, and Levi has no control at all, which puts me in a tactically superior position.

I feel the pressure of his hands. So I take my own hands and lock them around his wrists. I pull them off my skin. "Levi," I tell him softly. "I won't fight back. I won't hurt you."

These words, which I say as soothingly as I can, have the opposite effect I was hoping for. Levi backhands me. Hard. My surprise and the sting of pain gives him enough time to start strangling me again. I feel my airway closing down.

"Levi," I gurgle through the stronghold. *"Please."*

My plea brings his eyes to mine. He's looking right at me now. My body is slack. Not only am I not fighting, *I'm not even defending myself.* This is enough for him to pause. He releases the pressure at my neck and I gulp for air, but still, I don't dare move. I just keep looking at him, without judgment, without anger. I see the shift come over him physically. The Blood Lust drains out of him slowly, in small measures, like water from a sieve. He gets off of me and crawls over to the bed and sits on the edge of it. He covers his entire face with his forearms, scrunching his hair up in his fists. Levi is making himself as small as he possibly can. I know exactly the shame he's feeling. I know that telling him that everything is fine and that it's okay won't mean anything. Instead, I just sit up on the ground for a few moments so that his knees are touching the left side of my face.

"That was good," I croak out. I'm sure my esophagus is bruised. My neck is no doubt turning a deep purply black in the shape of his fingerprints. "You stopped. You didn't kill me. You didn't even hurt me all that much," I lie. My throat is on fire and the rest of my body feels whiplashed. My cheek still stings from his backhand.

Levi brings his elbow to his knees. I see his eyes, reddened, watery, look down at me. He's not crying, but he's close. "I could have. I *wanted* to." He barely manages to get out that last part.

"No—you didn't *want* to. You just *did* it. Because they did this to you, to us."

"Look," I say in a hoarse whisper. "I know you're used to being the best. To winning everything all the time. But the Blood Lust isn't something you can win. You've already lost too much to it. You can put it in its place, *the past*, as part of your history where it belongs. That's the best you can do. You did that tonight."

"Don't," he says as he jumps to his feet. "Don't be so nice, so understanding." He's pacing now and all I can do is look at him. "One minute we are practically having sex and the next minute I'm using you as a punching bag. It's fucked up, it's fucking *me* up, so stop normalizing it."

All I can do is give a kind of half laugh. "I think we should just eliminate words like that from our vocabulary. They've become irrelevant. 'Normal,' 'regular,' 'common,' 'logical.' Let's just stop using them because it just makes this whole thing more frustrating." I say this as I lean back on the bed's mattress. "I mean, look at us. We're in Morocco. Like, *Africa*. We didn't get here on a plane or a boat. We got here by traveling through a tear in the universe. Before that we were in Battle Ground, where another version of *me* helped us after you'd been shot by an unknown assassin. And before that we were in L.A. fighting as Roman gladiators. And *before* that—"

"Stop. I get it."

"Then get this. We will never be normal ever again, so let's stop trying. Give me the honor and respect I deserve as your fellow soldier, your equal, by letting yourself off the hook. You give me plenty of reasons to be pissed at you, but this isn't one of them. I don't need the extra emotional baggage of your guilt getting in the way of this mission, so let it go. *Now*."

Before he can say anything else, I get under the covers and turn off the small lamp beside the bed. I probably won't sleep, but I want him to understand the conversation is over.

I hear him grumbling to himself, unhappy that he's basically being dismissed. I don't care. I meant what I said. I'm not mad at him. If there's anyone I'm mad at, it's myself. I can keep on lying to him, pretend that what's happening is all part of the deprogramming process, because what does he know? He's never done it before and I doubt he's had a more sexual experience than the one we just had together. I, however, know better. What I felt tonight wasn't just about me helping him. It wasn't *professional*. My God, if the Blood Lust hadn't kicked in, I think I may very well have let what was happening between us play all the way out. I wanted him. I wanted him more in those moments than I wanted oxygen. I also know that it's wholly different from the way I want Ezra. Ezra is kind and nurturing. Ezra is safety and love. Levi is the exact opposite. He's a lit fuse. He's heat and intensity. With Ezra I remember who I am and forgive myself for the terrible things ARC commanded me to do. With Levi I forget everything—what I've done, where I am, what I want—forgiveness doesn't apply when I'm with him. I don't care about it. And because of that I have to think that what I'm feeling is just lust. It's a base emotion. You can't build a relationship of any real substance on something like that. I can only hope that when I tell Ezra about this, he'll be able to see this for what it is. A completely inexperienced girl suddenly being thrust into a world of emotions that she's never been allowed to have.

Never allowed *herself* to have.

After a few moments, I hear Levi crawl into bed beside me. I feel him reach for me and take my hand, and I fight the urge to pull closer and take comfort from him. At this moment, my thoughts are with Ezra. At least, they are until Levi speaks.

"I'm letting it go. I just want you to know that I understand what you're putting at risk every time you agree to help me. Thank you. It's inadequate, but it's all I've got." Instead of saying anything, I just squeeze his hand. I'm hurting all over and the part of me that needs to heal takes over. Tonight has been exhausting on every level. I close my eyes and drift off to sleep.

I don't know how much later it is when I find myself jerked awake, not by Levi or a prayer or the rising sunlight. A *feeling* wakes me up. I try to focus. What exactly am I feeling? A tug. A pull from somewhere. I look over at Levi. He's humming again. Loudly. I put an ear up to my own skin, and it's doing the same.

"Levi," I say quietly as I nudge him. Levi sits up and looks at me. "There's something . . . I don't know. Something's not right here." Levi immediately bounds out of bed and puts his uniform back on in the space of about two seconds. He attaches his belt, but he has to go into the hotel safe for his gun.

"Did you hear something?" he asks quietly.

"Well, yes, but please don't ask me to describe it. Mostly it's that I feel something. Like a wrongness, and we're both whistling again." I watch as Levi grits his teeth. I know he doesn't quite believe me. Or maybe he does believe me, up to a point. But he wants more than a vibe. He wants tangible proof. Still, I'm getting the benefit of the doubt here, seeing as he just beat the tar out of me a little while ago and owes me big time.

"So what do you want to do?"

"I suppose I want to go and check it out. Go outside, see if the feeling becomes stronger or weaker in any given direction."

Levi nods his head. "Sure," he agrees without enthusiasm, but at least he agrees. Levi makes his sensuit morph into his regular backpacker attire and I do the same, hiding our guns in the folds of our clothing. We walk out the door, but I'm in front of him, ready to guide us.

We leave the hotel and begin to walk. It's three A.M. The streets are quiet, but not deserted. Luckily the moon is full on this Earth, so there is plenty of light. I focus on the feeling. It's not queasiness or cramps, it's more like a fluttering of wings in my stomach, beating slower or faster depending on where we go. The wings flap less and I switch direction until they get rapid again. This lasts for about fifteen minutes. We find ourselves in the souk, where all the stalls are closed, their windows latched and chained, and large pieces of plywood covering tinier vendors.

To his credit, Levi says nothing, His steps mirror my own, but every once in a while I hear him give a deep, impatient sigh. I know he's frustrated and I'm also aware that every twist and turn we take over the uneven cobbled streets puts us at a tactical disadvantage. This place is a maze. Some avenues are only as wide as my outstretched hands. Some dead-end with no way to escape. Too many places for an ambush.

This is not the kind of place where a soldier feels comfortable.

We see him after we've rounded yet another corner. He's small in stature and his face is completely obscured by a shadow from a building overhead. I can tell he's wearing a long robe, a djellaba. Levi and I halt about twenty feet away.

"Interesting," the man says in a language that is most certainly not English, but I understand easily enough. "I have been waiting for quite some time, wondering if you would seek me out, and now here you are."

"Are you the asshole who shot me?" Levi asks in English. The man ignores him and continues to address me.

"We suspected that at least one of you would be Kir-Abisat.

I do not yet know if this is good or bad. Either way, it must be reported immediately." And with that, the man punches a button attached to his outfit, and I feel a greater, heavier tug, not just from my belly, but from my entire body. The Rift he opens swirls into action with alarming speed. Without even so much as a backward glance, the stranger steps through and the Rift closes again.

"Well, " I say with a wispy sigh, "shit."

"What?" Levi asks in a wary tone.

"He didn't look like one, but that man was speaking Karekin."

CHAPTER 17

We walk out of the next Rift into a fairy-tale forest. Fat, wide, bright green ferns cover the ground entirely. Towering conifers surround us, their branches puncturing tiny holes in the blue sky above, allowing little pockets of yellow sunlight to crisscross around us like a laser light show. Levi and I have not discussed the stranger we saw in the souk. There is not much to say. We did not get a look at his face. We have no idea where he was from or where he was going. All I know for sure is that he was speaking in the language of our enemies. He is a complication and a distraction. We are not Rifting across the Multiverse to ferret out the secrets of the Karekin. We have another mission. Find Ezra. Get intel. Get home.

Which means the mysterious Karekin stranger will have to wait.

Not that it's easy to put it out of my mind. Still, when you've been a soldier in one form or another since you were fourteen years old, it's not too hard to focus on the task at hand. And right now, that means surveying our surroundings and figuring out where the hell we are.

It's immediately clear we're not in Battle Ground. I don't even think we are in the Pacific Northwest. This is not an echo Earth. This place feels entirely too primeval. It takes me a couple of seconds to make this assessment . . . and then a couple more to realize that we are not alone. I glance at Levi. He has noticed this, too. Ever so slowly, we see them emerge from behind the trees and fallen logs. Immediately, Levi and I unhook our rifles and lift them up to our shoulders. The guns feel a bit over-the-top here in the enchanted forest, but I can't get an accurate read of how many of them there are (and how many are still hiding). Better safe than, well, dead.

They are a humanoid species, walking upright on two legs with arms and eyes. But the similarities end there. A female and male, with characteristics distinct enough to tell their gender, separate themselves from the others and step forward. They are a tall people, between seven and eight feet, but their height isn't the most remarkable thing about them. No, what really stands out are the giant ivory horns spiraling out from the sides of their heads—antlers. Their skin ranges in color from ochre to rust, and is covered with sleek, downy hair. Basically they are deer people. Or maybe antelope people? Or elk people? Whatever they are, they're—unsurprisingly—majestic.

The woman has braided some of her strawberry blond locks and wound them up and around her antlers. The rest of her hair hangs loose and down her back. Her antlers are decorated with tiny gold and silver charms that tinkle and sing when she moves her head. The male doesn't sport these decorations. Instead, he has symbols and pictures carved into the hard bone.

The two who approach us have open, kind faces, and they gesture clearly for us to follow them. When the rest of them fully emerge, about twenty in all, I see that they are all similarly dressed and styled.

"They were waiting for us. They knew we were coming, or else why would they know to gather right here, in this spot?" I remark, my voice soft and hoarse still from what happened last night. Sleep healed the brunt of my injuries, but I haven't recovered completely. There's still swelling in my vocal cords, and the bruises on my throat are the greenish yellow of mending skin.

"Yeah," Levi concurs. "I think you're right." I'm sure he noticed the frailty in my voice, but he's choosing not to remark on it, as if I insisted, and I'm grateful. Neither one of us can afford to be distracted by regrets while in this new place.

"I don't think they're hostile, though," I say. "I mean, if they wanted to hurt us, they're big enough. And they could have rushed us the moment we stepped through the Rift. I say we follow them."

"Fine," Levi agrees, but makes no move to lower his weapon. "We follow the . . . elk people. But we don't trust them."

I squint in his general direction. "They're an unknown, so I don't trust them, either. But I also don't feel comfortable pointing a rifle at their heads when they've done nothing even remotely hostile to provoke us," I throw out, my voice feeling stronger with every passing minute. I let go of my rifle and grudgingly, Levi does the same.

"The SenMachs weren't hostile, either, just remember that," Levi warns.

"Yeah and now we've got a powerful ally and an awesome computer that gives ATMs the ability to make it rain, so let's keep that in mind, too."

The male and female who had stepped out first wait for us as the others begin to walk ahead. I nod my head and start to move toward them. There's no way I'm going to get Levi to be less paranoid, or less of a hard-ass. I can't change the way he is, but I can change the way I feel about his behavior. This is just him. This is who he is. All the deprogramming in the world won't ever turn him into a shoulder shrugger—or an "I'm down for whatever" dude. He looks after his mom and sister. He's the man of the house and probably has been for a long time. Regardless of his Citadel status, he's just naturally cautious.

Our procession is brisk. With their long strides, our enhancements come in handy as we keep pace with them along a seemingly random path. To an untrained eye, it would probably look like we are wandering. My experience allows me to see something different. Evenly trod patches of dirt, broken-off twigs and branches, logs maneuvered in positions that are clearly not natural. This is a path, albeit a fairly hidden one.

I smell the village first: smoke, burning wood, maybe food. And then I see the evidence; the air is thicker, sootier. We push through a particularly dense thicket and into a clearing. Right away I know that these are not a nomadic people. The dwellings are made of logs and cemented clay. There are gardens, and we pass by what looks like a school—little elk children are at play in a yard in front of a disproportionately large wooden building. I notice small buds, the tiny acorns of antlers, forming on some of their heads. Everyone who sees us smiles politely, but they do not seem particularly curious or surprised at our presence. This leads me to only one very hopeful conclusion: We are not the first humans they have seen. And that means something else:

Ezra could be here.

I throw up a silent prayer. *Please let Ezra be here.*

"It kind of has a Renaissance fair vibe to it, right?" Levi observes.

"You go to a lot of Renaissance faires, m'lord?" I ask through a smile I can't even try to hide.

"My parents took my sister and me when we were kids. I *was* a kid once, you know."

"I mean, I know that in theory, but it seems almost impossible to actually imagine," I say. After what happened a few hours ago, I find it difficult to think of Levi as anything *but* a man. A very serious, *powerful* man, with strong hands and intense eyes and—

I cut off that line of thought, and instead focus on how badly I hope Ezra is here. If my boyfriend is in this village, Levi will know soon enough. It feels wrong for some reason, to verbalize how anxiously hopeful I am, especially considering the way that Levi just stole a glance at me. He's done that a few times today already. He looks at me now like we have a secret. I know this look. It's the look I had when Ezra was hiding in my attic. Pretty soon I won't be able to put this off. We're going to have to talk about it. Thankfully, it's not right now. Now, we have to work.

The bigger group has splintered off and we are left with the lead two as escorts. They take us to a smaller cabin set apart from the more densely populated part of the village. There is a large garden in the front with neat rows of lettuce and tall bean stalks. Dozens of wind chimes hang from the porch area, which runs entirely around the square building. The chimes—a collection of spoons, hollow reeds, and other delicate metal objects—are strung together with brightly colored yarn and deftly woven twine. They spin into one another in the light breeze, a domino effect of singing bells next to a large collection of various-colored hanging crystals in different states of polish. Wherever we are, no ordinary person dwells here. Our escorts look at the front door and bow their heads, encouraging us to go forward. Hoping that Ezra might be in there, I don't think twice: I give the two a grateful smile, and start toward the few steps that lead to the entrance.

Levi grabs my arm and pulls me closer to him. "Hey," he hisses. "This place just went from Sherwood Forest to 'Oh Right, This Is Where the Stupid White Kids Die,' in, like, every horror movie I've ever seen. You're not picking up on that at all with your new special powers?"

"No," I tell him honestly. "It feels peaceful here. Why? Have you got a bad feeling?"

"Ryn," he says with exasperation. "I've *always* got a bad feeling. And these people or whatever, *have antlers*. So maybe you could act a little less eager to walk into the scary cabin in the woods, and more like a soldier investigating a potential hostile?" I look over at our two escorts, who are still smiling broadly at us, and not in a remotely creepy way.

Not that I can actually tell what a creepy smile on an elk looks like, but I'm not going to tell Levi that.

"What do you think they're going to do? Eat us? They're basically deer, which makes them vegetarians." Levi raises a single eyebrow at me. "Okay, they are *probably* vegetarians. But if we go in and intimidate whoever is in that house by having our guns at the ready—or, worse, if we hurt them—we won't get any answers. And personally, I'd like to know how they knew we were coming. So let's be cool until it's not time to be cool. Okay?" I yank my arm away and give him a bright smile. Before I can even get to the door, though, a woman walks out to greet us. Her hair is pure silver and styled entirely of braids that wind up around her antlers. She has far more charms hanging from her horns than the other females I've seen.

The sleek fur covering her body is white as fresh snow, mottled here and there with tufts of steel gray, and she wears a long linen patchwork dress in various vibrant hues of purple and deep scarlet. Over the dress is an indigo-dyed apron. I can see where it has faded in places she has run her hands over it, around the front where it ties, and lower, from years of wiping them clean.

From the way our two guides are acting deferentially to her, it's clear this woman is someone who commands respect, possibly an elder of some sort. Since neither I nor Levi know these people's customs or traditions and we have no clue what will be considered respectful or taboo, we will need to tread carefully. Our best hope is to take our cues from her, to watch every move she makes in an attempt to copy her actions. Seeing how all our training was to always treat "others" as hostile first and let ARC ask the questions later, this is new territory for us. I've at least started down this path after my visits to the Village, but I can see Levi is coiled like a spring. I give him a small, solemn nod that I hope says *Just trust me*, and—miracle of miracles—he seems to do just that. It's subtle, but I've been around him long enough to see him relax just a bit. I look back at the silver-haired woman. She gives us both a brilliant smile. She is clearly pleased to see us. I return the open smile, and I am happy to see that Levi does the same.

She ushers us inside and closes the large door behind her. Her house is cozy and snug, but large enough for her to maneuver her tall, graceful body with ease. From the dozens of hanging dried plants and flowers attached to the rafters—and my extensive knowledge of fantasy novels—my initial guess is that she is some sort of healer. There is a significant hearth, and a makeshift kitchen off to one side with a large, smooth wooden table and copper and iron pots of various sizes sitting atop wide-planked shelves built in the wall. The common area is layered with many intricately patterned, handwoven rugs. It's big enough for more than a few of these elk people to gather together for meetings. I wouldn't say that this is *the* public meeting space, but there is ample room for this woman to hold an audience, and I get the sense she does that often.

The three of us simply stand there for a moment or two. The only sound is the music from the wind chimes outside. I make no move to sit on any of the chairs in the room. I don't speak, because I'm not sure if it's appropriate for me to say anything before she does. The woman maintains her happy, warm smile, and holds out her hands, which look human enough, apart from her nails, which are long and chestnut colored.

I take two strides, holding out my own hands, thinking that perhaps this is some sort of greeting. The moment that she takes hold of me, the room we are in disappears and I am assaulted with images. The elk woman as a child. The elk woman walking through the woods. I can see her without clothes, under the moonlight with others of her kind performing some kind of ritual with drums and dancing that she is leading. It's too much, too disorienting. I feel like I'm drowning in her memories, and my body, using its primal instinct, gulps for air. I pull my hands away from hers and take a step back. Her smile is gone, but she has a look that is clearly asking me to understand her.

"What?" Levi asks in alarm. "What happened?"

"I couldn't see. I mean, I could, but it was only pictures. I don't know, it was like a movie or something. I think it was

her, showing me things." I am aware that I am practically babbling, but the experience was incredibly intense. "I don't think
they can talk. I think they communicate with mind melds or
something."

Levi grimaces ever so slightly before stepping forward with
his own arms outstretched. He wants to see for himself. I
watch as the elk woman gently folds his hands into her own.
Levi practically gasps, and his green eyes glaze over. The
woman looks at him with just the barest hint of a smile on
her face. After a moment or two she releases him and nods
her head ever so slightly. Levi looks bewildered for a moment,
almost dazed. Then he clears his throat and nods almost im-
perceptibly back at her.

"You saw it, too, right?" I ask wildly. I take my pack off.
Whatever these people are, I don't believe they want to hurt
us, and the extra weight of my bag feels cumbersome and unnecessary. "Is that possible? I know we've experienced our fair
share of the bizarre when it comes to nonhuman species, but
psychics? Can that be a thing? For real?" I wonder.

"I don't see why not." Levi undoes his own pack and lets
it drop to his feet. I'm sure he would take his rifle off, as I
would, but this doesn't seem like an appropriate place for a
weapon. It looks right on us, but here? In this peaceful little
house? There's nowhere we could place them that wouldn't
feel wrong somehow. "Last night, a *feeling* woke you up and
we followed that feeling to a person, who then escaped into a
Rift. You're telling me that you can hear people's skin sing,
so I'm not sure why a species that uses ESP can't be in the
mix, too."

Just when I think I understand Levi, he turns around and
surprises me. I fold my arms, resting them on the strap of my
rifle. *I'm* supposed to be the open one. He's supposed to be the

shut-off, shut-down guy. I wonder what the woman showed him that could turn him into such an instant believer.

From what I can piece together from the vision she gave me, she is not only a healer, but some kind of shaman as well. If these people can communicate through telepathy, then perhaps there is also some way that they can see into the future. As improbable as that seems, it's also the most likely explanation as to how they knew we were coming.

The shaman gives me a slightly more determined look and once more reaches her hands out. I don't absolutely love the idea of my mind being invaded, no matter how well-meaning the intention, but it seems like this is the only way we are going to get any answers. I slowly lift my arms up and forward, and she takes them, the fur on her palms cool and reassuring.

The flood of images in my head is instantaneous. Only this time I know what to expect, so I steady myself mentally, bracing for the barrage.

Ezra. I see Ezra right here in this room!

My heart begins to race. Ezra being fed. Ezra sleeping. Ezra working on his computer. And then horribly, Karekins. Dozens of Karekins. Unlike the Karekins I deal with in Battle Ground, these ones do not trample everything and everyone around them. They move silently through the village. They have weapons, but they are not drawn.

I watch in horror as they enter the shaman's house. The wise woman steps out of their path with a bowed head, and Ezra, understandably, freaks out. The scene instantly goes dark, like a cap being screwed onto a lens. Then it opens up again. Ezra is going with the Karekins. He is going willingly, without a struggle, though his face is uneasy, his mouth fixed into a straight, determined line. He walks into a Rift with them and disappears.

I drop my hands and immediately cover my face. I don't know what's going on, and if I let that get to me I'll lose it. I close my eyes, relishing the absolute blackness, the peace I find in seeing nothing. I knew this trip would be confusing. I knew it would be difficult and even perilous, but I had no idea that I could ever feel so helpless, so incredibly small and insignificant.

I'm hearing things. I'm sensing things that make no logical sense. For years I've been reliant on what my body can do, trusting my strength and my physicality. I've used my mind to strategize, research, and plan, but what's happening now goes beyond intellect. I am walking into a world of spirit and energy. All the answers I need seem to be in this realm, and I am desperately unprepared to deal with it. For the first time in years, I feel my own age.

"Ezra was here," I finally say, softly in Levi's general direction. Immediately, Levi wants more information, but I have none to give. I try to explain that Karekins came and took him, but it doesn't make sense. The Karekins we know would have burned this village to the ground and killed everyone in it.

Throughout the course of this back-and-forth between us, the wise woman has gone about preparing us food. She takes wooden bowls from the shelf and ladles out some kind of stew or soup from the large iron cauldron hanging inside the fireplace. She puts the bowls on the table and pours tea into pint-size ceramic cups that she lays down gently beside our meals. Then she stands behind one of the big bent willow chairs and coughs.

Levi and I whip our heads around and look at her. "Nascha," she says in a voice that flutters like the bells swaying on her antlers, while pointing at her chest.

"I thought they couldn't talk," Levi says to me, like I'm some sort of expert.

"Well, I guess they can. Considering we don't know their language, I think the way they chose to communicate with us was far more effective," I reason.

Nascha points at me and says, "Ryn." This is not a question. She knows my name. Ezra, of course, has told her. She points at Levi and then shakes her head. The chimes shimmy and sway.

"Levi," he tells her immediately. Nascha nods. She has a look about her. Her eyes tell me that she isn't troubled per se, but concerned. I wonder what about.

"*Kipitay . . . migise owaantee,*" Nascha tells us while gesturing to the food she has laid out for us. She's asking us to eat. I smile gratefully at her and unclip my rifle. I check that the safety is on and put it at my feet before I sit down. I don't want to eat. I have about a dozen questions I'd like to fire at her instead, but I don't speak her language, and I'm not sure that the ESP works both ways. If I want answers, it's going to take patience and time, the two things I'm feeling pretty low on right about now.

I slide the heavy chair back and sit down and Levi follows my lead. These chairs are large and my boots barely scrape the bottom of the floor. He takes off his gun, too, but puts it beside him on the table. Nascha eyes it with irritation, which Levi either doesn't pick up on or, more likely, since he's hyper-observant, like me, ignores. I lift the bowl up to my mouth and take a gulp. The soup is surprisingly thick and filled with vegetables.

"Ezra?" I ask. She must know his name, since she knew mine.

"*Wai.*" Nascha nods, and the bells and chimes sing. "Ezra."

So *wai* must mean *yes*. That's one word down. Okay. I look around the room once more. I begin to notice the little things. Tiny brown and green bottles filled with liquids and powders. Light filtering through a thick glass window. This tells me their civilization has made some advancements. They make glass. They know how to keep and preserve materials. A large wooden bookshelf is tucked into the corner close to the hearth. It's filled with books covered with thinly shaved wood and bound together with some sort of glue and twine. This tells me that they are not necessarily a people dependent on oral (or in their case, psychic) traditions. They write down their stories and histories. I look around again, this time for something resembling a clock or some sort of apparatus that will tell time. No such luck on that front. It would be useful for me to know how long ago Ezra was here.

I finish my soup quickly and smile, then pat my tummy, showing that it was good. "Levi, Ryn," I say, gesturing to me and my partner, "and Ezra . . . human." I point to her and then shrug my shoulders and hold up my hands and then point to Nascha, hoping she'll give me the name of her people. She cocks her head to one side, then says, "Levi, Ryn—Citadel. Ezra, human." I am starting to get the feeling that Nascha knows much more than I am giving her credit for.

"Citadels, yes," Levi explains, "but humans, too." Nascha answers this with a little squeak, which sounds to me like a passive-aggressive way to politely disagree. She then points to her antlers and herself and says, "*Woon-Kwa*." I nod my head to indicate that I understand.

I can't see how else I'm going to get across the questions I need to ask other than to use a paper and pencil. I could try to mime them, but even then I'm not sure how I would do it.

I take out the pad of paper that's always tucked into one

of the leather pockets on the front of my uniform. There's a little pencil inside, too, which I grab. I draw a picture of the sun and show Nascha. I point at the window and say, "Day." I then draw a picture of the moon and stars. "Night," I tell her, once again looking out the window while shaking my head, hopefully indicating that it's not night outside. I then start counting on each of my fingers. "One, two, three . . . Ezra . . . Days? Nights?"

Nascha takes out her hand as well and begins to count. "*Sho, bin, tiv.*" One, two, three. But, Nascha emphasizes her three straight fingers. "*Tiv. Tiv saqwee.*" I get it. It's been three days since Ezra has left. I begin drawing again. I pencil out a sort of stick figure and point, saying Ezra's name. Then I draw a more intricate picture. I'm no artist by any means, but I get along well enough. I have no idea if this is my altered genes or real, raw talent. I feel a twinge of homesickness for my dad, who is a real artist, and my mom, who, as a designer, can sketch her ass off.

I shake away those feelings and use the pencil to my advantage, emphasizing shadows and highlights to depict a Karekin. I show the picture to Nascha. She nods. "*Karreekin,*" she tells me in her accented English.

"Yes. Karekin. Karekin bad." I scrunch up my face and scowl. I make a fist and slap it into my other palm. Nascha gives me a look that says she's not sure what I'm trying to say. I draw another picture of a Karekin beating up the figure I had designated as Ezra. I rip out the page from my pad and slide it over to her. I begin to scribble furiously again. In this picture, I draw a Karekin cutting the throat of a human. Nascha just shakes her head. She thrusts her hands out and her fingers wiggle. She wants me to see what she saw. This time I'm eager.

I have to stand to reach across the table, but I do so without hesitation. When I take her hands, I forget about how weird and intrusive it is to have someone inside my head. I simply pay attention to the images she is showing me.

The Karekins move through the village. They do not bother or threaten anyone. They certainly aren't killing any of the Woon-Kwa. As it did before, this disorients me. It contradicts everything I know of the Karekins—a ruthless and barbaric race that has never even wanted to parlay in all my experience as a Citadel. They come through the Rift and they try to kill as many of us as possible. That's all. Even though we outnumber and outflank them, they fight to the death every time. The one time we managed to capture a live Karekin he slit his own throat before he would be taken as a prisoner.

I watch a discussion happen between Ezra and one of the Karekins. The words are garbled and distorted. Nascha doesn't speak English, so I suppose this is how it would sound to her. I pay close attention to Ezra. He looks troubled. He keeps nodding his head, but his eyes shift nervously back and forth. Ultimately, I watch him go willingly with the Karekin. They don't lay a finger on him. If anything, they are scanning the Woon-Kwa to make sure that none *of them* are a threat, as if they were suddenly Ezra's bodyguards.

This time, it's Nascha who releases my hands. I sit back down on the chair, trying to make sense of things, but I just feel even more confused.

"Levi," Nascha says softly before pointing to the door. "*Kipitay. Fopaq.*"

Levi looks around, as if somehow she could be talking to someone else. His lip curls and a sound comes out of his mouth that is half snort and half chuckle.

"She wants me to leave? Seriously?" Nascha's expression does not change. It's clear she feels badly for asking him to go, but it's also clear she wants me alone.

"No way," Levi says with authority. "I'm not going anywhere. Anything that she wants to say, she can say it in front of me." I shrug my shoulders and look away. Levi leans in and practically whispers, "Ryn, has it occurred to you that maybe the Karekins didn't attack because these people are their *allies*? Have you considered that?"

I put my hand on his hand and give it a little squeeze. "I think she wants to talk to me about Ezra, and I don't think she wants you in the room for whatever she has to say or show me or whatever." Levi yanks his hand away and glowers. His teeth grind together, his jaw moving back and forth. I think for a moment he's going to say something. He opens his mouth for a second, and then he closes it again just as quickly. He scrapes his chair back so hard I'm afraid there might be a scuff mark on the soft wood floor. He grabs his gun, storms across the room, throws open the door, and slams it shut again behind him.

Embarrassed, I look at the table, waiting for Nascha to move or say something. Maybe Levi is right. Maybe I shouldn't be alone with any of these people. I know I can beat her in a fight, but she could have some crazy brain-melting superpower that could turn me into a vegetable. Right now, though, my concern for Ezra's safety overrides my own paranoia. I have to let Nascha take the lead. I hear the clamoring bells, the tiny chimes whistling and singing as she moves away from me. I bring my head up as she sets up two much more comfortable chairs in front of the fire. They aren't upholstered, but they are covered in layers and layers of pillows and knitted blankets. She takes a seat and gestures for me to do the same. I can't imagine what she wants to show me.

I walk over hesitantly and drop my body into the empty seat. The fire is warm, but not too hot. I look into Nascha's fascinating face. The flames catch on the charms hanging from her antlers. They sparkle and flicker on and off like stars. She holds out her hands and I lift up my own, a little slower than before. This time, Nascha takes my entire forearm. Her thumbs press down into the crease right below my elbow. The pressure doesn't hurt, but it's instant. She closes her eyes and I feel compelled to do the same. I hear her speaking her musical language. They are words I do not understand, but they are hypnotic, lulling. At first I try to resist, Levi's warning screaming in my head, but Nascha doesn't stop, and soon there's nothing I can do as I fall deeper into wherever it is she's taking me. The images slide into my head slowly. The outline comes first and then colors bloom, like film in a chemical bath.

The first thing I see is Levi. This is Levi when we first walked out of the Rift right here. Nascha was not there, so this must be a memory from one of our escorts—it seems the Woon-Kwa can transfer visions. As a secret keeper and a liar, I can't imagine living the way they do.

Nascha's grip intensifies and this time I feel her gentle probing inside my head like a knock on the door, a little *tap, tap, tap*. I'm no longer struggling. In fact, I *want* to know what she knows. I want to know what she didn't want Levi to see or feel. So I open my mind and she rushes in. She is fireflies and ballerina music boxes. She is sweetness and light. Then my own memories start to filter in. Levi and I in Morocco. First I am in his arms and then he is hitting me. Nascha and I both flinch as he attacks. There's no use explaining. If she now has access to my own memories, she will know everything about me and the Blood Lust.

A part of me is terrified to let anyone see so much of me,

and yet there is another, greater part, that is relieved. I never realized just how desperate I have always been for someone to really know me, to understand why I do the things I do.

She doesn't linger on that memory, though. Nascha is everywhere. She is rifling through everything in my head, but only bringing up the ones that can help her explain what she is trying to say. I see Levi in SenMach City curled up next to me on the bed. Levi and I on the beach the moment I say no to helping with the Blood Lust. I am seeing what she is seeing, how his body tenses when I get too near, but becomes even more rigid when I walk away. I see him volunteer for this mission. I watch him fight at the Rift in Battle Ground. Fight after fight, punching, hitting, kicking. He is fierce, strong, and focused, but somehow our eyes always seem to find each other when we are on duty together. I never realized it before. He is always watching out for me. *Always*. Nascha takes me back to the first time we met, when his sister, Flora, brought me to his house. The memory of this beautiful boy sitting on the couch with a bowl of cereal in his hands is visceral. I feel just like I did that day. My cheeks flush. I bite down on my lip.

My God, I had forgotten how much I liked him.

Then the visions are swept away as if they were nothing more than a thistle weed blown bare. They spin into the darkness of my mind and are replaced immediately with Ezra in this cottage. He looks so lost, not afraid but overwhelmed. I can tell that Nascha did her best to comfort him. I think she managed to. There is an image of Ezra working on his computer and he looks . . . maybe not happy, but centered and calm. The scene shifts. It's Levi pushing Ezra into the Rift to save my life. My heart sinks, but only for a moment, because Nascha does the most remarkable thing.

Here is Ezra at the Rift. This is my first memory of him.

He has just been spit out by it. He is disoriented, but strong. I am looking at him and then the perspective changes and he is looking at me. Nascha is sharing Ezra's own memories with me.

There is a constant back-and-forth. I am watching Ezra in his apartment in the Village, he is watching me, focusing on my neck and my mouth as I try to explain what we are as Citadels. There is a memory of my pacing, back and forth in my darkened living room waiting for him after he broke out of the Village prison. Then I stop moving, only to sit ram-rod straight on our couch for hours, waiting for him to walk through the door.

Nascha shows me the hidden room I had prepared for him. I am watching him at work, he is watching me, every move, paying attention to the smallest things. I watch myself broken at his feet when I figure out what the Roones had done to me, how they had lied to all of us. There is no magic chip inside our brains to turn our abilities off. We have been genetically altered forever. I feel Ezra's pain as he looks at me, his yearning to reach out.

I know what's coming next. Ezra deprogramming me. This is both beautiful and devastating to relive. The touching, slow fingers on smooth skin. The holding, the gentle prodding. But there is violence, too. I hit Ezra. I choke him. I almost kill him. Yet he never sees me as a monster. He loves me. I love him.

The images split in half, Ezra on one side, Levi on the other. Ezra is working on a computer. A whiteboard behind him is covered in equations, papers are flying. Levi is on the other side. In this memory we are fighting Karekins together in Battle Ground. Levi kicks one several feet in the air. I help the enemy land with my hand on his chest and then I whip my side arm around to shoot him in the head.

And then the images stop. Abruptly. Nascha releases the pressure on my forearms and I take them back. I dig my thumbs into the soft blankets puffed up around me. Nascha blinks hard and tilts her head to one side. A single tear falls from my left eye. It's not just seeing with the Woon-Kwa—it's feeling, too. I was swept up in the intensity of the memories. Like a ball of string, I am unwound. And now I'm scrambling, mentally, to roll it all back up into something tight and solid, without loops or knots. I wanted to be seen and known, but this is too much. *I'm* not even ready to face half the shit I've done, let alone ready for someone else to be witness to it. Not to mention all the feelings. There are so many damn feelings flying around here.

It's like a middle school boy-girl dance. Only *more* awkward.

And while Nascha's tribe seems capable of holding many emotions at once, I am not built to juggle so many. But, I can't break now; I've got to keep myself rolled up. It's not pride that is holding me together, but rather the knowledge that curling up into a fetal position and crying like a baby won't help me move forward. We have to go. We need to get to Ezra.

"Levi," she says, holding up one of her hands. "*Showw tai.*" Then she points at me. "Ryn. *Showw tai.*" Nascha's other hand goes up. "Ezra. *Kapa'a min. Fit showw tai.*"

I don't need to speak her language to understand what she's trying to say.

Levi and I are one thing. The same.

Ezra is different.

Fifteen minutes ago I would have said I knew exactly what my answer would be to these differences. Now, after she has shown me so much, a germ of doubt has crept in. I keep thinking that the Karekins and Roones and all the secrets and lies

I've been fed all these years are what's weighing heaviest on me. But Nascha has seen through me down to the truth. She will say what I cannot. Her visions show me what I can't bear to look at too closely. She is telling me what I have to do.

Choose.

And then it's too much, and I start to quietly cry.

CHAPTER 18

I suppose I don't cry like most people. If I let myself cry every time I felt miserable or overwhelmed, I would be a lunatic. I turn the pain inside out, like a pair of jeans before washing or flipping to the back page of a spiral notebook. I try to keep it all contained. Each tear that I let fall feels like an escaped prisoner.

With my eyes closed I will my body to be still, even as the drops leak through my lashes. The images Nascha showed me remain, the way some do after you've looked at something bright for too long. The outlines are there, movement, shape, form.

Ezra . . .

Levi . . .

What am I even doing? This isn't the time to be thinking these thoughts. Other teenage girls are free to while away hours, even days, lovestruck and boy crazy. I don't have this luxury. My feelings, whatever they are, are not useful right now. I'm a soldier, first and always. As I remind myself of that, I find myself suddenly shifting from sad and confused to truly annoyed. In that moment, I regain my composure.

I mean, couldn't Nascha have grabbed hold of a Karekin? Couldn't she have done the old woo-woo voodoo on one of them? Find out what the hell they want with Ezra? What their deal is? That at least would have served a greater purpose. This—this is verging on pathetic. My world, other worlds, thousands of lives on the line, and I get a vision quest about two guys and *cry* about it? Oh God. Am I becoming *that girl*? The "It's Armageddon! But which boy should I give my heart to?" girl?

No. No way.

I can choose not to be her. I can choose to focus on what's important. I'd like to convey the utter ridiculousness of this little love triangle to Nascha, but she's sitting there so serene and mystical, clearly believing that something sacred has gone on between us that I can only nod my head in thanks. There's no point in offending her, and I'm afraid if I tried to convince Nascha of my real priorities I would somehow only be proving her point.

I watch her slowly lift herself out of the chair and walk over to an intricately carved wooden box. God only knows what she wants to do to me now. If some kind of mushroom is involved I'm going to have to think about an exit strategy, pronto. Thankfully, all she does is take off a necklace that had been sitting beneath her clothes. When she holds it up it spins and glints in the light. It's not a locket or a charm. It's a key. Nascha fits it into a hammered brass lock on the box and turns it slowly to the right. The latch clicks and the lid opens.

From inside it she retrieves a sleek black object. Whatever it is, I can tell right away that it is not native to this Earth. When she hands it to me, I'm certain. It's some sort of flash drive. It's also Karekin tech. Shit.

I turn it over and over again in my hands. I'm so focused on what this little black thing could mean that I barely notice Nascha open the door. When I do, I see that she has called out to Levi. What really baffles me, though, is that Nascha does not seem conflicted by the different versions of Karekins she has seen in her visions. I don't understand it. What does she see that I can't? After reaching through my memories and experiencing firsthand—well, I guess it's secondhand really—the degenerate barbarism of the Karekins in Battle Ground, how can she be so unconcerned with the Karekins who took Ezra? The only reason I can think of is that Nascha will only involve herself with the things she can actually change. Or possibly, and more realistically, they are pacifists. The Karekins have come and gone. Levi and I are here.

Levi walks through the door and Nascha gives us a silent bow and walks outside. She's giving us our space. I appreciate this, but I'm not sure it's necessary. Despite the compelling things she has shown me, right now my focus is entirely on the piece of technology I am gripping in my hands. Ezra is with the Karekins.

I stand and hold my palm out and show Levi. He takes the small, black, oblong device and holds it up to his face, scrutinizing it. "She gave you this?" he finally asks.

"Yeah."

"Did she happen to mention or mime or vision quest the way in which she actually got it?" Levi asks, an obvious edge to his voice.

"She didn't and I don't think it matters. One of the Karekins who took Ezra left it behind. I bet if we put it in the SenMach computer, it will Rift us directly to where Ezra is being held."

"Riiiiggght. Or maybe it will blow up our computer and we'll be trapped here in Hippie Antler Land."

We stand there, facing each other as tiny motes of dust dance around in a shaft of sunlight shining between us. I understand his reluctance, but there's only so much wandering we can do out here in the Multiverse. This is our chance to get Ezra. It might not be the safest call, but since when do Citadels stick to what's safe?

"Okay," I begin, resting my hands on the back of the chair I had been sitting on. "What if, and I'm just throwing this out there, the Karekins are not necessarily the bad guys?" The thought surprises me as much as it does Levi, who returns my suggestion with nothing more than a blank stare. We stand there for a moment and then, annoyingly, he begins to laugh.

"Seriously? Have you totally lost it?"

"Don't," I warn. "Don't do that."

"Do what?"

"Be . . . *you*. Turn into a prick right now. I need you to think. Help me work this out. That guy who's been tracking us, *somehow*, he could have shot me in the gladiatorial ring. He could have busted down the door in Marrakech, caught us both unaware and killed us. And that guy, whoever he was, had Karekin tech, but he wasn't one of them. What if all the fighting we do in Battle Ground against the Karekins is nothing more than a protection detail? What if their beef is with the Roones?"

"You're grasping at straws, Ryn. The Karekins are vicious fucks. If they wanted to get to the Roones, why not just make a run for the base in formation? Why make a point to injure and kill as many Citadels as they can?"

I shrug. "Why not kill the Woon-Kwa? Why not just kill Ezra? They have no way of knowing whether or not he's a Citadel. We are missing a vital piece of information, and this," I say, holding up the drive, "could fill that gap. I think we should see what's on it and then make a decision."

"There is a ninety-nine percent chance it's a trap—you're aware of that, right?" Levi asks me flatly.

"Yes. But they've got Ezra, and that's where I'm going. Also, we *do have* another computer." I watch as Levi clamps down on his jaw. His head turns away so that I can't read his face. The wind chimes fall into each other on the porch outside. The music is metal and hollowed-out wood. As beautiful and exotic sounding as it is, it does nothing to fill the expanse of silence between us.

Finally, Levi speaks. "Just like that, huh? You're going to go. You don't have a plan. You don't even seem to care if I come with you. You're just going to leave. You're willing to Rift into a nest of Karekins, *for him*."

"Levi," I say softly, walking over to where he is standing. "This entire mission has been about Ezra, about saving him. Why are you acting like that's some kind of surprise twist? I risk my life every day in Battle Ground for strangers, to keep people I don't even know safe from the monsters that spill out of that Rift. Imagine how far I'm willing to go for someone I love."

"All I can imagine right now is that you're a fucking liar."

I take a step back. I'm this close to punching him.

"I warned you not to be a dick," I practically growl.

"Or what? Are we going to throw down in Grandma's love shack?"

"Stop it!" I throw my hands in the air. "Just . . . stop. Jesus.

Levi, I know it's complicated, or it's gotten complicated . . ." I try to reason, but even I'm not sure where I'm going with this.

"Complicated is a math problem, Ryn. Complicated is trying to figure out how to get out of a shift at work so you can make it to your mom's birthday dinner. This," he says, gesturing back and forth in the space between us, "this *is a thing* that you can't put down to deprogramming. You can't love someone *and* kiss me the way you did. I can hear your heartbeat. I see your face flush."

"So . . . what?"

"So *you* stop it."

I suddenly don't know what to do. Part of me feels like crying. Again! Part of me feels like throwing up. There is also a not-insignificant part of me that just wants to punch him. Instead, I take a deep, quivering gulp of air.

"You know what?" I say, "You're right. I don't know that much about relationships, practically nothing really, but I do know that you can love someone and be attracted to somebody else. It's chemistry, biology—it happens." Levi just looks at me stone-faced. Unconvinced. I continue anyway, because the words allow me not to think about taking action right now—whatever that action might be. "And we compartmentalize. That's what we do. One minute we're shooting someone and the next we're having dinner with our families. We're different. I mean, besides the supergenes. We can put important things away. We can lock them up so that they can't be touched by whatever is going on in that moment." Levi just shakes his head. The anger seems to have drained out of him completely. Now, he just looks tired.

The problem is, even as the words came out of my mouth, I wasn't sure if I believed them. Levi definitely doesn't.

"I don't *want* to kiss anyone else, Ryn. I'm not attracted to anyone else. You are the only person I want. Period. I don't need to compartmentalize anything, or put feelings away anywhere. I carry them around all the time. I have for a long time. I *want* to carry them around."

And there *it* is.

I swallow, gulp, actually. Levi is staring at me. Daring me to answer this. And now I really, really want to punch him, but then, just as quickly I want to hug him for admitting something that makes him so vulnerable.

"I think maybe you're confused—" I start to say, trying to calm things down.

"Oh, no you don't, Whittaker." He points his finger at me and raises his voice. "Don't you *dare* try to tell me that I don't feel what I'm feeling. You don't know how long it's taken me to feel. *Anything*. Don't take this away from me because it's inconvenient for you."

I cover up my face with both hands and then tuck my thumbs under my chin, breathing deeply into my palms. I knew this was coming. For God's sake, Nascha just warned me that exactly this was coming, but I thought it would be later, when Ezra was safe, and we had time to unpack and dissect these things.

"I don't want to hurt you," I say softly. "And I shouldn't dismiss the feelings you're having, either." I gulp again, and bite my lip. I have to say this and I hate it.

"I'm sorry, but I love him."

Levi says nothing.

"I know it. I know it like I know my own name. I know you want to feel, and I'm happy you're finally able to open up . . . but I don't think you should waste your feelings on me."

Levi gives me a slow, sad smile and then he walks over to

me. He takes both hands and runs them over my hair until they rest on my cheeks. Despite what I just said, I don't flinch at the intimate gesture, and I think he sees that. "What you're saying may be true, but it's not the truth," he says. "Not completely. Yeah, okay," he concedes, his thumb grazing beneath my eye as though I'm crying, "you still love Ezra. But you can't deny that whatever is between us has *changed* the love you have for him."

I look up into Levi's green eyes. I think back to that night at Flora's party, when I started to change, to question who I was and what we were doing as Citadels. Levi looked at me that night like he wanted to devour me whole. And maybe I knew there was something going on, but I pretended like there wasn't because, honestly, he scared me. Not in a physical way, but I was afraid of whatever was at the end of that look. I didn't want to be consumed by his affection—by *anyone's* affection—in that way. And now here we are, and all my fears are both justified and completely wrong—because *this* is what's on the other side. Intensity, loyalty, sacrifice. His love *is* ferocious, but it's honorable. He deserves my honesty.

I nod my head, as much as I can with him holding it. "I suppose it has changed things. Yeah. But don't take that as a victory, Levi. It makes me a cheat and an asshole. I'm being unfaithful to a person who's risked everything to help our cause. He could have just Rifted home. He didn't have to steal that stuff from the Roones. He's not a soldier. He's just a guy, a really good guy who wanted to help us find answers." I am desolate. My blood cells are razor blades, slicing my veins. I am cutting myself into pieces. "And look how I've repaid that kindness. Look what I've done. Look . . ."

Levi pulls me into his chest. It feels good, and that almost hurts worse. Because this is ultimately how I know the depth of Levi's feelings. He is holding me when I am hurting over another man.

Eventually, I pull away from him. I mentally shake off the pain I'm inflicting on myself. That's enough. I can't do this now.

"We'll go get him, Ryn. We'll get him and make sure he's safe. And if for some reason he isn't safe, we'll make the fuckers pay."

I look into his eyes—those fierce, vividly green eyes—and nod. I realize my voice is completely back and strong as ever when I say, "Roger that."

CHAPTER 19

The SenMach computer's tendrils absorb the information on the Karekin tech, and the screen bursts into binary life. A long series of zeros and ones scroll down the screen for over five minutes. I know then that whatever is happening is not just a simple command execution. If I have to guess, I'd say our QOINS are being rewritten. Each time a new page scrolls down, my heart beats a little faster. I have to stay positive and hope that Levi wasn't right. We could be changing our ability to Rift on a fundamental level. But if for some reason the tech is sabotaging our system, there is precious little we can do about it now, at least with this computer.

The screen goes dark, and Levi and I look at each other warily. There is nothing left to do now but go and see. Nascha strings a gorgeous gold necklace around my neck, a pendant with a smooth jet-black crystal topped with a crown of what looks to be tiny amethysts. To Levi she hands a similar crystal in a small wooden box, which Nascha insists he stick in his flak pocket, wanting him to keep it close.

There is a small audience outside Nascha's house. They stand tall, majestic, and beautiful, gathered in the shape of a crescent moon, giving us the space for what I assume they know is coming. Nascha sings a blessing over us. Her voice is haunting, somehow both full of hope and melancholy. I don't have many answers to much of anything and it seems like she has them all, so I really hope this isn't the last I'll see of her and her people. Besides, I never figured out how the Woon-Kwa knew we were coming. If they have a way to see into the future, it would be a pretty significant tactical advantage. I just wish that she had given me some kind of prescient clue as to what we are about to face.

Then again, it could be bad news, and, well, screw that.

We Rift out of the village, flying through the green expanse into what is most likely the most dangerous situation either of us has been in before. Inside the emerald waterfall of gravity and space, Levi and I find each other's hands. We clasp them together, needing the feel of skin on skin, clutching on to the hope that we will somehow find a way out of whatever situation we are about to face.

We keep our hands locked as we walk out of the Rift, but only for a moment. Once our feet touch solid ground we scramble to get our rifles unclipped. Levi is steady. He seems unfazed and not thrown in the slightest by where we are and I feel a little calmer.

I look around to get my bearings. We have landed in some sort of city center. This city, however, has been ravaged; at least three-quarters of the buildings have been hit by what I assume were bombs. They are empty shells, bricks and concrete falling out of their centers like spilled guts. A lot of the pavement is torn up and shredded. Curiously, in the distance, I see there are work crews. The damages to the city are being repaired. This doesn't tell me much, though, in terms of whether or not this location was on the winning or losing side of whatever war it suffered through. But it implies that the fighting is over.

I pull my binoculars out and try to get a better view of the workmen a quarter mile up ahead. There are smaller men on the detail, but I can also see quite clearly, yes:

Karekins.

I'm about to say something to Levi when I notice that, up above us, seemingly out of nowhere, hover two helicopter-like machines. They are much sleeker than the ones on our Earth, black and chrome and practically silent (not quite as futuristic as the SenMachs', though). In less than two seconds, twenty Karekins have leaped from the open doors of the helicopters and landed in front of us with weapons drawn.

"I know you want to run, Levi, or fight," I say quickly. "I know it, and so do I. Just remember, we're kind of here to get caught. So please, please cooperate." Levi glares at me. He knows what to do. Maybe that little speech was actually to myself.

"We're putting our weapons down!" I say in Karekin. Slowly, I bend over and drop my rifle on the pavement, kicking it away from me. I take my knife from my utility belt and throw that down as well. Levi does the same, including his remaining handgun, which reminds me of Ryn Two. I hope to God at this point that she didn't have to use mine.

I also hope I'm not going to regret not having that gun right now.

The Karekins have body armor strikingly similar to ours,

though theirs is entirely jet-black and they don't have any leather around their torsos, knees, or elbows. They certainly don't have pockets, but they do have belts like we do, to holster weapons and gadgets that would be useful on a mission. These Karekins are as tall as the ones we face back home, between seven and eight feet, though I will say they seem less feral. The Karekins that come through to Battle Ground are all hair, with beards that reach well down to their chests. The Karekins before us have beards as well, but these are much shorter, and their long hair is pulled back and away in multiple braids. Still, it seems like the majority of their faces are covered in hair, which has got to be itchy.

One of them, perhaps a commanding officer, bends down low in my face. I do not look away. I'm afraid—I'd be a particular kind of stupid not to be afraid—but I'm not about to let this asshole know that. My hands are up in surrender, but if I wanted, I know I could reach up and snap this monster's neck in less than three seconds. I'd be dead after that, and Levi, too, though, so I restrain myself.

The Karekin gets inches away from my face and I keep my eyes locked on his. I feel his unnerving exhalations on my cheeks, and I see his teeth are sharply pointed, as if they've been filed that way to rip flesh away from bone. As with the Karekins I'm used to, the man's eyes are tiny slits. I know they can barely see and that they use their other heightened senses to fight. This is why I'm not surprised that he's this close to me or that he takes a deep inhalation from his wide nostrils. He's obviously smelling me. And then he speaks.

"You do not seem so vicious. You are tiny."

I'm thrilled that Levi can't speak this language. If he did, I'm fairly certain this dick would see exactly how vicious we could be. Besides, what this guy thinks doesn't bother me.

Rather, because this Karekin has judged me based on my appearance, I now know he's not as smart as I am.

I remain silent, but I do offer just the barest hint of a smile, which I'm not even sure he can see. "You both are coming with us now. And do not try to run. You cannot hope to outrace us."

Again, I doubt that, but this is what we want, so I don't prove him wrong. The Karekins flank us, forming a circle around me and Levi. We begin to march at a pace that most people would find daunting. Obviously we're fine with it, and the only unfortunate thing about walking like this is that the Karekins are so tall and packed so tightly around us it's hard to see beyond them. I want to get a better scope of the city, see the extent of the damage, but it's nearly impossible. Still, I see enough to guess that this must have been, at one point, a thriving metropolis. Little glimpses reveal thoroughly modern architecture. I would say that it is similar to the Sen-Mach city, but there is an oddly retro feel. It reminds me of what people from our Earth's twentieth century assumed our twenty-first century would look like.

I can't believe I'm here. I've brought us to Karekin Earth. As noble as my intentions are, I can't help feeling that I might have just sacrificed Levi's life for Ezra's.

After about ten minutes we halt in front of a large, undamaged building. It is a long white rectangle with probably a hundred steps leading up to the doors. Fifteen-foot-long flags are draped along the front. They are blue with a white oval, and in the center is a black symbol. Like everything else, I only get a quick look at it, because as soon as I try to see it again we've moved past it. I *must* have seen it wrong. It was only a glimpse after all. Because if that symbol is what I think it is, then everything is about to get a million times more complicated.

We climb the steps, and I notice the Karekins are careful not to touch us. They herd me and Levi without so much as a single limb even accidentally brushing up against either one of us. I subtly lean toward one, and just as subtly he edges away. It's impressive. As we walk into the building, I still can't see much except the floor, which is a marble the color of lapis lazuli. There are a lot of tall windows casting light from outside, and it sounds like there are other people here, but my positioning makes it impossible to confirm.

We immediately veer left, like a giant school of fish all flittering in the same direction. We stop. We wait. Some of the Karekins break formation and circle back around us, which means I can finally see ahead of me. Unfortunately, we are facing an open elevator door. We are maneuvered inside the large car. I glance at Levi; his eyes narrow just a fraction. We might have had a fighting chance out in the open, but now we are trapped in an elevator with a dozen Karekins. There is no worse position for a Citadel to be in. Levi and I have both fought Karekins back home. We've been hurt by them and we've watched them kill more than a couple of our fellow soldiers. It's hard to keep those memories from surfacing. I am itching to kick one of these assholes in the throat and I know Levi is likely feeling the same. I steal another look at him and he is facing forward, not moving, barely even breathing. He's far from relaxed, but he looks indifferent, not furious. Finally, I think, we are on the same page here.

I keep thinking about that damned symbol. Shit . . . I feel us drop, and my ears pop. We must be going to a bunker, which would make sense given the condition on the surface. The elevator stops with a shudder and once again we are herded forward. This time, even though we are surrounded by these huge men, there are gaps, and I can see.

We've been brought to what looks like the Situation Room. There are at least eight massive tables with electronic displays. There are Karekins standing in front of these, but there is another race, too. Smaller, in uniform, but we are moving too fast for me to get a proper look at them.

There are also dozens and dozens of 2-D projections on the walls in lieu of monitor screens. I catch glimpses of codes, maps, equations, and different species. As I've always suspected, the Karekins may be violent, but they are not stupid. Now I can confirm that they are working with another species. It is rare, but not impossible, that two dominant species on a single Earth can thrive together concurrently. This must be what is going on here.

Finally, our bodyguards move away from us and I get a clear view of the room. At the far end there's a man sitting on a chair atop a dais. He is surrounded by more Karekins, including a few others who must be the same, unknown species. This must be the man in charge. He looks to be much shorter than the Karekins and slighter in weight. His eyes are somewhat small, too, but nothing like the tiny slivers of the Karekins. His long thick hair is pulled back in a puffy single braid that falls down the right side of his shoulder to his waist. He also has a beard. The thing that strikes me, though, the thing that is inescapable, is the color of his skin. Not just his skin, but the skin of his advisors around him, some of whom are women, the first we've seen. These are not the different shades of skin tones found on humans, which are really, at the end of the day, variations of the same.

These people are green, pink, jet-black, and amber. I take a closer look at the Karekin nearest to me and not just in the eyes, but his entire face. It's not something I've ever really done before. To my credit, I've generally been fighting for my life and mostly they've been obscured by hair. But now I can see that just under the surface of their skin hide tones of other, brighter shades as well.

The man sitting on the chair is the color of the marble floor in the building above us, the same color as the flags hanging from the roof. He is blue—not cheesy *Avatar* blue or as dark as navy, but lapis. I take him in and my eyes narrow. I think I know at least one part of the puzzle, and I don't know if I'm ready for it to come together.

"Thank you, Citadels, for joining us today. It was a brave and courageous thing to do," he says with a booming voice in accented English. How does he know English?

"Where's Ezra?" I demand. "I won't say another word until I can be assured that he is safe and unharmed." I watch as the people around him look at one another uneasily.

The man on the dais simply laughs, and the others, taking his cue, do the same. "You are hardly in a position to be making demands, little bird. My name is Iathan. I am the president of Ehwas."

I casually fold my arms and stare at him. I really don't give two fucks. He could be the president of Sesame Street for all his announcement means to me. I need assurance that Ezra is all right, and then we can discuss this guy's civic responsibilities.

"Tell me, Ryn Whittaker, Citadel, designation 473 and Beta Team leader . . ." Iathan grips both sides of the chair and lifts himself up. He isn't fragile or frail, I suspect this is more for dramatic effect, just like his use of my full name and rank. He is trying to intimidate me, but I'm beyond that now. If I can be surrounded by a full squadron of Karekins and keep it cool, Iathan's words, no matter how disturbing, are hardly going to back me into a corner. "Have you figured it out yet? They gave you speed and strength, but did they give you enough intelligence to know who I am? To know *what* I am?" Iathan smiles as if he's just eaten something delicious.

There is silence in the room. I close my eyes for just the briefest of seconds. The machines around us click and whir. I can hear the muffled hiss of electrical wires running out of the concrete walls. I focus. I zero in on the heartbeats of those that are closest to me, including Iathan's. It's barely audible. Another clue. I look down at the ARC patch on my uniform. I had been right. It's the same symbol, three interlocking, inverted triangles, that I saw on their flags. The same one that decorates their own patches on their black, sleek outfits. I can't believe I'm only now seeing it, but they are, after all, three feet taller than me. Besides, it doesn't matter—I wouldn't have been prepared anyway. I don't think there's enough time in the world for me to ever be prepared for *this*.

But fuck this guy if he thinks I'm going to be hot and bothered by it.

"I know exactly what you are. You're a Roone. Now bring me Ezra."

CHAPTER 20

"Excellent!" Iathan slaps his palms together, as if he's giving himself a high five. "Now, then, I imagine you must have many questions."

I glance at Levi. His body looks relaxed enough, but I know this posture well. It's right there, in his eyes, he wants to pounce. I get that there is some sort of game going on here, but Levi hates games. He'd rather just rip out your throat. Still, he is silent and hasn't killed anyone. Yet. I take that as progress.

"Yeah. I have some questions. And I've already asked my first one. *Where. Is. Ezra?* Is he hurt? Why won't you bring him out here?"

Iathan shakes his head and makes his way back to his seat. "You are very determined, Ryn Whittaker. However, you must earn the right to see Ezra Massad."

"I guess the fact that *I've traveled through the Multiverse to find him* doesn't count for much around here. Fine. What do you want, me to fight for it or something? 'Cause I promise you, if you make it a fair one, I'll earn that privilege."

Iathan simply sighs and puts both hands on his hips. "They really did *shoolack* with your mind. What's the word, Froome, in English? For *shoolack*?" Iathan gestures to one of his advisors, who steps forward gracefully. "I believe you've already met Froome, in Marrakech. He is one of our best agents. He's also very good with English, especially your colorful colloquialisms."

I understand why Iathan would choose Froome to spy for him among humans. His skin is neither light nor dark, but a fleshy pink that could easily pass for Caucasian. "Don't bother, Froome," I say loudly. "The word in English is 'mess' or 'screw.' I get it. And yes, we've been messed with. Badly. So please just go get Ezra, and then we can all participate in whatever *shoolacked* little play you're acting out."

"This is no act, I can assure you," Iathan says with hand over his heart. "Despite your training, violence is not the solution here. You have a saying on your Earth that I quite enjoy. 'If all you have is a hammer, then every problem looks like a nail.' Froome taught me that one." Iathan takes a seat and leans forward. "What is going on here, in this room on this Earth and yours and Ezra Massad's—it is not a bag of nails, little bird."

I throw my hands in the air in frustration. "My name is Ryn."

At this, Iathan chuckles, as do a few of his advisors. "Ah, yes, but I thought it was Wren, which is a little bird. We've made a point of learning all the Citadels' languages. Not me personally. But I do speak English and Russian, though admittedly not as well. There are nuances that someone like me, who is not a native speaker, find confusing."

"Fine. Call me whatever you want. Just tell me how to earn the right to see Ezra."

Iathan snaps his fingers and immediately two Karekins step forward with chairs. It is beyond bizarre to see them this way. It's not even that they are politely offering us a place to sit, which is crazy, but that they are calm. It's their general tranquility that's throwing me. It's taking more than a fair bit of my concentration not to stare too hard or think too much about them, because that would be bad. Very bad. I've already stopped myself from snarling when one of them gets too close. "The price to see Ezra is your patience and your ear. I want you to listen to my story in its entirety, without interrupting, and without hurrying me along to get what you want. Can you do that?"

Levi immediately takes a seat and even scoots it closer to the dais, nodding to me that he can do this, which means I can, too.

I sit down and sink deep into the black leather cushions, resting my hands lightly on the armrests. I lean back, hoping Iathan will believe that I am relaxing, ready to listen. And while I will be listening to every word he says, I am still ready to spring at the first hint of something else going on. I know when I am being lied to, even by someone like Iathan, who I'm sure has mastered the skill.

"I think I can keep it together long enough to listen to whatever you're going to say," I tell him coolly. Iathan looks at Froome and sighs as if I've already failed the task. I replace my smirk with a deadly serious stare. I *will not* let them goad me.

"Would you like some water? Some food?" he asks politely.

"We're fine," I answer.

"Unlike the Woon-Kwa, whose marvelous village you just Rifted from, I do not believe you are a telepath. How can you be so certain Levi Branach would not like some refreshment?" Iathan asks.

"If your spies gave you intimate knowledge of the Woon-Kwa," Levi says, "then I assume they would have also told you that they are a most hospitable race. We were fed well there. But maybe your spies aren't as thorough as you might want to believe?"

At this, Iathan gives us a broad, slow smile. "Well said, Levi Branach. I wondered if you had lost your voice, you've been so quiet."

"I speak when I have something to say. Right now I am here to listen. So please, begin." I bite my lip in an effort to keep from smiling. Levi has managed somehow to put the president firmly in his place while being completely respectful.

"So be it." Iathan's tone is no longer so congenial, and it's apparent Levi's calm has gotten to him. It's nice to know he can be rattled so easily.

"One hundred years ago, this city was a beacon of progress and prosperity. I know it might be hard to believe, looking at the sad place it has become, but once upon a time it shone. Like most great civilizations, it had taken centuries to secure world-wide peace and cooperation. This Earth has far less landmass than yours, roughly half, I believe. There was less to share, so believe me when I tell you that accomplishing global unity was an incredible achievement. Once our people began to share knowledge, our society grew in leaps and bounds. Not that it matters much in terms of this particular conversation, but the Roones used to be a society firmly rooted in the arts and philosophy. But then, for some reason our focus shifted on to technology and science. That was the beginning of the end, though, obviously, we did not see that coming. We thought we were being revolutionary.

"I think, perhaps, we thought ourselves gods."

Iathan stops. He strokes his beard, looking pensive. He doesn't seem that old, but it's like he was there, a witness to it all, and maybe he was. I never asked Edo her age. The Roones, even the ones here that look so different, do not have wrinkles or folds on their skin. And it's quite possible their life span is much longer than a human's. Given what they can do, it wouldn't surprise me if they have extended their life spans through science.

Iathan continues. "So. A hundred years ago, we made a discovery. We did something extraordinary. I think you can guess what that was, can't you, little bird?"

"You opened a Rift," I answer, my mask of indifference holding firm. It isn't too hard—it isn't the most astounding revelation at this point.

"Yes. We opened a Rift. Several, actually, quite by accident. We were doing research into harmonics and dark matter. We had no idea at first how we had even done it, let alone how to control it. One Rift turned into two, then four, then twenty. Ultimately, sixty-seven Rifts opened around our Earth, and we were ill prepared to deal with the repercussions. We had a peacekeeping force, but we had done away with the notion of soldiers and armies long before that. So what to do?

"As it is on your Earth, these Rifts were not so much doorways as revolving corridors. Day after day, hour after hour, our Earth was besieged by all manner of monsters. Thousands died, from both sides. It was a dark time. We believed that the Rifts were problems rooted in science and therefore the answers must lie in science as well. We knew we needed soldiers, but not just regular soldiers, for as you well know, the things that emerge from the Rift cannot be contained by conventional strength or speed. We needed monsters of our own.

And so, through genetic manipulation and mutation of Roon-ish volunteers, we created the Karekin. In our language, this word means *Citadel*."

Now *that* is a revelation.

Edo. That lying bitch.

I grip the handles of my chair. I grit my teeth. My mind spins in circles, almost tripping over itself when I imagine the scope of her lies. The Karekins *are* Roones, or they were . . .

I force my hands to relax. I clear my head. There's time to react later. Right now I will just do as he asked and listen.

Even though I want to show everyone in this room why thinking of me as a weak little bird is a *huge* mistake.

"The Karekins solved our immediate problems with the Rifts, but unlike you human Citadels, they did not have aug-mented brain capacity. We did not believe that we, on our own, as we were, would fully master the Rifts. So once again, we turned to science. Hundreds of volunteers offered them-selves up. They were the best and brightest scientific and mathematic minds. They saw what the gene therapy did to the Karekins, but they didn't care. All they wanted was to be smarter. At any cost. The Roones on your Earth are those vol-unteers. They made their skin as hard as the hardest rocks, almost as hard as metal, to protect their precious brains. They may not look it, but they turned into monsters, too. And for a while, I must admit, their gamble paid off. We learned how to close the Rifts. Then we learned how to navigate and control the Rifts. And I am sure, if we had learned how to do these things without so many of us becoming monsters, we would have found a way to explore and cultivate this newfound knowledge peacefully.

"However, the altered Roones weren't interested in peace or exploration. All they wanted was to exploit and dominate.

They believed that by crossing the genes of different species that Rifted here from different Earths, they could create better, stronger Citadels, though our need for more had diminished. It didn't matter—they were ruthless. They tortured many innocent souls in the name of science and progress until finally we felt that we had to put a stop to them.

"This city you Rifted into is a result of that decision. We drove the altered Roones off of this Earth. They took thousands of loyal Karekins with them. Thankfully, we had thousands of loyal Karekins on our side, too. The most important thing for you to know is that the altered Roones believe that they are in the right. They believe themselves to be healers and miracle workers. They truly think that they've given you a gift, and eventually, they'll want payment for that gift—help retaking this Earth, their home. It's the reason they continue as they do.

"But playing God, changing the destinies of other races, I think that game has become far more important to them. Still, the human Citadels are exactly what they have been waiting for. They were so smart to change you as children. They had never done that before, but it has cost them."

Levi and I look at each other. Is Iathan saying what I think he's saying? "Yes, little bird," Iathan says, as if reading my mind. "The Karekins were the first and you were the last, but there have been other Citadel races in between."

Iathan wisely pauses to let this information sink in. I'm sure he knows where my mind will go next: Taking down the Roones will not be easy. It may even be impossible, depending on how many other kinds of Citadels are out there in the Multiverse. All the Roones have to do is open a Rift and let them in. We can't even count on the entirety of the human Citadels to fight. The memory of those I had told before the Rift took Ezra—those like Duncan—is all the proof I need that we'd almost certainly be facing against our comrades. But if I needed more, all I'd have to do is look around the room at the Karekins and see how easily a seemingly united group can find itself tearing apart.

"So much of what you believe is a lie," Iathan says sadly. "Scientists on your Earth were fed false information, starting with the idea that the Rifts on your Earth were an accident. They weren't—they were deliberate, allowing the altered Roones to show up at *precisely* the right moment. Your people were desperate, so they gladly accepted their help, even if it meant sacrificing the lives of a few children. The altered Roones didn't sell it like that, of course. Remember, genetic manipulation is a gift in their minds. So it's not just the Roones on your Earth that are your enemy—your own people are complicit as well.

"Another lie they tell? That the Rift takes Immigrants randomly. Untrue. It was true at first, here, on this Earth. But they have mastered the Rifts. The majority of Immigrants are chosen and then kidnapped either for their intellect, as Ezra Massad was, or to sharpen your battle skills. This is why they send in their own Karekins, the only true match for you. We have a name for those lost men. We call them the *Settiku Hesh.* The Suicide Soldiers. They've been so drugged and so brainwashed they no longer ask questions. They are to try and kill as many other Citadels as possible and then kill themselves before they are taken. I know you hate the Karekins you fight at Battle Ground, but they deserve your pity. No other race has been as poorly used by the altered Roones.

"But perhaps the greatest lie, and one that pertains to you both, is that you were chosen for your averageness." At this, Iathan can't help but give a soft, melancholy chuckle. "The fact is, you were chosen because you were the smartest and the fastest, the most agile and the most dynamic thinkers. It is preposterous to believe that they would bestow what they consider the highest honor to a specimen they considered inferior. And you, little bird. They gave you something extra special, the gift of all gifts. You know what I am talking about, yes?"

I'm practically speechless at each new thing he says, but this is almost too much. Instead of rendering me mute, this smacks me in the face and awakens an anger I didn't realize was festering inside. I reply with an edge to my voice that makes Levi look at me with concern. "I assume it's the whole humming, whistling, screeching thing, yeah?"

I *really* dislike the fact that he knows something about me that I don't understand.

"Yes. The more direct exposure you get to—well, let's just call it a type of radiation that exists inside of a Rift—the more this gene expresses itself. You can tell when someone is on an Earth they don't belong to. But that's just the beginning. There are very few Citadels like you. Not even the altered Roones know exactly how far you can take this anomaly. That's why Edo let you go. It's not because she cares about you or Ezra or any other Citadel. All she cares about is measuring and tracking the mutation of this gene of yours they altered."

"Well, that was incredibly shortsighted of her."

At this, Iathan belly laughs. He even translates what I've said into Karekin, which is actually Roonish, now that I come to think about it, and the rest of the room chuckles at my comment.

"They are shortsighted indeed," he says. "They also have no idea how far my network of spies reaches out. They think they are untouchable and infallible. A dangerous position to take in any war. Now"—Iathan stands and walks down the dais—"you've heard my story. I understand you may be reluctant to believe it. You have been lied to all your life, so I can only assume you believe that is what people in positions of authority do. I promise you. Not one falsehood has crossed my lips. I have no reason to lie to you. I could have just killed you—many, many times—I've certainly had the opportunities. The state of this city, the craters where entire blocks used to be, is not enough. You and Levi are living reminders of why we fought this war. I would like to explore what working together might look like. Would that be of interest to you?"

I look around the room. These people have technology and answers that we need, but at the end of the day, they are Roones, and every Roone I've met, including Iathan, is an arrogant weirdo.

"Maybe," I say noncommittally. I glance over at Levi, who gives me a silent nod of approval.

I'm a bit surprised when Iathan agrees with my reluctance. "Yes—'maybe.' I understand your reservations, and honestly, I have my own. We would need to depend on one another in life-or-death situations, and truthfully, regardless of your many skills, you're a child. Not just that, you're a natural rule breaker and I'm not sure you can control your emotions."

"I can control my emotions just fine," I tell him without expression.

"Well, let us put that theory to the test, shall we?" He gestures to Froome, who leaves with a curt nod. While we are waiting, the tension in the air heightens. I don't like being tested and I really don't like being called a child.

I will cop to being a rule breaker, though.

Froome eventually returns, and limping quietly behind him is Ezra. If this is the test, it's a goddamn good one, because it takes all I have not to run to him as I watch them make slow progress toward us. Besides the fact that I'm so excited just to see him, I'm also anxious to get to him. Ezra is shirtless. His ribs are a patchwork of eggplant-colored bruises. His face is a wreck. His nose is clearly broken, and dried blood is caked all over his cheeks in scarlet striations. One eye is swollen completely shut. The other one is open, but the bright turquoise of his iris is ringed neon red. His entire face is falling at opposite angles, which makes me think his jaw has been broken. I dig my nails into my palms; the quick flash of pain holds me in check. I want to cry out to him.

I want to leap forward and kill them all.

I do nothing, though—nothing except file this away for later.

They hurt him. Badly. For all their big talk about the altered Roones being as bad as Nazi scientists, no altered Roone ever did this to one of us, at least not directly. If Iathan is trying to win me over, he has failed spectacularly. My breath quickens. I don't dare look at Levi because although I know he dislikes Ezra intensely, I also know he hates the idea of an unfair fight even more. If our eyes meet, we might slip back into Citadel behavior, where we protect the defenseless at all costs.

If Iathan suspects any of this going on inside me, he doesn't let it show as he says, "Now, I recognize that seeing your friend like this must be a shock. But please understand that we offered Ezra all our hospitality. In return, we caught him trying to access our mainframe to download sensitive information. This kind of breach cannot be tolerated. I hope you can understand our actions here."

Oh yeah, I understand. These Roones think *they're* the good guys. They want me to believe that Ezra basically asked for this beating. Maybe if he raped one of them or cut one of their dicks off (an option I'm seriously considering at this point), then I might see this as a proper way to treat him. But all he did was hack them. He didn't deserve this.

As I stare at Ezra, I hear him struggling. Each breath catches with reedy shallowness. He falls to his knees, swaying. He needs medical attention, *right now*. My heart starts ticking like a bomb. I review my options. There are at least one hundred Karekins and Roones in here. Levi and I are no match for that kind of manpower. So all I can do is get to Ezra. I can let him know I'm here, that I've come for him, and surely, with the SenMach biotech I have in my pack, I can ease his suffering. I take a step forward, well aware that everyone, including Levi, is watching me intently. Ezra is now right beside Iathan up on the dais. I walk up the steps in controlled measures and then crouch down on my knees.

"Ezra, I've got you. I'm right here." I gently reach my hand out to his shoulder and my fingers go right through him. I look at Iathan, who is observing me with a curious intent. I wave my hands inside Ezra's body, back and forth. This isn't him. It's a fucking projection. A hologram.

"Really?" I say as I leap up.

"Really," Iathan tells me in a tone more serious than I had yet to hear from him. "I do apologize. Especially after my great speech about honesty. But I had to make sure that you really could control yourself in a highly charged emotional situation. I simply had no other way to gauge your maturity."

"Here's a thought," I snap back, "maybe you could have just spent some time with me? Had a few conversations? Done some listening instead of talking nonstop." I pause to collect myself so that I can keep my voice level. "Don't you ever do that again. I don't like tests, and I like games even less. I think you get what I am in theory, but you really don't seem to understand. I am faster than you, I am stronger than you, and I am smarter than you. I am your enemy's greatest accomplishment. You remember that. You keep that thought in the back of your mind, and then maybe you can have this alliance you're so jazzed about."

"Little bird," Iathan coos.

I hold up a single finger. "And do *not* call me that. My name is Ryn." Iathan steps even closer to me. He smiles, and his skin picks up the light and glints subtly. I want to see it all covered in blood.

"I would not be so quick to dismiss my nickname for you," he says, not realizing that my being this close to him could be the most danger he's ever been in. "A little bird needs protection, it needs nurturing and special care, which is no small thing from the president of a nation. Ryn, however, is just a soldier. And soldiers, especially around here, do not always survive."

"Neither do petty little shits who talk a big game but are stupid enough to let someone who isn't exactly their friend get this close to them." In the blink of an eye, I grab his shirt and lift him up off his "throne." As Karekins shout and bring weapons to bear, I already have him back on his own feet and I'm standing with my hands behind my back, as if nothing has happened. "That feeling you have right now—that's the feeling that maybe you're not as in control as you think. And maybe this 'little bird' is more predatory than you give her credit for. But I think you know that, and that's why you want me on your side.

"So why don't you treat me—and Levi—with some fucking respect, okay? And do what you promised. Bring me Ezra. *Now*."

CHAPTER 21

The tension is dissipating from the room, but I barely notice; I'm a spinning needle on a compass. I blink my eyes and swallow. It feels like there isn't enough air in here. I want a window, a view, something I can look at outside even if it's just a ruin of a city so that I can get my bearings.

Without that, I do the only thing I can. I plant my boots on the concrete floor and hold my hands behind my back. I may not feel composed, but I'm not about to show it. Iathan has sent for Ezra, and while there is nothing I want more than to see him, I don't want it to be here, not surrounded by Roones and Karekins. And definitely not Levi. But for all the bravado I just showed, I really can't press my luck, meaning I have no say in how these next moments will play out. And that infuriates me. All I can do is stand here and wait. I grind my thumb into the joints of my index finger. I flex my toes inside my boots. I am not looking at Levi, but I can feel him. I can hear him. I don't want him to see this. I don't want him to see me seeing Ezra after all this time. The thought of hurting him makes my chest lurch in sympathy.

Finally, Ezra, *the real* Ezra, walks out from a door behind the dais, escorted by two Karekins. My stomach flutters. I tear my gaze from Ezra and look quickly to Iathan, who has folded his hands under his bottom lip. He is far too fascinated to see how this will play out. But I am *not* his experiment.

Screw it. Ezra is here and he looks fine, and good, *and safe.*

I bound toward him. And then, like a miracle, we are in each other's arms. I breathe him in, catching his woodsy smell at the nape of his neck. I hear his pulse soar. I can't believe it. I found him. And despite the terrible odds of him coming out of this not only alive but in one piece, he's okay. He really is. Ezra puts his hands around my face and pulls away. "You found me," he whispers.

"Of course. I wouldn't have stopped until I did."

"I'm sorry about all those paranoid e-mails I sent you. I suppose you've figured out it was the Roones. Tracking me."

"Yeah. I mean, I get it now. But how? How did they find you?"

"The QOINS is a lot more complex than they told us. The moment I activated it they were able to track me."

Of course. I blow out and nod my head. "It's a lot, right?" I put my hands into his. "God, we were so fucking stupid to think that it was just about Battle Ground. I bet Edo is laughing her ass off thinking about us, imagining our faces when we figured out how deep this goes."

"I doubt Edo is capable of laughing like that. I would put her emotional capacity at mildly amused," Levi pipes in from his chair. Ezra looks past my shoulder and I feel his body stiffen. His eyes narrow angrily. Why is he mad?

"Really?" Ezra explodes and releases my hands. "Of all the people to bring with you, you choose this guy? The guy who threw me into the Rift? Wow."

Riiiight—I wasn't thinking about that part. Ezra is beyond pissed—he's furious.

Levi wisely says nothing, simply stretches out his legs and crosses his arms. If there is a more universal sign for *Come at me, bruh* mixed with *I know you're threatened by me, but I'm so unconcerned by you, I don't even need to get up off my chair,* I can't think of it. I have to cut this off before it becomes a pissing contest—or worse.

"I brought the best soldier for the job. Beta Team needed to stay behind," I emphasize. "They're the only ones I trusted enough to keep Camp Bonneville under our control. I don't have to tell *you* how dangerous these jumps are. I had to have the most capable Citadel at my side." I don't need to look at Levi to know he's probably wearing a shit-eating grin on his face over that compliment.

"He tried to kill me," Ezra says, continuing to glower at Levi.

"No, he didn't," I say, taking a step forward and gently guiding his face until his eyes connect with mine. As they do, they soften, and I put my hands back on Ezra's body, as much for him as for me. *He's here.* My hands still need reassurance that he's right here. Safe. "He was trying to save me and he wasn't thinking."

Iathan and his advisors are looking at us and then back at Levi, like it's some kind of funny sketch we're putting on. I don't like it. It feels too exposed.

"Hey," Levi says. "These assholes"—Levi's hand casually sweeps the room, landing on Iathan's spy, Froome—"shot me. In the neck, with a tracker, like I was some kind of animal. But here I am. So bygones, dude, okay?"

I scratch an invisible itch behind my ear and moan internally. That is a truly dickhead apology. Actually, it's not an apology at all, but I know Ezra isn't going to get anything else right now.

"Your race is extremely confounding and awkward," Iathan says with amusement.

I glare at him, and the Roones' leader blessedly shuts up. So, for a beat, no one says anything, until finally Iathan sighs heavily. "Perhaps, over time, I will be able to get a better understanding of your people, but since time is against us, I propose we move forward. I felt it would be best if Ezra were to debrief you on the intel that he managed to collate with ours and Edo's computer files. Ezra? You have the floor."

"What?" Ezra has been staring at me, and it's a feeling I like a great deal. So when he shakes his head as if to snap out of a trance, I know exactly where he's coming from. "Right—okay."

Ezra walks over to a large black table, which is apparently some sort of central console. Levi and I both join him there, standing next to each other but across from him. Ezra immediately starts tapping away. Brief flashes of illuminated light appear beneath his fingers as they quickly buzz around the surface. Ezra's only been here three days, but given that he's a computer genius, I'm hardly surprised he's got it figured out. He's so damned brilliant. I know he has important things to say, but I just want to jump on him and kiss his face. I move my neck side to side as if cracking my spine is action enough. It isn't. Instead I just stare and fiddle with the zipper on my uniform.

"I'm assuming Iathan filled you in on the basics," he begins in a quiet voice. "The gaps that I've been able to cover concern the other Citadel races. There are five of them besides the

Karekins and you. The Roones here wondered if there might be more, but Edo's computer had daily briefings from each of the other Earths with Citadels, so it's just the five." Ezra clears his throat and runs his hand stiffly through his hair. "I suppose if you're a glass-half-full kind of person you could be grateful the number is so low. I gotta say, though, that it's hard to be optimistic when you see what they are, and what they can do."

Levi and I exchange worried looks. Ezra catches this and glares at me while typing harder on the console with his finger pads.

Well, that's me fucked.

If Ezra has a problem with a simple glance at my fellow Citadel and current partner, he's going to be pissed as hell when I tell him the rest of it. I try to ignore the ever-expanding pit of doom in my stomach. This information is too important to dilute with my personal life.

Ezra clears his throat to make sure he has all our attention. "Let's begin with the Spiradaels." A number of pictures pop up on the air, like floating TV screens, without the actual screen part. "These are the Spiradael Citadels. They were the first race to be converted after the other Roones were exiled. As you can see, they are tall, like the Karekins, which is one of the main reasons they were chosen. The altered Roones believed that if they could amp up their strength, they would be well matched to fight the remaining Karekins here. And while they didn't quite get to that level, don't let their scrawny appearance fool you. They are spindly but strong, and their hair, which, as you can see from this video here"—another image pops up of a Spiradael in a brawl with what looks like another humanoid race—"falls down to their ankles. They bind it in a thin alloy so that it becomes almost like a razor, and then they use it like a whip." The Spiradael Citadel in the video grabs hold of his mane and flicks it hard. It wraps around his opponent's neck and then, with a hard tug, the other guy's head is sliced clean away.

The video is graphic, but I am not frightened by it. I've faced worse. Hell—I've done worse. What has got my attention, though, is that I've had to sit through hundreds of informational meetings like this, but I've never seen anything like Ezra's briefing swag. It's like he's been doing this for years. He's calm, concise . . . and sexy as anything. I keep leaning my body forward toward him inch by inch.

Pretty soon I'm going to end up on the actual table.

"The advantage you have with Spiradaels is that their intelligence has not been genetically modified, and your uniforms should keep you safe enough. Just make sure you don't underestimate these skinny bastards. They aren't dumb, and they are strong and very fast."

Ezra takes his hand and seemingly collects the pictures in a single fist before throwing them up behind him, leaving room for the next race. "After the Spiradaels, the Roones made a gamble on brute force. The Spiradaels never quite achieved the level of the Karekins' sheer physicality, so the Roones then chose the Orsalines. As you can see, they kind of look like a cross between a grizzly and an Ewok."

I can't help it. I roll my eyes in disgust. "*Great.* Like I needed another reason to hate bears. They're useless *and* lethal. They're like the appendixes of the animal kingdom." The entire room looks at me. No one says anything, though I can tell my interruption was not appreciated by the varying looks of mild to downright irritation on everyone's faces.

Okay . . . so no with the witty banter, then.

Ezra continues as if I didn't say anything, and I worry he's annoyed with me, too. "They are also the most primitive of all the Citadels. In fact, according to Edo's notes, the altered Roones appeared to them as gods. The Rifts are hell mouths, like in *Buffy*, which is a special shout-out to you, Ryn," Ezra says with just the barest hint of a smile on his face, and then I know I was worried for nothing. Ezra gets my quirks.

"Woot," I say, raising a single hand, my heart gushing a little overtime as Ezra catches my eye for a second before getting back to work. I turn, still smiling, to Levi, who *is* annoyed. I shrug, and tuck an invisible piece of hair behind my ear. I'm sure that *woot* is probably the lamest word I could have used, but I couldn't help it. The shutting-up thing isn't working. I'm used to working out a problem with Ezra as a team, together, sharing information. This new role he's taken on is giving me way too much nervous energy. On one hand, I'm thrilled he's learned so much. On the other hand, I can't help but feel that this intel is too dangerous. He seems to be aware of how deadly these Citadels are but only from the vantage point of an observer. I'm having a hard time taking all this in and I've been training for years. He's been doing this for a few weeks and he's a gamer. Does this *actually feel* real to him? Does he know that he could be killed by any number of people or species for having this intel?

"The Orsalines are insanely strong. Probably the strongest of all the Citadels. But they aren't so fast, and they have average or below-average intelligence. We assume that, because of their genesis, they would be the most loyal of all the Citadel races. Maybe even impossible to turn." I notice Ezra's use of the word *we* and I wince a little. For all his brilliance, Ezra is new at this. A partnership with the Roones may be the best move, but until there's a human Citadel consensus, there can be no *we*, not yet.

I keep staring at the vivid, and quite gruesome, images of

the Orsalines. What an odd choice for the altered Roones to make. Strategically it's quite dumb. They look ridiculous, like bears in combat suits, like some fucked-up seventh-grader's idea of a funny Halloween costume, unless that's part of the strategy. I suppose if you're facing down a weird version of a roided-out circus bear, it might throw you.

Ezra tosses those pictures out of the way and a new crop levitates in front of our eyes. "Next we have the Daithi. From what I can tell, they were chosen for their stature. The Spiradaels are tall, like the Karekins; the Orsalines are strong; and this species is relatively tiny, like the altered Roones themselves. Not one of them is over five feet. The knot-work tattoos that cover their bodies might look familiar. They are very closely aligned with what we know from our history as the Celts, or Picts. All of them have black hair and blue eyes, without exception. I think the altered Roones looked at this warrior species as a way to bring stealth and speed into the equation. The Daithi are also the first race to create female Citadels. They ran extensive experiments to see if they made better or worse soldiers. Unsurprisingly, they found that there was no real difference. Up until this point, the altered Roones recruited species that already had qualities they believed they could enhance via genetic mutation. So the Daithi became faster and even more adept at subterfuge. However, once they came across the Faida, their thinking changed."

Ezra spreads his arms and a slew of new pictures lines up above us. I scrunch up my eyes and tilt my head. "Did the altered Roones do that?" I ask in genuine surprise.

"No. They're basically humans, with wings. I mean, the eyes are a little bigger, the bone structure a little sharper, but that's how they're born," Ezra answers.

"Angel Citadels. Fantastic," I mutter.

"Okay, so, here's what I got from Edo's research. The Karekin mutation was crudely done—no offense, dudes," Ezra says to the guards, who look back at him squarely. I doubt they speak English, but I suspect they would have remained silent anyway. "The altered Roones had been doing genetic experimentation with all the species that dumped out from their Rifts. So the Karekins are basically genetic Frankensteins. They've been altered with at least fifteen other races. The Roones altered themselves with some DNA splicing, which changed their appearance some, but mostly they managed to ramp up their intelligence by mutating their own genes. Over the years, the process got better and more efficient. Cross-species DNA splicing is always going to be part of the equation, but the Faida are such a remarkable race that they've figured, why not just enhance *everything* as opposed to just one or two of the species' already established characteristics? And that's what they did. They made them twice as fast. Twice as strong and twice as smart."

"So what made them change their MO?" Levi asks, intently staring at the photos and videos of the Faida, which not only look like footage from a big blockbuster movie, but are as intimidating as fuck.

"Hubris," Iathan says with a flick of disgust.

"Yeah, I mean, it makes a better Citadel, but"—I inhale quickly and look down at my uniform—"a Citadel that excels in just one thing, like the Daithi with their stealth, is going to be not only easier to control, but easier to deploy for certain missions."

I hear Iathan sigh a thin, reedy breath before he turns and addresses me. "That makes sense to you, but you must remember: Our rogue brothers and sisters do not believe they have done anything wrong. It's quite the opposite, in fact. And because of that, they don't worry about something like control. Rather, they believe that they are *entitled* to the Citadels' complete loyalty. And don't forget the kill switch and what you call the 'Blood Lust'—these are as effective controls as they need. Although, from the intelligence we've gathered, we can conclusively say that the Blood Lust was only used with the humans."

The term *Blood Lust* makes me twitch. The Blood Lust is the last friggin' thing I want to think about with both Ezra and Levi in the same room. Together. I stick a thumbnail between my teeth and bite.

"Something you want to say, Ryn?" Ezra asks. Had I actually groaned? Or is it my body language that's got him wondering? I shake the thoughts from my head and redirect my attention.

"Yeah, I'm just thinking about the ones, regardless of species, that *aren't* given the great gift of genetic fuckery. Conflict would be inevitable. History has proven that once one group believes it is superior to another it usually leads to war. I mean, eventually, after abuse and slavery," I say, exasperated.

"You don't really believe they care about that, do you?" Iathan says without emotion.

I shake my head deliberately. "Negative." I answer in a voice so deadpan it would give a Vulcan pause. Iathan simply flicks his thick eyebrows in my direction.

"Good," he says deliberately. "You may proceed."

"And finally," Ezra says, keeping us on track, "we have the Akshaji." Images of this fifth race pop up in the projection in front of us.

"Whoa" is about all I can manage.

"Yeah, they're pretty hard-core," Ezra agrees before continuing on. "The Akshaji are interesting for more than a few reasons. From Edo's notes we now know that the Akshaji actually already had Rift technology, or some approximation of it, a couple thousand years ago. They visited many iterations of Earth, including ones like our own. As you can see from the way they look, there's little doubt that their appearance kick-started Hinduism and Indian mythology. They have six hands and they adorn the basic Citadel uniform with a lot of extra-fancy gold stuff. I mean jewelry, if you can call it that.

"However, somewhere along the way the race took a step— well, several steps, *miles*, actually—backward. Infighting, revolutions, some basic extreme fundamentalism, and they lost most of their advanced technology, including the ability to Rift. That was the Roones' way in. They offered them limited Rift data in exchange for a fighting force that they could genetically alter.

"Again, they enhanced everything: speed, strength, stealth, and intelligence, by about a triple margin. You do not want to mess with an Akshaj. Not only are they insanely good soldiers, but they seem to be morally ambiguous. I think they *like* to kill, but that might be a by-product of their genetic mutation that the altered Roones deliberately left out of the human-Citadel cocktail."

I look all around the room, which is now absolutely teeming with pictures and videos of these incredibly diverse and interesting races. They are all so different, but I do notice one striking similarity: our patches. What a kick in the ass. We've been fighting all this time under a Roone banner. The observation leads me to the most obvious question.

"So why us?" I have to ask aloud. "I mean, why humans? We aren't that special. We aren't especially big or strong or smart and we have just the two hands."

"The altered Roones wanted to push it as far as they could," Ezra says as he, too, looks around the room at all the other

Citadels. "They needed to start with you as children in order to accomplish the kind of absolute genetic alterations they wanted to do. This meant that a lot of requirements had to be met. And believe me, according to Edo's records, many other races were considered. But humans on Earths like ours are technologically advanced enough to accept Roone technology without thinking it was mystical or magical. Beyond that, our Earths work within a geopolitical system that requires balance and secrecy in order to function effectively. They posited, and rightly so, that when the Rifts opened, governments would scramble to keep them hidden from the rest of the world in order to maintain that balance. And that's exactly what happened: The Rifts opened, ARC formed and then got desperate. Recruiting children seemed a fair enough trade to keep the world safe not only from Immigrants, but from total socioeconomic collapse.

"And it turns out humans make great Citadels. Our bodies are incredibly well proportioned. We have an excellent capacity to store energy inside our cells, and even more important, the plasticity of our brains is exceptional. On paper, human Citadels are the fastest, strongest, and smartest. But against *all* the other Citadels? You can't beat the Roones alone. You're going to have to convert at least two other races. Statistically, anyway."

I clench my jaw and gulp. The weight of this new information doesn't hit me so much as land on my back and jump up and down, squeezing my ribs and compacting my lungs. It's too much. It seems impossible, insurmountable. How do we get at least two other Citadel races on our side when a civil war broke out over control at Battle Ground—and we were all human?

Well, Ryn—you got what you wanted.

Because I had wanted answers. And now I have them—kind of. Edo warned me that her laptop would give them to me, but she also said that I wouldn't necessarily get to the truth. She was right. There is no *one* truth here. Everyone has an agenda and everyone believes that they are the only ones fighting the good fight. I understand why Iathan keeps saying that Edo and the altered Roones don't consider themselves anything other than the heroes in this epic they've created. This is important because, at some point, if I'm going to get close enough to neutralize her and the others, I am going to have to feed into this delusion. I'm going to have to bow and scrape and kneel in gratitude to them. Convince them that I believe I've been saved from the boring life of a regular human being.

In that moment, I make a decision. I forgive myself for all the lies I've ever told, because it was all just practice. Practice for the most important lie I am ever going to tell—that I understand why Edo did what she did, and that I am thankful that they chose me.

So that I can then kill her.

I turn my attention to Iathan. "You've clearly done extensive recon on the other Citadels, but have you approached any of them? Or have any of your spies ever been caught?"

"I was about to ask the same thing," Levi chimes in.

Iathan looks at the videos and photos that are swimming around all our heads like a swarm of bees. The willow-thin Spiradaels, the furry bulk of the Orsalines, the lightning-fast reactions of the Daithi, the angelic majesty of the Faida, and the ferocious whirling hands of the Akshaji. "No," he says rather quietly. "We felt that the most prudent course of action was to wait for at least one Citadel race to see the altered Roones for the evil lunatics they really are."

Even on the surface that seems like a tragically stupid plan.

Iathan is about to continue, but I hold up my hand and close my eyes. "Stop," I tell him. The weight continues to press and squeeze. Each breath is now being pushed out in short, laborious huffs. "I'm going to clarify something before we go any further. You need to know that I don't care about this Earth. And it's not because it's your people who started all this." Iathan starts to object, but I speak over him. "I told you to stop." He shuts his mouth.

"Believe me, I get it. It wasn't really you, at least not from your perspective. But from mine, you're all Roones. That said, I have to concede that our options are limited, which is why I'm willing to at least discuss an alliance. All the same, though, let's not disrespect this process when it's at its most fragile by building it on a foundation of bullshit. You need us and we need you. The only thing we have in common is an enemy."

Iathan strokes his beard and looks down at the floor for a moment. "You are right," he finally says, with a tone that is more regretful than I expected. "My main concern is rebuilding this Earth free from the fear that we will be attacked by the other Roones. However," he says as he leans in toward me and Levi, "if you are under the impression that I do not care what was done to you, or that I do not feel some measure of responsibility, then you are wrong. I am the leader of my people, and perhaps if we had fought harder or smarter, none of this would have happened to you or the other Citadels. Admittedly, I . . ." Iathan pauses and swallows. I see the Karekins in the room suddenly take significantly more interest in him, and even his spies move in closer, as if to shield him. If we were wolves, he would be leaving his throat exposed with this admission. The others don't have to understand his words to see how his body language has changed, and they clearly want to protect the alpha. For perhaps the first time since I've met him, I actually feel a twinge of respect for him as he goes through with it anyway. "I am regretful," Iathan says softly, solemnly. "So while you might not care what happens to us, I assure you, Ryn, I most certainly do not share your apathy."

I dig my nails into my palm for just the briefest of seconds. I get fighting and running, and sometimes (obviously not all the time) following orders, but nuance is hard for me. It's hard for me to take a definitive stand when I am surrounded by conditions that are both right *and* wrong.

"Okay," I say while folding my hands in front of me. "I guess the view from where I'm sitting right now is entirely self-serving. But I've been in enough battles to know that view can change. And the victors are almost always the ones who are willing to shift perspective. I am a lot of things, but fortune-teller is not one of them. Who knows what the future will bring? For the immediate future, let's just call this a mutually beneficial alliance and start with a plan."

"I say we pick a Citadel race and capture a single soldier," Levi offers. "We give them the facts. We show them irrefutable proof of what the Roones are and what they've done and what they're most likely to do—which is enslave them—and turn them into another version of the Settiku Hesh. All it takes is one person to start asking questions. Ryn is proof of that."

It's a sound argument. As I take a hard look at all the evidence floating around me, I realize there are a few problems, first of which is that, while these species are Citadels, they are not humans. They will not act or react like us. But it's not like all humans reacted with a parade when we told them about what Ezra and I had learned.

God—how long ago was that?

"Well," I say finally, "I think there's merit to Levi's suggestion." From across the room, in Ezra's direction, I hear a little snort. Without advanced hearing, I doubt anyone else besides Levi and I would have heard the same. I am going to have to deal with this. And it's going to suck. Right now, though, there are far more important things to consider than Ezra's feelings. Add to that the fact that *he* hasn't supplied any solutions of his own means—so right now Levi is more valuable. So I build on what he's given us.

"One major concern is the drugs," I say. "We can't forget that it's the drugs that are keeping the majority of the Citadels in line. At least, I think so. Iathan? Does your recon include that information? Or, Ezra? Does Edo mention it?"

"The Citadels are all given various doses, combining different compounds based on each species' biology, but yes, the mind-controlling drugs are in play," Ezra says with authority.

"That means this can't be done in the field. We'll have to capture someone and bring them back here. We wait for the cocktail to clear their system and while we're doing that, we create a red pill made specifically for their body chemistry. I assume you can do that, Mr. President?" Amazingly, Levi says this without irony.

He does love an appropriate chain of command.

One of Iathan's spies leans over and whispers something in his ear. Iathan's small eyes narrow to thumbnail slivers. The spy backs away, melting among his comrades.

"That is quite a significant security risk for us," Iathan states. He does not agree or disagree. I know what he's looking for.

"So is having people whispering secrets to you as if we can't be trusted," I say. "But forget that for now, because I think I share your concerns. So I'll say this: If we can't convince the other Citadels to reason—if they are intent on remaining blindly aligned with the altered Roones—then we execute them."

"Ryn!" Ezra cries.

"What? If they don't come over to our side, we'll have to kill them anyway. There's going to be a *war*, Ezra. If we can't convince the other Citadels to break ties with the people who are controlling them—and *us*—what do you think our options are?"

Ezra gapes as he looks at me. He's making a strange noise with his mouth, almost an airless grunt. I glance at Levi. He is blessedly looking at the floor—an attempt, no doubt, to be diplomatic, given where we are. I swear to God, if I so much as hear him snigger . . .

Finally, Ezra speaks: "You can't just kill thousands of people who don't agree with you, especially if they've been brainwashed. Ryn, *come on*."

I shake my head in disbelief. Why does Ezra suddenly believe that I *want* to kill people? Am I twiddling my fingers together like some mustache-twirling villain and maniacally laughing like a psycho? He *knows* me.

Or . . . at least, I thought he did.

I wonder if Levi was right when he said I'd only known Ezra a short time. That I couldn't be sure of anything because it really hasn't been all that long for us. Sure, Levi was being an asshole when he said it, but right now it feels like Ezra and I are nowhere close to being on the same page. In fact, it's almost as if he's *baiting* me.

And it's really starting to piss me off.

"No," I say, holding up my hands, palms out. "No way. Your help is invaluable when it comes to the computer stuff and the decryption, but the tactical part of this equation? The strategy when it comes to fighting and winning? The *morality* of possibly having to take lives when it's us who might have to do it? No—that has to be our call."

"'The computer stuff'? That's what you want to call my

contribution?" Ezra folds his arms. His chin is set and his brilliant blue eyes focus on me with laser-like precision. But if he thinks I'm intimidated, then he *really* doesn't know me. I meet his gaze with the same intensity. It's naive of him to assume there won't be collateral damage if we want to get out from under this. And it's petulant of him to think I was trying to denigrate what he's provided this mission. What he's given *me*. I try to remember that one of the reasons I love Ezra is his optimism and his faith that people deserve the chance to be saved. This kind of reasoning is all well and good in a safe room, deep underground and far from harm.

The problem is, optimism doesn't hold up all that well on the battlefield.

"You know that's not true, Ezra," I say. I take in a big gulp of air—I seem to have been doing that a lot lately—to get my simmering anger under control. I keep my eyes locked on his, though, because I want him to see that what I'm saying is sincere. "We're here right now because of you. There's a bigger picture here, though. Speculating on how we proceed in the future is pointless unless we have as much information as possible. We won't get that information without grabbing another Citadel. Let's just start from there."

"Agreed," Levi says while leaning forward. God—of course he'd chime in right now. While I'm grateful for his support— and he's definitely in his element with all this talk of kidnapping and war—the last thing I need is for Ezra to be reminded that I have more in common with Levi than with him.

Ezra remains silent. He shakes his head and his brown hair falls into his eyes. He swoops it back, exposing the strain on his face.

"I say we take a Spiradael," I suggest, hoping to get us past this current awkward moment. "We are faster than them, and stronger, and our body armor should protect us from their weird machete hair. More important, they're probably the easiest to break, as they aren't brainless thugs like the Orsalines, naturally crafty like the Daithi, or had their intelligence enhanced like the others."

"I concur," Iathan says while pointing at all the other Citadel races in the projections around the room. He makes a slight flick of his thumb and index finger so that they all disappear until all that's left are the photos and footage of the Spiradaels. "We had, through our assets, a basic knowledge of their language, but Edo's files provided an entire lexicon of the language."

"Perfect. Levi and I can learn it tonight and we'll go tomorrow." There. A plan. I've had enough of this for today. Right now, I want to be alone with Ezra.

"Very well. I think we could all use some time to reflect on what we have learned from each other today. Ezra Massad informed me that you would wish to share his living quarters with him. Is that still the case, Ryn?"

I can't tell if Iathan is being polite or if this is another of his tests. I can't help but suspect at least some of it is the latter, as he's watching all of us intently, Levi most of all. Of course, it might be that something dawned on him—I'd have been shocked if he hadn't picked up on the tension between us, considering it's been growing by the minute. The air in this large room is thickening with unsaid words and wandering suspicions. I don't have the courage to steal a look at Levi in the face. We might have been on the same page when it came to a battle plan, but this is an entirely different kind of fight, one that he won't win. And then there's the fact that Ezra wouldn't like it if I looked at Levi, either—and that makes me both upset and mad, as if I have to explain myself to him.

Fuck!

I hate having to answer Iathan aloud. I feel like he's making me choose in front of all these people for no reason other than to get a little payback for the way I'd manhandled him earlier. I shake my head. *Petty little shit.*

"Yes," I finally say. "Ezra and I will be sharing a room."

CHAPTER 22

With my admission, Iathan and his minions dismissed us without ceremony and we are being escorted down a long hallway by two Karekins. Levi is walking ahead. Ezra is beside me. I want him to take my hand, but he has not. I should reach for him, but I don't. The concrete walls are smooth, with tiny deposits of minerals that flicker in the overhead lights. I could trail my fingers across it. It would be good to touch something solid, something my own skin might recognize as familiar as Ezra continues to keep his distance. But I know that would be inappropriate. Something a teenager might do instead of a soldier. In this place, in front of others, at least, I must always be a soldier.

I don't want to, though.

So instead I glance at Ezra, whose lips curve upward in the barest hint of a smile. I grin in response and of course it's that one moment when Levi finally looks back, right at us. He quickly whips his head forward once more. I keep my eyes locked on to Ezra's face and pretend I didn't see Levi look. Just like touching the walls, it's probably juvenile to be feeling happy when I'm pretty certain Levi is feeling shitty. One feeling should cancel out the other, I think. I bite my tongue to stop myself from asking Ezra about how I should feel. Ezra would know the answer, but obviously he's the last person I should be asking. I can't even believe it crossed my mind. I'm so stupid in the romance department it's laughable.

We stop in front of a painted metal door. "There's no handle," I remark.

"The Roone technology is all about sound," Ezra informs me with a little shrug. "*Open door*," he says, and I hear a click. The metal swings open silently. The Karekins escorting Levi continue once again down the hallway.

"I'll see you tomorrow!" I holler in a tone that sounds overly saccharine, even to me. I'm overcompensating. I know it. Levi says nothing in response. He doesn't even turn around. He just waves a single hand above his head. It's there for only a second and then it's back down at his side. I stare at his back as he walks away. I know he's upset. I'm not a person who just hurts people—at least, I don't hurt their *feelings*. That's probably not true, either. I can be brusque, bossy even. But I would never go out of my way to hurt anyone.

"Do you want to go in?" Ezra asks with an edge to his voice. "Or would you like to watch Levi walk all the way to his own room?" I exhale loudly to show I'm not exactly pleased with comments like that and push past him into the living quarters. I hear Ezra command the door to shut and finally we are alone. And as rough as it's been to get here, I knew I would finally make it. I knew if I just held on and stayed focused, I could find Ezra, and now, here we are.

Surrounded by silence.

The space is large and mostly concrete, warmed with a folksy but colorfully abstract tapestry on one wall—a leftover, I guess, from when the Roones were artists and philosophers. Another wall is painted cobalt blue and the bed is large with ivory linens. On either side sit two lamps on wooden bedside tables, providing ample light for the space. There is a large desk where Ezra has made himself at home. Papers with his handwriting are scattered about next to his and Edo's laptops, which are open but not powered up. There's also a computer interface built right into the metal of the desk, just like in the war room.

It's like a cozy home, with none of the welcome.

I drop my pack to the floor. I look at Ezra and he looks at me. He doesn't say anything, but by the set of his jaw it's clear that he's pissed. While he's got a lot to be upset about, I would think seeing me would be more than enough to get us past that, at least in the short-term. I really *am* naive about relationship stuff. Because even though I get where he's coming from, his being pissed pisses me off. I'm ready to get into this, to ask him what the hell his problem is . . . but not in my damn uniform. I have the sudden urge to just feel like a normal girl. "I'm going to take a shower and change," I announce, hoping he'll stop me, hug me, kiss me, *anything* me.

But he doesn't, and my stomach drops.

"The bathroom is right through that door," Ezra says indifferently. I don't bother to answer. I do, however, rummage around optimistically in my pack for a toothbrush. When I find one, I walk to the door he indicated without even looking at him.

Two can play this game.

Unlike the bedroom, the bathroom is purely utilitarian. It's gray everywhere, with a stainless steel sink and toilet that, while it blessedly has an actual seat, still reminds me of one you'd see in prison movies. I move quickly. It's not the kind of space to luxuriate in. Once I'm showered and dry, I use the cuff to change into navy sweats and a long-sleeved knitted top with lots of ease. Not exactly sexy, but I have a hard time figuring out what to wear at the best of times, and right now I don't know what would be appropriate. See-through and sexy just isn't me, and jeans feel too formal. I think this is the right outfit because I could both sleep and go to Starbucks in it.

I open the door and the steam from the shower escapes into the windowless room, my face flushing with the heat. Or maybe I'm flushed because I see Ezra lying on the bed, staring at the ceiling. He maybe looks slightly less annoyed, but he's playing it pretty cool. I wish *I* could play things cool. When it comes to Ezra, I'm about as subtle as a gunshot. He sits up when he sees me, and leans back against the wall behind the mattress, drawing his legs up so his forearms can rest on his knees.

"Where did you get those clothes?"

I smile and hold up my right hand to show him the cuff. "It's actually technology that we acquired from an amazing race of . . . ummm . . . 'people' would be the wrong word. They're robots, I guess. They call themselves SenMachs, and I can't wait to tell you all about them. Later."

Ezra shakes his head and sighs. "Right. Because obviously a magical bracelet given to you by robots is just another day at the office around here." Any other time this might have been nothing more than a little barb, a joke. Right now, the statement feels loaded. And once more there's distance between us.

I try to bridge that gap, just a little, by sitting down on the bed next to him. The mattress is surprisingly comfortable, it being a war bunker and all. I put my hand on his knee. "Look, I know you're pissed about Levi being here—" I begin delicately.

"'Pissed' doesn't even begin to cover it," he says, cutting me off. "Why him? Of all the Citadels? *Him?*"

"I told you already. He was the best choice, for my safety and the safety of everyone at Camp Bonneville. We're soldiers, Ezra, and this made the most sense tactically." Ezra is ignoring my hand, and resting it on him suddenly feels awkward and forced, so I take it back and put it in my lap.

"I'm not stupid," Ezra practically spits. "I can see there's something going on between you two. The way he looks at you. It's so obvious. Actually, I think even a stupid person would be able to pick up on it. So what exactly is going on? When I left your Earth you didn't even *like* Levi."

The air in the room suddenly feels thicker, hotter. I lift my top up by the collar and fan myself. "I . . . I don't know where to begin."

"Why don't you start with the truth?"

"Ezra—I've never lied to you. *Ever.*"

"Fine. But you're holding something back. Something you must know is pretty messed up. Or else you'd have just said there's nothing going on between you two. That he's infatuated with you but that you don't feel that way." He looks at me, and I stare back, unsure how to respond. He snorts. "And you can't even do that."

"Why are you being like this? What have I done to make you so angry at me? I came to find *you.*"

"With *him.*"

"Yes," I say quietly. I knew I'd have to tell Ezra—I always planned on telling him. I just never, you know, actually planned *how* I would tell him. Swallowing hard, I look down at my hands. I've faced monsters. I've survived a toxic Earth. Been in more fights than I can count, many where my life was on the line.

And this is the hardest thing I've ever had to do.

"Well?"

I look up, and those blue eyes almost destroy me. How they're somehow fire and ice at the same time makes no sense, and—as if I'm in a trance—the words spill out. "I've been deprogramming him and it's a little more complicated than I anticipated."

"You've been what?" Ezra asks in a voice that is chillingly calm.

"I *had* to. It was unsafe for us to travel together and not get his Blood Lust under control, not just for myself but for anyone else we might meet along the way. Back home we can isolate ourselves from situations where it can overtake us, but out here in the field there were just too many variables to leave to chance. It could have taken weeks to find you, months even. I was hoping that it would be this fast, but I had no idea."

Ezra closes his eyes for a moment, his arms crossed tightly across his chest. "Oh my God, Ryn."

"Look," I say, getting up on my knees, tucking my feet beneath me. I put my hands on either side of his face. "It doesn't matter. I could give you a million reasons why I did it and you could turn around and tell me why they're all bullshit. The only thing you need to know is that I did what I did to get to you. I had"—I pull his hands away from his chest and hold them in my own—"to get to you."

Ezra opens his mouth. I think he's going to say something, but then his eyes change. For a fleeting moment the look reminds me of the way Levi gets when the Blood Lust is about to kick in—anger and despair and intense passion. It is an expression that suggests he doesn't quite have control. Since I know Ezra would never hurt me physically, I happily know where this is going and I'm not surprised when he kisses me. At first his mouth is gentle. I close my eyes and say a thousand prayers of gratitude. Are there even gods on this Earth? It feels like it. This kiss feels like redemption and sanctuary. Ezra's lips get more insistent, desperate even, and I respond in kind. His tongue pushes into my mouth and skillfully rolls around my own. We both move up so that we're both on our knees, another prayer.

Ezra pulls away long enough to get his shirt off and then he tries to help me with my own but of course he can't. It's the sensuit. It doesn't separate. "Cuff," I say softly. The suit slides off my arms and legs like an oily slick. It flows away from me back into my bracelet. I am totally naked. Ezra gapes at me. He drinks me in. Up and down his eyes eat my skin. He scrambles to get his pants and boxers off.

Ever so gently he nudges me down with his face in my neck. He kisses my collarbone. He licks the space between my breasts. When he takes one of them in his mouth, I groan. It occurs to me then that I have never done this before, that I actually don't know what to do. Am I supposed to do something? I can feel how hard he is against my thigh. I wrap my hand around him, my palm ready to move back and forth, but he takes my hand away.

"If you touch me like that, I won't last long," Ezra whispers playfully. He maneuvers himself around so that he is lying beside me. He takes his hand and runs it down the length of my entire body, making each hair stand on end until he gets to that place where I am wet and pulsing. He pushes one of my thighs away so he can get to the center of me. I bite down on my bottom lip as he spreads me open and finds that one perfect, sweet spot. He flicks and swirls and then dips his finger inside me. At first it's just the tip of his finger, but as his movements become faster, he goes farther in, all the way inside. My hips buck. I start to pant. My muscles clench; my entire body feels like a live wire.

"Ryn, let go," he whispers in my ear, "just come for me." I groan and move my pelvis up to his finger. I clutch the bed and my knuckles go white against the fabric. After a few more moments I do let go. I moan and shiver all the way through the orgasm as it jolts like electricity, making my whole body shiver.

I don't exactly know what is happening. All I know is that I want more.

I pull him on top of me and he settles between my legs. Ezra looks at me. He's making sure that this is what I want. I lick my lips and pull his face to my own, kissing my response. He guides himself inside me, slowly. I know this part is going to hurt. I understand that much and I'm glad for it. For a person like me, pain can be a kind of love song. For so long, it was the only physical thing my body could feel. I've read and seen enough to know that there is no "normal" when it comes to sex. Everyone has a thing and my thing happens to be that I like a little bit of pain, which seems, all things considered, totally appropriate.

Ezra tries to take it slow, but I put both hands on his ass and pull him all the way in. The sensation makes me yelp. It makes my back arch. It makes me think that I might be close to coming again.

"Move," I tell him, grinding my hips up and against him. Ezra happily obliges. I wrap a leg around his torso and he lifts his body up, bringing my leg and ass with him under his hand. I use my other foot as leverage so that I can bring him closer and deeper.

Unsurprisingly, sex is full of contradictions. It is push and pull. It is ache and pleasure. It is stop and go, fast and slow. It is something you feel. It is all body and limbs, but at the same time, it is a place. It's a world that two people create with their wanting. It has its own language and geography. I am sure this city we have made with need and urgency can only be traveled by Ezra and me. I could have sex with different men, but none of them would take me to the same place.

I dig my fingers into his toffee-colored flesh. Ezra keeps on kissing my throat, my shoulder, and then rearing up to reach different places inside of me. I think he might be saying my name or he might just be groaning. I don't care. I hear his breathing start to quicken. I feel his body tense, and then he goes silent, as if he's sucking the sound of his voice back inside, drawing it in so he can focus all his energy on climaxing. When he does, I actually feel it, which shocks me.

I'm amazed by the feeling. Not just about the fire that poured through me, but of my hands on Ezra. During, his entire body was forged steel, rippling and reforming, but always powerful and strong. And right before he came, it somehow got *harder*, and as much as anything, that's what drove me over the edge. Now, though, it's still hot—his skin, his breath, his place between my legs—but somehow it's liquid. And if we had been close before—as close as two people could be—this is somehow even more intimate.

The . . . after.

We lie like that for a while, and I'm sure there's nowhere—no Earth, no world—I'd rather be on than the one we've just created together. Eventually, though, Ezra moves so that he's by my side. A minute ago it was like we were one person and now we are two again. It's the strangest sensation, letting someone in and then letting them go.

I give him a quick kiss on the nose and then make my way to the bathroom because that's another thing I didn't know about sex: It requires some cleanup. When I come back, Ezra is still there, lazing. I get into the bed and curl up against him.

"So," I say as I wrap my fingers around his.

"So," he answers back in a swaggy kind of way that's cheese ball enough to make me giggle.

"Can we do that again? Like right now?" I ask him earnestly.

"You're not sore?"

"Well, yeah, but with the job and all, I'm kind of in a constant state of soreness and this is kind of a good sore?" I blush. "That didn't come out right."

Ezra smiles at me and brings my hand to his naked chest. "We can absolutely do it again, but maybe in a few minutes? I am young, but you do know it works different with guys . . ." Ezra tapers the sentence off.

"I'm aware. I just don't know the actual mechanics of it." I snuggle up even closer to him and put my face in the crook of his arm.

"Are you happy, Ryn?"

"Very."

"We're good, right? What we just did. You do know what that means?" Ezra's tone takes on an unexpectedly serious tone.

"That I'm a woman now?" I say playfully. I trace my finger over his skin and he grabs my hand.

"It means that we're *together*, together. Whatever happened before this, whatever happened between you and Levi, it's forgotten. It's done."

What the actual fuck?

Immediately, I sit up, bringing the sheet up with me. "I

thought we were together before. Hence the 'jumping into the Multiverse and its many perils to find you to make sure that you were safe' thing that I did."

Now its Ezra's turn to sit up. "As much as I love the whole emasculating 'I rescued you' routine, that's not what I'm talking about. Once you have sex with someone, it makes the relationship more solid, more committed. Those are, like, the rules." Ezra is explaining this like I'm a baby or an idiot. How did this turn so quickly? I don't get it. We *were just* having sex.

I also don't get where he's coming up with these rules. "The rules according to who? Pilgrims?"

"No. To monogamy."

I shake my head. "I'm not sure what you're saying."

Ezra closes and opens his eyes slowly. His frustration is palpable, and mine is starting to grow, too. "I'm saying that as much as it kills me to imagine, I can see why you would deprogram Levi. You felt like you had to do it in order to complete your mission. But you've completed your mission. You found me. And I forgive you, for whatever you did."

Ezra's declaration sinks in. It goes deep, into my veins. I had felt bad about what had happened between me and Levi, but that was before. There was so much I didn't understand before I had sex. I opened myself up to love and realized that my capacity for holding it and giving it was boundless.

Ezra's forgiveness isn't coming from that place.

In fact, it feels petty and mean. He doesn't understand. I mean, I don't think I entirely understand, either, but at least I'm not pretending I do. At least I'm not pretending like this whole situation is normal and normal rules apply. His hypocrisy or stupidity (or both) gets my back up.

"Well, I'm *so* glad I have your forgiveness," I throw at him. "And you know what? I *forgive you.* I forgive you for getting sucked into the Rift and then being so completely fucking inept that you were thrown back in it. I forgive you for all the crazy medical procedures they did on me and my skin melting off and, oh yeah, that time I was a slave."

Ezra narrows his eyes at me. "I don't know what the hell you're talking about," he practically growls. "But the stuff I kinda know you're talking about wasn't my fault, so I don't need your forgiveness."

"Exactly!"

Ezra puts his face in his hands and then slowly slides his fingers down, changing the shape of his face. "I don't know why we're fighting. All I'm saying is that the past is the past. Let's leave it there." The thing is, though, there is no softness in his voice, no proof at all that he is capable of doing such a thing.

"So," I tell him, not bothering to hide the disappointment in my voice. "You're saying that I can't finish deprogramming Levi."

Ezra throws up his hands, leaving his lean torso completely exposed. "Yeah. Obviously. What are you going to do, Ryn? Are you going to have sex with me and then run to Levi and let him *touch* you? That's not how couples work. You can't be intimate with someone else. It's one person or another. You have to choose. I get that you think you're special and normal rules don't apply to you, but in this one area they do. It's me or Levi. You can't have us both."

At that, I leap off the bed. "There is nothing about this situation that is normal. Loungewear, present day," I say to my cuff, and the sensuit flowers out of the bracelet and turns into a pair of gray sweats and a long-sleeved V-neck. "I have done so much for you, gone through so much, and so has Levi. What if another Citadel—a female Citadel—had been pushed into the Rift with you that day? What if you had to deprogram her? For safety? Would the idea of you two being intimate piss me off? Yeah it would. But I would find a way to understand that it was temporary and being done for the greater good. I would feel confident enough in you and me to know we'd get through it. And if I didn't, I would ask for reassurance."

Ezra furrows his brow, his mouth agape. "You *cannot* be serious. You can't base an entire argument on something that didn't even happen!" Ezra's anger has shifted gears. It's taken on an incredulous tone as if, somehow, he's above all this speculating. I could almost laugh. *I'm a soldier.* I live and die by what-if scenarios.

"Sure I can. Unless, sorry, is that not allowed? Is that what's written down in your mysterious Rule Book for Relationships?"

"This is not funny, Ryn."

"I'm not laughing, and I'm definitely not trying to be funny, but I feel like you're messing with me. You've *got* to be, because you know better than anyone that if I stop deprogramming Levi now, at this critical time in the process, it could ruin his chances to recover. If I abandon and hurt him when he's made himself so vulnerable to me, he might never get over the Blood Lust. He doesn't deserve that. I can't do that to him. How could you?"

Ezra gets up himself and throws on his own sweats. Speaking of vulnerability, I don't think he wants to have this conversation stark naked. "Regardless of what Levi's done—and make no mistake, he hasn't helped *me* at all—it's all been for you. Don't kid yourself on that front. I really don't give two fucks about Levi's sex life and neither should you. That's the point."

Ezra's words are like a slap in the face. "Okay," I say softly, resolutely. "You want me to choose? All right. *I choose me.* I choose myself. Because you know, recently, it's come to my attention that for the past few years I've been manipulated and controlled and abused and treated like a thing, like property. I don't like that feeling. That feeling makes me cranky. Sometimes, it even makes me kill people."

Ezra's eyes widen as he freezes.

Now that is disappointing.

"Seriously? I'm not going to kill you. I'm just trying to convey how much I hate the idea of someone thinking I belong to them. I hate it so much that I *would* kill thousands, hundreds of thousands, to ensure my freedom. So, I'm sure as fuck not gonna let *you* dictate to me—because of some 'monogamy rule' that seems ridiculous in our present circumstances—what I can or cannot do with Levi."

"I should have known," Ezra says. "I should have known that you could only see this in terms of some sort of battle. You want me to fight Levi for you? Is that it? I mean, it's hardly a fair fight—only if we're talking physical strength, of course."

I grab my head with both hands. I want to scream, but I also partly want to throttle him. "Really? That's what you got from my whole 'I Know Why the Caged Bird Sings' speech? You think I want you to fight? That's the last friggin' thing I want."

Ezra folds his arms together. He lifts his chin haughtily. "Then what do you want? Really? Because I'm starting to think that this whole deprogramming thing is a smoke screen, Ryn."

I glare at Ezra straight on. Jealousy I can understand. It's irrational, but that irrationality has a basis. But an accusation? Based on his own paranoia? Screw that. He's hurt me. He's practically gutted me. Maybe asking him to accept this was too much, I honestly don't know. I do know that I had sex with him to feel close to him, to show him, without words, how deeply

I cared for him. I think maybe he had sex with me to make a point, too. Except right now, the edge of that point feels like it's stabbing me in the back.

"I want you to leave."

"What?"

"Get. *Out!*"

Once again, Ezra opens his mouth to say something, but he slams it shut again and grits his teeth. His turquoise eyes shoot me a look that is equal parts despair and disgust. I take a step back, against the wall. He grabs his things and starts shoving them inside his pack with furious intensity. Neither one of us says anything else. The silence is visceral. It is a living thing, the third person in this room, or maybe it's the fourth. Maybe Levi has been here all along. I didn't ask for Levi's presence. It was Ezra who kept bringing him up, but I have to admit that I never quite banished him, either.

Ezra collects his papers from the desk, crumpling them in a single hand and pushing them hastily inside the backpack. "Open," he says to the door angrily. The lock clicks, and Ezra pushes the door open with considerable force before disappearing into the hallway.

I look at the bed. The sheets are crumpled, uneven. The top sheet is half off the mattress. I feel the sudden urge to make it, to put it back. I lift the sheet and shake it out. It flutters like a parachute, suspended in the air. I look at the spot where Ezra and I had just been together. I guess I'm looking for blood. How much blood does virginity spill? There isn't anything but a stretch of white. Somewhere along the way, either through fighting, or God knows what else, ARC stole that from me, too, I guess.

I fold the sheet under the mattress, hospital corners. And I shake out the duvet so that it's as smooth as glass. I run my hand over it, giving it tiny yanks to make it perfect. I replace the pillows and sit back down. I feel angry, but also really sad, and I find that these emotions cancel each other out. It's as if they've pushed me out of the way and I'm just swirling them around, thinking about them but not actually feeling them. I am hollow.

Are Ezra and I still together? Was that just a fight? Or did I break up with him or did he just break up with me? I laugh out loud because I actually don't know.

I'm at sixes and sevens. That's what my grandmother would say. She would wring her hands and fly about the house when there was dinner on the stove and someone at the door and her book club still to get to. Sixes and sevens. I don't really have the luxury to be all over the place, though, do I? I have a hostage to take and a language to learn. War is coming, one way or another. So really, should my relationship status even be a thing?

No. I don't think so.

CHAPTER 23

I walk over to my pack, pull out my SenMach laptop, and put it on the Roone console.

"Download every pertinent file about the Roones, the altered Roones, and the Citadels. Make sure to include the decrypted files from Edo's computer." The luminescent tendrils squirm out of my machine and unfold across the desk. I'm going to know it all now, even the stuff Iathan might not necessarily want me to know, and he'll have no idea. The SenMachs' technology is far more advanced than the Roones', and it will leave no trace. Alliances are well and good, but at the end of the day, the Roones are a species of spies and mad scientists. I want to know what they've got.

"It will take approximately thirteen minutes to download this information. Do you still wish to proceed, Ryn Whittaker?" I can't help but jolt at the familiar voice coming from my wrist. It's Doe. I put the cuff up to my ear. Is there a speaker in there?

"You can talk?" I ask, a little self-conscious, in the empty room.

"Yes."

"Then why haven't you ever talked before?"

"It has never been necessary. I am only addressing you now because the amount of data you are requesting to download is quite significant. It will take up nine point eight percent of what you would call my 'memory storage.' I wanted to make sure this operation was what you intended."

Even though I just lost my virginity to a guy who may or may not still be my boyfriend, I can't help but feel a little pumped about the idea of my own personal Jarvis.

"Can you manifest into a hologram?" I wonder aloud. Seeing Tim Riggins would go a long way toward making me feel better.

"I could rewrite some of the Roone code they use for visual interface in combination with our own holographic programming and do an approximation, if you wish. It will take another seven minutes to create this application."

I think seriously about it and then decide it's not really a priority. That said, I might want the Fortress of Solitude option at some later date, so I say, "Go ahead and create the program, but I don't need to use it right now. What I would like is the Spiradael language files so that I can start to learn it. Please display them in an order which would most efficiently expedite that process."

"Affirmative." The files start popping up in front of me, projected by what looks like four outputs from the desk. Interesting. They know where I am in relation to the room and are adjusting accordingly.

"Great—and in the future, please just say 'okay' or 'yes' or 'no.' Don't speak 'robot.' It makes me feel like I'm in a movie where you're about to take over the world."

There is a slight pause.

"Okay," I hear the computer say. I pinch my nose with my thumb and forefinger. I have to focus. I have to learn this. I mentally push everything back. I concentrate on the floating images above me. It's time to go to work.

"*Veen. Trak. Teesh. Sohn. Kowf.* One. Two. Three. Four. Five." An actual Spiradael voice is speaking from somewhere. I think it's my cuff, but it could be a speaker from somewhere in the room. All things considered, it hardly matters really.

"Just play more audio of them conversing. For now." I close my eyes and listen to the spiky, guttural language of the Spiradael. I get a sense of it. I can almost feel it slide from my ears to my throat. "Stop," I command. "Let's start with basic phrases. Something that I will probably need."

I lean back against the wall behind the bed, which is layered with pillows.

"How do you say 'I am a Citadel'?"

A BREAKFAST TRAY IS DELIVERED to my room. There is a plate full of something that looks like scrambled eggs but is the color of a neon pumpkin. There's also a something that might be meat, possibly bacon, but it smells like feet. I decide to go with the SenMach cubes. I take another shower, because God only knows when I might get another chance to do so. I then make my way to the war room. When I get there, Levi is browsing a topographical map of an area around the Spiradael Rift. He stares at me, and then behind me, noticing that I'm alone. His green eyes get just a fraction smaller as he registers that I'm by myself and then he goes back to looking at the hovering maps. Before I can walk over to him, Ezra enters from an entirely different direction than I did and stands beside me. Levi notices that, too, and just for a moment, I see a flicker of a smile on his face. Cocky bastard.

"Hi," I say to Ezra hesitantly. I don't know what I'm supposed to do here. I am sorry that things went down but not sorry enough to start acting deferential.

"Hi," he responds coolly. Okay, then. An impasse. This is going to be awesome. At that moment, Iathan strides in with his lackeys behind him.

"Excellent, we're all here. I hope the two of you were able to learn the language in the time you had?"

"Yeah," and "Pretty much," Levi and I answer respectively while looking at each other. Ten hours was more than enough, but it's not like we're going to admit that. Iathan will get information about us on a need-to-know basis only.

"Excellent," Iathan remarks as he walks over to the largest console table and leans his hands on the sleek black metal. "Any ideas, then, on how best to proceed?"

"I've spent the past hour studying different Rift sites on the Spiradael Earth, looking for ideal entry locations," Levi begins. "There are only two Rifts on that Earth." Levi opens his arms and pushes them together, causing two images to illuminate above all of us, side by side. "One site is in a desert. I would eliminate that one for obvious reasons." He makes another motion with his fingers outstretched and flicks them backward so that now, only one picture is highlighted. "This site is in a forested area. I say we Rift in here, about a klick away from the base, and try to grab a Spiradael from the reserves. If they operate like we do, there will be a large contingent of troops around the permanent Rift and then another fifty or sixty holding positions closer to their command, guarding it from Immigrants who might slip through the first line of defense, but they will be far more spread out."

I fold my arms and study the photo, which looks like it comes from a drone image. "We can't be sure they operate like we do. If there are only two Rifts on that Earth, there's a chance that there are far fewer Spiradael Citadels."

"They do not operate like human Citadels. I can tell you that much from our intelligence work," Iathan says.

"Can you elaborate?" I ask, though I don't know why I should have to.

Iathan looks momentarily caught up in a memory. I don't think he's withholding, but there is something about what he knows of this race that troubles him. He clears his throat—and presumably the memory. "They do not hide. They stand and wait at the Rift's mouth. There are some reserves, but in terms of operations, they do not bother with subterfuge. They've also had years and years to establish a Citadel race. Which, unfortunately, means we do not know the exact numbers. It is intel we were never able to accurately collect, and Edo conveniently left out actual troop numbers in her coded files. I can assure you, though, there are many."

"Could you maybe take an educated guess?" I ask.

Iathan knits his brows together and strokes his beard. "Anywhere from thirty to fifty thousand?"

Jesus . . .

Levi and I look at each other across the table. This is not good. I keep forgetting the scope of this. But it's hard for me to imagine there are so many others like me, and even harder to imagine a war based on those numbers.

However, as I turn it over in my head some more, a glimmer of hope breaks through. "But they won't all be there," I say. "That's impossible. Too many Citadels at any given Rift site can actually be less effective. It's difficult to coordinate a thousand troops. It's much easier to command a couple hundred."

"True," Ezra interjects to my surprise. Then again, he knows a lot about human Citadels from me. He knows about the other Citadel races from Edo's files and through extensive research here in the Roone world, and he also probably knows more than I do about the altered Roones. He's hardly an expert, but he's a guy who loves data. As unlikely as it seems, given how new he is to this game, he's got valuable insight. "But human Citadels are stronger and more capable than Spiradael Citadels. They would need more troops on the ground to accomplish what fewer of you can do."

"Well, then, I suppose the question goes back to numbers," Iathan says bluntly. "Do you want a full unit to escort you, or a simple strike force?"

"Wait," I say, holding up a single hand. "You want us to bring Karekins along? I don't know about that."

"Hear him out, Ryn," Levi says in a tone that sounds more like a command than a request. Up until now I have been in charge, but I have to admit that Levi is great at this kind of strategy. He has a kind of sixth sense about enemy troop movement that I don't possess. As much as it irritates me, I have to loosen the reins of my control a little bit and let Levi do what he's good at. Ego has no place when lives are on the line. And honestly, the idea of having Karekins with us had never dawned on me. But why wouldn't they come along—or, at least, why wouldn't Iathan assume they'd be coming along? I don't like it—don't *trust* it—but I can trust Levi when it comes to something like this, so I nod my head and look at Iathan.

"Yes, it would be unwise to dismiss our offer of help so quickly. As you've seen, the Karekins—*our* Karekins—are much different from the ones you have faced. They are not mindless drones, drugged out of their minds. They are strong and capable, and should you encounter more than just a few Spiradaels, they could be the difference between you getting out of there alive or being taken prisoner."

"And they will concede command to us? Without question?" I have to ask.

"I think perhaps that is a question better left to our Karekin general." Iathan looks over to one of the Karekins standing in the room and beckons him over. I listen as he explains my trepidation in Roonish, and the large man nods his head.

"Citadel Ryn Whittaker, my name is Vlock," the Karekin leader says in Roonish. I am surprised by the gentle cadence of his voice, the soft, lilting rise and fall of his words. It's the total opposite of the guttural screeches I've heard while fighting a column of Karekins in Battle Ground. I give Vlock my full attention, and he continues. "I am in charge of the Karekin troops. I understand your reluctance to trust us. All you know of my kind is violence and brutality, but I can assure you that we are nothing like the Settiku Hesh that infiltrate your Earth. We have all fought, and many of us perished, in an attempt to ensure that what happened to you would never come to pass. We failed in that mission. Please be assured that we will do everything in our power to address that grievous wrongdoing. My men will be yours to command. They are good fighters, and loyal to our common cause." Vlock pauses and relaxes ever so slightly before speaking on. "I stopped apologizing long ago for the actions of our rogue brothers. I had to, because the guilt and the shame of it made us weak. But please do not condemn us for the actions of our misguided brethren. They are hardly men anymore. They have no free will. They have no morality. It has been stripped away by the enemy.

You can trust us, human Citadel. We will protect you with our lives." Vlock steps back, and I must admit I am moved by his speech.

It has been hard being around these Karekins. They have been mute ghosts during my time here, easy to dismiss and subconsciously ignored for all the reasons that Vlock spoke of. But they are victims, too. Just like me. I think about crazy Audrey, who's still in a coma back at Battle Ground. She's a Citadel, just like me, and we fought on different sides when the truth came out about ARC. Sadly, this is no different.

"Very well," I say in both English and Roonish. "However, I do believe that a small strike force would be more effective in this situation."

"I agree," Levi says. I bet he learned Roonish last night. It would have been the most strategic move and I could tell when Vlock was speaking that Levi was paying attention to more than just his deferential body language and tone. "Let's bring five of your best men and the two of us. That should be more than enough to fight off even a large force of Spiradaels if necessary. Though hopefully it won't be necessary. Our goal is to capture a Spiradael and Rift back immediately, before anyone knows he's been taken."

"And me. I'm going," Ezra says. Levi swallows a chuckle between clenched lips and I throw him a dirty look before turning to Ezra.

"I don't think that's the best idea, Ezra. If I'm worried about keeping you safe, I won't be able to fight as well."

Surprisingly, Ezra starts talking in Arabic, effectively cutting everyone else out of the conversation. "'inna dhahib."

I'm going.

"We shouldn't be discussing this here," I answer in Arabic.

"Please, stop treating me like I'm incapable of defending

myself. Like I'm some sort of fragile thing that will break. It is beyond condescending."

Shit. This is dangerous territory. If I say what I really want to say—that *he is* fragile, that *he will* break when a Spiradael Citadel tries to slice his guts out with a hair braid—I'll sound like an emasculating asshole. However, if I stroke Ezra's ego, he might actually think he has half a chance against these guys. He doesn't. "I just don't think it's a good idea," I say reluctantly.

"There are soldiers all over the world, an infinite number of worlds, that actually fight without superpowers," Ezra counters. And now, he's just kind of pissing me off. Clearly after last night he feels like he has something to prove, to me, to Levi, to himself, but the Spiradael Earth is not the place to do it.

"Well, let's be clear about something," I say, putting a single fist on my hip. "Every truly good soldier knows where his strengths are, and where he or she can be most useful to the team. And a big part of that is that they've *trained* to be soldiers. To grow those strengths. Your strengths are not on the battlefield. I'm sorry, but that's just the way it is. You are, however, invaluable, irreplaceable even, when it comes to computing."

"I don't care where my strengths are," Ezra says.

At this, Iathan interjects, "I dislike this foreign banter *intensely*. Speak English," he commands, which saves me from lashing out at Ezra for being a petulant child.

Ezra ignores him, though, and continues in Arabic. "I am not going to be left behind again. No way. What if you die on this mission? Am I supposed to trust that these Roones will get me back home? Do *you* trust them absolutely? Because think about it: I could very well spend the rest of my life here if you don't."

"Have they tried to keep you here against your will? Have

320 / AMY S. FOSTER

they ever told you that you couldn't leave?" Ezra looks at Iathan and then back at me.

"No."

"You've already jumped far more times than Levi and me.
On one hand you're totally capable of defending yourself, but
on the other, what? You're afraid of the Multiverse now? Of
being able to get home? Which is it?" I lean in and look at
him directly, intently, last night's argument still tender like a
newly stitched wound. "Because you can't have it *both* ways,
Ezra."

"I'm going," he says in English.

"You're actually not. And right now you're doing more harm
than good. This is not personal. I'm sorry if you feel my command decision is pussy-whipping your masculine sensibilities,
but the fact that we're still talking about this is proof enough
that you don't belong on a combat mission. So, no." Ezra's eyes
narrow at me, but he's reading the room. He knows that there
is no possible argument he could offer that would actually
make any kind of sense.

Whenever Levi shit-talks Ezra he calls him the Golden Boy
or the Wonder Kid. I'm beginning to understand that that isn't
how Levi sees Ezra, but rather how Ezra sees himself. He's gorgeous, he's a music and math prodigy, he had already finished
his undergraduate degree at MIT, and he's only eighteen. He
is, in a word, amazing. But I'm beginning to see that Ezra, for
all his brilliance—or *because* of his brilliance—isn't used to
the word *no*.

He's . . . *spoiled*.

"Whatever," Ezra says, shaking his head. I expect him to
leave at that point, but he doesn't. He just stands there, angrily,
in a sulk.

Like so many other things, I don't have time to worry about that right now.

"Okay," Levi says with determination. Like me, he's not interested in this drama. Right now, he is all mission. "Let's get squared away. Can we all agree to adjust our Rift entry location exactly to here," Levi says, pointing to an outcropping of trees. "Once we've arrived we can send out the drones and get a full picture of how to proceed on the ground."

"You have drones?" Iathan asks with a lick of suspicion in his tone. "And you've managed to calibrate your QOINS to Rift in with that kind of precision?"

"We do have stealth drones," I answer, "and yes we can Rift in to an exact location, since you have the exact coordinates to that Earth in your system along with these topographical maps." There is an uncomfortable silence as the Karekins look at one another warily and then back at me. "It's tech we picked up on our travels."

For the first time I see Iathan's congenial mask slip. He knows we have something valuable, and like a child with restricted access to a playground, he doesn't like it. His blue eyes dart back and forth and his lips purse as he grips the sides of the console tight enough for his knuckles to whiten. Iathan is a seasoned politician, and likely much older than he looks, certainly over a century. He is also a man who understands the value of patience. The mask slides back on and he gives me the slickest of smiles.

"I'd very much like to know more about them."

"And I think we need to focus on the mission. We can talk when we return."

"Very well, I look forward to having a discussion of that nature *as soon* as you get back," Iathan emphasizes. There's no mistaking that as a threat. Now I need a plan for this as well. How much to share, how much to hold back. I look briefly at Levi—he needs to be part of the discussion. Maybe we'll get a chance to speak when we're on the Spiradael Earth.

"I have a few things that need attending to," Iathan says suddenly. "You can firm up your entry and exit strategies. Just make sure to brief Vlock and his team. I'll meet you back here shortly to see you off." Iathan walks away. I don't love that all my gear is back in my bedroom, but I also have a sliver of pity for anyone who would dare attempt to use it. The Roones aren't human and I get the sense that Doe could do some serious damage to protect the tech.

Ezra leaves as well, without a word. I watch his back disappear down the cement archway. I feel us cracking apart. Last night feels like ash in my mouth. I can't say he's wrong, about any of it. I see all his points and they are valid.

They're just not valid enough.

Levi walks over and stands close, but we are hardly alone. There are over a dozen Roones and Karekins still present, including Vlock and the strike force. I assume Levi's going to ask about sharing the SenMach tech. Instead, he asks, *"Ça va?"* I just nod my head.

"There's trouble between you and Ezra," he states, remaining in French so we're not overheard. But it's not really a question. He knows.

I slide my tongue over my teeth. "It's complicated. Relationships are complicated. But they are also not a priority. Not today."

Levi reaches over and gently squeezes the top of my arm. *"Je suis desolé."* I give him a grateful smile because I think he means it. I think he actually is sorry that I'm upset.

"Let's just nail this, okay?" I say. "This has to be precise. We all have to work together and anticipate every possible contingency so that there are backups for our backups."

"Roger that."

About an hour later, Levi and I have collected our things from our rooms, and are waiting in the war room for everyone who will be going with us and those who want to wish us good luck. Ezra comes in first, wearing a bulky sweater and sweats. He looks rough. I know he's mad and hurt. I hate having to leave with things the way they are between us. He keeps his distance from me, with his back hunched and his eyes looking at everyone and everything going on except for me. I walk up to him and he takes a small step back.

"Just go," he tells me sadly. "Don't make a big deal out of it or else I'm gonna feel like you're not coming back."

"Ezra," I sigh, moving once again toward him as he takes another giant step backward. It's clear he doesn't want any affection from me and I'm sure as hell not going to embarrass myself any further by demanding it. I walk away from him, toward the bigger group.

Iathan finally walks in, his silent lackeys moving like ghosts behind him. Vlock and his soldiers are ready, too. I nod respectfully in their direction and he gives me a similar nod in return.

"So," Iathan says loudly, "this is a momentous occasion indeed. The first joint mission between the human Citadels and Karekins. It's quite an achievement."

Are we all about to get a slow-clap pep talk? I don't have the patience for that kind of thing on a good day, and this is *not* a good day. More important than my personal shit, though, today is all about the mission. Nothing else. Before Iathan can continue I say, "Roger that," in a tone that makes it clear that a speech right now would not be welcome.

Iathan reads the look on my face and smiles deferentially. "I assume you are going to be the ones to call up the Rift with your new mysterious technology," he wonders out loud, and I am grateful that we can just get on with it.

"Affirmative," I say as I tighten the straps of my much lighter pack. Just taking the essentials with us today. "We're ready. Everybody squared away?" I ask in English and Roonish, ignoring Iathan's pointed comment. The others voice their assent. "Great, we'll see you soon," I say, specifically in Ezra's direction. He gives me the tightest of nods. I tighten the pack on my shoulders and make eye contact with Levi. He's ready. "Rift to Spiradael Earth with Citadels. Use the exact coordinates Levi has pinpointed on the satellite map," I say, though purposefully not into my cuff. I don't want Iathan to make that connection, not yet. Still, Iathan gives me an incredulous, yet speculative, look.

There's no mistaking now that I can hear the Rift before it opens. It sounds like a sustained piano chord played underwater. I unconsciously hum along, and I can feel Levi's eyes on me. I shrug. The Rift opens, a shining emerald doorway, sized exactly proportionate to the space we are in. As we planned, the Karekins walk in first and Levi and I take up the rear. I try not to think too hard about what's on the other side. I let my own personal drama fall away like a woolen cardigan on a blistering-hot day. I cannot let what happened last night distract me from what's coming next. I push my shoulders back and walk though. And then I hear something else, a grunt, maybe a whoosh, someone saying or screaming something. I look behind me in the green expanse and there, nose-diving like a pro, is Ezra.

If the Spiradaels don't kill him, I just might.

CHAPTER 24

I see the exit coming and adjust my body, as we all do vertically. Our misfit team walks out the other side of the Rift easily, as if we were walking from one room to another. The moment my feet touch the ground I whip around to Ezra.

"Now, Ryn," he starts, talking fast, his hands up, palms out. "I know you're pissed, but I just couldn't stay back there. I'm part of this team. I can be useful and you need to see that."

I want to punch him so bad my fists are practically aching. Instead I just say, "You're a fucking moron."

"Hey, I am a lot of things, but I am not stupid. You're going to see that. You're going to see that not every problem can be solved at the end of a gun."

I dig my nails into my palm. I push them in so deep I puncture the skin. "I know that. We all know that," I swing my arm around, gesturing to the rest of the crew. "I get that you have some weird need to prove something to me. But I would never just walk into your computer lab and start pressing buttons. I respect you too much to try to act like I belong there as much as you do. As if being smart earned me that right. But here you are thinking just that. This is my house, Ezra, and I told you to stay outside."

"Well, we'll have to agree to disagree on that one," he says dismissively as he throws off his sweater and pants, revealing a Karekin uniform complete with two guns strapped to his thighs. "And I'm here, so get over it."

"I thought you said not every problem can be solved at the end of a gun," I tell him sarcastically as I look at his weapons.

"These are more like phasers, really, than guns—they shoot laser beams. Well, you know, they issued you the same ones, didn't they?" Ezra pushes a button on his forearm and I hear a little hiss and then watch as the hard shell on the back of his uniform swings around almost to the front. It's like a back-pack of sorts, or, I guess *storage compartment* would be more accurate. Ezra stuffs his clothes inside. "I really am sorry," he says to me genuinely as the molded backpack swings around and attaches to his back again. "I'm not trying to be a dick or disrespectful, but I had to do what I felt was right, what I felt was best for me. I am not trying to prove anything to you. This is my fight, just as much as it is yours."

I could almost laugh. Only someone who's never actually been in a fight for his life would say something so incredibly dumb. I've got half a mind to drug the guy and tie him up so he can't get in my way, but that might be even more of a disaster.

"You have no idea what you've done. The danger you've put us in." A tiny hint of a smile begins to form on his lips, but as he looks at the rest of the team, the smile disappears. One of these things is not like the others: His fantasy, his macho musings, where he imagines himself as some kind of hero, are catching up to the reality of the situation. He thinks he's Han Solo. He's only just getting, at this very moment, that Han Solo, while iconically cool, was also lightsabered. *To death.*

I glance over at Levi. His face betrays nothing. I'm sure he's just as pissed as I am, but he can be detached. He probably doesn't care one way or the other if Ezra gets himself killed. The Karekins don't speak English, but they understand well enough that Ezra is not supposed to be here.

"Just try to keep up. Don't do anything unless I tell you to, and most importantly, if it comes down to a fight, you run. One of us will track you down later. And if we don't, it means we're dead and if we're dead, that means you'll be dead soon, too. Got it?"

"Yeah, okay," Ezra says softly. I don't know what he expects. Does he think I'm the same girl who had her legs wrapped around him a few hours ago? That girl isn't here. There is no girl here. There is only a soldier, a soldier who doesn't like surprises or planning for a potentially lethal contingency that would be totally unnecessary if Ezra had just listened to me in the first place.

"Great. Let's move out." Levi and I take point. The outcropping of trees that we saw in the overhead images are exactly where we thought they would be. Levi and I signal for the rest of the team to walk into them and take cover. We open our packs and release our drones. I pull out my laptop and everyone eyes the slender, silver machine in the air with wonder. I get it. I mean, it's mine, but I have no clue as to how the thing actually flies, either.

It doesn't take long for images to start popping up on the screen. It's clear right away that Iathan's intel was correct. The

328 / AMY S. FOSTER

Spiradaels do things much differently than we do back home. The Rift is the same constant tower of green, but the other Citadels are not hiding. They are standing at attention in front of it. The column is ten deep and twenty across. Two hundred men. That's not a number we can fight and beat.

The drone continues to gather intel, finding reserves farther back—hundreds of them.

Shit.

I watch as their Rift opens on the monitor. Even from this distance I can feel the same familiar tug and hear the sound—the sonic boom and harmonic resonance is just a whisper of a song, but still it's there. The black at the center of the Rift deepens and widens until the entire thing is one inky patch of darkness in the middle of the trees that are as bony and thin as the Spiradaels themselves.

Eight people come tumbling out. Eight normal humans who look like they were on their way to work. One is a young woman, not a child but a girl about my brother's age. Without a moment's hesitation, without an attempt to take them away, much less any kind of warning, the first column of Spiradaels pick up their rifles, aim, and open fire. The eight Immigrants are pummeled with live rounds. The entire process takes ten seconds. They fall in a bloody heap to the dusty ground below.

I bring my hands to my face in horror.

"Oh my God," I whisper to no one in particular. We are all just standing there, huddled around the laptop in disbelief. We're supposed to align ourselves with these people? These murderers? I can't even begin to imagine it. "This may be a lost cause. Our best recourse might be to return to the Roone Earth, get some big-ass bombs, and burn this place to the ground," I say out loud.

"If this is some kind of vote, then Ryn has mine on this one," Ezra chimes in.

The Karekins remain silent, though Vlock looks visibly distressed. Levi is crouched down. He has one muscled forearm dug into the earth and the other is resting on his knee, the cuff close to his mouth. "Just wait," he tells us. I shake my head but continue to watch. The Spiradaels who shot the innocent Immigrants step out of formation. They pick the dead up by the arms and legs, as if they are nothing but roadkill, and drag the bodies about a hundred feet to a floating platform, some kind of hover-board cart. My nose twitches. These assholes get cool flying shit? How is that in any way fair? My shock is quickly turning to white-hot anger. It's getting difficult to sit still.

"Drone 1, follow the Spiradael with the bodies. Drone 2, stay above the Rift," Levi commands his cuff. We watch as the computer split-screens the action. The Spiradael column takes a step forward so that the second row is now the first row. In short order, Citadels from the reserves join the troops at the back.

Meanwhile, we watch the twenty who walked away. They are escorting the floating morgue table through the forest. I notice that there are no birds here, no other kind of wildlife at all. Nature knows when to stay away. They are taking a path that winds around to the west of the Rift, back toward their base. I know what Levi is doing. He's seeing if the killers are passing by or through the reserves. They aren't. The Spiradaels are on a well-worn path, more of a road. The backup Citadels are hiding, cloistered among the brush and rocky outcrops well away from the ones on their way back to base. Some are in foxholes, but there are no nests. The freaky Tim Burton–like trees don't look like they could support the weight of one. It takes the Spiradaels about five minutes at their quick clip to make it back to their headquarters.

The drone zooms out. Their base of operations is a series of tall, thin, ivory buildings. As slender as matchsticks cut to varying lengths, the tops of each one end in a surprising flourish, like the swirl of an ice-cream cone. It's such a big compound, and my guess is that there is no basement or bunker. Strategically, it's a stupid choice. A military installation should be intimidating, not impressive. This tells me something, too. The Spiradaels are arrogant. One side of my mouth curls into the tiniest of smiles. That's the first good news I've managed to glean since we got here. When an opponent's ego comes first, they're much weaker.

"It's not a lot of time, but we could take the next unit that leaves the Rift," Levi tells us. It's not really a suggestion. I go to translate to Vlock, but Levi interrupts me and speaks in Roonish himself. I knew it. *He did* learn the language last night. Vlock says that he was about to suggest the same thing, and I find I'm relieved. I wasn't sure that we would be able to get past our history with the Karekins, but this is working out fine. We'll need this kind of cohesion if we want the next part of this mission to succeed.

"There are twenty of them and eight of us," Ezra says slowly.

"Yeah," Levi responds as he stands up and stretches out his neck. "And if your intel is correct, then we'll be fine. Shit. If it came right down to it, Ryn and I could probably take out those twenty on our own." He shrugs. "Maybe."

"So we just wait for them to kill more people? That's your great plan? We just stand by and let them execute whatever comes out of the Rift next and count ourselves lucky that we have an opening?" Ezra is getting more agitated as he speaks. He begins to pace.

Ezra is so ignorant when it comes to combat theater that he doesn't understand there can be only *one* leader. On this mission, that leader is me and I've already warned him. He's distracting me and he truly doesn't get how dangerous that is. "Ezra, I told you to keep your mouth shut. And stop moving around."

"But—" he starts to speak.

"But nothing. You see, we have to fight *some* of them so we don't have to fight *all* of them. Thousands of them."

"I know you think I'm an idiot about battle strategy, but I'm not completely clueless," Ezra says. "The strike force was your idea. We could have brought hundreds of troops with us. Karekin troops. We could have even Rifted to Battle Ground and grabbed a bunch of our own Citadels. We could have taken out all these skinny fucks today. We could have ended this. So whoever they murder next, that blood is on your hands."

I hold my ground even though Ezra's words sting. Levi grits his teeth, his jaw clamps. Ezra might not be aware of how badly he's just insulted me, but Levi is, and his body language is making it quite clear he doesn't like it.

"That statement right there just proved how clueless you are," I hiss at him. "Go to Battle Ground? Really? Just let the altered Roones know how much we know? I understand what we saw from the drones was downright disgusting, but *welcome*, Ezra, this is war. Fun, right? Glad you came? Capturing a Spiradael Citadel might save countless lives down the road, but we might have to kill to do it, so that's the devil's bargain. There's no winning today. It's not like we're high-fiving each other and whipping our dicks out. All of this would be happening whether we were here or not, so seriously, shut. The. Fuck. Up."

"I love how you just go straight for 'the ends justify the

means' routine. Do you even hear yourself sometimes? You get that you don't really sound much different from Edo, right?"

I open my mouth to protest, but before I can manage a single word, Levi leaps toward Ezra. In a microsecond he takes one of Ezra's guns from the holster, grabs the front of his uniform, putting his forearm across his neck, and shoves the gun squarely under Ezra's chin.

"Now you listen to me, you whiny douche," Levi growls, and a part of me wants to intervene, but another, more sensible part of me hangs back. I'm tired of justifying myself and my actions. For whatever reason I can't fathom, Ezra just won't listen to me. I've tried reason. I've used my super-hard-core bitch voice (which I *really* dislike using), too. If we're going to get out of here alive, then clearly, Ezra needs to be scared into submission.

And Levi's got to be the one to do it.

"You think we're on campus, college boy? You think this is part of your ethics seminar where you can debate and philosophize and ponder the use of force? You're in the shit, man. One wrong move and you're dead. I'd honestly kill you myself, and trust me, there's a case for it, if it wasn't for Ryn."

Vlock does not look happy. He takes one giant step toward both of them.

Levi ignores Vlock's movements, though, and calmly continues, his voice intimidatingly throaty. "Look how fast I got the drop on you. You can't fight. You're nothing but a liability and now you want to make everything ten times harder by guilt-tripping Ryn? Look around you. Look at these fucking trees and the color of the dirt on this Earth. Death lives here, man, and it's on the prowl. If you don't want it to come for you, then do as our commanding officer says and shut your damn mouth before I shut it for you. Permanently." With that,

Levi gives him a good shove, though to Ezra's credit, he stays on his feet. I hate that it's come to this, but I also hate that Ezra is basically calling me a coldhearted murdering bitch. I'm kinda Team Levi on this one.

"Both of you humans," Vlock says with icy authority. Ezra of course won't be able to understand him, but his tone is clear enough. "I was under the impression you were soldiers. This is a mission. Whatever is happening between you all is not part of the mission. Ryn, get your men under control. Immediately."

Of course Vlock is absolutely right and I am momentarily ashamed that as the leader here, a *Karekin* needed to intervene. I need to do better. Right now.

"Please tell me that I don't have to translate that," I say in Ezra's direction. "We need to put everything else away and focus. No more." I stare down both of them. Ezra doesn't know any better, but Levi and I certainly do. As if reading my mind, Levi gives me a curt nod.

"Fine," Ezra says sharply. But instead of backing off, he steps up and snatches his gun back from Levi. There isn't any point in checking his bravado. He's clueless. "I'll leave the soldiering to you, but don't for one minute," Ezra says as he points a finger in Levi's face, "tell me that I don't deserve to have an opinion about watching a bunch of innocent people being gunned down. I wouldn't be able to live with myself if I didn't at least try to prevent that."

"Fine. Duly noted. You object for an ethical reason, but that is all you can do—*object*. So stay out of our way," I warn, because pretending that he isn't even here is probably the best chance we have of getting through this. I walk back over to the open laptop and sit on the ground in front of it. Levi and Ezra sit on either side of me and the Karekins remain standing.

"Doe. Identify the next species that Rifts through as soon as you can," I tell the cuff.

"Why are talking to your bracelet? Wait," Ezra says as he looks at Levi's wrist, "why do you guys have *matching* bracelets?"

"And why did you just call our operating system Doe?" Levi asks. "I mean, I get it. I can't say I haven't asked 'What would Tim Riggins do' more than a few times myself, but is this taking it too far maybe?"

I don't even bother to answer. Either one of them.

Boys.

I drag my thoughts back to the mission. I focus on where we are and what we've just seen and combine it with the intel we have. When I think about that slaughter, there's no room in my mind for anything else. There is no logic to this. The altered Roones control the Rifts. This is the second-oldest Citadel species. No one coming through here is doing so *randomly*. There's only one reason to pull innocent people through only to have them gunned down in an instant.

Control.

These Citadels kill without question or hesitation. I can't imagine a lie big enough to justify that. So now, I have to assume, there is no lie. There are only orders. Kill everyone. The altered Roones have scared, drugged, and brainwashed the Spiradaels out of any sense of conscience. I don't know if we can undo that. And even if we could, would there be any semblance of reason left?

And the most terrifying part?

They could do this *to us*.

I'm so glad I'm recording this on our SenMach computer. The troops back home need to see this. They need to see these Citadels, wearing the same patch as we are, just open fire on innocent civilians. Maybe that will stop a civil war. Vlock and his men could help on that front, too. *This* is the mission. We cannot end up like these soldiers.

I run strategies for disseminating this information to all the other Citadels, on all the other Earths. There are so many variables, I still can't see through to a real solution. We need time. We need allies, but more than that, if we want to win, we have to know *why*. What could the altered Roones want so badly that they would make the Spiradaels do this? It can't just be to have their own Earth back. That kind of thinking is too small considering the scope of this. There has to be more. What could be motivating this kind of absolute disregard for the sanctity of life? Power? Wealth? Land? Religion? I shake my head at those concepts—what motivates humans doesn't necessarily motivate the altered Roones. And then it hits me: It's science with them. It's genetics and playing God. But how does *that* fit? With this? I mull it all over in my head until the Rift opens again. This time, it's only five Immigrants. I stare at the screen and squint my eyes.

"Wait . . ."

Doe's voice comes through softly. "Immigrant species, Roonish."

"He followed you here?" Levi says with clear annoyance, not letting it go. I sigh loudly enough to let him know that I'm not about to answer such a stupid question. The Roones huddle together, four males and one female. They are asking the Spiradaels what is going on, afraid and near hysteria. The Spiradael Citadels lower their rifles.

"What are they doing? They aren't going to shoot them?" Ezra asks in confusion.

"They're swapping out their ammo," Levi answers as he stares harder at the laptop screen.

"Why?" Ezra wisely touches the laptop as if it were an iPad and enlarges the image so that we can see what they are doing in detail. Levi swats his hand away and takes the picture wide again.

"I'm guessing it's tranqs," I say. "I did wonder about the numbers. So many Karekins coming through all the Rifts on our Earth, but none of them ever surviving. It's like they have an endless supply. They don't, obviously—they just make more. I can't believe I didn't put it all together before."

"Which parts?" Ezra asks. This time he's not being a dick. He's just genuinely curious.

"I guess I thought that somehow, the Roonish Earth was unique in an infinite number of Earths, but statistically that's impossible. There are other Roone Earths, of course there are. There have to be. There are just no other *altered* Roones. Although technically, since it is the Multiverse, there could be."

Levi follows my logic. "And . . . no other Roones besides the altered ones have ever, not once, Rifted to our Earth."

"Not one," I say as we all watch the Spiradaels bring up their rifles. The Roones begin to scream. "We know now that the Rifts on our Earth don't open at random. That's why we've never seen a normal Roone Rift to our Earth." As I say these words aloud I let them sink in.

How many people have I hurt? Have I killed because of the Rifts? It all could have been prevented. What am I even thinking? *I* could have been prevented. There was never any global threat to our Earth. Except of course, from the altered Roones. I sigh deeply. I have to lock those thoughts away. I can't feel this. I can't think about this. I clear my throat.

"They're going to tranq the men and kill the woman," I say grimly. Sure enough, the four men are hit with darts from the front line. The line separates. Ten take two steps to the left, ten take two steps to the right. A lone gunman from the second row aims and fires a bullet into the female's head. The screaming stops and everything is silent again.

"How did you know that was going to happen?" Ezra asks.

"Because I've never seen a female Karekin. Have you?"

CHAPTER 25

We run, hard and fast, through the trees that reach out like finger bones, our uniforms protecting our skin from the needles on their branches—faded green porcupine quills that whisper "hush" when we pass them. We have little time, so we push it, the pads of our feet barely touching the uneven ground beneath us. Ezra cannot keep up, which is definitely for the best. He'll join us eventually, hopefully when the fighting is over.

We explode out of the trees onto the path directly in front of the Spiradael Citadels. We heard them, Levi and I. They had long, light strides, but still we heard them, over our own breaths and from a distance. But they did not hear us. The Roones haven't given them that particular gift. I wonder if, when they find out the truth about who the alternate Roones really are, if that will mean anything.

Expecting an immediate show of force, I drop my pack

swiftly on the ground the moment I see the unit, but they don't attack. They look at us curiously, probably wondering how we got through the Rift without being detected. We've caught them by surprise and so I take the opening they've given us to try to reason with them. They need to hear what I have to say.

"We're all Citadels! Look at my patch!" I say in Spiradael, speaking calmly with my hands stretched out, hoping the similarities in our patches will give them even the briefest pause as some kind of proof. "The Roones have been lying to you. We've come to tell you the truth—"

With lightning-quick speed, before we can even reach for our own guns, the five Spiradaels in the front of the group separate and whip out their long black braids. Most of the Karekins manage to dodge the razor hair in time, but one of them does not. The hair whips around his throat, and the Spiradael gives a quick tug. The Karekin's thick neck is broken and then sliced so that his head, mostly decapitated, falls to his shoulder.

So much for diplomacy.

I take out both of my new Roonish guns and manage to shoot three Spiradaels in the skull before I have to roll to dodge a spray of bullets. I try to keep track of the others. Levi shoots four, and the Karekins take out seven more. That means there are only six left. I hear Ezra crash through behind us. He runs to the large floating platform and crouches, with his gun aimed and ready to fire. I'm sure with us moving so fast he's afraid he'll shoot one of us. He's going to see, right now, with sickening accuracy, just how out of his league he is here.

I deliberately get close enough to one of the Spiradaels so that we can actually fight. I want to knock him out and take him with us, yes, but I also want to see what these Citadels can do. The hair is a thing, of course, but this isn't *Avatar*—it doesn't move on its own—so unless I'm planning on standing there so he can choke me with it, it won't do much good in close combat.

I am right up next to him now. His skin is the color of the pages in an old book, faded, not yellow, more of an ecru. He is at least two feet taller than me. Every joint on his skinny frame looks nobbled, the way arthritics' hands and elbows sometimes do, but I don't think this pains him. The larger joints may give him a greater range of motion and therefore a farther reach. He regards me with jet-black eyes absent of pupils.

Creepy.

I wait for him to throw the first punch. I want him to be on the offensive so I can study his fighting style. His left fist reaches out with alarming speed as he attempts a right hook. Shit he's fast. Not faster than me, though. I continue to move out of his way, my forearms blocking whatever punches he's landing when I'm not ducking and swaying beneath his arms, which are almost too fast for my eyes to track. No feet. No legs. He doesn't kick.

But I do.

He moves in to take another swing at me, but I catch his hand, crushing his slender wrist as I do. I expect the bone to break, but it doesn't. As fragile as these Spiradaels seem, their bodies are actually much denser than they appear. I use all my strength and clamp down harder until I hear a snap and then I kick out, my foot connecting to his stomach as he goes hurtling through the air. He lands on his back but is up again faster than I can get to him. I judge the distance between us and take off, using the power in my thighs to sprint, and then I leap, wrapping my legs around his neck and squeezing his throat with deadly intensity as I pull him down.

His black eyes widen in surprise. I'm sure he's fought a few baddies from the Rift, but nothing like me and he knows it. He tries to get my thighs away from his neck with his hands, but I am much stronger than him. I ease the tension ever so slightly so I won't kill him, but even then he can't shake me. I know nothing of Spiradael physiology, but I think I've probably bruised his windpipe to a significant degree. I untangle my legs but keep my arms on him, using all my weight to pin him, but there isn't much he can do. He still can't get any air. He's not even trying to get me off of him. I sit up. I'm straddling his chest now. I can feel his bony rib cage through my uniform.

"Listen to me," I say loudly in his own language. "*I am a Citadel*. But they did more to me. They enhanced more of my genes. They are lying to you. Do you understand me? They're giving you drugs to brainwash you!" His pale face is turning purple. I think I may have injured him more badly than I intended, and his eyes, deep and black, are impossible to read. I don't know if I'm getting through to him at all.

I feel a sharp pain at my neck. I can't see it, but I know what this is—hair. I quickly reach down to my calf, pulling out my long bowie knife, and start hacking away at the braid, even though it's tearing the flesh of my palms to shreds. It takes a few breathless seconds, but eventually I cut myself loose. I keep my hands on the braid and pull, using all my strength to quickly yank the black hair forward, and the Spiradael it's attached to comes flying over.

I jump out of the way so that I can guide his tall slender body as it lands firmly facedown on top of the other Spiradael. I still have the braid in my hand and I use it to hog-tie him together. The bind won't last but it's good enough for now.

"I have two!" I scream. "Kill the rest, let's go!" I hear gunshots, but I keep my focus on the squirming Spiradael that I have a hold of, one elbow on his neck and my other hand locking his legs in place. "Ezra! Grab the packs," I shout, and then watch as he dodges quickly out from the floating table to retrieve both my and Levi's things, strapping one pack on his front and the other on his back.

I'm about to tell the cuff to open a Rift to the Roone Earth, when Vlock is shot right between the eyes. His massive body falls to the ground with a thud. I stare for a moment, shocked that I can feel anything besides hatred for a Karekin, let alone regret.

"Uhhh . . . Ryn?" Ezra says in a voice that is quiet enough for me to know that he's too scared to yell. I look around and see Spiradaels everywhere, hundreds of them, running at breakneck speed from every direction. What happened? I didn't hear any of them call for backup. There must be cameras. But where? In the trees? Not even we surveil every inch of the roads leading to the base. It must have been their drones, which I didn't see or hear. I was thinking human technology. Stupid. They might not be as advanced or stealthy as SenMach tech, but obviously they're cloaked enough for us not to have noticed.

There are only two Karekins left and the three of us. Five against hundreds. There's no way we can fight. We'll have to open a Rift and hope we can fling ourselves through before they get to us. I use the handle of my knife to hit the Spiradael I have tied up hard enough to knock him unconscious, while I leave the other one, still gulping and wheezing, on the ground. We don't need two—even one might be a liability—but I am not leaving here without him. This can't have been for nothing.

I pick him up and heave him over my shoulders, but it's too late. A bullet hits me square in the chest, sending me staggering back, knocking the wind out of me. It didn't penetrate the suit, but shit, it hurts. More shots come at us and then the Spiradaels are only a few feet away. I try to use the Citadel I have on my shoulder as cover, but he's heavier than he looks and my chest is burning.

We aren't going to make it anywhere.

And then the barrage of bullets stops, or at least, they stop shooting us. I'm panting, trying to breathe through the pain and bruised ribs. The rapid fire continues, but the Spiradaels have stopped aiming at us. Bewildered, I look to the direction they are shooting. The sky. What? I stare up, craning my neck as I attempt to see over the Spiradael I have slung over my shoulder. There are dozens and dozens of them up there in some kind of formation coming right for us.

Angels.

No—*Faida*.

I don't see a single one fall to the ground, so miraculously— and yes, I get what that word means in this context—none of them have been shot. They shift their flying direction all at once, like a massive murmuration, and begin to land around us, the dry, cracked earth trembling beneath our feet as they do. They are beautiful. Stunning. *Breathtaking*. Their wings are massive, as wide as they are tall, in various shades of black, ivory, and gray. All of them are at least six feet tall with wavy copper or blond hair. Their eyes are piercing blue, but unlike Ezra's, which are more turquoise, theirs are the color of ice caps.

Two of them immediately surround me, their wings creating a feathered cage, which must be bulletproof somehow, though aerodynamically I don't see how that's possible. Then again, the Faida are *flying people*, so anything could be possible.

I hear a loud careening whistle, which is unmistakably coming from the Faida themselves. It's an alarm like a migraine letting me know they don't belong to this Earth. There's also a faint buzz, like an electrical kiss, coming from their wings. Instinctively, I reach my hand out and brush my fingers against them. The field around the pure white feathers ripples and glows in a neon grid before quickly disappearing. It makes sense. The wings are cool as hell but an obvious target, so the Roones gave them a shield. A bulletproof vest for their wings with no extra weight. Neat trick.

I look up, right into the eyes of the Faida in front of me. He's so gorgeous, he doesn't even look real. He looks like Charlie Hunnam but hotter, if that's even possible.

"Do you speak English?" I whisper. No answer.

"Do you speak Roonish?" I ask again. This time, I hear his pulse rate go up. That's triggered something. He looks down at me in all his insanely gorgeous glory and whispers in my ear. The first thing I think is, *Jesus, I am so grateful that I don't have the Blood Lust because this guy would be toast.* Then I think, *He knows Roonish. Is he working with them? Or against them?*

"If you can open a Rift, human girl child, you must do so, *right now*."

"You can't open one yourselves?" I ask incredulously. The fact that he can't open a Rift somehow is shocking. Also shocking? He called me a "girl child."

I kind of bristle at that.

"Obviously not, or I would not have asked," the Faida says. He seems to be bristling, too.

Well. *That's interesting.*

"Rift. Pandora," I say over the near-deafening gunfire. We

need to get out of here immediately, but I'm not taking these guys anywhere near the Roonish Earth.

I hear the sonic boom of a Rift opening instantly. I can also now hear that the discordant hum sounds different from the last one I heard coming here. Well that's certainly fun and new but hardly important right now.

The Faida behind me pulls the Spiradael off my shoulders.

"Don't do that!" I holler in Roonish. "I need him. I need to question him." The female Faida raises an eyebrow at the male who is still holding on to me. He nods, which I can only assume means that she will do as I've asked. While still clutching on to his limp body she crouches into position as if getting ready to launch. The Faida in front of me grabs hold of my waist with more urgency and pulls me close to him so that my face is buried in his chest. He's so quick and efficient that I'm not one hundred percent positive I could break free even if I wanted to. After all, the Spiradaels are everywhere, and right now, assuming the winged Citadels have snatched the rest of my team (I have to hope they would because it's looking like they need us just as much as we need them to get out of here), the Faida are our best chance at escape.

In seconds we are off the ground. I feel another bullet hit my leg, but for the most part my uniform and the Faida's wings protect me. I frantically whip my head back and forth, trying to see past the flurry of feathers, and I'm beyond relieved when I see that another Faida has Ezra and the packs. Also, slightly ahead of us and to the right, a male Faida has Levi.

Below us, the remaining Karekins lie motionless on the ground. The Faida did not protect them with their Tron wings and I feel another pang of regret. Maybe Ezra had been right. Maybe we should have come in with a full company. Doing so might have escalated things before we were ready, but at least

Vlock and his men might not have died, and maybe we could have actually made it back without now having to deal with this new unknown equation of the Faida.

We nose-dive in the air through the Rift. I no longer hear ambient birdsong. Instead, I can pick out the millions of individual notes as they play on the inside of my eardrum. The Faida does not let me go; if anything, he holds on tighter, and I uncomfortably wonder why.

It's not like I can escape. We are all going to the same place. Is he so sure I'll fight him the minute we emerge? Well I might, but he did just save my life, so I'd probably talk to him first. I guess he wouldn't know that, though.

I close my eyes. The music of the Rift runs through my entire body. The Faida smells annoyingly good, like mint and teak. Do angels lie? Yes, they do if they're Citadels. I wonder what story he's going to spin when we get through the Rift—if he cares to spin one at all. They have the numbers, but apparently not the technology. I don't know what they were doing on the Spiradael Earth, but clearly they were trapped there. Unless that, too, was a lie to see what we've acquired on our travels and possibly to observe me and my special singing genes near a Rift.

I think that maybe getting to the truth will be far more difficult than it was when I walked onto the Roone Earth and it was basically served up like a Christmas dinner. I haven't yet read the files that Doe hacked, so maybe Iathan, with his covetous looks and condescending manner, is not telling the truth at all. I suppose the real question is, how far am I willing to go to get it?

When we arrive at whatever Earth the computer has chosen for us, there will be fight or there will be a discussion. Am I willing to kill all these gorgeous beings to get to the answers I need?

Yes I am.

It might take a different approach. I might have to act dumb. I might have to play at being a "human girl child." Maybe the Faida, with his movie-star good looks, was just using that term as a show of dominance and he doesn't really see me as a girl at all. And now that things are so fucked up with Ezra, I'm not above flirting or even spy-banging one of these hotties if that's what it takes to get what I want, either. There isn't anything I wouldn't do and any length I wouldn't go to, because the game has changed. The altered Roones don't just have an army at their disposal, but *armies* of armies. I dipped my toe into the waters of diplomacy. I've taken up reason and logic instead of taking aim. It's felt good to feel like something other than a weapon, or at least a different kind of weapon. But all that has changed. Rules will be broken. Lies will be told. Alliances will hold only so long as they benefit *us*.

I see the white slit of the Rift's exit and feel its gravitational pull. The music will end soon. The Pandora Earth is seconds away. We may have a new partnership with the Faida, giving us the advantage we desperately need. Or, because we have not taken them to the Roonish Earth, or the Citadel base on our own human one, they may well try to kill us. This could be the end.

But if it is, I'm sure as hell not going down without a fight.

I see a glimpse of Ezra ahead of me aligning his body so he can walk out of the Rift. Levi is to my right. I cannot see his face. I can't signal to him to prepare. I can't tell him to get ready. Then again, I probably don't have to. The Faida angles our bodies upward. We are face-first instead of headfirst. This

Earth has me in its clutches. In this space of a few heartbeats my feet will be on solid ground.

I brace myself for the atmospheric change in pressure and my ears pop a little when we emerge. I don't know what to expect. Adrenaline is pluming like ink through my bloodstream. The Faida who held me lets go. I don't know where we are or when we are, but there is nothing here but a wide-open glade surrounded by tall evergreens. I put my hands on my pistols. I'm ready to draw. I'm also ready to listen, but none of that happens. The entire squadron of Faida, without warning or explanation, explode into the air like winged rockets.

What the fuck?

The unconscious Spiradael is splayed out at my feet, and when I look over to Ezra and Levi, they seem as baffled as I am. I crane my neck up to the sky and cup my hand over my eyes to watch them. They are flying in formation, like birds. It's hypnotic, this aerial dance. A murder of crows, a watch of nightingales, an affliction of starlings—what would a group of Faida be called? A clamor? A flush? A lamentation?

They break off in threes and fours, flying in each direction until some of them disappear.

"Are they coming back?" Ezra asks hesitantly.

"Yes," Levi says in an aggravated tone. "I think they're just trying to prove a point."

I watch them circle and dip and then regroup. "No. I mean, that might be part of it, but they're scouting. It's no different from sending out drones, really."

"Except that drones are expendable," Levi points out.

"Yeah, well, maybe that's how the altered Roones see the Faida." I keep my gaze skyward, at the cloudless blue expanse. They're coming back.

"What do you think is going on, Ryn?" Levi asks. "Why were they there? Why did you have to open a Rift?" He asks calmly, but there is a dangerous edge to his voice. Levi is a brilliant strategist, but he needs to know where he is and what's going on to make a plan.

Like I said, though: I'm great at improvising.

I watch them land so hard it seems as if the Earth might crack open and swallow them whole. They start to run at us. "I think speculating is a waste of energy," I respond as I keep my eyes fixed as they move toward us. I don't think Levi and I can take on this many. If Ezra were a Citadel we'd have a decent shot, but the fact that they can fly will make fighting them hand to hand extremely difficult. All it would take is for *one* of them isolate us. Just one to pull us into the air and take us so high that the landing would be lethal.

I reach for my gun, because shooting as many of them as possible before they can get near us is the smartest move here, but instead of attacking, they *surround* us in a circle and keep their backs to us.

"Human children!" the one who had me, the one who must be the leader, screams. "Prepare to defend yourselves."

"Well—yeah, okay. But I usually don't just shoot people in the back . . . maybe just turn around so this won't feel like a complete massacre."

The leader does whip his head back to give me a look that I can only interpret as complete annoyance. "You don't have to defend yourselves against *us*! Why would we kill you after we just saved you from the Spiradael filth?"

"Well, technically, we opened the Rift, so maybe we were saving you."

"Human girl child, there is something coming. Many, many

coming things. They are large and they are fast. They have teeth. We have clearly encroached on their territory and I believe they mean to defend it."

I look past them, into the dense crop of trees beyond. I don't see anything yet, but I do hear something, a rumbling, feet on dirt, branches snapping.

"Describe the threat," Levi demands.

"What is it? What's happening? Why are they surrounding us like this?" Ezra asks in a rush.

"Just get your weapons out and be ready to shoot. The Faida saw something, from the air." Ezra's eyes widen. I can hear his heartbeat, which was already going pretty strong, get even faster.

"They are very tall," another Faida answers. "At least eight feet, and round shaped. Their flesh is a milky pink. Their ears are pointed and their noses are flat and circular. They do not have weapons, but they have claws."

I scratch the top of my head. I wonder briefly if the Faida are fucking with us, but I don't think they have it in them. "Uhhh, like a pig?"

"I do not know this word, 'pig.' You have faced this enemy before?" the leader asks brusquely.

"On a sandwich with lettuce and tomato, yeah."

He turns around now, to face me. "You are telling me that the humans eat these creatures? They are for hunting?"

"Well, not every human eats pork. Sometimes it's a religious choice. I do like bacon, though," I say, but I let myself trail off, because now I can hear them. And they are loud. It's not just movement; they are actually squealing. The sound is unsettling, like backward screaming. "Well, okay, I think maybe on this Earth the pigs are a little different. They're domesticated back home. We raise them on farms. They're animals. They walk on all fours."

"Are we being attacked by giant pigs?" Ezra asks, eyeing the tree line.

"These pigs run on two cloven hooves," the leader says. "And I believe if there is to be consumption, it would be us that would be eaten."

"How many?" Levi asks.

"Hundreds."

"Look," I say to the leader. "I appreciate the circle of friendship here, but you don't need to protect us. Let's spread out. Half your squadron can take to the air and act as snipers. You do have ammo, right?"

"Some, not a lot."

Shit.

In one thunderous boom the pigs break through the trees. They do not look like Babe. They are not cute. They are huge, lumbering animals with tusks that curl over very sharp teeth. I don't know that much about pigs except that they taste good, and that in the movies, if you want to get rid of a body, you can throw it in a sty and they will eat the whole thing. Bones and all.

Shit.

I probably should not have made the sandwich joke.

The Faida break formation and some do indeed begin to soar. I feel better knowing they can shoot these things from the air. But the scout was right—there are hundreds. I don't think we even have enough bullets to kill them all. This is not going to be fun. Or it could be very fun depending on how they fight.

"Human girl child," the leader announces stoically, "I have heard that the Citadels on your Earth are the Roones' greatest achievement. I hope that was not an exaggeration. We will defend you and you will defend us. We will fight together and let this battle cement our alliance. And after we have tasted victory, there will be much to discuss. Are you ready?"

The pigs are running full-out now, the ground shaking at their approach. The truth is, I trust the Faida about as much as I trust the pink monsters (who have ruined *Charlotte's Web* forever now, thanks) that want to rip us apart. The squealing is overwhelming, a dissonant symphony of wind instruments being blown into by middle-schoolers. But I am getting better now at turning down the sounds that undo me. I will fight these things, and after, I'll get to the question of the Faida. The altered Roones have broken us all in one way or another. I'll have to see where the Faida have cracked and how deep those cuts run before I can ever trust them.

The familiar wave of adrenaline begins to crest in my bloodstream. It builds with towering ferocity until it breaks, washing over every pulsing muscle and joint. I *want* this. I'm aching for this. An enemy who doesn't need anything from me besides my death. A battle without an agenda. ARC, the Roones, the Faida, Ezra, Levi—all of it, all of *them* and their noise and their half-truths and manipulations—can just go away. I don't need to be anyone here other than a soldier. Screw politics. Diplomacy doesn't make my skin tingle. It doesn't make me feel this alive. The future can wait. Hell, I don't know if I'll ever win that war. But this one?

This is a battle I can win.

Shots begin to ring out and I draw my pistols. I'm ready. I was, after all, made for this very thing.

"Let's do this." I take aim. I pull the trigger.

I fight.

ACKNOWLEDGMENTS

Writing *The Rift Uprising* was a fairly solitary affair. I had an idea and I got to work. This book, however, was a totally different experience. There was no wondering if this book would ever get published or who might read it. I knew where *The Rift Frequency* was headed and because of that, I needed to rely on many people who have become integral to the process of delivering a trilogy.

First off, there is my agent and partner in crime, Yfat Reiss Gendell. Thank you for being an amazing agent, but also for being a true friend. You always said you could get me here. You must be some kind of fortune-teller because it took years! And it didn't seem like it was ever going to happen, but you stuck by me, and I am so grateful. Jessica Felleman, your right-hand lady, has become my right-hand lady, too! Jessica, thank you for all your patience through my Chicken Little moments! You're the best. And, Richie Kern—thank you for bringing Hollywood to the table. Also at Foundry I'd like to give a shout-out to Kirsten Neuhaus and Heidi Gall in the foreign rights department. The contract peeps—Deirdre Smerillo, Melissa Moorehead, and Hayley Burdett—and the money guys: Sara DeNobrega, Alex Rice, and Colette Grecco.

At HarperCollins I really need to thank my incredible editor, David Pomerico, who took a huge chance on Ryn and her world. You're the only other person who knows it as well as I do. You made this book better. Thank you. I would also like to thank Priyanka Krishnan, Jessie Edwards, Shawn Nicholls, Angela Craft, Liate Stehlik, and Jeanne Reina for all their hard work in getting the Rift out there to the people.

Elena Stokes and Brianna Robinson at Wunderkind PR, you genius gals, you are fabulous at your jobs and I know we have a lot of work to do still. I'm looking forward to it all. Marni Wadner, Kelly Ann Collins, and Mary Thayer at Sneak Attack Media, because of you all, I'm verified on social media, which turned me into an actual cool mom! But more than that, you opened up a whole new world for me and it's been a game changer. Thanks so much. I'd also like to give a shout-out to Section 101 for the kick-ass website.

On a personal note I would like to thank my mom and my dad and my sisters. I love you all. I would also like to thank my friends in Portland and Nashville. I know I'm a bit of a hermit, but you all keep me connected to the world—which I *really* need. In particular I'd like to thank Lisa Rockower—the best friend and beta reader a girl could ask for. Claire Coffee, who narrated *The Rift Uprising* (thirty hours reading a book out loud—that's real friendship); Melissa Sher, an excellent friend and PDX PR lady; and Samantha Brickman, who has been an absolute rock and rock star. Sammy, you know what you've done—thank you. I'd also like to give a shout-out once again to Elaine Lui, who hooked me up in Canada and who is pretty much the best advice giver. Ever. Sam Maggs, you brilliant lil munchkin—we got plans.

On the musical side I want to thank Stephanie Cox, who is an awesome all-around mama bear. Your faith in me keeps me going. Jesse Willoughby, Chris Lakey, Derek Anderson, and everyone at Kobalt, who helped me create a sound track and gave me a record deal, really, so that I could put out songs that I wrote for this series. On that note (ha!) Micah Wilshire, you musical monster. I love every minute I'm in the studio with you. QOINS forever.

I would also like to thank Dr. Daniel Barton for such steadfast navigation, Lt. Col. Matt Fandre of the 101st for the military technical advice, and for being *such* a cool guy. I would also like to thank Kim Newport Mimram of Pink Tartan for the support (and the amazing clothes) and Heather Reisman for the sage council.

Finally, I would like to thank my incredibly brave and smart and funny and gorgeous firefighting husband, Matt Freeman, who sends me on my way to my office/condo once a week for my own twenty-four-hour shift so that I can have a full day of uninterrupted writing—I love you. And my kids, Mikaela, Eva, and Vaughn—thank you for being patient with all of this. You are all special, funny, brilliant, and beautiful. I adore you. Always.

DON'T MISS THE THRILLING CONCLUSION TO
THE RIFT UPRISING TRILOGY BY AMY S. FOSTER

THE RIFT CODA

Coming in October 2018
from Harper Voyager

Read on for a sneak peek!

HARPER Voyager
An Imprint of HarperCollins*Publishers*

Today we're going to do our homework. We're going to be soldiers. We're going to pore over every intel file we have on the other Citadel races. We're going to learn their languages. We're going to see how they fight. And we're going to make sure that Iathan and the Roones back on their Earth aren't hiding anything from us. I'm not about to get blindsided again.

"Okay," Levi says finally, snapping me out of my own head. "Where do you want to start?"

"With the Spiradaels. Those pig things ate the one hostage we had, and I want to know more about them."

"I don't think they can be turned, Ryn."

"Neither do I. I just want to figure out the best way to kill them."

"Other than getting eaten by pigs?" He holds up his hand

to make it clear that's a joke and pulls out his laptop so we can begin.

We spend hours learning their guttural language, which lacks any sort of flair and only a handful of words that are more than three syllables. We pore over the footage we have of the giant, spindly Citadel race. We watch how they use their hair as razor-like whips. We see how they block and punch. From fighting them personally, I know they don't use their legs. It's all upper body with them. I think I understand it now. It seems the joints on their arms, necks, and shoulders allow them to contort these appendages almost 360 degrees. I don't think their knees do the same, so they focus on the chest and hair to win.

Over and over again we watch their fighting style and then we practice on one another, blocking and overcoming Spiradael attacks. I never could understand why the Blood Lust doesn't kick in during sparring, but it never has. This is yet another mystery of how ARC works—how specific they were when they programmed us with the Blood Lust. It never interferes with our ability to fight an enemy. It inserts itself only if we try to have a life off the battlefield.

After we finish with the Spiradaels, we begin with the Orsalines. It takes all of an hour and forty-five minutes to learn their language. They simply don't have that many words. I still can't believe the altered Roones would choose them. If their genetic fuckery is this big gift, why waste it on dumb bear people? The secret must lie in not just their strength, which I am learning is far greater than I gave them credit for, but their devotion to the altered Roones. It's religious with the Orsalines. They're zealots, and that might make them the most dangerous Citadels of all.

Levi and I study their fighting style. It's actually not so

much as a style as out and out berserker mode. They don't kick, because bear legs. They don't exactly punch, either, as much as they do maul. Mostly what they do is either claw an opponent to death or squeeze them until their organs burst. Sometimes they will just hurl a boulder at them. Or a tree.

Once again, Levi and I do maneuvers and I am grateful for this huge, almost empty room with its cathedral-like ceilings so that we can use the walls and beams to hang and jump from. Technically, we are stronger than the Orsalines. We have more physical strength than any other Citadel, but I would hate to be on the receiving end of one of those hugs. We each find effective ways to get out of these holds and keep moving to make sure their nails can't get at us. They couldn't penetrate the uniform of course, but a lucky swipe at the neck while going for our faces would lead to death pretty quickly.

After that, we hurry ourselves to the canteen, grab something that looks like a sandwich with some kind of meat and bottles of water with additional electrolytes. We've got a lot of work to do and not much time until the council we've agreed to have tomorrow.

The Daithi are the next Citadels we study. Their language is nuanced and many words are difficult to pronounce as they don't use a lot of vowels, almost like Welsh. While the pronunciation and grammar is harder to grasp, the Daithi lexicon is more straightforward than most. There are very few words that mean the same thing and it is abnormally absent of adverbs and adjectives. It is a language of nouns and verbs, of naming and doing. This in and of itself gives us further insight into their culture. The Daithi are as small as children, but that doesn't make them any less dangerous. They are remarkably fast and their fighting style is more like a dance than combat. They move in quickly with deadly accuracy and move to another place in the blink of an eye. The Daithi rarely block. They seem to have little use for defensive fighting because in the footage we've seen where they engage, no one—not even the Settiku Hesh—gets close enough to land a punch.

Levi and I quickly realize that the only way to defeat the Daithi is if we don't rely on sight. We need to use our other senses—smell, hearing their heart beats and the whirring rush of air when a fist or leg rushes toward a body. This is especially difficult for me because of the stupid Kir-Abisat and the sound my own body is throwing off, but in a way, it's a good practice. It forces me to learn how to dampen it even more.

Levi blindfolds me like the Jedi I've always wanted to be and begins to attack. The first hurdle is just getting out of the way. I focus on his heartbeat and the heat signature his body gives off. When he lunges, eventually I get the hang of spinning away, ducking and rolling in a different direction. As cool as this is, it won't actually help us defeat the Daithi. Together, Levi and I come up with strategies that will help us strike immediately after deflection. For this, we not only use combinations of punches and kicks from very strange angles, but our knives as well. Guns would be the most useful, of course. I'm never above just shooting someone, but if things go down the way they did with the Spiradael, we're going to need to fight them off long enough to talk to them.

We don't bother leaving the room for dinner. We stuff our faces with the tasteless gel cubes provided by the SenMachs. They will give us the nutrition we need and save us valuable time. Besides, I'm not in any mood to deal with Ezra. I'm actually enjoying today. It feels good to be doing something I'm actually good at as opposed to all this fumbling around, second-guessing every word I say and how it will be interpreted.

When we move on to the Akshaj for the first time, I begin to feel truly afraid. I had been worried up till this point and anxious because of the sheer volume of puzzle pieces the altered Roones were trying to put together. The Akshaj are barely Citadels. They've been enhanced, certainly, but it's clear they see the Rifts not as a call to duty, but as a form of endless entertainment.

The language does not take us long to learn, and soon we're able to converse in Akshaj as we study their fighting. But while learning Akshaj is easy enough, learning how to defend yourself and beat a race of Citadels with six arms is another story entirely. Levi and I use the SenSuits to give us the illusion of this, a visual, just so we know what to avoid and how, but other than looking terrifying, it's a fairly useless way to train as the four "pretend" arms just kind of hover. In the end, Levi and I devise a high-low strategy and just have to hope it will work.

We spar, taking turns being Akshaj. As humans, we aim for the feet and calves in attempt to get them off-balance, on the ground preferably. Alternately, we go right for the head and throat, aiming killing blows there or using the leverage of what's around us to jump up and straddle our legs around the neck. Again, guns are always a bonus, but in the case of the Akshaj, we wonder if machetes or scimitars wouldn't be preferable. It would be a lot easier to just hack off those extra appendages than try to avoid them.

It is near midnight when we finish, but our day is hardly done. We ask Doe to show us any pertinent documents about the Roones that might help us. I had Doe download their entire database when I was on their Earth—unbeknownst to them, of course. We ask Doe to look for anomalies and inconsistencies in the data when compared to the story we were given by Iathan. Doe shows us videos, official documents, health records, experiment hypotheses, the various species the Roones spliced with their own to create the "altered" Roones and the Karekin. Doe assures us that the story Iathan told us is the truth, or at least, the Roones' version of the truth. The altered Roones would have a very different take on things.

So, for all of Iathan's arrogance and posturing, he wasn't lying. We can trust him as an ally. This should make me feel better, but for some reason it doesn't. It's so obvious from the research that a civil war was inevitable. I saw it coming years before it actually arrived. Politicians at each other's throats, rhetoric and propaganda about superior species. There were demonstrations and marches and strikes. The Roones didn't like what was happening to the Immigrants. The Roones practiced civil disobedience, but it was their civility that was their downfall. There is no reasoning with crazy. There is no compromising with tyranny. None of them thought in a million years the conflict would get to where it would and when it did, the Roones were more offended at first than they were tactical.

When we finally finish studying, I feel tired in a way that I haven't for a while. It is the exhaustion of a full day of hard work, of goals accomplished and the odd clarity you can sometimes find through busywork. I stretch my legs out on the carpet, flexing the arches of my feet and rolling my neck clockwise to get the kinks out. Levi is sitting on the only chair in the room. His back is resting against it, but there is an intensity to his gaze which lets me know he's far from relaxed.

"What?" I ask him hesitantly.

"We have to talk about this, Ryn. You need to tell me what the hell is going on with you and Ezra, because it's messy and it makes us all look bad." I don't answer Levi right away. Instead, I walk over to the tall leaded glass window. It is pitch black outside and all I can see is my reflection. Why don't these windows open? It's not like the Faida would be worried about someone falling out. I inspect the seams, I run my fingers over the cool metal, and I hear the window shift and creak. I move my hand away and the sound stops. I wave my hand over the window again and this time it swings open fully. Motion sensors. That's the kind of thing you might want to tell a guest.

I open the remaining three windows and a cool breeze rushes in to wash away the stale air. There is the faintest smell of eucalyptus and burning wood. The night creeps in slowly like a tired ghost. It's one thing to see the hour and quite another to actually feel it.

"I had sex with him," I tell Levi boldly. There's no point in lying. Ezra and I were together—though, perhaps, the reality was our togetherness was more of a technicality. Still, I believed I loved Ezra and maybe I did or even still do, but it was an indulgent love. It was selfish and myopic, as almost all first loves are.

Yet I also cannot deny that there was—and always has been—something between Levi and me. I can't say for certain what it is, though Levi seems to have a better idea of it. I also know that he hasn't allowed himself to feel much of anything for years which means his feelings cannot necessarily be trusted. His emotions are just unfurling. They are gilded petals, bright and shining, too fragile yet to pluck and examine.

I watch his body change with this admission. His knuckles

turn white as they grip the wooden armrests. His back molars grind together, squaring off his jaw. "Okay," he says softly. "Then what happened."

I bite the corner of my lower lip. I don't want to talk about this with him. It's none of his business. But . . . it *is* his business, and he's right to ask. There's too much obvious tension amongst us three right now, and that puts us at a disadvantage. Whatever we feel for each other, at this moment we humans have to put up a united front here. What's at stake is just too important.

"Everything changed."

ABOUT THE AUTHOR

AMY S. FOSTER is a celebrated and award-winning songwriter, best known as Michael Bublé's writing partner, and has collaborated with Beyoncé, Diana Krall, Andrea Bocelli, Josh Groban, and a host of other artists. She is also the author of *When Autumn Leaves*. When she's not in a studio in Nashville, she lives in the Pacific Northwest with her family.

CPSIA information can be obtained
at www.ICGtesting.com
Printed in the USA
LVHW031005290820
664525LV00031B/2621